Eleanor

Autor

Contents

PART I. 7
CHAPTER I 7
CHAPTER II 24
CHAPTER III 46
CHAPTER IV 60
CHAPTER V 72
CHAPTER VI 88
CHAPTER VII 106
CHAPTER VIII 121
CHAPTER IX 139
CHAPTER X 157
CHAPTER XI 172
CHAPTER XII 185
CHAPTER XIII 198
CHAPTER XIV 218
PART II. 236
CHAPTER XV 236
CHAPTER XVI 245
CHAPTER XVII 265
CHAPTER XVIII 276
CHAPTER XIX 293
CHAPTER XX 310
CHAPTER XXI 322
CHAPTER XXII 331
CHAPTER XXIII 344
CHAPTER XXIV 362
CHAPTER XXV 375

ELEANOR

BY

Autor

TO ITALY THE BELOVED AND BEAUTI-
FUL,
INSTRUCTRESS OF OUR PAST,
DELIGHT OF OUR PRESENT,
COMRADE OF OUR FUTURE:--
THE HEART OF AN ENGLISHWOMAN
OFFERS THIS BOOK.

PART I.

'I would that you were all to me,
You that are just so much, no more.
Nor yours nor mine, nor slave nor free!
Where does the fault lie? What the core
O' the wound, since wound must be?'

CHAPTER I

Let us be quite clear, Aunt Pattie--when does this young woman arrive?'
'In about half an hour. But really, Edward, you need take no trouble! she is coming to visit me, and I will see that she doesn't get in your way. Neither you nor Eleanor need trouble your heads about her.'

Miss Manisty--a small elderly lady in a cap--looked at her nephew with a mild and deprecating air. The slight tremor of the hands, which were crossed over the knitting on her lap, betrayed a certain nervousness; but for all that she had the air of managing a familiar difficulty in familiar ways.

The gentleman addressed shook his head impatiently.

'One never prepares for these catastrophes till they actually arrive,' he muttered, taking up a magazine that lay on the table near him, and restlessly playing with the leaves.

'I warned you yesterday.'

'And I forgot--and was happy. Eleanor--what are we going to do with Miss

Foster?'

A lady, who had been sitting at some little distance, rose and came forward.

'Well, I should have thought the answer was simple. Here we are fifteen miles from Rome. The trains might be better--still there are trains. Miss Foster has never been to Europe before. Either Aunt Pattie's maid or mine can take her to all the proper things--or there are plenty of people in Rome--the Westertons--the Borrows?--who at a word from Aunt Pattie would fly to look after her and take her about. I really don't see that you need be so miserable!'

Mrs. Burgoyne stood looking down in some amusement at the aunt and nephew. Edward Manisty, however, was not apparently consoled by her remarks. He began to pace up and down the salon in a disturbance out of all proportion to its cause. And as he walked he threw out phrases of ill-humour, so that at last Miss Manisty, driven to defend herself, put the irresistible question--

'Then why--why--my dear Edward, did you make me invite her? For it was really his doing--wasn't it, Eleanor?'

'Yes--I am witness!'

'One of those abominable flashes of conscience that have so much to answer for!' said Manisty, throwing up his hand in annoyance.--'If she had come to us in Rome, one could have provided for her. But here in this solitude--just at the most critical moment of one's work--and it's all very well--but one can't treat a young lady, when she is actually in one's house, as if she were the tongs!'

He stood beside the window, with his hands on his sides, moodily looking out. Thus strongly defined against the sunset light, he would have impressed himself on a stranger as a man no longer in his first youth, extraordinarily handsome so far as the head was concerned, but of a somewhat irregular and stunted figure; stunted, however, only in comparison with what it had to carry; for in fact he was of about middle height. But the head, face and shoulders were all remarkably large and powerful; the colouring--curly black hair, grey eyes, dark complexion--singularly vivid; and the lines of the brow, the long nose, the energetic mouth, in their mingled force and perfection, had made the stimulus of many an artist before now. For Edward Manisty was one of those men of note whose portraits the world likes to paint: and this 'Olympian head' of his was well known in many a French and English studio, through a fine drawing of it made by Legros when Manisty was still a youth at Oxford. 'Begun by David--and finished by Rembrandt': so a young French painter had once described Edward Manisty.

The final effect of this discord, however, was an effect of power--of personality--of something that claimed and held attention. So at least it was described by Manisty's friends. Manisty's enemies, of whom the world contained no small number, had other words for it. But women in general took the more complimentary view.

The two women now in his company were clearly much affected by the force--wilfulness--extravagance--for one might call it by any of these names--that breathed from the man before them. Miss Manisty, his aunt, followed his movements with her small blinking eyes, timidly uneasy, but yet visibly conscious all the time that she had done nothing that any reasonable man could rationally complain of; while in the manner towards him of his widowed cousin Mrs. Burgoyne, in the few words of banter or remonstrance that she threw him on the subject of his aunt's expected visitor, there was an indulgence, a deference even, that his irritation scarcely deserved.

'At least, give me some account of this girl'--he said, breaking in upon his aunt's explanations. 'I have really not given her a thought--and--good heavens!--she will be here, you say, in half an hour. Is she young--stupid--pretty? Has she any experience--any conversation?'

'I read you Adele's letter on Monday,' said Miss Manisty, in a tone of patience--'and I told you then all I knew--but I noticed you didn't listen. I only saw her myself for a few hours at Boston. I remember she was rather good-looking--but very shy, and not a bit like all the other girls one was seeing. Her clothes were odd, and dowdy, and too old for her altogether,--which struck me as curious, for the American girls, even the country ones, have such a natural turn for dressing themselves. Her Boston cousins didn't like it, and they tried to buy her things--but she was difficult to manage--and they had to give it up. Still they were very fond of her, I remember. Only she didn't let them show it much. Her manners were much stiffer than theirs. They said she was very countrified and simple--that she had been brought up quite alone by their old uncle, in a little country town--and hardly ever went away from home.'

'And Edward never saw her?' inquired Mrs. Burgoyne, with a motion of the head towards Manisty.

'No. He was at Chicago just those days. But you never saw anything like the kindness of the cousins! Luncheons and dinners!'--Miss Manisty raised her little gouty hands--'my dear--when we left Boston I never wanted to eat again. It would be simply indecent if we did nothing for this girl. English people are so ungrateful this side of the water. It makes me hot when I think of all they do for us.'

The small lady's blanched and wrinkled face reddened a little with a colour which became her. Manisty, lost in irritable reflection, apparently took no notice.

'But why did they send her out all alone?' said Mrs. Burgoyne. 'Couldn't they have found some family for her to travel with?'

'Well, it was a series of accidents. She did come over with some Boston people--the Porters--we knew very well. And they hadn't been three days in London before one of the daughters developed meningitis, and was at the point of death. And of course they could go nowhere and see nothing--and poor Lucy Foster felt herself in the way. Then she was to have joined some other people in Italy, and *they* changed their plans. And at last I got a letter from Mrs. Porter--in despair--asking me if I knew of anyone in Rome who would take her in and chaperon her. And then--well, then you know the rest.'

And the speaker nodded again, still more significantly, towards her nephew.

'No, not all,' said Mrs. Burgoyne, laughing. 'I remember he telegraphed.'

'Yes. He wouldn't even wait for me to write. No--"Of course we must have the girl!" he said. "She can join us at the villa. And they'll want to know, so I'll wire." And out he went. And then that evening I had to write and ask her to stay as long as she wished--and--well, there it is!'

'And hence these tears,' said Mrs. Burgoyne. 'What possessed him?'

'Well, I think it was conscience,' said the little spinster, plucking up spirit. 'I know it was with me. There had been some Americans calling on us that day--you remember--those charming Harvard people? And somehow it recalled to us both what a fuss they had made with us--and how kind everybody was. At least I suppose that was how Edward felt. I know I did.'

Manisty paused in his walk. For the first time his dark whimsical face was crossed by an unwilling smile--slight but agreeable.

'It is the old story,' he said. 'Life would be tolerable but for one's virtues. All this time, I beg to point out, Aunt Pattie, that you have still told us nothing about the young lady--except something about her clothes, which doesn't matter.'

Mrs. Burgoyne's amused gesture showed the woman's view of this remark. Miss Manisty looked puzzled.

'Well--I don't know. Yes--I have told you a great deal. The Lewinsons apparently thought her rather strange. Adele said she couldn't tell what to be at with her--you never knew what she would like or dislike. Tom Lewinson seems to have liked her better than Adele did. He said "there was no nonsense about her--and she never kept a fellow waiting." Adele says she is the oddest mixture of knowledge and ignorance. She would ask the most absurd elementary questions--and then one morning Tom found out that she was quite a Latin scholar, and had read Horace and Virgil, and all the rest.'

'Good God!' said Manisty under his breath, resuming his walk.

'And when they asked her to play, she played--quite respectably.'

'Of course:--two hours' practising in the morning,--I foresaw it,' said Manisty, stopping short. 'Eleanor, we have been like children sporting over the abyss!'

Mrs. Burgoyne rose with a laugh--a very soft and charming laugh--by no means the least among the various gifts with which nature had endowed her.

'Oh, civilisation has resources,' she said--'Aunt Pattie and I will take care of you. Now we have got a quarter of an hour to dress in. Only first--one must really pay one's respects to this sunset.'

And she stepped out through an open door upon a balcony beyond. Then turning, with a face of delight, she beckoned to Manisty, who followed.

'Every night more marvellous than the last'--she said, hanging over the balustrade--'and one seems to be here in the high box of a theatre, with the sun playing pageants for our particular benefit.'

Before them, beneath them indeed, stretched a scene, majestic, incomparable. The old villa in which they stood was built high on the ridge of the Alban Hills. Below it, olive-grounds and vineyards, plough-lands and pine plantations sank, slope after slope, fold after fold, to the Campagna. And beyond the Campagna, along the whole shining line of the west, the sea met the sunset; while to the north, a dim and scattered whiteness rising from the plain--was Rome.

The sunset was rushing to its height through every possible phase of violence

and splendour. From the Mediterranean, storm-clouds were rising fast to the as-
sault and conquest of the upper sky, which still above the hills shone blue and
tranquil. But the north-west wind and the sea were leagued against it. They sent
out threatening fingers and long spinning veils of cloud across it--skirmishers that
foretold the black and serried lines, the torn and monstrous masses behind. Below
these wild tempest shapes, again,--in long spaces resting on the sea--the heaven was
at peace, shining in delicate greens and yellows, infinitely translucent and serene,
above the dazzling lines of water. Over Rome itself there was a strange massing and
curving of the clouds. Between their blackness and the deep purple of the Campagna, rose the city--pale phantom--upholding one great dome, and one only, to
the view of night and the world. Round and above and behind, beneath the long flat
arch of the storm, glowed a furnace of scarlet light. The buildings of the city were
faint specks within its fierce intensity, dimly visible through a sea of fire. St. Peter's
alone, without visible foundation or support, had consistence, form, identity.--And
between the city and the hills, waves of blue and purple shade, forerunners of the
night, stole over the Campagna towards the higher ground. But the hills themselves
were still shining, still clad in rose and amethyst, caught in gentler repetition from
the wildness of the west. Pale rose even the olive-gardens; rose the rich brown fallows, the emerging farms; while drawn across the Campagna from north to south,
as though some mighty brush had just laid it there for sheer lust of colour, sheer joy
in the mating it with the rose,--one long strip of sharpest, purest green.

Mrs. Burgoyne turned at last from the great spectacle to her companion.

'One has really no adjectives left,' she said. 'But I had used mine up within a
week.'

'It still gives you so much pleasure?' he said, looking at her a little askance.

Her face changed at once.

'And you?--you are beginning to be tired of it?'

'One gets a sort of indigestion.--Oh! I shall be all right to-morrow.'

Both were silent for a moment. Then he resumed.--

'I met General Fenton in the Borgia rooms this morning.'

She turned, with a quick look of curiosity.

'Well?'

'I hadn't seen him since I met him at Simla three years ago. I always found him particularly agreeable then. We used to ride together and talk together,--and he put me in the way of seeing a good many things. This morning he received me with a change of manner--can't exactly describe it; but it was not flattering! So I presently left him to his own devices and went on into another room. Then he followed me, and seemed to wish to talk. Perhaps he perceived that he had been unfriendly, and thought he would make amends. But I was rather short with him. We had been real friends; we hadn't met for three years; and I thought he might have behaved differently. He asked me a number of questions, however, about last year, about my resignation, and so forth; and I answered as little as I could. So presently he looked at me and laughed--"You remind me," he said, "of what somebody said of Peel--that he was bad to go up to in the stable!--But what on earth are you in the stable for?--and not in the running?"'

Mrs. Burgoyne smiled.

'He was evidently bored with the pictures!' she said, dryly.

Manisty gave a shrug. 'Oh! I let him off. I wouldn't be drawn. I told him I had expressed myself so much in public there was nothing more to say. "H'm," he said, "they tell me at the Embassy you're writing a book!" You should have seen the little old fellow's wizened face--and the scorn of it! So I inquired whether there was any objection to the writing of books. "Yes!"--he said--"when a man can do a d----d sight better for himself--as you could! Everyone tells me that last year you had the ball at your feet." "Well,"--I said--"and I kicked it--and am still kicking it--in my own way. It mayn't be yours--or anybody else's--but wait and see." He shook his head. "A man with what *were* your prospects can't afford escapades. It's all very well for a Frenchman; it don't pay in England." So then I maintained that half the political reputations of the present day were based on escapades. "Whom do you mean?"--he said--"Randolph Churchill?--But Randolph's escapades were always just what the man in the street understood. As for your escapade, the man in the street can't make head or tail of it. That's just the, difference."'

Mrs. Burgoyne laughed--but rather impatiently.

'I should like to know when General Fenton ever considered the man in the street!'

'Not at Simla certainly. There you may despise him.--But the old man is right enough as to the part he plays in England.--I gathered that all my old Indian friends thought I had done for myself. There was no sympathy for me anywhere. Oh!--as to the cause I upheld--yes. But none as to the mode of doing it.'

'Well--there is plenty of sympathy elsewhere! What does it matter what dried-up officials like General Fenton choose to think about it?'

'Nothing--so long as there are no doubts inside to open the gates to the General Fentons outside!'

He looked at her oddly--half smiling, half frowning.

'The doubts are traitors. Send them to execution!' He shook his head.

'Do you remember that sentence we came across yesterday in Chateaubriand's letters "As to my career--I have gone from shipwreck to shipwreck." What if I am merely bound on the same charming voyage?'

'I accept the comparison,' she said with vivacity. 'End as he did in re-creating a church, and regenerating a literature--and see who will count the shipwrecks!'

Her hand's disdainful gesture completed the sally.

Manisty's face dismissed its shadow.

As she stood beside him, in the rosy light--so proudly confident--Eleanor Burgoyne was very delightful to see and hear. Manisty, one of the subtlest and most fastidious of observers, was abundantly conscious of it. Yet she was not beautiful, except in the judgment of a few exceptional people, to whom a certain kind of grace--very rare, and very complex in origin--is of more importance than other things. The eyes were, indeed, beautiful; so was the forehead, and the hair of a soft ashy brown folded and piled round it in a most skilful simplicity. But the rest of the face was too long; and its pallor, the singularly dark circles round the eyes, the great thinness of the temples and cheeks, together with the emaciation of the whole delicate frame, made a rather painful impression on a stranger. It was a face of experience, a face of grief; timid, yet with many strange capacities and suggestions both of vehemence and pride. It could still tremble into youth and delight. But in general it held the world aloof. Mrs. Burgoyne was not very far from thirty, and either physical weakness, or the presence of some enemy within more destructive still, had emphasised the loss of youth. At the same time she had still a voice, a hand, a carriage that lovelier women had often envied, discerning in them those subtleties of race and personality which are not to be rivalled for the asking.

To-night she brought all her charm to bear upon her companion's despondency, and succeeded as she had often succeeded before. She divined that he needed flattery, and she gave it; that he must be supported and endorsed, and she had soon pushed General Fenton out of sight behind a cloud of witness of another sort.

Manisty's mood yielded; and in a short time he was again no less ready to admire the sunset than she was.

'Heavens!' she said at last, holding out her watch.--'Just look at the time--and Miss Foster!'

Manisty struck his hand against the railing.

'How is one to be civil about this visit! Nothing could be more unfortunate. These last critical weeks--and each of us so dependent on the other--Really it is the most monstrous folly on all our parts that we should have brought this girl upon us.'

'Poor Miss Foster!' said Mrs. Burgoyne, raising her eyebrows. 'But of course you won't be civil!--Aunt Pattie and I know that. When I think of what I went through that first fortnight--'

'Eleanor!'

'You are the only man I ever knew that could sit silent through a whole meal. By to-morrow Miss Foster will have added that experience to her collection. Well--I shall be prepared with my consolations--there's the carriage--and the bell!'

They fled indoors, escaping through the side entrances of the salon, before the visitor could be shown in.

*   *   *   *   *

'Must I change my dress?'

The voice that asked the question trembled with agitation and fatigue. But the girl who owned the voice stood up stiffly, looking at Miss Manisty with a frowning, almost a threatening shyness.

'Well, my dear,' said Miss Manisty, hesitating. 'Are you not rather dusty? We can easily keep dinner a quarter of an hour.'

She looked at the grey alpaca dress before her, in some perplexity.

'Oh, very well'--said the girl hurriedly.--'Of course I'll change. Only'--and the voice fluttered again evidently against her will--'I'm afraid I haven't anything very nice. I must get something in Rome. Mrs. Lewinson advised me. This is my afternoon dress,--I've been wearing it in Florence. But of course--I'll put on my other.--Oh! please don't send for a maid. I'd rather unpack for myself--so much rather!'

The speaker flushed crimson, as she saw Miss Manisty's maid enter the room in answer to her mistress's ring. She stood up indeed with her hand grasping her trunk, as though defending it from an assailant.

The maid looked at her mistress. 'Miss Foster will ring, Benson, if she wants you'--said Miss Manisty; and the black-robed elderly maid, breathing decorous fashion and the ways of 'the best people,' turned, gave a swift look at Miss Foster, and left the room.

'Are you sure, my dear? You know she would make you tidy in no time. She arranges hair beautifully.'

'Oh quite--quite sure!--thank you,' said the girl with the same eagerness. 'I will be ready,--right away.'

Then, left to herself, Miss Foster hastily opened her box and took out some of its contents. She unfolded one dress after another,--and looked at them unhappily.

'Perhaps I ought to have let cousin Izza give me those things in Boston,' she thought. 'Perhaps I was too proud. And that money of Uncle Ben's--it might have been kinder--after all he wanted me to look nice'--

She sat ruefully on the ground beside her trunk, turning the things over, in a misery of annoyance and mortification; half inclined to laugh too as she remembered the seamstress in the small New England country town, who had helped her own hands to manufacture them. 'Well, Miss Lucy, your uncle's done real handsome by you. I guess he's set you up, and no mistake. There's no meanness about him!'

And she saw the dress on the stand--the little blonde withered head of the dressmaker--the spectacled eyes dwelling proudly on the masterpiece before them.--

Alack! There rose up the memory of little Mrs. Lewinson at Florence--of her gently pursed lips--of the looks that were meant to be kind, and were in reality so critical.

No matter. The choice had to be made; and she chose at last a blue and white check that seemed to have borne its travels better than the rest. It had looked so fresh and striking in the window of the shop whence she had bought it. 'And you know, Miss Lucy, you're so tall, you can stand them chancy things'--her little friend had said to her, when *she* had wondered whether the check might not be too large.

And yet only with a passing wonder. She could not honestly say that her dress had cost her much thought then or at any other time. She had been content to be very simple, to admire other girls' cleverness. There had been influences upon her own childhood, however, that had somehow separated her from the girls around her, had made it difficult for her to think and plan as they did.

She rose with the dress in her hands, and as she did so, she caught the glory of the sunset through the open window.

She ran to look, all her senses flooded with the sudden beauty,--when she heard a man's voice as it seemed close beside her. Looking to the left, she distinguished a balcony, and a dark figure that had just emerged upon it.

Mr. Manisty--no doubt! She closed her window hurriedly, and began her dressing, trying at the time to collect her thoughts on the subject of these people whom she had come to visit.

Yet neither the talk of her Boston cousins, nor the gossip of the Lewinsons at Florence had left any very clear impression. She remembered well her first and only sight of Miss Manisty at Boston. The little spinster, so much a lady, so kind, cheerful and agreeable, had left a very favourable impression in America. Mr. Manisty had left an impression too--that was certain--for people talked of him perpetually. Not many persons, however, had liked him, it seemed. She could remember, as it were, a whole track of resentments, hostilities, left behind. 'He cares nothing about us'--an irate Boston lady had said in her hearing--but he will exploit us! He despises us,--but he'll make plenty of speeches and articles out of us--you'll see!'

As for Major Lewinson, the husband of Mr. Manisty's first cousin,--she had been conscious all the time of only half believing what he said, of holding out against it. He must be so different from Mr. Manisty--the little smart, quick-tempered soldier--with his contempt for the undisciplined civilian way of doing things. She did not mean to remember his remarks. For after all, she had her own ideas of what Mr. Manisty would be like. She had secretly formed her own opinion. He had been a man of letters and a traveller before he entered politics. She remembered--nay, she would never forget--a volume of letters from Palestine, written by him, which had reached her through the free library of the little town near her home.

She who read slowly, but, when she admired, with a silent and worshipping ardour, had read this book, had hidden it under her pillow, had been haunted for days by its pliant sonorous sentences, by the colour, the perfume, the melancholy of pages that seemed to her dreaming youth marvellous, inimitable. There were descriptions of a dawn at Bethlehem--a night wandering at Jerusalem--a reverie by the sea of Galilee--the very thought of which made her shiver a little, so deeply had they touched her young and pure imagination.

And then--people talked so angrily of his quarrel with the Government--and his resigning. They said he had been foolish, arrogant, unwise. Perhaps. But after all it had been to his own hurt--it must have been for principle. So far the girl's secret instinct was all on his side.

Meanwhile, as she dressed, there floated through her mind fragments of what she had been told as to his strange personal beauty; but these she only entertained shyly and in passing. She had been brought up to think little of such matters, or rather to avoid thinking of them.

She went through her toilette as neatly and rapidly as she could, her mind all the time so full of speculation and a deep restrained excitement that she ceased to trouble herself in the least about her gown, As for her hair, she arranged it almost mechanically, caring only that its black masses should be smooth and in order. She fastened at her throat a small turquoise brooch that had been her mother's; she clasped the two little chain bracelets that were the only ornaments of the kind she possessed, and then without a single backward look towards the reflection in the glass, she left her room--her heart beating fast with timidity and expectation.

*   *   *   *   *

'Oh! poor child--poor child!--what a frock!'

Such was the inward ejaculation of Mrs. Burgoyne, as the door of the salon was thrown open by the Italian butler, and a very tall girl came abruptly through, edging to one side as though she were trying to escape the servant, and looking anxiously round the vast room.

Manisty also turned as the door opened. Miss Manisty caught his momentary expression of wonder, as she herself hurried forward to meet the new-comer.

'You have been very quick, my dear, and I am sure you must be hungry.--This is an old friend of ours--Mrs. Burgoyne--my nephew--Edward Manisty. He knows all your Boston cousins, if not you. Edward, will you take Miss Foster?--she's the stranger.'

Mrs. Burgoyne pressed the girl's hand with a friendly effusion. Beyond her was a dark-haired man, who bowed in silence. Lucy Foster took his arm, and he led her through a large intervening room, in which were many tables and many books, to the dining-room.

On the way he muttered a few embarrassed words as to the weather and the lateness of dinner, walking meanwhile so fast that she had to hurry after him. 'Good heavens, why she is a perfect chess-board!' he thought to himself, looking askance at her dress, in a sudden and passionate dislike--'one could play draughts upon her. What has my Aunt been about?'

The girl looked round her in bewilderment as they sat down. What a strange place! The salon in her momentary glance round it had seemed to her all splendour. She had been dimly aware of pictures, fine hangings, luxurious carpets. Here on the other hand all was rude and bare. The stained walls were covered with a series of tattered daubs, that seemed to be meant for family portraits--of the Malestrini family perhaps, to whom the villa belonged? And between the portraits there were rough modern doors everywhere of the commonest wood and manufacture which let in all the draughts, and made the room not a room, but a passage. The uneven brick floor was covered in the centre with some thin and torn matting; many of the chairs ranged against the wall were broken; and the old lamp that swung above the table gave hardly any light.

Miss Manisty watched her guest's face with a look of amusement.

'Well, what do you think of our dining-room, my dear? I wanted to clean it and put it in order. But my nephew there wouldn't have a thing touched.'

She looked at Manisty, with a movement of the lips and head that seemed to implore him to make some efforts.

Manisty frowned a little, lifted his great brow and looked, not at Miss Foster, but at Mrs. Burgoyne--

'The room, as it happens, gives me more pleasure than any other in the villa.'

Mrs. Burgoyne laughed.

'Because it's hideous?'

'If you like. I should only call it the natural, untouched thing.'

Then while his Aunt and Mrs. Burgoyne made mock of him, he fell silent again, nervously crumbling his bread with a large wasteful hand. Lucy Foster stole a look at him, at the strong curls of black hair piled above the brow, the moody embarrassment of the eyes, the energy of the lips and chin.

Then she turned to her companions. Suddenly the girl's clear brown skin flushed rosily, and she abruptly took her eyes from Mrs. Burgoyne.

Miss Manisty, however--in despair of her nephew--was bent upon doing her own duty. She asked all the proper questions about the girl's journey, about the cousins at Florence, about her last letters from home. Miss Foster answered quickly, a little breathlessly, as though each question were an ordeal that had to be got through. And once or twice, in the course of the conversation, she looked again at Mrs. Burgoyne, more lingeringly each time. That lady wore a thin dress gleaming with jet. The long white arms showed under the transparent stuff. The slender neck and delicate bosom were bare,--too bare surely,--that was the trouble. To look at her filled the girl's shrinking Puritan sense with discomfort. But what small and graceful hands!--and how she used them!--how she turned her neck!--how delicious her voice was! It made the new-comer think of some sweet plashing stream in her own Vermont valleys. And then, every now and again, how subtle and startling was the change of look!--the gaiety passing in a moment, with the drooping of eye and mouth, into something sad and harsh, like a cloud dropping round a goddess. In her elegance and self-possession indeed, she seemed to the girl a kind of goddess--heathenishly divine, because of that mixture of unseemliness, but still divine.

Several times Mrs. Burgoyne addressed her--with a gentle courtesy--and Miss Foster answered. She was shy, but not at all awkward or conscious. Her manner had the essential self-possession which is the birthright of the American woman. But it suggested reserve, and a curious absence of any young desire to make an effect.

As for Mrs. Burgoyne, long before dinner was over, she had divined a great many things about the new-comer, and amongst them the girl's disapproval of herself. 'After all'--she thought--'if she only knew it, she is a beauty. What a trouble it must have been first to find, and then to make that dress!--Ill luck!--And her hair! Who on earth taught her to drag it back like that? If one could only loosen it, how beautiful it would be! What is it? Is it Puritanism? Has she been brought up to go to meetings and sit under a minister? Were her forbears married in drawing-rooms and under trees? The Fates were certainly frolicking when they brought her here! How am I to keep Edward in order?'

And suddenly, with a little signalling of eye and brow, she too conveyed to Manisty, who was looking listlessly towards her, that he was behaving as badly as even she could have expected. He made a little face that only she saw, but he turned to Miss Foster and began to talk,--all the time adding to the mountain of crumbs beside him, and scarcely waiting to listen to the girl's answers.

'You came by Pisa?'

'Yes. Mrs. Lewinson found me an escort--'

'It was a mistake--' he said, hurrying his words like a schoolboy. 'You should have come by Perugia and Spoleto. Do you know Spello?'

Miss Foster stared.

'Edward!' said Miss Manisty, 'how could she have heard of Spello? It is the first time she has ever been in Italy.'

'No matter!' he said, and in a moment his moroseness was lit up, chased away by the little pleasure of his own whim--'Some day Miss Foster must hear of Spello. May I not be the first person to tell her that she should see Spello?'

'Really, Edward!' cried Miss Manisty, looking at him in a mild exasperation.

'But there was so much to see at Florence!' said Lucy Foster, wondering.

'No--pardon me!--there is nothing to be seen at Florence--or nothing that one ought to wish to see--till the destroyers of the town have been hung in their own new Piazza!'

'Oh yes!--that is a real disfigurement!' said the girl eagerly. 'And yet--can't one understand?--they must use their towns for themselves. They can't always be thinking of them as museums--as we do.'

'The argument would be good if the towns were theirs,' he said, flashing round upon her. 'One can stand a great deal from lawful owners.'

Miss Foster looked in bewilderment at Mrs. Burgoyne. That lady laughed and bent across the table.

'Let me warn you, Miss Foster, this gentleman here must be taken with a grain of salt when he talks about poor Italy--and the Italians.'

'But I thought'--said Lucy Foster, staring at her host--

'You thought he was writing a book on Italy? That doesn't matter. It's the new Italy of course that he hates--the poor King and Queen--the Government and the officials.'

'He wants the old times back?'--said Miss Foster, wondering--'when the priests tyrannised over everybody? when the Italians had no country--and no unity?'

She spoke slowly, at last looking her host in the face. Her frown of nervousness had disappeared. Manisty laughed.

'Pio Nono pulled down nothing--not a brick--or scarcely. And it is a most excellent thing, Miss Foster, to be tyrannised over by priests.'

His great eyes shone--one might even say, glared upon her. His manner was not agreeable; and Miss Foster coloured.

'I don't think so'--she said, and then was too shy to say any more.

'Oh, but you will think so,'--he said, obstinately--'only you must stay long enough in the country. What people are pleased to call Papal tyranny puts a few people in prison--and tells them what books to read. Well!--what matter? Who knows what books they ought to read?'

'But all their long struggle!--and their heroes! They had to make themselves a nation--'

The words stumbled on the girl's tongue, but her effort, the hot feeling in her young face became her.--Miss Manisty thought to herself, 'Oh, we shall dress, and improve her--We shall see!'--

'One has first to settle whether it was worth while. What does a new nation matter? Theirs, anyway, was made too quick,' said Manisty, rising in answer to his aunt's signal.

'But liberty matters!' said the girl. She stood an instant with her hand on the back of her chair, unconsciously defiant.

'Ah! Liberty!' said Manisty--'Liberty!' He lifted his shoulders contemptuously.

Then backing to the wall, he made room for her to pass. The girl felt almost as though she had been struck. She moved hurriedly, appealingly towards Miss Manisty, who took her arm kindly as they left the room.

'Don't let my nephew frighten you, my dear'--she said--'He never thinks like anybody else.'

'I read so much at Florence--and on the journey'--said Lucy, while her hand trembled in Miss Manisty's--'Mrs. Browning--Mazzini--many things. I could not put that time out of my head!'

CHAPTER II

On the way back to the salon the ladies passed once more through the large book-room or library which lay between it and the dining-room. Lucy Foster looked round it, a little piteously, as though she were seeking for something to undo the impression--the disappointment--she had just received.

'Oh! my dear, you never saw such a place as it was when we arrived in March'--said Miss Manisty. 'It was the billiard-room--a ridiculous table--and ridiculous balls--and a tiled floor without a scrap of carpet--and the *cold*! In the whole apartment there were just two bedrooms with fireplaces. Eleanor went to bed in one; I went to bed in the other. No carpets--no stoves--no proper beds even. Edward of course said it was all charming, and the climate balmy. Ah, well!--now we are really quite comfortable--except in that odious dining-room, which Edward will have left in its sins.'

Miss Manisty surveyed her work with a mild satisfaction. The table indeed had been carried away. The floor was covered with soft carpets. The rough uneven walls painted everywhere with the interlaced M's of the Malestrini were almost hidden by well-filled bookcases; and, in addition, a profusion of new books, mostly French and Italian, was heaped on all the tables. On the mantelpiece a large recent photograph stood propped against a marble head. It represented a soldier in a striking dress; and Lucy stopped to look at it.

'One of the Swiss Guards--at the Vatican'--said Mrs. Burgoyne kindly. 'You know the famous uniform--it was designed by Michael Angelo.'

'No--I didn't know'--said the girl, flushing again.--'And this head?'

'Ah, that is a treasure! Mr. Manisty bought it a few months ago from a Roman noble who has come to grief. He sold this and a few bits of furniture first of all. Then he tried to sell his pictures. But the Government came down upon him--you know your pictures are not your own in Italy. So the poor man must keep his pictures and go bankrupt. But isn't she beautiful? She is far finer than most of the things in the Vatican--real primitive Greek--not a copy. Do you know'--Mrs. Burgoyne stepped back, looked first at the bust, then at Miss Poster--'do you know you are really very like her--curiously like her!'

'Oh!'--cried Miss Foster in confusion--'I wish--'

'But it is quite true. Except for the hair. And that's only arrangement. Do you think--would you let me?--would you forgive me?--It's just this band of hair here, yours waves precisely in the same way. Would you really allow me--I won't make you untidy?'

And before Miss Poster could resist, Mrs. Burgoyne had put up her deft hands, and in a moment, with a pull here, and the alteration of a hairpin there, she had loosened the girl's black and silky hair, till it showed the beautiful waves above the ear in which it did indeed resemble the marble head with a curious closeness.

'I can put it back in a moment. But oh--that is so charming! Aunt Pattie!'

Miss Manisty looked up from a newspaper which had just arrived.

'My dear!--that was bold of you I But indeed it *is* charming! I think I would forgive you if I were Miss Foster.

The girl felt herself gently turned towards the mirror that rose behind the Greek head. With pink cheeks she too looked at herself for a moment. Then in a shyness beyond speech, she lifted her hands.

'Must you'--said Mrs. Burgoyne appealingly. 'I know one doesn't like to be untidy. But it isn't really the least untidy--It is only delightful--perfectly delightful!'

Her voice, her manner charmed the girl's annoyance.

'If you like it'--she said, hesitating--'But it will come down!'

'I like it terribly--and it will not think of coming down! Let me show you Mr. Manisty's latest purchase.'

And, slipping her arm inside Miss Foster's, Mrs. Burgoyne dexterously turned her away from the glass, and brought her to the large central table, where a vivid charcoal sketch, supported on a small easel, rose among the litter of books.

It represented an old old man carried in a chair on the shoulders of a crowd of attendants and guards. Soldiers in curved helmets, courtiers in short velvet cloaks and ruffs, priests in floating vestments pressed about him--a dim vast multitude stretched into the distance. The old man wore a high cap with three lines about it; his thin and shrunken form was enveloped in a gorgeous robe. The face, infinitely old, was concentrated in the sharply smiling eyes, the long, straight, secret mouth. His arm, supporting with difficulty the weight of the robe, was raised,--the hand blessed. On either side of him rose great fans of white ostrich feathers, and the old man among them was whiter than they, spectrally white from head to foot, save for the triple cap, and the devices on his robe. But into his emaciation, his weakness, the artist had thrown a triumph, a force that thrilled the spectator. The small figure, hovering above the crowd, seemed in truth to have nothing to do with it, to be alone with the huge spaces--arch on arch--dome on dome--of the vast church through which it was being borne.--

'Do you know who it is?' asked Mrs. Burgoyne, smiling.

'The--the Pope?' said Miss Foster, wondering.

'Isn't it clever? It is by one of your compatriots, an American artist in Rome. Isn't it wonderful too, the way in which it shows you, not the Pope--but the Papacy--not the man but the Church?'

Miss Foster said nothing. Her puzzled eyes travelled from the drawing to Mrs. Burgoyne's face. Then she caught sight of another photograph on the table.

'And that also?'--she said--For again it was the face of Leo XIII.--feminine, priestly, indomitable--that looked out upon her from among the books.

'Oh, my dear, come away,' said Miss Manisty impatiently. 'In my days the Scarlet Lady **was** the Scarlet Lady, and we didn't flirt with her as all the world does now. Shrewd old gentleman! I should have thought one picture of him was enough.'

*   *   *   *   *

As they entered the old painted salon, Mrs. Burgoyne went to one of the tall windows opening to the floor and set it wide. Instantly the Campagna was in the room--the great moonlit plain, a thousand feet below, with the sea at its further edge, and the boundless sweep of starry sky above it. From the little balcony, one might, it seemed, have walked straight into Orion. The note of a nightingale bubbled up from the olives; and the scent of a bean-field in flower flooded the salon.

Miss Foster sprang to her feet and followed Mrs. Burgoyne. She hung over the balcony while her companion pointed here and there, to the line of the Appian Way,--to those faint streaks in the darkness that marked the distant city--to the dim blue of the Etrurian mountains.--

Presently, however, she drew herself erect, and Mrs. Burgoyne fancied that she shivered.

'Ah! this is a hill-air,' she said, and she took from her arm a light evening cloak, and threw it round Miss Foster.

'Oh, I am not cold!--It wasn't that!'

'What was it?' said Mrs. Burgoyne pleasantly. 'That you feel Italy too much for you? Ah! you must got used to that.'

Lucy Foster drew a long breath--a breath of emotion. She was grateful for being understood. But she could not express herself.

Mrs. Burgoyne looked at her curiously.

'Did you read a good deal about it before you came?'

'Well, I read some--we have a good town library--and Uncle Ben gave me two or three books--but of course it wasn't like Boston. Ours is a little place.'

'And you were pleased to come?'

The girl hesitated.

'Yes'--she said simply. 'I wanted to come.--But I didn't want to leave my uncle. He is getting quite an old man.'

'And you have lived with him a long time?'

'Since I was a little thing. Mother and I came to live with him after Father died. Then Mother died, five years ago.'

'And you have been alone--and very good friends?'

Mrs. Burgoyne smiled kindly. She had a manner of questioning that seemed to Miss Foster the height of courtesy. But the girl did not find it easy to answer.

'I have no one else--' she said at last, and then stopped abruptly.

'She is home-sick'--said Mrs. Burgoyne inwardly--'I wonder whether the Lewinsons treated her nicely at Florence?'

Indeed as Lucy Foster leant over the balcony, the olive-gardens and vineyards faded before her. She saw in their stead, the snow-covered farms and fields of a New England valley--the elms in along village street, bare and wintry--a rambling wooden house--a glowing fire, in a simple parlour--an old man sitting beside it.--

It *is* chilly'--said Mrs. Burgoyne--'Let us go in. But we will keep the window open. Don't take that off.'

She laid a restraining hand on the girl's arm. Miss Foster sat down absently not far from the window. The mingled lights of lamp and moon fell upon her, upon the noble rounding of the face, which was grave, a little austere even, but still sensitive and delicate. Her black hair, thanks to Mrs. Burgoyne's devices, rippled against the brow and cheek, almost hiding the small ear. The graceful cloak, with its touches of sable on a main fabric of soft white, hid the ugly dress; its ample folds height-ened the natural dignity of the young form and long limbs, lent them a stately and muse-like charm. Mrs. Burgoyne and Miss Manisty looked at each other, then at Miss Foster. Both of them had the same curious feeling, as though a veil were being drawn away from something they were just beginning to see.

'You must be very tired, my dear'--said Miss Manisty at last, when she and Mrs. Burgoyne had chatted a good deal, and the new-comer still sat silent--'I wonder what you are thinking about so intently?'

Miss Foster woke up at once.

'Oh, I'm not a bit tired--not a bit! I was thinking--I was thinking of that pho-tograph in the next room--and a line of poetry.'

She spoke with the *naivete* of one who had not known how to avoid the con-fession. 'What line?' said Mrs. Burgoyne.

'It's Milton. I learnt it at school. You will know it, of course,' she said timidly. 'It's the line about "the triple tyrant" and "the Babylonian woe"'--

Mrs. Burgoyne laughed.

'Their martyred blood and ashes sow
O'er all the Italian fields, where still doth sway
The triple tyrant--

Was that what you were thinking of?'

Miss Foster had coloured deeply.

'It was the cap--the tiara, isn't it?--that reminded me,' she said faintly; and then she looked away, as though not wishing to continue the subject.

'She wonders whether I am a Catholic,' thought Mrs. Burgoyne, amused, 'and whether she has hurt my feelings.'--Aloud, she said--'Are you very, very Puritan still in your part of America? Excuse me, but I am dreadfully ignorant about America.'

'We are Methodists in our little town mostly'--said Miss Foster. 'There is a Presbyterian church--and the best families go there. But my father's people were always Methodists. My mother was a Universalist.'

Mrs. Burgoyne frowned with perplexity. 'I'm afraid I don't know what that is?' she said.

'They think everybody will be saved,' said Miss Foster in her shy deep voice. 'They don't despair of anybody.'

And suddenly Mrs. Burgoyne saw a very soft and tender expression pass across the girl's grave features, like the rising of an inward light.

'A mystic--and a beauty both?' she thought to herself, a little scornfully this time. In all her politeness to the new-comer so far, she had been like a person stealthily searching for something foreseen and desired. If she had found it, it would have been quite easy to go on being kind to Miss Foster. But she had not found it.

At that moment the door between the library and the salon was thrown open, and Manisty appeared, cigarette in hand.

'Aunt Pattie--Eleanor--how many tickets do you want for this function next Sunday?'

'Four tribune tickets--we three'--Miss Manisty pointed to the other two ladies--'and yourself. If we can't get so many, leave me at home.'

'Of course we shall have tribune tickets--as many as we want,' said Manisty a little impatiently.--'Have you explained to Miss Foster?'

'No, but I will. Miss Foster, next Sunday fortnight the Pope celebrates his 'Capella Papale'--the eighteenth anniversary of his coronation--in St. Peter's. Rome is very full, and there will be a great demonstration--fifty thousand people or more. Would you like to come?'

Miss Foster looked up, hesitating. Manisty, who had turned to go back to his room, paused, struck by the momentary silence. He listened with curiosity for the girl's reply.

'One just goes to see it like a spectacle?' she said at last, slowly. 'One needn't do anything oneself?'

Miss Manisty stared--and then laughed. 'Nobody will see what you do in such a crowd--I should think,' she said. 'But you know one can't be rude--to an old old man. If others kneel, I suppose we must kneel. Does it do anyone harm to be blessed by an old man?'

'Oh no!--no!' cried Miss Foster, flushing deeply. Then, after a moment, she added decidedly--'Please--I should like to go very much.'

Manisty grinned unseen, and closed the door behind him.

Then Miss Foster, after an instant's restlessness, moved nearer to her hostess.

'I am afraid--you thought I was rude just now? It's so lovely of you to plan things for me. But--I can't ever be sure whether it's right to go into other people's churches and look at their services--like a show. I should just hate it myself--and I felt it once or twice at Florence. And so--you understand--don't you?'--she said imploringly.

Miss Manisty's small eyes examined her with anxiety. 'What an extraordinary girl!' she thought. 'Is she going to be a great bore?'

At the same time the girl's look--so open, sweet and modest--disarmed and attracted her. She shrugged her shoulders with a smile.

'Well, my dear--I don't know. All I can say is, the Catholics don't mind! They walk in and out of their own churches all the time mass is going on--the children run about--the sacristans take you round. You certainly needn't feel it on their account.'

'But then, too, if I am not a Catholic--how far ought one to be taking part--in--in what--'

'In what one disapproves?' said Mrs. Burgoyne, smiling. 'You would make the world a little difficult, wouldn't you, if you were to arrange it on that principle?'

She spoke in a dry, rather sharp voice, unlike that in which she had hitherto addressed the new-comer. Lucy Foster looked at her with a shrinking perplexity.

'It's best if we're all straightforward, isn't it?'--she said in a low voice, and then, drawing towards her an illustrated magazine that lay on the table near her she hurriedly buried herself in its pages.

*   *   *   *   *

Silence had fallen on the three ladies. Eleanor Burgoyne sat lost in reverie, her fair head thrown back against her low chair.

She was thinking of her conversation with Edward Manisty on the balcony-- and of his book. That book indeed had for her a deep personal significance. To think of it at all, was to be carried to the past, to feel for the hundredth time the thrill of change and new birth.

When she joined them in Rome, in mid-winter, she had found Manisty strug- gling with the first drafts of it,--full of yeasty ideas, full also of doubts, confusions and discouragements. He had not been at all glad to see his half-forgotten cousin- -quite the contrary. As she had reminded him, she had suffered much the same things at his hands that Miss Foster was likely to suffer now. It made her laugh to think of his languid reception of her, the moods, the silences, the weeks of just civil acquaintanceship; and then gradually, the snatches of talk--and those great black brows of his lifted in a surprise which a tardy politeness would try to mask:--and at last, the good, long, brain-filling, heart-filling talks, the break-down of reserves- -the man's whole mind, its remorses, ambitions, misgivings, poured at her feet-- ending in the growth of that sweet daily habit of common work--side by side, head close to head--hand close to hand.--

Eleanor Burgoyne lay still and motionless in the soft dusk of the old room, her white lids shut--Lucy Foster thought her asleep.--

He had said to her once, quoting some Frenchman, that she was 'good to con- sult about ideas.' Ah well!--at a great price had she won that praise. And with an unconscious stiffening of the frail hands lying on the arms of the chair, she thought of those bygone hours in which she had asked herself--'what remains?' Religious faith?--No!--Life was too horrible! Could such things have happened to her in a world ruled by a God?--that was her question, day and night for years. But books, facts, ideas--all the riddle of this various nature--*that* one might still amuse oneself with a little, till one's own light went out in the same darkness that had already engulfed mother--husband--child.

So that 'cleverness,' of which father and husband had taken so little account, which had been of so little profit to her so far in her course through circumstance, had come to her aid. The names and lists of the books that had passed through her hands, during those silent years of her widowhood, lived beside her stern old father, would astonish even Manisty were she to try and give some account of them. And first she had read merely to fill the hours, to dull memory. But gradually there had sprung up in her that inner sweetness, that gentle restoring flame that comes from the life of ideas, the life of knowledge, even as a poor untrained woman may approach it. She had shared it with no one, revealed it to no one. Her nature dreaded rebuffs; and her father had no words sharp enough for any feminine ambition beyond the household and the nursery.

So she had kept it all to herself, till Miss Manisty, shocked as many other people had begun to be by her fragile looks, had bearded the General, and carried her off to Rome for the winter. And there she had been forced, as it were, into this daily contact with Edward Manisty, at what might well turn out to be the most critical moment of his life; when he was divided between fierce regrets for the immediate past, and fierce resolves to recover and assert himself in other ways; when he was taking up again his earlier function of man of letters in order to vindicate himself as a politician and a man of action. Strange and challenging personality!--did she yet know it fully?

Ah! that winter--what a healing in it all!--what a great human experience! Yet now, as always, when her thoughts turned to the past, she did not allow them to dwell upon it long. That past lay for her in a golden haze. To explore it too deeply, or too long,--that she shrank from. All that she prayed was to press no questions, force no issues. But at least she had found in it a new reason for living; she meant to live; whereas last year she had wished to die, and all the world--dear, kind Aunt Pattie first and foremost--had thought her on the road for death.

But the book?--she bent her brows over it, wrestling with various doubts and difficulties. Though it was supposed to represent the thoughts and fancies of an Englishman wandering through modern Italy, it was really Manisty's Apologia-- Manisty's defence of certain acts which had made him for a time the scandal and offence of the English political party to which ancestrally he belonged, in whose interests he had entered Parliament and taken office. He had broken with his party on the ground that it had become a party of revolution, especially in matters connected with Religion and Education; and having come abroad to escape for a time from the personal frictions and agitations which his conduct had brought upon him, he had thrown himself into a passionate and most hostile study of Italy--Italy, the new country, made by revolution, fashioned, so far as laws and government can do it, by the lay modern spirit--as an object-lesson to England and the world. The book was in reality a party pamphlet, written by a man whose history and antecedents, independently of his literary ability, made his work certain of readers and of vogue.

That, however, was not what Mrs. Burgoyne was thinking of.--She was anxiously debating with herself certain points of detail, points of form.

These fragments of poetical prose which Manisty had interspersed amid a serious political argument--were they really an adornment of the book, or a blur upon it? He had a natural tendency towards colour and exuberance in writing; he loved to be leisurely, and a little sonorous; there was something old-fashioned and Byronic in his style and taste. His sentences, perhaps, were short; but his manner was not brief. The elliptical fashion of the day was not his. He liked to wander through his subject, dreaming, poetising, discussing at his will. It was like a return to *vetturino* after the summary haste of the railway. And so far the public had welcomed this manner of his. His earlier book (the 'Letters from Palestine'), with its warm, overladen pages, had found many readers and much fame.

But here--in a strenuous political study, furnished with all the facts and figures that the student and the debater require--representing, too, another side of the man, just as vigorous and as real, were these intrusions of poetry wise or desirable? Were they in place? Was the note of them quite right? Was it not a little turbid--uncertain?

That prose poem of 'The Priest of Nemi,' for example?

Ah! Nemi!--the mere thought of it sent a thrill of pleasure through her. That blue lake in its green cup on the edge of the Campagna, with its ruins and its legends--what golden hours had she and Manisty spent there! It had caught their fancy from the beginning--the site of the great temple, the wild strawberry fields, the great cliffs of Nemi and Genzano, the bright-faced dark-eyed peasants with their classical names--Aristodemo, Oreste, Evandro.

And that strange legend of the murdered priest--
  'The priest who slew the slayer,

  And shall himself be slain'--
--what modern could not find something in that--some stimulus to fancy--some hint for dreaming?

Yes--it had been very natural--very tempting. But!--

... So she pondered,--a number of acute, critical instincts coming into play. And presently her thoughts spread and became a vague reverie, covering a multitude of ideas and images that she and Manisty now had in common. How strange that she and he should be engaged in this work together!--this impassioned defence of tradition, of Catholicism and the Papacy, as the imperishable, indestructible things--'chastened and not killed--dying, and behold they live'--let the puny sons of modern Italy rage and struggle as they may. He--one of the most thorough sceptics of his day, as she had good reason to know--she, a woman who had at one time ceased to believe because of an intolerable anguish, and was now only creeping slowly back to faith, to hope, because--because--

Ah!--with a little shiver, she recalled her thought, as a falconer might his bird, before it struck. Oh! this old, old Europe, with its complexities, its manifold currents and impulses, every human being an embodied contradiction--no simplicity, no wholeness anywhere--none possible!

She opened her eyes languidly, and they rested on Lucy Foster's head and profile bent over her book. Mrs. Burgoyne's mind filled with a sudden amused pity for the girl's rawness and ignorance. She seemed the fitting type of a young crude race with all its lessons to learn; that saw nothing absurd in its Methodists and Universalists and the rest--confident, as a child is, in its cries and whims and prejudices. The American girl, fresh from her wilds, and doubtful whether she would go to see the Pope in St. Peter's, lest she should have to bow the knee to Antichrist--the image delighted the mind of the elder woman. She played with it, finding fresh mock at every turn.

*   *   *   *   *

'Eleanor!--now I have rewritten it. Tell me how it runs.'

Lucy Poster looked up. She saw that Mr. Manisty, carrying a sheaf of papers in his hand, had thrown himself into a chair behind Mrs. Burgoyne. His look was strenuous and absorbed, his tumbling black hair had fallen forward as though in a stress of composition; he spoke in a low, imperative voice, like one accustomed to command the time and the attention of those about him.

'Read!' said Mrs. Burgoyne, turning her slender neck that she might look at him and hear. He began to read at once in a deep, tremulous voice, and as though he were quite unconscious of any other presence in the room than hers. Miss Foster, who was sitting at a little distance, supposed she ought not to listen. She was about to close her book and rise, when Miss Manisty touched her on the arm.

'It disturbs him if we move about!' said the little spinster in a smiling whisper, her finger on her lip. And suddenly the girl was conscious of a lightning flash from lifted eyes--a look threatening and peremptory. She settled herself into her chair again as quietly as possible, and sat with head bent, a smile she could not repress playing round her lips. It was all she could do indeed not to laugh, so startling and passionate had been the monition conveyed in Mr. Manisty's signal. That the great man should take little notice of his aunt's guest was natural enough. But to be frowned upon the first evening, as though she were a troublesome child!--she did not resent it at all, but it tickled her sense of humour. She thought happily of her next letter to Uncle Ben; how she would describe these rather strange people.

And at first she hardly listened to what was being read. The voice displeased her. It was too emphatic--she disliked its tremolo, its deep bass vibrations. Surely one should read more simply!

Then the first impression passed away altogether. She looked up--her eyes fastened themselves on the reader--her lips parted--the smile changed.

*   *   *   *   *

What the full over-rich voice was calling up before her was a little morning scene, as Virgil might have described it, passing in the hut of a Latian peasant farmer, under Tiberius.

It opened with the waking at dawn of the herdsman Caeculus and his little son, in their round thatched cottage on the ridge of Aricia, beneath the Alban Mount. It showed the countryman stepping out of his bed into the darkness, groping for the embers on the hearth, re-lighting his lamp, and calling first to his boy asleep on his bed of leaves, then to their African servant, the negro slave-girl with her wide mouth, her tight woolly hair. One by one the rustic facts emerged, so old, so ever new:--Caeculus grinding his corn, and singing at his work--the baking of the flat wheaten cakes on the hot embers--the gathering of herbs from the garden--the kneading them with a little cheese and oil to make a relish for the day--the harnessing of the white steers under the thonged yoke--the man going forth to his ploughing, under the mounting dawn, clad in his goatskin tunic and his leathern hat,--the boy loosening the goats from their pen beside the hut, and sleepily driving them past the furrows where his father was at work, to the misty woods beyond.

With every touch, the earlier world revived, grew plainer in the sun, till the listener found herself walking with Manisty through paths that cut the Alban Hills in the days of Rome's first imperial glory, listening to his tale of the little goatherd, and of Nemi.

*   *   *   *   *

'So the boy--Quintus--left the ploughed lands, and climbed a hill above the sleeping town. And when he reached the summit, he paused and turned him to the west.

'The Latian plain spreads beneath him in the climbing sun; at its edge is the sea in a light of pearl; the white fishing-boats sparkle along the shore. Close at his feet runs a straight road high upon the hill. He can see the country folk on their laden mules and donkeys journeying along it, journeying northwards to the city in the plain that the spurs of the mountain hide from him. His fancy goes with them, along the Appian Way, trotting with the mules. When will his father take him again to Rome to see the shops, and the Forum, and the new white temples, and Caesar's great palace on the hill?

'Then carelessly his eyes pass southward, and there beneath him in its hollow is the lake--the round blue lake that Diana loves, where are her temple and her shadowy grove. The morning mists lie wreathed above it; the just-leafing trees stand close in the great cup; only a few patches of roof and column reveal the shrine.

'On he moves. His wheaten cake is done. He takes his pipe from his girdle, touches it, and sings.

'His bare feet as he moves tread down the wet flowers. Bound him throng the goats; suddenly he throws down his pipe; he runs to a goat heavy with milk; he presses the teats with his quick hands; the milk flows foaming into the wooden cup he has placed below; he drinks, his brown curls sweeping the cup; then he picks up his pipe and walks on proudly before his goats, his lithe body swaying from side to side as he moves, dancing to the music that he makes. The notes float up into the morning air; the echo of them runs round the shadowy hollow of the lake.

'Down trips the boy, parting the dewy branches with his brown shoulders. Around him the mountain side is golden with the broom; at his feet the white cistus covers the rock. The shrubs of the scattered wood send out their scents; and the goats browse upon their shoots.

'But the path sinks gently downward--winding along the basin of the lake. And now the boy emerges from the wood; he stands upon a knoll to rest.

'Ah! sudden and fierce comes the sun!--and there below him in the rich hollow it strikes the temple--Diana's temple and her grove. Out flame the white columns, the bronze roof, the white enclosing walls. Piercingly white the holy and famous place shines among the olives and the fallows; the sun burns upon the marble; Phoebus salutes his great sister. And in the waters of the lake reappear the white columns; the blue waves dance around the shimmering lines; the mists part above them; they rise from the lake, lingering awhile upon the woods.

'The boy lays his hands to his eyes and looks eagerly towards the temple. Nothing. No living creature stirs.

'Often has he been warned by his father not to venture alone within the grove of the goddess. Twice, indeed, on the great June festivals has he witnessed the solemn sacrifices, and the crowds of worshippers, and the torches mirrored in the lake. But without his father, fear has hitherto stayed his steps far from the temple.

'To-day, however, as the sun mounts, and the fresh breeze breaks from the sea, his youth and the wildness of it dance within his blood. He and his goats pass into an olive garden. The red-brown earth has been freshly turned amid the twisted trunks; the goats scatter, searching for the patches of daisied grass still left by the plough. Guiltily the boy looks round him--peers through the olives and their silvery foam of leaves, as they fall past him down the steep. Then like one of his own kids he lowers his head and runs; he leaves his flock under the olives; he slips into a dense ilex-wood, still chill with the morning; he presses towards its edge; panting he climbs a huge and ancient tree that flings its boughs forward above the temple wall; he creeps along a branch among the thick small leaves,--he lifts his head.

'The temple is before him, and the sacred grove. He sees the great terrace, stretching to the lake; he hears the little waves plashing on its buttressed wall.

'Close beneath him, towards the rising and the midday sun there stretches a great niched wall girdling the temple on two sides, each niche a shrine, and in each shrine a cold white form that waits the sun--Apollo the Far-Darter, and the spear-bearing Pallas, and among them that golden Caesar, of whom the country talks, who has given great gifts to the temple--he and his grandson, the young Gaius.

'The boy strains his eye to see, and as the light strikes into the niche, flames on the gleaming breastplate, and the uplifted hand, he trembles on his branch for fear. Hurriedly he turns his look on the dwellings of the priestesses, where all still sleeps; on the rows of shining pillars that stand round about the temple; on the close-set trees of the grove that stands between it and the lake.

'Hark!--a clanging of metal--of great doors upon their hinges. From the inner temple--from the shrine of the goddess, there comes a man. His head is bound with the priest's fillet; sharply the sun touches his white pointed cap; in his hand he carries a sword.

'Between the temple and the grove there is a space of dazzling light. The man passes into it, turns himself to the east, and raises his hand to his mouth; drawing his robe over his head, he sinks upon the ground, and prostrate there, adores the coming god.

'His prayer lasts but an instant. Rising in haste, he stands looking around him, his sword gathered in his hand. He is a man still young; his stature is more than the ordinary height of men; his limbs are strong and supple. His rich dress, moreover, shows him to be both priest and king. But again the boy among his leaves draws his trembling body close, hiding, like a lizard, when some passing step has startled it from the sun. For on this haggard face the gods have written strange and terrible things; the priest's eyes deep sunk under his shaggy hair dart from side to side in a horrible unrest; he seems a creature separate from his kind--possessed of evil-- dedicate to fear.

'In the midst of the temple grove stands one vast ilex,--the tree of trees, sacred to Trivia. The other trees fall back from it in homage; and round it paces the priest, alone in the morning light.

'But his is no holy meditation. His head is thrown back; his ear listens for every sound; the bared sword glitters as he moves ...

'There is a rustle among the further trees. Quickly the boy stretches his brown neck; for at the sound the priest crouches on himself; he throws the robe from his right arm; and so waits, ready to strike. The light falls on his pale features, the tor- ment of his brow, the anguish of his drawn lips. Beside the lapping lake, and under the golden morning, he stands as Terror in the midst of Peace.

'Silence again:--only the questing birds call from the olive-woods. Panting, the priest moves onward, racked with sick tremors, prescient of doom.

'But hark! a cry!--and yet another answering--a dark form bursting from the grove--a fierce locked struggle under the sacred tree. The boy crawls to the furthest end of the branch, his eyes starting from his head.

'From the temple enclosure, from the further trees, from the hill around, a crowd comes running; men and white-robed priestesses, women, children even-- gathering in haste. But they pause afar off. Not a living soul approaches the place of combat; not a hand gives aid. The boy can see the faces of the virgins who serve the temple. They are pale, but very still. Not a sound of pity escapes their white lips; their ambiguous eyes watch calmly for the issue of the strife.

'And on the further side, at the edge of the grove stand country folk, men in goatskin tunics and leathern hats like the boy's father. And the little goatherd, not knowing what he does, calls to them for help in his shrill voice. But no one heeds; and the priest himself calls no one, entreats no one.

'Ah! The priest wavers--he falls--his white robes are in the dust. The bright steel rises--descends:--the last groan speeds to heaven.

*   *   *   *   *

'The victor raised himself from the dead, all stained with the blood and soil of the battle. Quintus gazed upon him astonished. For here was no rude soldier, nor swollen boxer, but a youth merely--a youth, slender and beautiful, fair-haired, and of a fair complexion. His loins were girt with a slave's tunic. Pallid were his young features; his limbs wasted with hunger and toil; his eyes blood-streaked as those of the deer when the dogs close upon its tender life.

'And looking down upon the huddled priest, fallen in his blood upon the dust, he peered long into the dead face, as though he beheld it for the first time. Shudders ran through him; Quintus listened to hear him weep or moan. But at the last, he lifted his head, fiercely straightening his limbs like one who reminds himself of black fate, and things not to be undone. And turning to the multitude, he made a sign. With shouting and wild cries they came upon him; they snatched the purple-striped robe from the murdered priest, and with it they clothed his murderer. They put on him the priest's fillet, and the priest's cap; they hung garlands upon his neck; and with rejoicing and obeisance they led him to the sacred temple....

'And for many hours more the boy remained hidden in the tree, held there by the spell of his terror. He saw the temple ministers take up the body of the dead, and carelessly drag it from the grove. All day long was there crowd and festival within the sacred precinct. But when the shadows began to fall from the ridge of Aricia across the lake; when the new-made priest had offered on Trivia's altar a white steer, nourished on the Alban grass; when he had fed the fire of Vesta; and poured offerings to Virbius the immortal, whom in ancient days great Diana had snatched from the gods' wrath, and hidden here, safe within the Arician wood,--when these were done, the crowd departed and the Grove-King came forth alone from the temple.

'The boy watched what he would do. In his hand he carried the sword, which at the sunrise he had taken from the dead. And he came to the sacred tree that was in the middle of the grove, and he too began to pace about it, glancing from side to side, as that other had done before him. And once when he was near the place where the caked blood still lay upon the ground, the sword fell clashing from his hand, and he flung his two arms to heaven with a hoarse and piercing cry--the cry of him who accuses and arraigns the gods.

'And the boy, shivering, slipped from the tree, with that cry in his ear, and hastily sought for his goats. And when he had found them he drove them home, not staying even to quench his thirst from their swollen udders. And in the shepherd's hut he found his father Caeculus; and sinking down beside him with tears and sobs he told his tale.

'And Caeculus pondered long. And without chiding, he laid his hand upon the boy's head and bade him be comforted. "For," said he, as though he spake with himself--"such is the will of the goddess. And from the furthest times it has happened thus, before the Roman fathers journeyed from the Alban Mount and made them dwellings on the seven hills--before Romulus gave laws,--or any white-robed priest had climbed the Capitol. From blood springs up the sacred office; and to blood it goes! No natural death must waste the priest of Trivia's tree. The earth is hungry for the blood in its strength--nor shall it be withheld! Thus only do the trees bear, and the fields bring forth."

'Astonished, the boy looked at his father, and saw upon his face, as he turned it upon the ploughed lands and the vineyards, a secret and a savage joy. And the little goatherd's mind was filled with terror--nor would his father tell him further what the mystery meant. But when he went to his bed of dried leaves at night, and the moon rose upon the lake, and the great woods murmured in the hollow far beneath him, he tossed restlessly from side to side, thinking of the new priest who kept watch there--of his young limbs and miserable eyes--of that voice which he had flung to heaven. And the child tried to believe that he might yet escape.--But already in his dreams he saw the grove part once more and the slayer leap forth. He saw the watching crowd--and their fierce, steady eyes, waiting thirstily for the spilt blood. And it was as though a mighty hand crushed the boy's heart, and for the first time he shrank from the gods, and from his father,--so that the joy of his youth was darkened within him.'

* * * * *

As he read the last word, Manisty flung the sheets down upon the table beside him, and rising, he began to pace the room with his hands upon his sides, frowning and downcast. When he came to Mrs. Burgoyne's chair he paused beside her--

'I don't see what it has to do with the book. It is time lost'--he said to her abruptly, almost angrily.

'I think not,' she said, smiling at him. But her tone wavered a little, and his look grew still more irritable.

'I shall destroy it!'--he said, with energy--'nothing more intolerable than orna-ment out of place!'

'Oh don't!--don't alter it at all!' said a quick imploring voice.

Manisty turned in astonishment.

Lucy Foster was looking at him steadily. A glow of pleasure was on her cheek, her beautiful eyes were warm and eager. Manisty for the first time observed her, took note also of the loosened hair and Eleanor's cloak.

'You liked it?' he said with some embarrassment. He had entirely forgotten that she was in the room.

She drew a long breath.

'Yes!'--she said softly, looking down.

He thought that she was too shy to express herself. In reality her feeling was divided between her old enthusiasm and her new disillusion. She would have liked to tell him that his reading had reminded her of the book she loved. But the man, standing beside her, chilled her. She wished she had not spoken. It began to seem to her a piece of forwardness.

'Well, you're very kind'--he said, rather formally--'But I'm afraid it won't do. That lady there won't pass it.'

'What have I said?'--cried Mrs. Burgoyne, protesting.

Manisty laughed. 'Nothing. But you'll agree with me.' Then he gathered up his papers under his arm in a ruthless confusion, and walked away into his study, leav-ing discomfort behind him.

Mrs. Burgoyne sat silent, a little tired and pale. She too would have liked to praise and to give pleasure. It was not wonderful indeed that the child's fancy had been touched. That thrilling, passionate voice--her own difficulty always was to resist it--to try and see straight in spite of it.

*   *   *   *   *

Later that evening, when Miss Foster had withdrawn, Manisty and Mrs. Burgoyne were lingering and talking on a stone balcony that ran along the eastern front of the villa. The Campagna and the sea were behind them. Here, beyond a stretch of formal garden, rose a curved front of wall with statues and plashing water showing dimly in the moonlight; and beyond the wall there was a space of blue and silver lake; and girdling the lake the forest-covered Monte Cavo rose towering into the moonlit sky, just showing on its topmost peak that white speck which once was the temple of the Latian Jupiter, and is now, alas! only the monument of an Englishman's crime against history, art, and Rome. The air was soft, and perfumed with scent from the roses in the side-alleys below. A monotonous bird-note came from the ilex darkness, like the note of a thin passing bell. It was the cry of a small owl, which, in its plaintiveness and changelessness, had often seemed to Manisty and Eleanor the very voice of the Roman night.

Suddenly Mrs. Burgoyne said--'I have a different version of your Nemi story running in my head!--more tragic than yours. My priest is no murderer. He found his predecessor dead under the tree; the place was empty; he took it. He won't escape his own doom, of course, but he has not deserved it. There is no blood on his hand--his heart is pure. There!--I imagine it so.'

There was a curious tremor in her voice, which Manisty, lost in his own thoughts, did not detect. He smiled.

'Well!--you'll compete with Renan. He made a satire out of it. His priest is a moral gentleman who won't kill anybody. But the populace soon settle that. They knock him on the head, as a disturber of religion.'

'I had forgotten--' said Mrs. Burgoyne absently.

'But you didn't like it, Eleanor--my little piece!' said Manisty, after a pause. 'So don't pretend!'

She roused herself at once, and began to talk with her usual eagerness and sympathy. It was a repetition of the scene before dinner. Only this time her effect was not so great. Manisty's depression did not yield.

Presently, however, he looked down upon her. In the kind, concealing moonlight she was all grace and charm. The man's easy tenderness awoke.

'Eleanor--this air is too keen for that thin dress.'

And stooping over her he took her cloak from her arm, and wrapped it about her.

'You lent it to Miss Foster'--he said, surveying her. 'It became her--but it knows its mistress!'

The colour mounted an instant in her cheek. Then she moved further away from him.

'Have you discovered yet'--she said--'that that girl is extraordinarily handsome?'

'Oh yes'--he said carelessly--'with a handsomeness that doesn't matter.'

She laughed.

'Wait till Aunt Pattie and I have dressed her and put her to rights.'

'Well, you can do most things no doubt--both with bad books, and raw girls,'--he said, with a shrug and a sigh.

They bade each other good-night, and Mrs. Burgoyne disappeared through the glass door behind them.

*   *   *   *   *

The moon was sailing gloriously above the stone-pines of the garden. Mrs. Burgoyne, half-undressed, sat dreaming in a corner room, with a high painted ceiling, and both its windows open to the night.

She had entered her room in a glow of something which had been half torment, half happiness. Now, after an hour's dreaming, she suddenly bent forward and, parting the cloud of fair hair that fell about her, she looked in the glass before her, at the worn, delicate face haloed within it--thinking all the time with a vague misery of Lucy Foster's untouched bloom.

Then her eyes fell upon two photographs that stood upon her table. One represented a man in yeomanry uniform; the other a tottering child of two.

'Oh! my boy--my darling!'--she cried in a stifled agony, and snatching up the picture, she bowed her head upon it, kissing it. The touch of it calmed her. But she could not part from it. She put it in her breast, and when she slept, it was still there.

CHAPTER III

Eleanor--where are you off to?'

'Just to my house of Simmon,' said that lady, smiling. She was standing on the eastern balcony, buttoning a dainty grey glove, while Manisty a few paces from her was lounging in a deck-chair, with the English newspapers.

'What?--to mass? I protest. Look at the lake--look at the sky--look at that patch of broom on the lake side. Come and walk there before *dejeuner*--and make a round home by Aricia.'

Mrs. Burgoyne shook her head.

'No--I like my little idolatries,' she said, with decision. It was Sunday morning. The bells in Marinata were ringing merrily. Women and girls with black lace scarves upon their heads, handsome young men in short coats and soft peaked hats, were passing along the road between the villa and the lake, on their way to mass. It was a warm April day. The clouds of yellow banksia, hanging over the statued wall that girdled the fountain-basin, were breaking into bloom; and the nightingales were singing with a prodigality that was hardly worthy of their rank and dignity. Nature in truth is too lavish of nightingales on the Alban Hills in spring! She forgets, as it were, her own sweet arts, and all that rareness adds to beauty. One may hear a nightingale and not mark him; which is a *lese majeste*.

Mrs. Burgoyne's toilette matched the morning. The grey dress, so fresh and elegant, the broad black hat above the fair hair, the violets dewy from the garden that were fastened at her slender waist, and again at her throat beneath the pallor of the face,--these things were of a perfection quite evident to the critical sense of Edward Manisty. It was the perfection that was characteristic. So too was the faded fairness of hair and skin, the frail distinguished look. So, above all, was the contrast between the minute care for personal adornment implied in the finish of the dress, and the melancholy shrinking of the dark-rimmed eyes.

He watched her, through the smoke wreaths of his cigarette,--pleasantly and lazily conscious both of her charm and her inconsistencies.

'Are you going to take Miss Foster?' he asked her.

Mrs. Burgoyne laughed.

'I made the suggestion. She looked at me with amazement, coloured crimson, and went away. I have lost all my chances with her.'

'Then she must be an ungrateful minx'--said Manisty, lowering his voice and looking round him towards the villa, 'considering the pains you take.'

'*Some* of us must take pains,' said Mrs. Burgoyne, significantly.

'Some of us do'--he said, laughing. 'The others profit.--One goes on praying for the primitive,--but when it comes--No!--it is not permitted to be as typical as Miss Foster.'

'Typical of what?'

'The dissidence of Dissent, apparently--and the Protestantism of the Protestant religion. Confess:--it was an odd caprice on the part of high Jove to send her here?'

'I am sure she has a noble character--and an excellent intelligence!'

Manisty shrugged his shoulders.

'--Her grandfather'--continued the lady--'was a divinity professor and wrote a book on the Inquisition!'--

Manisty repeated his gesture.

'--And as I told you last night, she is almost as handsome as your Greek head--and very like her.'

'My dear lady--you have the wildest notions!'

Mrs. Burgoyne picked up her parasol.

'Quite true.--Your aunt tells me she was so disappointed, poor child, that there was no church of her own sort for her to go to this morning.'

'What!'--cried Manisty--'Did she expect a conventicle in the Pope's own town!'

For Marinata owned a Papal villa and had once been a favourite summer residence of the Popes.

'No--but she thought she might have gone into Rome, and she missed the trains. I found her wandering about the salon looking quite starved and restless.'

'Those are hungers that pass!--My heart is hard.--There--your bell is stopping.'

Eleanor!--I wonder why you go to these functions?'

He turned to look at her, his fine eye sharp and a little mocking.

'Because I like it.'

'You like the thought of it. But when you get there, the reality won't please you at all. There will be the dirty floor, and the bad music,--and the little priest intoning through his nose--and the scuffling boys,--and the abominable pictures--and the tawdry altars. Much better stay at home--and help me praise the Holy Roman Church from a safe distance!'

'What a hypocrite people would think you, if they could hear you talk like that!' she said, flushing.

'Then they would think it unjustly.--I don't mean to be my own dupe, that's all.'

'The dupes are the happiest,' she said in a low voice. 'There is something between them, and--Ah! well, never mind!'--

She stood still a moment, looking across the lake, her hands resting lightly on the stone balustrade of the terrace. Manisty watched her in silence, occasionally puffing at his cigarette.

'Well, I shall be back very soon,' she said, gathering up her prayer-book and her parasol. 'Will it then be our duty to take Miss Foster for a walk?'

'Why not leave her to my aunt?'

She passed him with a little nod of farewell. Presently, through the openings of the balustrade, Manisty could watch her climbing the village street with her dress held high above her daintily shod feet, a crowd of children asking for a halfpenny following at her heels. Presently he saw her stop irresolutely, open a little velvet bag that hung from her waist and throw a shower of *soldi* among the children. They swooped upon it, fighting and shrieking.

Mrs. Burgoyne looked at them half smiling, half repentant, shook her head and walked on.

'Eleanor--you coward!' said Manisty, throwing himself back in his chair with a silent laugh.

Under his protection, or his aunt's, as he knew well, Mrs. Burgoyne could walk past those little pests of children, even the poor armless and legless horrors on the way to Albano, and give a firm adhesion to Miss Manisty's Scotch doctrines on the subject of begging. But by herself, she could not refuse--she could not bear to be scowled on--even for a moment. She must yield--must give herself the luxury of being liked. It was all of a piece with her weakness towards servants and porters and cabmen--her absurdities in the way of tips and gifts--the kindnesses she had been showing during the last three days to the American girl. Too kind! Insipidity lay that way.

Manisty returned to his newspapers. When he had finished them he got up and began to pace the stone terrace, his great head bent forward as usual, as though the weight of it were too much for the shoulders. The newspapers had made him restless again, had dissipated the good humour of the morning, born perhaps of the mere April warmth and *bien etre*.

'Idling in a villa--with two women'--he said to himself, bitterly--'while all these things are happening.'

For the papers were full of news--of battles lost and won, on questions with which he had been at one time intimately concerned. Once or twice in the course of these many columns he had found his own name, his own opinion quoted, but only as belonging to a man who had left the field--a man of the past--politically dead.

As he stood there with his hands upon his sides, looking out over the Alban Lake, and its broom-clad sides, a great hunger for London swept suddenly upon him, for the hot scent of its streets, for its English crowd, for the look of its shops and clubs and parks. He had a vision of the club writing-room--of well-known men coming in and going out--discussing the news of the morning, the gossip of the House--he saw himself accosted as one of the inner circle,--he was sensible again of those short-lived pleasures of power and office. Not that he had cared half as much for these pleasures, when he had them, as other men. To affirm with him meant to be already half way on the road to doubt; contradiction was his character. Nevertheless, now that he was out of it, alone and forgotten--now that the game was well beyond his reach--it had a way of appearing to him at moments intolerably attractive!

Nothing before him now, in these long days at the villa, but the hours of work with Eleanor, the walks With Eleanor, the meals with his aunt and Eleanor--and now, for a stimulating change, Miss Foster! The male in him was restless. He had been eager to come to the villa, and the quiet of the hills, so as to push this long delaying book to its final end. And, behold, day by day, in the absence of the talk and distractions of Rome, a thousand discontents and misgivings were creeping upon him. In Rome he was still a power. In spite of his strange detached position, it was known that he was the defender of the Roman system, the panegyrist of Leo XIII., the apologist of the Papal position in Italy. And this had been more than enough to open to him all but the very inmost heart of Catholic life. Their apartments in Rome, to the scandal of Miss Manisty's Scotch instincts, had been haunted by ecclesiastics of every rank and kind. Cardinals, Italian and foreign, had taken their afternoon tea from Mrs. Burgoyne's hands; the black and white of the Dominicans, the brown of the Franciscans, the black of the Jesuits,--the staircase in the Via Sistina had been well acquainted with them all. Information not usually available had been placed lavishly at Manisty's disposal; he had felt the stir and thrill of the great Catholic organisation as all its nerve-threads gather to its brain and centre in the Vatican. Nay, on two occasions, he had conversed freely with Leo XIII. himself.

All this he had put aside, impatiently, that he might hurry on his book, and accomplish his *coup*. And in the tranquillity of the hills, was he beginning to lose faith in the book, and the compensation it was to bring him? Unless this book, with its scathing analysis of the dangers and difficulties of the secularist State, were not only a book, but *an event*, of what use would it be to him? He was capable both of extravagant conceit, and of the most boundless temporary disgust with his own doings and ideas. Such a disgust seemed to be mounting now through all his veins, taking all the savour out of life and work. No doubt it would be the same to the end,--the politician in him just strong enough to ruin the man of letters--the man of letters always ready to distract and paralyse the politician. And as for the book, there also he had been the victim of a double mind. He had endeavoured to make it popular, as Chateaubriand made the great argument of the *Genie du Christian-isme* popular, by the introduction of an element of poetry and romance. For the moment he was totally out of love with the result. What was the plain man to make of it? And nowadays the plain man settles everything.

Well!--if the book came to grief, it was not only he that would suffer.--Poor Eleanor!--poor, kind, devoted Eleanor!

Yet as the thought of her passed through his meditations, a certain annoyance mingled with it. What if she had been helping to keep him, all this time, in a fool's paradise--hiding the truth from him by this soft enveloping sympathy of hers?

His mind started these questions freely. Yet only to brush them away with a sense of shame. Beneath his outer controlling egotism there were large and generous elements in his mixed nature. And nothing could stand finally against the memory of that sweet all-sacrificing devotion which had been lavished upon himself and his work all the winter!

What right had he to accept it? What did it mean? Where was it leading?

He guessed pretty shrewdly what had been the speculations of the friends and acquaintances who had seen them together in Rome. Eleanor Burgoyne was but just thirty, very attractive, and his distant kinswoman. As for himself, he knew very well that according to the general opinion of the world, beginning with his aunt, it was his duty to marry and marry soon. He was in the prime of life; he had a property that cried out for an heir; and a rambling Georgian house that would be the better for a mistress. He was tolerably sure that Aunt Pattie had already had glimpses of Eleanor Burgoyne in that position.

Well--if so, Aunt Pattie was less shrewd than usual. Marriage! The notion of its fetters and burdens was no less odious to him now than it had been at twenty. What did he want with a wife--still more, with a son? The thought of his own life continued in another's filled him with a shock of repulsion. Where was the sense of infusing into another being the black drop of discontent that poisoned his own? A daughter perhaps--with the eyes of his mad sister Alice? Or a son--with the contradictions and weaknesses, without the gifts, of his father? Men have different ways of challenging the future. But that particular way called paternity had never in his most optimistic moments appealed to Manisty.

And of course Eleanor understood him! He had not been ungrateful. No!--he knew well enough that he had the power to make a woman's hours pass pleasantly. Eleanor's winter had been a happy one; her health and spirits had alike revived. Friendship, as they had known it, was a very rare and exquisite thing. No doubt when the book was done with, their relations must change somewhat. He confessed that he might have been imprudent; that he might have been appropriating the energies and sympathies of a delightful woman, as a man is hardly justified in doing, unless--. But, after all, a few weeks more would see the end of it; and friends, dear, close friends, they must always be.

For now there was plenty of room and leisure in his life for these subtler bonds. The day of great passions was gone by. There were one or two incidents in his earlier manhood on which he could look back with the half-triumphant consciousness that no man had dived deeper to the heart of feeling, had drunk more wildly, more inventively, of passion than he, in more than one country of Europe, in the East as in the West. These events had occurred in those wander-years between twenty and thirty, which he had spent in travelling, hunting and writing, in the pursuit, alternately eager and fastidious, of as wide an experience as possible. But all that was over. These things concerned another man, in another world. Politics and ambition had possessed him since, and women now appealed to other instincts in him--instincts rather of the diplomatist and intriguer than of the lover. Of late years they had been his friends and instruments. And by no unworthy arts. They were delightful to him; and his power with them was based on natural sympathies and divinations that were perhaps his birthright. His father had had the same gift. Why deny that both his father and he had owed much to women? What was there to be ashamed of? His father had been one of the ablest and most respected men of his day and so far as English society was concerned, the son had no scandal, nor the shadow of one, upon his conscience.

How far did Eleanor divine him? He raised his shoulder with a smile. Probably she knew him better than he knew himself. Besides, she was no mere girl, brimful of illusions and dreaming of love-affairs. What a history!--Good heavens! Why had he not known and seen something of her in the days when she was still under the tyranny of that intolerable husband? He might have eased the weight a little--protected her--as a kinsman may. Ah well--better not! They were both younger then.--

As for the present,--let him only extricate himself from this coil in which he stood, find his way back to activity and his rightful place, and many things might look differently. Perhaps--who could say?--in the future, when youth was still further forgotten by both of them, he and Eleanor might after all take each other by the hand--sit down on either side of the same hearth--their present friendship pass into one of another kind? It was quite possible, only--

The sudden crash of a glass door made him look round. It was Miss Foster who was hastening along the enclosed passage leading to the outer stair. She had miscalculated the strength of the wind on the north side of the house, and the glass door communicating with the library had slipped from her hand. She passed Manisty with a rather scared penitent look, quickly opened the outer door, and ran down-stairs.

Manisty watched her as she turned into the garden. The shadows of the ilex-avenue chequered her straw bonnet, her prim black cape, her white skirt. There had been no meddling of freakish hands with her dark hair this morning. It was tightly plaited at the back of her head. Her plain sun-shade, her black kid gloves were neatness itself--middle-class, sabbatical neatness.

Manisty recalled his thoughts of the last half-hour with a touch of amusement. He had been meditating on 'women'--the delightfulness of 'women,' his own natural inclination to their society. But how narrow is everybody's world!

His collective noun of course had referred merely to that small, high-bred, cosmopolitan class which presents types like Eleanor Burgoyne. And here came this girl, walking through his dream, to remind him of what 'woman,' average virtuous woman of the New or the Old World, is really like.

All the same, she walked well,--carried her head remarkably well. There was a free and springing youth in all her movements that he could not but follow with eyes that noticed all such things as she passed through the old trees, and the fragments of Graeco-Roman sculpture placed among them.

*   *   *   *   *

That afternoon Lucy Foster was sitting by herself in the garden of the villa. She had a volume of sermons by a famous Boston preacher in her hand, and was alternately reading--and looking. Miss Manisty had told her that some visitors from Rome would probably arrive between four and five o'clock, and close to her indeed the little butler, running hither and thither with an anxiety, an effusion that no English servant would have deigned to show, was placing chairs and tea-tables and putting out tea-things.

Presently indeed Alfredo approached the silent lady sitting under the trees, on tip-toe.

Would the signorina be so very kind as to come and look at the tables? The signora--so all the household called Miss Manisty--had given directions--but he, Alfredo, was not sure--and it would be so sad if when she came out she were not satisfied!

Lucy rose and went to look. She discovered some sugar-tongs missing. Alfredo started like the wind in search of them, running down the avenue with short, scudding steps, his coat-tails streaming behind him.

What a child-like eagerness to please! Yet he had been five years in the cavalry; he was admirably educated; he wrote a better hand than Manisty's own, and when his engagement at the villa came to an end he was already, thanks to a very fair scientific knowledge, engaged as manager in a firework factory in Rome.

Lucy's look pursued the short flying figure of the butler with a smiling kindness. What was wrong with this clever and loveable people that Mr. Manisty should never have a good word for their institutions, or their history, or their public men? Unjust! Nor was he even consistent with his own creed. He, so moody and silent with Mrs. Burgoyne and Miss Manisty, could always find a smile and a phrase for the natives. The servants adored him, and all the long street of Marinata welcomed him with friendly eyes. His Italian was fluency itself; and his handsome looks perhaps, his keen commanding air gave him a natural kingship among a susceptible race.

But to laugh and live with a people, merely that you might gibbet it before Europe, that you might show it as the Helot among nations--there was a kind of treachery in it! Lucy Foster remembered some of the talk and feeling in America after the Manistys' visit there had borne fruit in certain hostile lectures and addresses on the English side of the water. She had shared the feeling. She was angry still. And her young ignorance and sympathy were up in arms so far on behalf of Italy. Who and what was this critic that he should blame so freely, praise so little?

Not that Mr. Manisty had so far confided any of his views to her! It seemed to her that she had hardly spoken with him since that first evening of her arrival. But she had heard further portions of his book read aloud; taken from the main fabric this time and not from the embroideries. The whole villa indeed was occupied, and pre-occupied by the book. Mrs. Burgoyne was looking pale and worn with the stress of it.

Mrs. Burgoyne! The girl fell into a wondering reverie. She was Mr. Manisty's second cousin--she had lost her husband and child in some frightful accident--she was not going to marry Mr. Manisty--at least nobody said so--and though she went to mass, she was not a Catholic, but on the contrary a Scotch Presbyterian, by birth, being the daughter of a Scotch laird of old family--one General Delafield Muir--?

'She is very kind to me,' thought Lucy Foster in a rush of gratitude mixed with some perplexity.--'I don't know why she takes so much trouble about me. She is so different--so--so fashionable--so experienced. She can't care a bit about me. Yet she is very sweet to me--to everybody, indeed. But--'

And again she lost herself in ponderings on the relation of Mr. Manisty to his cousin. She had never seen anything like it. The mere neighbourhood of it thrilled her, she could not have told why. Was it the intimacy that it implied--the intimacy of mind and thought? It was like marriage--but married people were more reserved, more secret. Yet of course it was only friendship. Miss Manisty had said that her nephew and Mrs. Burgoyne were 'very great friends.' Well--One read of such things--one did not often see them.

* * * * *

The sound of steps approaching made her lift her eyes.

It was not Alfredo, but a young man, a young Englishman apparently, who was coming towards her. He was fair-haired and smiling; he carried his hat under his arm; and he wore a light suit and a rose in his button-hole--this was all she had time to see before he was at her side.

'May I introduce myself? I must!--Miss Manisty told me to come and find you. I'm Reggie Brooklyn--Mrs. Burgoyne's friend. Haven't you heard of me? I look after her when Manisty ought to, and doesn't; I'm going to take you all to St. Peter's next week.'

Lucy looked up to see a charming face, lit by the bluest of blue eyes, adorned moreover by a fair moustache, and an expression at once confident and appealing.

Was this the 'delightful boy' from the Embassy Mrs. Burgoyne had announced to her? No doubt. The colour rose softly in her cheek. She was not accustomed to young gentlemen with such a manner and such a ***savoir faire***.

'Won't you sit down?' She moved sedately to one side of the bench.

He settled himself at once, fanning himself with his hat, and looking at her discreetly.

'You're American, aren't you? You don't mind my asking you?'

'Not in the least. Yes; it's my first time in Europe.'

'Well, Italy's not bad; is it? Nice place, Rome, anyway. Aren't you rather knocked over by it? I was when I first came.'

'I've only been here four days.

'And of course nobody here has time to take you about. I can guess that! How's the book getting on?'

'I don't know,' she said, opening her eyes wide in a smile that would not be repressed, a smile that broke like light in her grave face.

Her companion looked at her with approval.

'My word! she's dowdy'--he thought--'like a Sunday-school teacher. But she's handsome.'

The real point was, however, that Mrs. Burgoyne had told him to go out and make himself agreeable, and he was accustomed to obey orders from that quarter.

'Doesn't he read it to you all day and all night?' he asked. 'That's his way.'

'I have heard some of it. It's very interesting.'

The young man shrugged his shoulders.

'It's a queer business that book. My chief here is awfully sick about it. So are a good many other English. Why should an Englishman come out here and write a book to run down Italy?--And an Englishman that's been in the Government, too--so of course what he says'll have authority. Why, we're friends with Italy-- we've always stuck up for Italy! When I think what he's writing--and what a row it'll make--I declare I'm ashamed to look one's Italian friends in the face!--And just now, too, when they're so down on their luck.'

For it was the year of the Abyssinian disasters; and the carnage of Adowa was not yet two months old.

Lucy's expression showed her sympathy.

'What makes him--'

'Take such a twisted sort of a line? O goodness! what makes Manisty do anything? Of course, I oughtn't to talk. I'm just an understrapper--and he's a man of genius,--more or less--we all know that. But what made him do what he did last year? I say it was because his chief--he was in the Education Office you know--was a Dissenter, and a jam manufacturer, and had mutton-chop whisker. Manisty just couldn't do what he was told by a man like that. He's as proud as Lucifer. I once heard him tell a friend of mine that he didn't know how to obey anybody--he'd never learnt. That's because they didn't send him to a public school--worse luck; that was his mother's doing, I believe. She thought him so clever--he must be treated differently to other people. Don't you think that's a great mistake?'

'What?'

'Why--to prefer the cross-cuts, when you might stick to the high road?'

The American girl considered. Then she flashed into a smile.--

'I think I'm for the cross-cuts!'

'Ah--that's because you're American. I might have known you'd say that. All your people want to go one better than anybody else. But I can tell you it doesn't do for Englishmen. They want their noses kept to the grindstone. That's my experience! Of course it was a great pity Manisty ever went into Parliament at all. He'd been abroad for seven or eight years, living with all the big-wigs and reactionaries everywhere. The last thing in the world he knew anything about was English politics.--But then his father had been a Liberal, and a Minister for ever so long. And when Manisty came home, and the member for his father's division died, I don't deny it was very natural they should put him in. And he's such a queer mixture, I dare say he didn't know himself where he was.--But I'll tell you one thing--'

He shook his head slowly,--with all the airs of the budding statesman.

'When you've joined a party,--you must *dine* with 'em:--It don't sound much--but I declare it's the root of everything. Now Manisty was always dining with the other side. All the great Tory ladies,--and the charming High Churchwomen, and the delightful High Churchmen--and they *are* nice fellows, I can tell you!--got hold of him. And then it came to some question about these beastly schools--don't you wish they were all at the bottom of the sea?--and I suppose his chief was more annoying than usual--(oh, but he had a number of other coolnesses on his hands by that time--he wasn't meant to be a Liberal!) and his friends talked to him--and so--Ah! there they are!'

And lifting his hat, the young man waved it towards Mrs. Burgoyne who with Manisty and three or four other companions had just become visible at the further end of the ilex-avenue which stretched from their stone bench to the villa.

'Why, that's my chief,'--he cried--'I didn't think he was to be here this afternoon. I say, do you know my chief?'

And he turned to her with the brightest, most confiding manner, as though he had been the friend of her cradle.

'Who?'--said Lucy, bewildered--'the tall gentleman with the white hair?'

'Yes,--that's the ambassador. Oh! I'm glad you'll see him. He's a charmer, is our chief! And that's his married daughter, who's keeping house for him just now.--I'll tell you something, if you'll keep a secret'--he bent towards her,--'He likes Mrs. Burgoyne of course,--everybody does--but he don't take Manisty at his own valuation. I've heard him say some awfully good things to Manisty--you'd hardly think a man would get over them.--Who's that on the other side?'

He put his hand over his eyes for a moment, then burst into a laugh.--

'Why, it's the other man of letters!--Bellasis. I should think you've read some of his poems--or plays? Rome has hardly been able to hold the two of them this winter. It's worse than the archaeologists. Mrs. Burgoyne is always trying to be civil to him, so that he mayn't make uncivil remarks about Manisty. I say--don't you think she's delightful?'

He lowered his voice as he looked round upon his companion, but his blue eyes shone.

'Mrs. Burgoyne?'--said Lucy--'Yes, indeed!--She's so--so very kind.'

'Oh! she's a darling, is Eleanor Burgoyne. And I may call her that, you know, for I'm her cousin, just as Manisty is--only on the other side. I have been trying to look after her a bit this winter in Rome; she never looks after herself. And she's not a bit strong.--You know her history of course?'

He lowered his voice with young importance, speaking almost in a whisper, though the advancing party were still far away. Lucy shook her head.

'Well, it's a ghastly tale, and I've only a minute.--Her husband, you see, had pneumonia--they were in Switzerland together, and he'd taken a chill after a walk--and one night he was raving mad, mad you understand with delirium and fever--and poor Eleanor was so ill, they had taken her away from her husband, and put her to bed on the other side of the hotel.--And there was a drunken nurse--it's almost too horrible, isn't it?--and while she was asleep Mr. Burgoyne got up, quite mad--

and he went into the next room, where the baby was, without waking anybody, and he took the child out asleep in his arms, back to his own room where the windows were open, and there he threw himself and the boy out together--headlong! The hotel was high up,--built, one side of it, above a rock wall, with a stream below it.-- There had been a great deal of rain, and the river was swollen. The bodies were not found for days.--When poor Eleanor woke up, she had lost everything.--Oh! I dare say, when the first shock was over, the husband didn't so much matter--he hadn't made her at all happy.--But the child!'--

He stopped, Mrs. Burgoyne's gay voice could be heard as she approached. All the elegance of the dress was visible, the gleam of a diamond at the throat, the flowers at the waist. Lucy Foster's eyes, dim with sudden tears, fastened themselves upon the slender, advancing form.

CHAPTER IV

The party grouped themselves round the tea-tables. Mrs. Burgoyne laid a kind hand on Lucy Foster's arm, and introduced one or two of the new-comers.

Then, while Miss Manisty, a little apart, lent her ear to the soft chat of the ambassador, who sat beside her, supporting a pair of old and very white hands upon a gold-headed stick, Mrs. Burgoyne busied herself with Mr. Bellasis and his tea. For he was anxious to catch a train, and had but a short time to spare.

He was a tall stiffly built man, with a heavy white face, and a shock of black hair combed into a high and bird-like crest. As to Mrs. Burgoyne's attentions, he received them with a somewhat pinched but still smiling dignity. Manisty, meanwhile, a few feet away, was fidgetting on his chair, in one of his most unmanageable moods. Around him were two or three young men bearing the great names of Rome. They all belonged to the Guardia Nobile, and were all dressed by English tailors. Two of them, moreover, were the sons of English mothers. They were laughing and joking together, and every now and then they addressed their host. But he scarcely replied. He gathered stalk after stalk of grass from the ground beside him, nibbled it and threw it away--a constant habit of his when he was annoyed or out of spirits.

"So you have read my book?" said Mr. Bellasis pleasantly, addressing Mrs. Burgoyne, as she handed him a cup of tea. The book in question was long; it revived the narrative verse of our grandfathers; and in spite of the efforts of a 'set' the world was not disposed to take much notice of it.

'Yes, indeed! We liked it so much.--But I think when I wrote to you I told you what we thought about it?'

And she glanced towards Manisty for support. He, however, did not apparently hear what she said. Mr. Bellasis also looked round in his direction; but in vain. The poet's face clouded.

'May I ask what reading you are at?' he said, returning to his tea.

'What reading?'--Mrs. Burgoyne looked puzzled.

'Have you read it more than once?'

She coloured.

'No--I'm afraid--'

'Ah!--my friends tell me in Rome that the book cannot be really appreciated except at a second or third reading--'

Mrs. Burgoyne looked up in dismay, as a shower of gravel descended on the tea-table. Manisty has just beckoned in haste to his great Newfoundland who was lying stretched on the gravel path, and the dog bounding towards him, seemed to have brought the path with him.

Mr. Bellasis impatiently shook some fragments of gravel from his coat, and resumed:--

'I have just got a batch of the first reviews. Really criticism has become an ab-surdity! Did you look at the "Sentinel"?'

Mrs. Burgoyne hesitated.

'Yes--I saw there was something about the style--'

'The style!'--Mr. Bellasis threw himself back in his chair and laughed loud--'Why the style is done with a magnifying-glass!--There's not a phrase,--not a word that I don't stand by.'

'Mr. Bellasis'--said the courteous voice of the ambassador--'are you going by this train?'

The great man held out his watch.

'Yes indeed--and I must catch it!' cried the man of letters. He started to his feet, and bending over Mrs. Burgoyne, he said in an aside perfectly audible to all the world--'I read my new play to-night--just finished--at Madame Salvi's!'

Eleanor smiled and congratulated him. He took his leave, and Manisty in an embarrassed silence accompanied him half way down the avenue.

Then returning, he threw himself into a chair near Lucy Foster and young Brooklyn, with a sigh of relief.

'Intolerable ass!'--he said under his breath, as though quite unconscious of any bystander.

The young man looked at Lucy with eyes that danced.

*   *   *   *   *

'Who is your young lady?' said the ambassador.

Miss Manisty explained.

'An American? Really? I was quite off the scent, But now--I see--I see! Let me guess. She is a New Englander--not from Boston, but from the country. I remember the type exactly. The year I was at Washington I spent some weeks in the summer convalescing at a village up in the hills of Maine.--The women there seemed to me the salt of the earth. May I go and talk to her?'

Miss Manisty led him across the circle to Lucy, and introduced him.

'Will you take me to the terrace and show me St. Peter's? I know one can see it from here,' said the suave polished voice.

Lucy rose in a shy pleasure that became her. The thought flashed happily through her, as she walked beside the old man, that Uncle Ben would like to hear of it! She had that 'respect of persons' which comes not from snobbishness, but from imagination and sympathy. The man's office thrilled her, not his title.

The ambassador's shrewd eyes ran over her face and bearing, taking note of all the signs of character. Then he began to talk, exerting himself as he had not exerted himself that morning for a princess who had lunched at his table. And as he was one of the enchanters of his day, known for such in half a dozen courts, and two hemi-spheres, Lucy Foster's walk was a walk of delight. There was only one drawback. She had heard some member of the party say 'Your Excellency'--and somehow her lips would not pronounce it! Yet so kind and kingly was the old man, there was no sign of homage she would not have gladly paid him, if she had known how.

They emerged at last upon the stone terrace at the edge of the garden looking out upon the Campagna.

'Ah! there it is!'--said the ambassador, and, walking to the corner of the terrace, he pointed northwards.

And there--just caught between two stone pines--in the dim blue distance rose the great dome.

'Doesn't it give you an emotion?' he said, smiling down upon her.--'When I first stayed on these hills I wrote a poem about it--a very bad poem. There's a kind of miracle in it, you know. Go where you will, that dome follows you. Again and again, storm and mist may blot out the rest--that remains. The peasants on these hills have a superstition about it. They look for that dome as they look for the sun. When they can't see it, they are unhappy--they expect some calamity.--It's a symbol, isn't it, an idea?--and those are the things that touch us. I have a notion'--he turned to her smiling, 'that it will come into Mr. Manisty's book?'

Their eyes met in a smiling assent.

"Well, there are symbols--and symbols. That dome makes my old heart beat because it speaks of so much--half the history of our race. But looking back--I remember another symbol--I was at Harvard in '69; and I remember the first time I ever saw those tablets--you recollect--in the Memorial Hall--to the Harvard men that fell in the war?"

The colour leapt into her cheek. Her eyes filled.

"Oh yes! yes!"--she said, half eager, half timid--"My father lost two brothers--both their names are there."

The ambassador looked at her kindly.--"Well--be proud of it!--be proud of it! That wall, those names, that youth, and death--they remain with me, as the symbol of the other great majesty in the world! There's one,"--he pointed to the dome,--"that's Religion. And the other's Country. It's country that Mr. Manisty forgets--isn't it?"

The old man shook his head, and fell silent, looking out over the cloud-flecked Campagna.

"Ah, well"--he said, rousing himself--"I must go. Will you come and see me? My daughter shall write to you."

And five minutes later the ambassador was driving swiftly towards Rome, in a good humour with himself and the day. He had that morning sent off what he knew to be a masterly despatch, and in the afternoon, as he was also quite conscious, he had made a young thing happy.

*   *   *   *   *

Manisty could not attend the ambassador to his carriage. He was absorbed by another guest. Mrs. Burgoyne, young Brooklyn, and Lucy, paid the necessary civilities.

When they returned, they found a fresh group gathered on the terrace. Two persons made the centre of it--a grey-haired cardinal--and Manisty.

Lucy looked at her host in amazement. What a transformation! The man who had been lounging and listless all the afternoon--barely civil to his guests--making no effort indeed for anyone, was now another being. An hour before he had been in middle age; now he was young, handsome, courteous, animating, and guiding the conversation around him with the practised ease of one who knew himself a master.

Where was the spell? The Cardinal?

The Cardinal sat to Manisty's right, one wrinkled hand resting on the neck of the Newfoundland. It was a typical Italian face, large-cheeked and large-jawed, with good eyes,--a little sleepy, but not unspiritual. His red-edged cassock allowed a glimpse of red stockings to be seen, and his finely worked cross and chain, his red sash, and the bright ribbon that lit up his broad-brimmed hat, made spots of cheerful colour in the shadow of the trees.

He was a Cardinal of the Curia, belonging indeed to the Congregation of the Index. The vulgar believed that he was staying on the hills for his health.

The initiated, however, knew that he had come to these heights, bringing with him the works of a certain German Catholic professor threatened with the thunders of the Church. It was a matter that demanded leisure and a quiet mind.

As he sat sipping Miss Manisty's tea, however, nothing could be divined of those scathing Latin sheets on which he had left his secretary employed. He had the air of one at peace with all the world--hardly stirred indeed by the brilliance of his host.

'Italy again!'--said Reggie Brooklyn in Lucy's ear--poor old Italy!--one might be sure of that, when one sees one of these black gentlemen about.'

The Cardinal indeed had given Manisty his text. He had brought an account

of some fresh vandalism of the Government--the buildings of an old Umbrian convent turned to Government uses--the disappearance of some famous pictures in the
process, supposed to have passed into the bands of a Paris dealer by the connivance
of a corrupt official.

The story had roused Manisty to a white heat. This maltreatment of religious
buildings and the wasting of their treasures was a subject on which he was inex-
haustible. Encouraged by the slow smile of the Cardinal, the laughter and applause
of the young men, he took the history of a monastery in the mountains of Spoleto,
which had long been intimately known to him, and told it,--with a variety, a passion, an irony, that only he could achieve--that at last revealed indeed to Lucy Foster, as she sat quivering with antagonism beside Miss Manisty, all the secret of the
man's fame and power in the world.

For gradually--from the story of this monastery, and its suppression at the
hands of a few Italian officials--he built up a figure, typical, representative, according to him, of the New Italy, small, insolent, venal,--insulting and despoiling the
Old Italy, venerable, beautiful and defenceless. And then a natural turn of thought,
or a suggestion from one of the group surrounding him, brought him to the scandals
connected with the Abyssinian campaign--to the charges of incompetence and corruption which every Radical paper was now hurling against the Crispi government.
He gave the latest gossip, handling it lightly, inexorably, as one more symptom
of an inveterate disease, linking the men of the past with the men of the present,
spattering all with the same mud, till Italian Liberalism, from Cavour to Crispi, sat
shivering and ugly--stripped of all those pleas and glories wherewith she had once
stepped forth adorned upon the page of history.

Finally--with the art of the accomplished talker--a transition! Back to the
mountains, and the lonely convent on the heights--to the handful of monks left
in the old sanctuary, handing on the past, waiting for the future, heirs of a society
which would destroy and outlive the New Italy, as it had destroyed and outlived
the Old Rome,--offering the daily sacrifice amid the murmur and solitude of the
woods,--confident, peaceful, unstained; while the new men in the valleys below
peculated and bribed, swarmed and sweated, in the mire of a profitless and purposeless corruption.

And all this in no set harangue--but in vivid broken sentences; in snatches of paradox and mockery; of emotion touched and left; interrupted, moreover, by the lively give and take of conversation with the young Italians, by the quiet comments of the Cardinal. None the less, the whole final image emerged, as Manisty meant it to emerge; till the fascinated hearers felt, as it were, a breath of hot bitterness and hate pass between them and the spring day, enveloping the grim phantom of a ruined and a doomed State.

The Cardinal said little. Every now and then he put in a fact of his own knowledge--a stroke of character--a phrase of compassion that bit more sharply even than Manisty's scorns--a smile--a shake of the head. And sometimes, as Manisty talked with the young men, the sharp wrinkled eyes rested upon the Englishman with a scrutiny, instantly withdrawn. All the caution of the Roman ecclesiastic,--the inheritance of centuries--spoke in the glance.

It was perceived by no one, however, but a certain dark elderly lady, who was sitting restlessly silent beside Miss Manisty. Lucy Foster had noticed her as a newcomer, and believed that her name was Madame Variani.

As for Eleanor Burgoyne, she sat on Manisty's left while he talked--it was curious to notice how a place was always made for her beside him!--her head raised a little towards him, her eyes bright and fixed. The force that breathed from him passed through her frail being, quickening every pulse of life. She neither criticised nor accepted what he said. It was the man's splendid vitality that subdued and mastered her.

Yet she alone knew what no one else suspected. At the beginning of the conversation Manisty had placed himself behind an old stone table of oblong shape and thick base, of which there were several in the garden. Round it grew up grasses and tall vetches which had sown themselves among the gaping stones of the terrace. Nothing, therefore, could be seen of the talker as he leant carelessly across the table but the magnificent head, and the shoulders on which it was so freely and proudly carried.

Anybody noticing the effect--for it was an effect--would have thought it a mere happy accident. Eleanor Burgoyne alone knew that it was conscious. She had seen the same pose, the same concealment practised too often to be mistaken. But it made no difference whatever to the spell that held her. The small vanities and miseries of Manisty's nature were all known to her--and alas! she would not have altered one of them!

*   *   *   *   *

When the Cardinal rose to go, two Italian girls, who had come with their brother, the Count Casaleschi, ran forward, and curtseying kissed the Cardinal's ring. And as he walked away, escorted by Manisty, a gardener crossed the avenue, who also at sight of the tall red-sashed figure fell on his knees and did the same. The Cardinal gave him an absent nod and smile, and passed on.

'Ah! *j'etouffe*!'--cried Madame Variani, throwing herself down by Miss Manisty. 'Give me another cup, *chere Madame*. Your nephew is too bad. Let him show us another nation born in forty years--that has had to make itself in a generation--let him show it us! Ah! you English--with all your advantages--and your proud hearts.--Perhaps we too could pick some holes in you!'

She fanned herself with angry vigour. The young men came to stand round her arguing and laughing. She was a favourite in Rome, and as a French woman, and the widow of a Florentine man of letters, occupied a somewhat independent position, and was the friend of many different groups.

'And you--young lady, what do you think?'--she said suddenly, laying a large hand on Lucy Foster's knee.

Lucy, startled, looked into the sparkling black eyes brought thus close to her own.

'But I just *long*'--she said, catching her breath--'to hear the other side.'

'Ah, and you shall hear it, my dear--you shall!' cried Madame Variani. '*N'est-ce pas, Madame?*' she said, addressing Miss Manisty--'We will get rid of all those priests--and then we will speak our mind? Oh, and you too,'--she waved her hand with a motherly roughness towards the young men,--'What do you know about it, Signor Marchese? If there were no Guardia Nobile, you would not wear those fine uniforms.--That is why you like the Pope.'

The Marchese Vitellucci--a charming boy of two and twenty, tall, thin-faced and pensive,--laughed and bowed.

'The Pope, Madame, should establish some *dames d'honneur*. Then he would have all the ladies too on his side.

'*O, mon Dieu!*--he has enough of them,' cried Madame Variani. 'But here comes Mr. Manisty, I must drink my tea and hold my tongue. I am going out to dinner to-night, and if one gets hot and cross, that is not good for the complexion.'

Manisty advanced at his usual quick pace, his head sunk once more between his shoulders.

Young Vitellucci approached him. 'Ah! Carlo!' he said, looking up affectionately--'dear fellow!--Come for a stroll with me.'

And linking his arm in the young man's, he carried him off. Their peals of laughter could be heard coming back from the distance of the ilex-walk.

Madame Variani tilted back her chair to look after them.

'Ah! your nephew can be agreeable too, when he likes,' she said to Miss Manisty. 'I do not say no. But when he talks of these poor Italians, he is *mechant--mechant*!'

As for Lucy Foster, as Manisty passed out of sight, she felt her pulses still tingling with a wholly new sense of passionate hostility--dislike even. But none the less did the stage seem empty and meaningless when he had left it.

*   *   *   *   *

Manisty and Mrs. Burgoyne were closeted in the library for some time before dinner. Lucy in the salon could hear him pacing up and down, and the deep voice dictating.

Then Mrs. Burgoyne came into the salon, and not noticing the girl who was hidden behind a great pot of broom threw herself on the sofa with a long sigh of fatigue. Lucy could just see the pale face against the pillow and the closed eyes. Thus abandoned and at rest, there was something strangely pitiful in the whole figure, for all its grace.

A wave of feeling rose in the girl's breast. She slipped softly from her hiding-place, took a silk wrap that was lying on a chair, and approached Mrs. Burgoyne.

'Let me put this over you. Won't you sleep before dinner? And I will shut the window. It is getting cold.'

Mrs. Burgoyne opened her eyes in astonishment, and murmured a few words of thanks.

Lucy covered her up, closed the window, and was stealing away, when Mrs. Burgoyne put out a hand and touched her.

'It is very sweet of you to think of me.'

She drew the girl to her, enclosed the hand she had taken in both hers, pressed it and released it. Lucy went quietly out of the room.

Then till dinner she sat reading her New Testament, and trying rather piteously to remind herself that it was Sunday. Far away in a New England village, the bells were ringing for the evening meeting. Lucy, shutting her eyes, could smell the spring scents in the church lane, could hear the droning of the opening hymn. A vague mystical peace stole upon her, as she recalled the service; the great words of 'sin,' 'salvation,' 'righteousness,' as the Evangelical understands them, thrilled through her heart.

Then, as she rose to dress, there burst upon her through the open window the sunset blaze of the Campagna with the purple dome in its midst. And with that came the memory of the afternoon,--of the Cardinal--and Manisty.

Very often, in these first days, it was as though her mind ached, under the stress of new thinking, like something stretched and sore. In the New England house where she had grown up, a corner of the old-fashioned study was given up to the books of her grandfather, the divinity professor. They were a small collection, all gathered with one object,--the confuting and confronting of Rome. Like many another Protestant zealot, the old professor had brooded on the crimes and cruelties of persecuting Rome, till they became a madness in the blood. How well Lucy remembered his books--with their backs of faded grey or brown cloths, and their grim titles. Most of them she had never yet been allowed to read. When she looked for a book, she was wont to pass this shelf by in a vague horror. What Rome habitually did or permitted, what at any rate she had habitually done or permitted in the past, could not--it seemed--be known by a pure woman! And she would glance from the books to the engraving of her grandfather above them,--to the stern and yet delicate face of the old Calvinist, with its high-peaked brow, and white neckcloth supporting the sharp chin; lifting her heart to him in a passionate endorsement, a common fierce hatred of wrong and tyranny.

She had grown older since then, and her country with her. New England Puritanism was no longer what it had been; and the Catholic Church had spread in the land. But in Uncle Ben's quiet household, and in her own feeling, the changes had been but slight and subtle. Pity, perhaps, had insensibly taken the place of hatred. But those old words 'priest' and 'mass' still rung in her ears as symbols of all that man had devised to corrupt and deface the purity of Christ.

And of what that purity might be, she had such tender, such positive traditions! Her mother had been a Christian mystic--a 'sweet woman,' meek as a dove in household life, yet capable of the fiercest ardours as a preacher and missionary, gathering rough labourers into barns and by the wayside, and dying before her time, worn out by the imperious energies of religion. Lucy had always before her the eyes that seemed to be shining through a mist, the large tremulous mouth, the gently furrowed brow. Those strange forces--'grace'--and 'the spirit'--had been the realities, the deciding powers of her childhood, whether in what concerned the great emotions of faith, or the most trivial incidents of ordinary life--writing a letter--inviting a guest--taking a journey. The soul bare before God, depending on no fleshly aid, distracted by no outward rite; sternly defending its own freedom as a divine trust:--she had been reared on these main thoughts of Puritanism, and they were still through all insensible transformation, the guiding forces of her own being.

Already, in this Catholic country, she had been jarred and repelled on all sides. Yet she found herself living with two people for whom Catholicism was not indeed a personal faith--she could not think of that side of it without indignation--but a thing to be passionately admired and praised, like art, or music, or scenery. You might believe nothing, and yet write pages and pages in glorification of the Pope and the Mass, and in contempt of everything else!--in excuse too of every kind of tyranny so long as it served the Papacy and 'the Church.'

She leaned out to the sunset, remembering sentence after sentence from the talk on the terrace--hating or combating them all.

Yet all the time a new excitement invaded her. For the man who had spoken thus was, in a sense, not a mere stranger to her. Somewhere in his being must be the capacity for those thoughts and feelings that had touched her so deeply in his book--for that magical insight and sweetness--

Ah!--perhaps she had not understood his book--no more than she understood him now. The sense of her own ignorance oppressed her--and of all that **might** be said, with regard apparently to anything whatever. Was there nothing quite true-- quite certain--in the world?

So the girl's intense and simple nature entered like all its fellows, upon the old inevitable struggle. As she stood there, with locked hands and flushed cheeks, conscious through every vein of the inrush and shock of new perceptions, new comparisons, she was like a ship that leaves the harbour for the open, and feels for the first time on all her timbers the strain of the unplumbed sea.

And of this invasion, this excitement, the mind, in haunting debate and antagonism, made for itself one image, one symbol--the face of Edward Manisty.

CHAPTER V

While he was thus--unknowing--the cause of so many new attractions and repulsions in his guest's mind, Manisty, after the first shock of annoyance produced by her arrival was over, hardly remembered her existence. He was incessantly occupied by the completion of his book, working late and early, sometimes in high and even extravagant spirits, but, on the whole, more commonly depressed and discontented.

Eleanor Burgoyne worked with him or for him many hours in each day. Her thin pallor became more pronounced. She ate little, and Miss Manisty believed that she slept less. The elder lady indeed began to fidget and protest, to remonstrate now and then with Manisty himself, even to threaten a letter to 'the General.' Eleanor's smiling obstinacy, however, carried all before it. And Manisty, in spite of a few startled looks and perfunctory dissuasions, whenever his aunt attacked him, soon slipped back into his normal ways of depending on his cousin, and not being able to work without her. Lucy Foster thought him selfish and inconsiderate. It gave her one more cause of quarrel with him.

For she and Mrs. Burgoyne were slowly but surely making friends. The clearer it became that Manisty took no notice of Miss Foster, and refused to be held in any way responsible for her entertainment, the more anxious, it seemed, did Eleanor show herself to make life pleasant for the American girl. Her manner, which had always been kind, became more natural and gay. It was as though she had settled some question with herself, and settled it entirely to Lucy Foster's advantage.

Not much indeed could be done for the stranger while the stress of Manisty's work lasted. Aunt Pattie braced herself once or twice, got out the guide-books and took her visitor into Rome to see the sights. But the little lady was so frankly worn out by these expeditions, that Lucy, full of compunctions, could only beg to be left to herself in future. Were not the garden and the lake, the wood-paths to Rocca di Papa, and the roads to Albano good enough?

So presently it came to her spending many hours alone in the terraced garden on the hill-side, with all the golden Campagna at her feet. Her young fancy, however, soon learnt to look upon that garden as the very concentration and symbol of Italy. All the Italian elements, the Italian magics were there. Along its topmost edge ran a vast broken wall, built into the hill; and hanging from the brink of the wall like a long roof, great ilexes shut out the day from the path below. Within the thickness of the wall--in days when, in that dim Rome upon the plain, many still lived who could remember the voice and the face of Paul of Tarsus--Domitian had made niches and fountains; and he had thrown over the terrace, now darkened by the great ilex boughs, a long portico roof supported on capitals and shafts of gleaming marble. Then in the niches round the clear fountains, he had ranged the fine statues of a still admirable art; everywhere he had lavished marbles, rose and yellow and white, and under foot he had spread a mosaic floor, glistening beneath the shadow-play of leaf and water, in the rich reflected light from the garden and the Campagna outside; while at intervals, he had driven through the very crest of the hill long tunnelled passages, down which one might look from the garden and see the blue lake shining at their further end.

And still the niches and the recesses were there,--the huge wall too along the face of the hill; all broken and gashed and ruinous, showing the fine reticulated brickwork that had been once faced with marble; alternately supported and torn by the pushing roots of the ilex-trees. The tunnelled passages too were there, choked and fallen in; no flash of the lake now beyond their cool darkness! And into the crumbling surface of the wall, rude hands had built fragments of the goddesses and the Caesars that had once reigned there, barbarously mingled with warm white morsels from the great cornice of the portico, acanthus blocks from the long buried capitals, or dolphins orphaned of Aphrodite.

The wreck was beautiful, like all wrecks in Italy where Nature has had her way. For it was masked in the gloom of the overhanging trees; or hidden behind dropping veils of ivy; or lit up by straggling patches of broom and cytisus that thrust themselves through the gaps in the Roman brickwork and shone golden in the dark. At the foot of the wall, along its whole length, ran a low marble conduit that held still the sweetest liveliest water. Lilies of the valley grew beside it, breathing scent into the shadowed air; while on the outer or garden side of the path, the grass was purple with long-stalked violets, or pink with the sharp heads of the cyclamen. And a little further, from the same grass, there shot up in a happy neglect, tall camellia-trees ragged and laden, strewing the ground red and white beneath them. And above the camellias again, the famous stone-pines of the villa climbed into the high air, overlooking the plain and the sea, peering at Rome and Soracte.

So old it was!--and yet so fresh with spring! In the mornings at least the spring was uppermost. It silenced the plaint of outraged beauty which the place seemed to be always making, under a flutter of growth and song. Water and flowers and night-ingales, the shadow, the sunlight, and the heat, were all alike strong and living,--Italy untamed. It was only in the evenings that Lucy shunned the path. For then, from the soil below and the wall above, there crept out the old imprisoned forces of sadness, or of poison, and her heart flagged or her spirits sank as she sat or walked there. Marinata has no malaria; but on old soils, and as night approaches, there is always something in the shade of Italy that fights with human life. The poor ghosts rise from the earth--jealous of those that are still walking the warm ways of the world.

But in the evenings, when the Fountain Walk drove her forth, the central hot zone of the garden was divine, with its roses and lilacs, its birds, its exquisite grass alive with shining lizards, jewelled with every flower, breathing every scent; and at its edge the old terrace with its balustrade, set above the Campagna, commanding the plain and the sea, the sky and the sunsets.

Evening after evening Lucy might have been found perched on the stone cop-ing of the balustrade, sometimes trying, through the warm silent hours, by the help of this book or that, to call up again the old Roman life; sometimes dreaming of what there might still be--what the archaeologists indeed said must be--buried beneath her feet; of the marble limbs and faces pressed into the earth, and all the other ruined things, small and great, mean or lovely, that lay deep in a common grave below the rustling olives, and the still leafless vineyards; and sometimes the mere passive companion of the breeze and the sun, conscious only of the chirping of the crickets, or the loudness of the nightingales, or the flight of a hoopoe, like some strange bright bird of fairy-tale, flashing from one deep garden-shadow to another.

Yet the garden was not always given up to her and the birds. Peasant folk coming from Albano or the olive-grounds between it and the villa would take a short cut through the garden to Marinata; dark-faced gardeners, in blue linen suits, would doff their peaked hats to the strange lady; or a score or two of young black-frocked priestlings from a neighbouring seminary would suddenly throng its paths, playing mild girlish games, with infinite clamour and chatter, running races as far and fast as their black petticoats would allow, twisting their long overcoats and red sashes meanwhile round a battered old noseless bust that stood for Domitian at the end of a long ilex-avenue, and was the butt for all the slings and arrows of the day,--poor helpless State, blinded and buffeted by the Church!

Lucy would hide herself among the lilacs and the arbutus when the seminary invaded her; watching through the leaves the strapping Italian boys in their hindering womanish dress; scorning them for their state of supervision and dependence; pitying them for their destiny!

And sometimes Manisty, disturbed by the noise, would come out--pale and frowning. But at the sight of the seminarists and of the old priest in command of them, his irritable look would soften. He would stand indeed with his hands on his sides, laughing and chatting with the boys, his head uncovered, his black curls blown backward from the great furrowed brow; and in the end Lucy peering from her nook would see him pacing up and down the ilex-walk with the priest,--haranguing and gesticulating--the old man in a pleased wonder looking at the Englishman through his spectacles, and throwing in from time to time ejaculations of assent, now half puzzled, and now fanatically eager. "He is talking the book!"--Lucy would think to herself--and her mind would rise in revolt.

One day after parting with the lads he came unexpectedly past her hiding-place, and paused at sight of her. "Do the boys disturb you?" he said, glancing at her book, and speaking with the awkward abruptness which with him could in a moment take the place of ease and mirth.

"Oh no--not at all."

He fidgeted, stripping leaves from the arbutus tree under which she sat.

"That old priest who comes with them is a charming fellow!"

Her shyness gave way.

"Is he?--He looks after them like an old nurse. And they are such babies--those great boys!"

His eye kindled.

"So you would like them to be more independent--more brutal. You prefer a Harvard and Yale football match--with the dead and wounded left on the ground?"

She laughed, daring for the first time to assert herself.

"No. I don't want blood! But there is something between. However--"

She hesitated. He looked down upon her half irritable, half smiling.

"Please go on."

"It would do them no good, would it--to be independent?"

"Considering how soon they must be slaves for life? Is that what you mean?"

Her frank blue eyes raised themselves to his. He was instantly conscious of something cool and critical in her attitude towards him. Very possibly he had been conscious of it for some time, which accounted for his instinctive avoidance of her. In the crisis of thought and production through which he was passing he shrank from any touch of opposition or distrust. He distrusted himself enough. It was as though he carried about with him wounds that only Eleanor's soft touch could be allowed to approach. And from the first evening he had very naturally divined in this Yankee girl, with her mingled reserve and transparency, her sturdy Protestant-isms of all sorts, elements antagonistic to himself.

She answered his question, however, by another--still referring to the seminar-ists.

'Isn't that the reason why they take and train them so young--that they may have no will left?'

'Well, is that the worst condition in the world--to give up your own will to an idea--a cause?'

She laughed shyly--a low musical sound that suddenly gave him, as it seemed, a new impression of her.

'You call the old priest an "idea"?'

Both had the same vision of the most portly and substantial of figures. Manisty smiled unwillingly.

'The old priest is merely the symbol.'

She shook her head obstinately.

'He is all they know anything about. He gives orders, and they obey. Soon it will be some one else's turn to give them the orders--'

'Till the time comes for them to give orders themselves?--Well, what is there to object to in that?' He scanned her severely. 'What does it mean but that they are parts of a great system, properly organised, to a great end? Show me anything better?'

She coloured.

'It is better, isn't it, that--sometimes--one should give oneself orders?' she said in a low voice.

Manisty laughed.

'Liberty to make a fool of oneself--in short. No doubt,--that's the great modern panacea.' He paused, staring at her without being conscious of it, with his absent brilliant eyes. Then he broke out--'Well! so you despise my little priests! Did you ever think of inquiring, however, which wears best--their notion of human life, which after all has weathered 1900 years, and is as strong and prevailing as it ever was--or the sort of notion that their enemies here go to work upon? Look into the history of this Abyssinian war--everybody free to make fools of themselves, in Rome or Africa--and doing it magnificently! Private judgment--private aims everywhere--from Crispi to the smallest lieutenant. Result--universal wreck and muddle--thousands of lives thrown away--a nation brought to shame. Then look about you at what's going on--here--this week--on these hills. It's Holy Week. They're all fasting--they're all going to mass--the people working in the fields, our servants, the bright little priests. To-morrow's Holy Thursday. From now till Sunday, nobody here will eat anything but a little bread and a few olives. The bells will cease to-morrow. If a single church-bell rang in Rome--over this plain, and these mountains--through the whole of Italy--from mass to-morrow till mass on Saturday--a whole nation would feel pain and outrage. Then on Saturday--marvellous symbol!--listen for the bells. You will hear them all loosed together, as soon as the Sanctus begins--all over Italy. And on Sunday--watch the churches. If it isn't Matthew Arnold's "One common wave of thought and joy--Lifting mankind amain,"--what is it? To me, it's what keeps the human machine running. Make the comparison!--it will repay you. My little muffs of priests with their silly obedience won't come so badly out of it.'

Unconsciously he had taken a seat beside her, and was looking at her with a sharp imperious air. She dimly understood that he was not talking to her but to a much larger audience, that he was still in fact in the grip of "the book." But that he should have anyway addressed so many consecutive sentences to her excited her after these many days of absolute neglect and indifference on his part; she felt a certain tremor of pulse. Instead, however, of diminishing self-command, it bestowed it.

'Well, if that's the only way of running the machine--the Catholic way I mean,'--her words came out a little hurried and breathless--'I don't see how *we* exist.'

'You? America?'

She nodded.

'*Do* you exist?--in any sense that matters?'

He laughed as he spoke; but his tone provoked her. She threw up her head a little, suddenly grave.

'Of course we know that you dislike us.'

He showed a certain embarrassment.

'How do you know?'

'Oh!--we read what you said of us.'

'I was badly reported,' he said, smiling.

'No,'--she insisted. 'But you were mistaken in a great many things--very, very much mistaken. You judged much too quickly.'

He rose, a covert amusement playing round his lips. It was the indulgence of the politician and man of affairs towards the little backwoods girl who was setting him to rights.

'We must have it out,' he said, 'I see I shall have to defend myself. But now I fear Mrs. Burgoyne will be waiting for me.'

And lifting his hat with the somewhat stately and excessive manner, which he could always substitute at the shortest notice for *brusquerie* or inattention, he went his way.

Lucy Foster was left with a red cheek. She watched him till he had passed into the shadow of the avenue leading to the house; then with an impetuous movement she took up a book which had been lying beside her on the bench, and began to read it with a peculiar ardour--almost passion. It was the life of one of the heroes of the Garibaldian expedition of 1860-61.

For of late she had been surrounding herself--by the help of a library in Rome to which the Manistys had access--with the books of the Italian *Risorgimento*, that great movement, that heroic making of a nation, in which our fathers felt so passionate an interest, which has grown so dim and far away now, not only in the mind of a younger England, but even in that of a younger Italy.

But to Lucy--reading the story with the plain of Rome, and St. Peter's in sight, her wits quickened by the perpetual challenge of Manisty's talk with Mrs. Burgoyne, or any chance visitor,--Cavour, Garibaldi, Mazzini; all the striking figures and all the main stages in the great epic; the blind, mad, hopeless outbreaks of '48; the hangings and shootings and bottomless despairs of '49; the sullen calm of those waiting years from '49 to '58; the ecstasy of Magenta and Solferino, and the fierce disappointment of Villafranca; the wild golden days of Sicily in 1860; the plucking of Venice like a ripe fruit in '66; of Rome, in 1870; all the deliriums of freedom, vengeance, union--these immortal names and passions and actions, were thrilling through the girl's fresh poetic sense, and capturing all her sympathies. Had Italy indeed been 'made too quick'? Was all the vast struggle, and these martyred lives for nothing--all to end like a choked river in death and corruption? Well, if so, whose fault was it, but the priests'?--of that black, intriguing, traitorous Italy, headed by the Papacy, which except for one brief moment in the forties, had upheld every tyranny, and drenched every liberty in blood, had been the supporter of the Austrian and the Bourbon, and was now again tearing to pieces the Italy that so many brave men had died to make?

The priests!--the Church!--Why!--she wondered, as she read the story of Charles Albert, and Metternich and the Naples Bourbons, that Italy still dared to let the ignorant, persecuting brood live and thrive in her midst at all! Especially was it a marvel to her that any Jesuit might still walk Italian streets, that a nation could ever forgive or forget such crimes against her inmost life as had been the crimes of the Jesuits. She would stand at the end of the terrace, her hands behind her clasping her book, her eyes fixed on the distant dome amid the stone-pines. Her book opened with the experiences of a Neapolitan boy at school in Naples during the priest-ridden years of the twenties, when Austrian bayonets, after the rising of '21, had replaced Bourbons and Jesuits in power, and crushed the life out of the young striving liberty of '21, as a cruel boy may crush and strangle a fledgling bird. 'What did we learn,' cried the author of the memoir--'from that monkish education which dwarfed both our mind and body? How many have I seen in later life groaning over their own ignorance, and pouring maledictions on the seminary or the college, where they had wasted so many years and had learnt nothing!'

'That monkish education which dwarfed both our mind and body'--

Lucy would repeat the words to herself--throwing them out as a challenge to that great dome hovering amid the sunny haze. That old man there, among his Cardinals--she thought of him with a young horror and revolt; yet not without a certain tremor of the imagination. Well!--in a few days--Sunday week--she was to see him, and judge for herself.

*   *   *   *   *

Meanwhile visitors were almost shut out. The villa sank into a convent-like quiet; for in a week, ten days, the book was perhaps to be finished. Miss Manisty, as the crisis approached, kept a vigilant eye on Mrs. Burgoyne. She was in constant dread of a delicate woman's collapse; and after the sittings in the library had lasted a certain time she had now the courage to break in upon them, and drive Manisty's Egeria out of her cave to rest and to the garden.

So Lucy, as the shadows lengthened in the garden, would hear the sound of a light though languid step, and would look up to see a delicate white face smiling down upon her.

'Oh! how tired you must be!' she would say, springing up. 'Let me make a place for you here under the trees.'

'No, no. Let us move about. I am tired of sitting.'

And they would pace up and down the terrace and the olive-garden beyond, while Mrs. Burgoyne leant upon Lucy's arm, chatting and laughing with an evident relief from tension which only betrayed the mental and physical fatigue behind.

Lucy wondered to see how exquisite, how dainty, she would emerge from these wrestles with hard work. Her fresh white or pale dresses, the few jewels half-hidden at her wrists or throat, the curled or piled masses of the fair hair, were never less than perfection, it seemed to Lucy; she was never more the woman of fashion and the great world than when she came out from a morning's toil that would have left its disturbing mark on a strong man, her eyes shining under the stress and ardour of those 'ideas,' as to which it was good to talk with her.

But how eagerly she would throw off that stress, and turn to wooing and winning Lucy Foster! All hanging back in the matter was gone. Certain vague thoughts and terrors were laid to sleep, and she must needs allow herself the luxury of charming the quiet girl, like all the rest--the dogs, the servants or the village children. There was a perpetual hunger for love in Eleanor's nature which expressed itself in a thousand small and piteous ways. She could never help throwing out tendrils, and it was rarely that she ventured them in vain.

In the case of Lucy Foster, however, her fine tact soon discovered that caresses were best left alone. They were natural to herself, and once or twice as the April days went by, she ventured to kiss the girl's fresh cheek, or to slip an arm round her waist. But Lucy took it awkwardly. When she was kissed she flushed, and stood passive; and all her personal ways were a little stiff and austere. After one of these demonstrations indeed Mrs. Burgoyne generally found herself repaid in some other form, by some small thoughtfulness on Lucy's part--the placing of a stool, the fetching of a cloak--or merely perhaps by a new softness in the girl's open look. And Eleanor never once thought of resenting her lack of response. There was even a kind of charm in it. The prevailing American type in Rome that winter had been a demonstrative type.

Lucy's manner in comparison was like a cool and bracing air. 'And when she does kiss!' Eleanor would say to herself--'it will be with all her heart. One can see that.'

Meanwhile Mrs. Burgoyne took occasional note of the Mazzinian literature that lay about. She would turn the books over and read their titles, her eyes sparkling with a little gentle mischief, as she divined the girl's disapproval of her host and his views. But she never argued with Lucy. She was too tired of the subject, too eager to seek relief in talking of the birds and the view, of people and *chiffons*.

Too happy perhaps--also. She walked on air in these days before Easter. The book was prospering; Manisty was more content; and as agreeable in all daily ways and offices as only the hope of good fortune can make a man. 'The Priest of Nemi'--indeed, with several other prose poems of the same kind, had been cast out of the text; which now presented one firm and vigorous whole of social and political discussion. But the Nemi piece was to be specially bound for Eleanor, together with some drawings that she had made of the lake and the temple site earlier in the spring. And on the day the book was finished--somewhere within the next fortnight--there was to be a festal journey to Nemi--divine and blessed place!

So she felt no fatigue, and was always ready to chatter to Lucy of the most womanish things. Especially, as the girl's beauty grew upon her, was she anxious to carry out those plans of transforming her dress and hair,--her gowns and hats and shoes--the primness of her brown braids, which she and Miss Manisty had confided to each other.

But Lucy was shy--would not be drawn that way. There were fewer visitors at the villa than she had expected. For this quiet life in the garden, and on the country roads, it seemed to her that her dresses did very well. The sense of discomfort excited by the elegance of her Florentine acquaintance died away. And she would have thought it wrong and extravagant to spend unnecessary money.

So she had quietly ceased to think about her dress; and the blue and white check, to Eleanor's torment, had frequently to be borne with.

Even the promised invitation to the Embassy had not arrived. It was said that the Ambassador's daughter had gone to Florence. Only Lucy wished she had not written that letter to Uncle Ben from Florence:--that rather troubled and penitent letter on the subject of dress. He might misunderstand--might do something foolish.

*   *   *   *   *

And apparently Uncle Ben did do something foolish. For a certain letter arrived from Boston on the day after the seminarists' invasion of the garden. Lucy after an hour's qualms and hesitations, must needs reluctantly confide the contents of it to Miss Manisty. And that lady with smiles and evident pleasure called Mrs. Burgoyne--and Eleanor called her maid,--and the ball began to roll.

* * * * *

On Saturday morning early, Mrs. Burgoyne's room indeed was in a bustle--delightful to all but Lucy. Manisty was in Rome for the day, and Eleanor had holiday. She had never looked more frail--a rose-leaf pink in her cheek--nor more at ease. For she was at least as good to consult about a skirt as an idea.

'Marie!'--she said, giving her own maid a little peremptory push--'just run and fetch Benson--there's an angel. We must have all the brains possible. If we don't get the bodice right, it won't suit Miss Foster a bit.'

Marie went in all haste. Meanwhile in front of a large glass stood a rather red and troubled Lucy arrayed in a Paris gown belonging to Mrs. Burgoyne. Eleanor had played her with much tact, and now had her in her power.

'It is the crisis, my dear,' Miss Manisty had said in Eleanor's ear, as they rose from breakfast, with a twinkle of her small eyes. 'The question is; can we, or can we not, turn her into a beauty? *You* can!'

Eleanor at any rate was doing her best. She had brought out her newest gowns and Lucy was submissively putting them on one after the other. Eleanor was in pursuit first of all of some general conceptions. What was the girl's true style?--what were the possibilities?

'When I have got my lines and main ideas in my head,' she said pensively, 'then we will call in the maids. Of course you *might* have the things made in Rome. But as we have the models--and these two maids have nothing to do--why not give ourselves the pleasure of looking after it?'

Pleasure! Lucy Foster opened her eyes.

Still, here was this absurd, this most extravagant cheque from Uncle Ben, and these peremptory commands to get herself everything--everything--that other girls had. Why, it was demanded of her, had she been economical and scrupulous before starting? Folly and disobedience! He had been told of her silly hesitations, her detestable frugalities--he had ferreted it all out. And now she was at a disadvantage--was she? Let her provide herself at once, or old as he was, he would take train and steamer and come and see to it!

She was not submissive in general--far from it. But the reading of Uncle Ben's letter had left her very meek in spirit and rather inclined to cry.

Had Uncle Ben really considered whether it was right to spend so much money on oneself, to think so much about it? Their life together had been so simple, the question had hardly emerged. Of course it was right to be neat and fresh, and to please his taste in what she wore. But--

The net result of all this internal debate, however, was to give a peculiar charm, like the charm of rippled and sensitive water, to features that were generally too still and grave. She stood silently before the long glass while Mrs. Burgoyne and the maids talked and pinned. She walked to the end of the room and back, as she was bid; she tried to express a preference, when she was asked for one; and as she was arrayed in one delicious gown after another, she became more and more alive to the beauty of the soft stuffs, the invention and caprice with which they were combined, the daintiness of their pinks and blues, their greys and creams, their lilacs and ivories. At last Mrs. Burgoyne happened upon a dress of white crape, opening upon a vest of pale green, with thin edges of black here and there, disposed with the tact, the feeling of the artist; and when Lucy's tall form had been draped in this garment, her three attendants fell back with one simultaneous cry:

'Oh my dear!' said Mrs. Burgoyne drawing a long breath.--'Now you see, Marie--I told you!--that's the cut. And just look how simple that is, and how it falls! That's the green. Yes, when Mathilde is as good as that she's divine.--Now all you've got to do is just to copy that. And the materials are just nothing--you'll get them in the Corso in half-an-hour.'

'May I take it off?' said Lucy.

'Well yes, you may'--said Mrs. Burgoyne, reluctantly--'but it's a great pity. Well now, for the coat and skirt,'--she checked them off on her slim fingers--'for the afternoon gown, and one evening dress, I think I see my way--'

'Enough for one morning isn't it?' said Lucy half laughing, half imploring.

'Yes,'--said Mrs. Burgoyne absently, her mind already full of further developments.

The gowns were carried away, and Aunt Pattie's maid departed. Then as Lucy in her white cotton wrapper was retiring to her own room, Mrs. Burgoyne caught her by the arm.

'You remember,'--she said appealingly,--'how rude I was that evening you came--how I just altered your hair? You don't know how I long to do it properly! You know I shall have a little trouble with these dresses--trouble I like--but still I shall pretend it's trouble, that you may pay me for it. Pay me by letting me experiment! I just long to take all your hair down, and do it as it ought to be done. And you don't know how clever I am. *Let* me!'

And already, before the shamefaced girl could reply, she was gently pushed into the chair before Mrs. Burgoyne's dressing-table, and a pair of skilled hands went to work.

'I can't say you look as though you enjoyed it,' said Mrs. Burgoyne by the time she had covered the girl's shoulders with the long silky veil which she had released from the stiff plaits confining it. 'Do you think it's wrong to do your hair prettily?' Lucy laughed uneasily.

'I was never brought up to think much about it. My mother had very strict views.'

'Ah!'--said Eleanor, with a discreet intonation. 'But you see, at Rome it is really so much better for the character to do as Rome does. To be out of the way makes one self-conscious. Your mother didn't foresee that.'

Silence,--while the swift white fingers plaited and tied and laid foundations.

'It waves charmingly already'--murmured the artist--'but it must be just a little more *ondule* in the right places--just a touch--here and there. Quick, Marie!--bring me the stove--and the tongs--and two or three of those finest hairpins.'

The maid flew, infected by the ardour of her mistress, and between them they worked to such purpose that when at last they released their victim, they had turned the dark head into that of a stately and fashionable beauty. The splendid hair was raised high in small silky ripples above the white brow. The little love-locks on the temples had been delicately arranged so as to complete the fine oval of the face, and at the back the black masses drawn lightly upwards from the neck, and held in place there by a pearl comb of Mrs. Burgoyne's, had been piled and twisted into a crown that would have made Artemis herself more queenly.

'Am I really to keep it like this?' cried Lucy, looking at herself in the glass.

'But of course you are!' and Mrs. Burgoyne instinctively held the girl's arms, lest any violence should be offered to her handiwork--'And you must put on your *old* white frock--*not* the check--the nice soft one that's been washed, with the pink sash--Goodness, how the time goes! Marie, run and tell Miss Manisty not to wait for me--I'll follow her to the village.'

The maid went. Lucy looked down upon her tyrant--

You are very kind to me'--she said with a lip that trembled slightly. Her blue eyes under the black brows showed a feeling that she did not know how to express. The subdued responsiveness, indeed, of Lucy's face was like that of Wordsworth's Highland girl struggling with English. You felt her 'beating up against the wind,'--in the current, yet resisting it. Or to take another comparison, her nature seemed to be at once stiff and rich--like some heavy church stuff, shot with gold.

'Oh! these things are my snare,' said Eleanor, laughing--'If I have any gift, it is for *chiffons*.'

'Any gift!' said Lucy wondering--'when you do so much for Mr. Manisty?'

Mrs. Burgoyne shrugged her shoulders.

'Ah! well--he wanted a secretary--and I happened to get the place,' she said, in a more constrained voice.

'Miss Manisty told me how you helped him in the winter. And she and Mr. Brooklyn--have--told me--other things--' said Lucy. She paused, colouring deeply. But her eyes travelled timidly to the photographs on Mrs. Burgoyne's table.

Eleanor understood.

'Ah!--they told you that, did they?'--The speaker turned a little white. 'And you wonder--don't you?--that I can go on talking about frocks, and new ways of doing one's hair?'

She moved away from Lucy, a touch of cold defensive dignity effacing all her pliant sweetness.

Lucy followed and caught her hand.

'Oh no! no!'--she said--'it is only so brave and good of you--to be able still--to take an interest--'

'Do I take it?' said Eleanor, scornfully, raising her other hand and letting it fall.

Lucy was silenced. After a moment Eleanor looked round, calmly took the photograph of the child from the table, and held it towards Lucy.

'He was just two--his birthday was four days before this was taken. It's the picture I love best, because I last saw him like that--in his night-gown. I was very ill that night--they wouldn't let me stay with my husband--but after I left him, I came and rocked the baby and tucked him up--and leant my face against his. He was so warm and sweet always in his sleep. The touch of him--and the scent of him--his dear breath--and his curls--and the moist little hands--sometimes they used to intoxicate me--to give me life--like wine. They did me such good--that night.'

Her voice did not tremble. Tears softly found their way down Lucy's face. And suddenly she stooped, and put her lips, tenderly, clingingly, to Mrs. Burgoyne's hand.

Eleanor smiled. Then she herself bent forward and lightly kissed the girl's cheek.

'Oh! I am not worthy either to have had him--or lost him--' she said bitterly. There was a little pause, which Eleanor broke. 'Now really we must go to Aunt Pattie--mustn't we?'

CHAPTER VI

A h! here you are! Don't kill yourselves. Plenty of time--for us! Listen-- there's the bell--eight o'clock--now they open the doors. Goodness!-- Look at the rush--and those little Italian chaps tackling those strapping priests. Go it, ye cripples!'

Lucy tamed her run to a quick walk, and Mr. Reggie took care of her, while Manisty disappeared ahead with Mrs. Burgoyne, and Aunt Pattie fell to the share of a certain Mr. Vanbrugh Neal, an elderly man tall and slim, and of a singular elegance of bearing, who had joined them at the Piazza, and seemed to be an old friend of Mr. Manisty's.

Lucy looked round her in bewilderment. Before the first stroke of the bell the Piazza of St. Peter's had been thickly covered with freely moving groups, all advancing in order upon the steps of the church. But as the bell began to speak, there was a sudden charge mostly of young priests and seminarists--black skirts flying, black legs leaping--across the open space and up the steps.

'Reminds me of nothing so much'--said Reggie laughing back over his shoulder at a friend behind--'as the charge of the Harrow boys at Lord's last year--when they stormed the pavilion--did you see it?--and that little Harrow chap saved the draw? I say!--they've broken the line!--and there'll be a bad squash somewhere.'

And indeed the attacking priests had for a moment borne down the Italian soldiers who were good-naturedly guarding and guiding the Pope's guests from the entrance of the Piazza to the very door of the church. But the little men--as they seemed to Lucy's eyes--recovered themselves in a twinkling, threw themselves stoutly on the black gentry, like sheep dogs on the sheep, worried them back into line, collared a few bold spirits here, formed a new cordon there, till all was once more in tolerable order, and a dangerous pressure on the central door was averted.

Meanwhile Lucy was hurried forward with the privileged crowd going to the tribunes, towards the sacristy door on the south.

'Let's catch up Mrs. Burgoyne'--said the young man, looking ahead with some anxiety--'Manisty's no use. He'll begin to moon and forget all about her. I say!--Look at the building--and the sky behind it! Isn't it stunning?'

And they threw up a hasty glance as they sped along at the superb walls and apses and cornices of the southern side--golden ivory or wax against the blue.--The pigeons flew in white eddies above their heads; the April wind flushed Lucy's cheek, and played with her black mantilla. All qualms were gone. After her days of seclusion in the villa garden, she was passionately conscious of this great Rome and its magic; and under her demure and rather stately air, her young spirits danced and throbbed with pleasure.

'How that black lace stuff does become all you women!'--said Reggie Brooklyn, throwing a lordly and approving glance at her and his cousin Eleanor, as they all met and paused amid the crowd that was concentrating itself on the sacristy door; and Lucy, instead of laughing at the lad's airs, only reddened a little more brightly and found it somehow sweet--April sweet--that a young man on this spring morning should admire her; though after all, she was hardly more inclined to fall in love with Reggie Brooklyn than with Manisty's dear collie puppy, that had been left behind, wailing, at the villa.

At the actual door the young man quietly possessed himself of Mrs. Burgoyne, while Manisty with an unconscious look of relief fell behind.

'And you, Miss Foster,--keep closer--my coat's all at your service--it'll stand a pull. Don't you be swept away--and I'll answer for Mrs. Burgoyne.'

So on they hurried, borne along with the human current through passages and corridors, part of a laughing, pushing, chatting crowd, containing all the types that throng the Roman streets--English and American tourists, Irish or German or English priests, monks white and brown, tall girls who wore their black veils with an evident delight in the new setting thus given to their fair hair and brilliant skins, beside older women to whom, on the contrary, the dress had given a kind of unwonted repose and quietness of look, as though for once they dared to be themselves in it, and gave up the struggle with the years.

Reggie Brooklyn maintained a lively chatter all the time, mostly at Manisty's expense. Eleanor Burgoyne first laughed at his sallies, then gently turned her head in a pause of the general advance and searched the crowd pressing at their heels. Lucy's eyes followed hers, and there far behind, carried forward passively in a brown study, losing ground slightly whenever it was possible, was Manisty. The fine significant face was turned a little upward; the eyes were full of thoughts; he was at once the slave of the crowd, and its master.

And across Eleanor's expression--unseen--there passed the slightest, subtlest flash of tenderness and pride. She knew and understood him--she alone!

*   *   *   *   *

At last the doors are passed. They are in the vast barricaded and partitioned space, already humming with the talk and tread of thousands,--the 'Tu es Petrus' overhead. Reggie Brooklyn would have hurried them on in the general rush for the tribunes. But Mrs. Burgoyne laid a restraining hand upon him. 'No--we mustn't separate,' she said, gently peremptory. And for a few minutes Mr. Reggie in an anguish must needs see the crowd flow past him, and the first seats of Tribune D filled. Then Manisty appeared, lifting his eyebrows in a frowning wonder at the young man's impatience;--and on they flew.

At last!--They are in the third row of Tribune D, close to the line by which the Pope must pass, and to the platform from which he will deliver the Apostolic Benediction. Reggie the unsatisfied, the idealist, grumbles that they ought to have been in the very front. But Eleanor and Aunt Pattie are well satisfied. They find their acquaintance all around them. It is a general flutter of fans, and murmur of talk. Already people are standing on their seats looking down on the rapidly filling church. In press the less favoured thousands from the Piazza, through the Atrium and the Eastern door--great sea of human life spreading over the illimitable nave behind the two lines of Swiss and Papal Guards, in quick never-ending waves that bewilder and dazzle the eye.

Lucy found the three hours' wait but a moment. The passing and re-passing of the splendid officials in their Tudor or Valois dress; the great names, 'Colonna,' 'Barberini,' 'Savelli,' 'Borghese' that sound about her, as Mrs. Burgoyne who knows everybody, at least by sight, laughs and points and chats with her neighbour, Mr. Neal; the constant welling up of processions from behind,--the Canons and Monsi-

gnori in their fur and lace tippets, the red Cardinals with their suites; the entry of
the Guardia Nobile, splendid, incredible, in their winged Achillean helmets above
their Empire uniforms--half Greek, half French, half gods, half dandies, the costli-
est foolishest plaything that any court can show; and finally as the time draws on,
the sudden thrills and murmurs that run through the church, announcing the great
moment which still, after all, delays: these things chase the minutes, blot out, the
sense of time.

Meanwhile, again and again, Lucy, the sedate, the self-controlled, cannot prevent herself from obeying a common impulse with those about her--from leaping
on her chair--straining her white throat--her eyes. Then a handsome chamber-
lain would come by, lifting a hand in gentle protest, motioning to the ladies--'De
grace, mesdames--mesdames, de *grace*!--' Or angry murmurs would rise from
those few who had not the courage or the agility to mount--'*Giu! giu!*--Descen-
dez, mesdames!--qu'est-ce que c'est done que ces manieres?'--and Lucy, crimson
and abashed, would descend in haste, only to find a kind Irish priest behind smiling at her,--prompting her,--'Never mind them!--take no notice!--who is it you're
harmin'?'--And her excitement would take him at his word--for who should know
if not a priest?

And from these risky heights she looked down sometimes on Manisty--won-
dering where was emotion, sympathy. Not a trace of them! Of all their party he
alone was obviously and hideously bored by the long wait. He leant back in his
chair, with folded arms, staring at the ceiling--yawning--fidgetting. At last he took
out a small Greek book from his pocket, and hung over it in a moody absorption.
Once only, when a procession of the inferior clergy went by, he looked at it closely,
turning afterwards to Mrs. Burgoyne with the emphatic remark: 'Bad faces!--aren't
they?--almost all of them?'

Yet Lucy could see that even here in this vast crowd, amid the hubbub and
bustle, he still counted, was still remembered. Officials came to lean and chat across
the rope; diplomats stopped to greet him on the way to the august seats beyond the
Confession. His manner in return showed no particular cordiality; Lucy thought
it languid, even cold. She was struck with the difference between his mood of the
day, and that brilliant and eager homage he had lavished on the old Cardinal in the
villa garden. What a man of change and fantasy! Here it was he *qui tendait la joue*.

Cold, distant, dreamy--one would have thought him either indifferent or hostile to the whole great pageant and its meanings.

Only once did Lucy see him bestir himself--show a gleam of animation. A white-haired priest, all tremulous dignity and delicacy, stood for a moment beside the rope-barrier, waiting for a friend. Manisty bent over and touched him on the arm. The old man turned. The face was parchment, the cheeks cavernous. But in the blue eyes there was an exquisite innocence and youth.

Manisty smiled at him. His manner showed a peculiar almost a boyish deference. 'You join us afterwards--at lunch?'

'Yes, yes.' The old priest beamed and nodded; then his friend came up and he was carried on.

*   *   *   *   *

'A quarter to eleven,' said Manisty with a yawn, looking at his watch. 'Ah!--listen!'

He sprang to his feet. In an instant half the occupants of Tribune D were on their chairs, Lucy and Eleanor among them. A roar came up the church--passionate--indescribable. Lucy held her breath.

There--there he is,--the old man! Caught in a great shaft of sunlight striking from south to north, across the church, and just touching the chapel of the Holy Sacrament--the Pope emerges. The white figure, high above the crowd, sways from side to side; the hand upraised gives the benediction. Fragile, spiritual as is the apparition, the sunbeam refines, subtilises, spiritualises it still more. It hovers like a dream above the vast multitudes--surely no living man!--but thought, history, faith, taking shape; the passion of many hearts revealed. Up rushes the roar towards the Tribunes. 'Did you hear?' said Manisty to Mrs. Burgoyne, lifting a smiling brow, as a few Papalino cries--'Viva il Papa Re'--make themselves heard among the rest. Eleanor's thin face turns to him with responsive excitement. But she has seen these things before. Instinctively her eyes wander perpetually to Manisty's, taking their colour, their meaning from his. It is not the spectacle itself that matters to her--poor Eleanor! One heart-beat, one smile of the man beside her outweighs it all. And he, roused at last from his nonchalance, watching hawk-like every movement of the figure and the crowd, is going mentally through a certain page of his book, repeating certain phrases--correcting here--strengthening there.

Lucy alone--the alien and Puritan Lucy--Lucy surrenders herself completely. She betrays nothing, save by the slightly parted lips, and the flutter of the black veil fastened on her breast; but it is as though her whole inner being were dissolving, melting away, in the flame of the moment. It is her first contact with decisive central things, her first taste of the great world-play, as Europe has known it and taken part in it, at least since Charles the Great.

Yet, as she looks, within the visible scene, there opens another: the porch of a plain, shingled house, her uncle sitting within it, his pipe and his newspaper on his knee, sunning himself in the April morning. She passes behind him, looks into the stiff leaf-scented parlour--at the framed Declaration of Independence on the walls, the fresh boughs in the fire-place, the Bible on its table, the rag-carpet before the hearth. She breathes the atmosphere of the house; its stern independence and simplicities; the scorns and the denials, the sturdy freedoms both of body and soul that it implies--conscience the only master--vice-master for God, in this His house of the World. And beyond--as her lids sink for an instant on the pageant before her--she hears, as it were, the voices of her country, so young and raw and strong!--she feels within her the throb of its struggling self-assertive life; she is conscious too of the uglinesses and meannesses that belong to birth and newness, to growth and fermentation. Then, in a proud timidity--as one who feels herself an alien and on sufferance--she hangs again upon the incomparable scene. This is St. Peter's; there is the dome of Michael Angelo; and here, advancing towards her amid the red of the cardinals, the clatter of the guards, the tossing of the flabellae, as though looking at her alone--the two waxen fingers raised for her alone--is the white-robed triple-crowned Pope.

She threw herself upon the sight with passion, trying to penetrate and possess it; and it baffled her, passed her by. Some force of resistance within her cried out to it that she was not its subject--rather its enemy! And august, unheeding, the great pageant swept on. Close, close to her now! Down sink the crowd upon the chairs; the heads fall like corn before the wind. Lucy is bending too. The Papal chair borne on the shoulders of the guards is now but a few feet distant; vaguely she wonders that the old man keeps his balance, as he clings with one frail hand to the arm of the chair, rises incessantly--and blesses with the other. She catches the very look and meaning of the eyes--the sharp long line of the closed and toothless jaw. Spirit and spectre;--embodying the Past, bearing the clue to the Future.

'*Yeux de police!*'--laughed Reggie Brooklyn to Mrs. Burgoyne as the procession passed--'don't you know?--that's what they say.'

Manisty bent forward. The flush of excitement was still on his cheek, but he threw a little nod to Brooklyn, whose gibe amused him.

Lucy drew a long breath--and the spell was broken.

*   *   *   *   *

Nor was it again renewed, in the same way. The Pope and his cortege disappeared behind the Confession, behind the High Altar, and presently, Lucy, craning her neck to the right, could see dimly in the furthest distance, against the apse, and under the chair of St. Peter, the chair of Leo XIII. and the white shadow, motionless, erect, within it, amid a court of cardinals and diplomats. As for the mass that followed, it had its moments of beauty for the girl's wondering or shrinking curiosity, but also its moments of weariness and disillusion. From the latticed choir-gallery, placed against one of the great piers of the dome, came unaccompanied music--fine, pliant, expressive--like a single voice moving freely in the vast space; and at the High Altar, Cardinals and Bishops crossed and recrossed, knelt and rose, offered and put off the mitre; amid wreaths of incense, long silences, a few chanted words; sustained, enfolded all the while by the swelling tide of *Gloria*, or *Sanctus*.

At last--the elevation!--and at the bell the whole long double line of soldiers, from the Pope's chair at the western end to the eastern door, with a rattle of arms that ran from end to end of the church, dropped on one knee--saluted. Then, crac!--and as they had dropped, they rose, the stiff white breeches and towering helmets of the Guardia Nobile, the red and yellow of the Swiss, the red and blue of the Papal guards--all motionless as before. It was like the movement of some gigantic toy. And who or what else took any notice? Lucy looked round amazed. Even the Irish priest behind her had scarcely bowed his head. Nobody knelt. Most people were talking. Eleanor Burgoyne indeed had covered her face with her long delicate fingers. Manisty leaning back in his chair, looked up for an instant at the rattle of the soldiers, then went back sleepily to his Greek book. Yet Lucy felt her own heart throbbing. Through the candelabra of the High Altar beneath the dome, she can see the moving figures of the priests, the wreaths of incense ascending. The face of the celebrant Cardinal, which had dropped out of sight, reappears. Since it was last visible, according to Catholic faith, the great act of Catholic worship has been accomplished--the Body and Blood are there--God has descended, has mingled with a mortal frame. And who cares? Lucy looks round her at the good-humoured indifference, vacancy, curiosity, of the great multitude filling the nave; and her soul frees itself in a rush of protesting amazement.

*   *   *   *   *

One more 'moment' however there was,--very different from the great moment of the entry, yet beautiful. The mass is over, and a temporary platform has been erected between the Confession and the nave. The Pope has been placed upon it, and is about to chant the Apostolic Benediction.

The old man is within thirty feet of Manisty, who sits nearest to the barrier. The red Cardinal holding the service-book, the groups of guards, clergy and high officials, every detail of the Pope's gorgeous dress, nay every line of the wrinkled face, and fleshless hands, Lucy's eyes command them all. The quavering voice rises into the sudden silence of St. Peter's. Fifty thousand people hush every movement, strain their ears to listen.

Ah! how weak it is! Surely the effort is too great for a frame so enfeebled, so ancient. It should not have been exacted--allowed. Lucy's ears listen painfully for the inevitable break. But no!--The Pope draws a long sigh--the sigh of weakness,--('Ah! poveretto!' says a woman, close to Lucy, in a transport of pity),--then once more attempts the chant--sighs again--and sings. Lucy's face softens and glows; her eyes fill with tears. Nothing more touching, more triumphant, than this weakness and this perseverance. Fragile indomitable face beneath the Papal crown! Under the eyes of fifty thousand people the Pope sighs like a child, because he is weak and old, and the burden of his office is great; but in sighing, keeps a perfect simplicity, dignity, courage. Not a trace of stoical concealment; but also not a trace of flinching. He sings to the end, and St. Peter's listens in a tender hush.

Then there seems to be a moment of collapse. The long straight lips close as though with a snap, the upper jaw protruding; the eyelids drop; the emaciated form sinks upon itself.--

But his guards raise the chair, and the Pope's trance passes away. He opens his eyes, and braces himself for the last effort. Whiter than the gorgeous cope which falls about him, he raises himself, clinging to the chair; he lifts the skeleton fingers of his partially gloved hand; his look searches the crowd.

Lucy fell on her knees, a sob in her throat. When the Pope had passed, some influence made her look up. She met the eyes of Edward Manisty. They were instantly withdrawn, but not before the mingling of amusement and triumph in them had brought the quick red to the girl's cheek.

*   *   *   *   *

And outside, in the Piazza, amid the out-pouring thousands, as they were rushing for their carriage, Manisty's stride overtook her.

'Well--you were impressed?'--he said, looking at her sharply.

The girl's pride was somehow nettled by his tone.

'Yes--but by the old man--more than by the Pope,'--she said quickly.

'I hope not,' he said, with emphasis.--'Otherwise you would have missed the whole point.'

'Why?--Mayn't one feel it was pathetic, and touching--'

'No--not in the least!' he said, impatiently. 'What does the man himself matter, or his age?--That's all irrelevant,--foolish sentiment. What makes these ceremonies so tremendous is that there is no break between that man and Peter--or Linus, if you like--it comes to the same thing:--that the bones, if not of Peter, at any rate of men who might have known Peter, are there, mingled with the earth beneath his feet--that he stands there recognised by half the civilised world as Peter's successor--that five hundred, a thousand years hence, the vast probability is there will still be a Pope in St. Peter's to hand on the same traditions, and make the same claims.'

'But if you don't acknowledge the tradition or the claims!--why shouldn't you feel just the human interest?'

'Oh, of course, if you want to take the mere vulgar, parochial view--the halfpenny interviewer's view--why, you must take it!' he said, almost with violence, shrugging his shoulders.

Lucy's eyes sparkled. There was always something of the overgrown, provoking child in him, when he wanted to bear down an opinion or feeling that displeased him. She would have liked to go on walking and wrangling with him, for the great ceremony had excited her, and made it easier for her to talk. But at that moment Mrs. Burgoyne's voice was heard in front--'Joy! there is the carriage, and Reggie has picked up another.--Edward, take Aunt Pattie through--we'll look after ourselves.'

*   *   *   *   *

And soon the whole party were driving in two of the little Roman victorias through streets at the back of the Capitol, and round the base of the Palatine, to the Aventine, where it appeared they were to lunch at an open-air *trattoria*, recommended by Mr. Brooklyn.

Mrs. Burgoyne, Lucy and Mr. Vanbrugh Neal found themselves together. Mrs. Burgoyne and Mr. Neal talked of the function, and Lucy, after a few shy expressions of gratitude and pleasure, fell silent, and listened. But she noticed very soon that Mrs. Burgoyne was talking absently. Amid the black that fell about her slim tallness, she was more fragile, more pale than ever; and it seemed to Lucy that her eyes were dark with a fatigue that had not much to do with St. Peter's. Suddenly indeed, she bent forward and said in a lowered voice to Mr. Neal--

'You have read it?'

He too bent forward, with a smile not quite free from embarrassment--

'Yes, I have read it--I shall have some criticisms to make.--You won't mind?'

She threw up her hands--

'Must you?'

'I think I must--for the good of the book,'--he said reluctantly. 'Very likely I'm all wrong. I can only look at it as one of the public. But that's what he wants,'--what you both want--isn't it?'

She assented. Then she turned her head away, looked out of the carriage and said no more. But her face had drooped and dimmed, all in a moment; the lines graven in it long years before, by grief and delicacy, came out with a singular and sudden plainness.

The man sitting opposite to her was of an aspect little less distinguished than hers. He had a long face, with a high forehead, set in grizzled hair, and a mouth and chin of peculiar refinement. The shortness of the chin gave a first impression of weakness, which however was soon undone by the very subtle and decided lines in which, so to speak, the mouth, and indeed the face as a whole, were drawn. All that Lucy knew of him was that he was a Cambridge don, a man versed in classical archaeology who was an old friend and tutor of Mr. Manisty's. She had heard his name mentioned several times at the Villa, and always with an emphasis that marked it out from other names. And she understood from various signs that before finally passing his proofs for publication, Mr. Manisty had taken advantage of his old friend's coming to Rome to ask his opinion on them.

How brilliant was the April day on the high terrace of the Aventine ***trattoria***! As Lucy and Aunt Pattie stood together beside the little parapet looking out through the sprays of banksia rose that were already making a white canopy above the restaurant tables, they had before them the steep sides and Imperial ruins of the Palatine; the wonderful group of churches on the Coelian; the low villa-covered ridges to the right melting into the Campagna; and far away, the blue, Sabine mountains--'suffused with sunny air'--that look down with equal kindness on the refuge of Horace, and the oratory of St. Benedict. What sharpness of wall and tree against the pearly sky--what radiance of blossom in the neighbouring gardens--what ruin everywhere, yet what indomitable life!

Beneath on a lower terrace, Manisty and Mr. Vanbrugh Neal were walking up and down.

'He's such a clever man,' sighed Aunt Pattie, as she looked down upon them. 'But I do hope he won't discourage Edward.'

Whereupon she glanced not at Manisty but at Eleanor, who was sitting near them, pretending to talk to Reggie Brooklyn--but in reality watching the conversation below.

Presently some other guests arrived, and amongst them the tall and fine-faced priest who had spoken to Manisty in St. Peter's. He came in very shyly. Eleanor Burgoyne received him, made him sit by her, and took charge of him till Manisty should appear. But he seemed to be ill at ease with ladies. He buried his hands in the sleeves of his soutane, and would answer little more than Yes and No.

'There'll be a great fuss about him soon,' whispered Aunt Pattie in Lucy's ear--'I don't quite understand--but he's written a book that's been condemned; and the question is, will he submit? They give you a year apparently to decide in. Edward says the book's quite right--and yet they were quite right to condemn him. It's very puzzling!'

When Manisty and Mr. Neal answered to the call of luncheon, Mr. Neal mounted the steps leading to the open-air restaurant, with the somewhat sheepish air of the man who has done his duty, and is inclined to feel himself a meddler for his pains. The luncheon itself passed without gaiety. Manisty was either moodily silent, or engaged in discussions with the strange priest, Father Benecke, as to certain incidents connected with a South German University, which had lately excited Catholic opinion. He scarcely spoke to any of the ladies--least of all to Eleanor Burgoyne. She and Aunt Pattie must needs make all the greater efforts to carry off the festa. Aunt Pattie chattered nervously like one in dread of a silence, while Eleanor was merry with young Brooklyn, and courteous to the other guests whom Manisty had invited--a distinguished French journalist for instance, an English member of Parliament and his daughter, and an Italian senator with an English wife.

Nevertheless when the party was breaking up, Reggie who had thrown her occasional glances of disquiet, approached Lucy Foster and said to her in a low voice, twirling an angry moustache--

'Mrs. Burgoyne is worn out. Can't you look after her?'

Lucy, a little scared by so much responsibility, did her best. She dissuaded Aunt Pattie from dragging Mrs. Burgoyne through an afternoon of visits. She secured an early train for the return to Marinata, and so earned a special and approving smile from Mr. Reggie, when at last he had settled the three ladies safely in their carriage, and was raising his hat to them on the platform. Manisty and Mr. Neal were to follow by a later train.

No sooner were they speeding through the Campagna than Eleanor sank back in her corner with a long involuntary sigh.

'My dear--you are very tired!'--exclaimed Miss Manisty.

'No.--'

Mrs. Burgoyne took off the hat which had by now replaced the black veil of the morning, and closed her eyes. Her attitude by its sad unresistingness appealed to Lucy as it had done once before. And it was borne in upon her that what she saw was not mere physical fatigue, but a deep discouragement of mind and heart. As to the true sources of it Lucy could only guess. She guessed at any rate that they were somehow connected with Mr. Manisty and his book; and she was indignant again--she hardly knew why. The situation suggested to her a great devotion ill-repaid, a friendship, of which the strong tyrannous man took advantage. Why should he behave as though all that happened ill with regard to his book was somehow Mrs. Burgoyne's fault? Claim all her time and strength--overstrain and overwork her--and then make her tacitly responsible if anything went amiss! It was like the petulant selfishness of his character. Miss Manisty ought to interfere!

*   *   *   *   *

Dreary days followed at the Villa.

It appeared that Mr. Vanbrugh Neal had indeed raised certain critical objections both to the facts and to the arguments of one whole section of the book, and that Manisty had been unable to resist them. The two men would walk up and down the ilex avenues of the garden for hours together, Mr. Neal gentle, conciliating, but immovable; Manisty violent and excited, but always submitting in the end. He would defend his point of view with obstinacy, with offensiveness even, for an afternoon, and then give way, with absolute suddenness. Lucy learnt with some astonishment that beneath his outward egotism he was really amazingly dependent on the opinions of two or three people, of whom Mr. Neal seemed to be one. This dependence turned out indeed to be even excessive. He would make a hard fight for his own way; but in the end he was determined that what he wrote should please his friends, and please a certain public. At bottom he was a rhetorician writing for this public--the slave of praise, and eager for fame, which made his complete indifference as to what people thought of his actions all the more remarkable. He lived to please himself; he wrote to be read; and he had found reason to trust the instinct of certain friends in this respect, Vanbrugh Neal among them.

To do him justice, indeed, along with his dependence on Vanbrugh Neal's opinion, there seemed to go a rather winning dependence on his affection.

Mr. Neal was apparently a devout Anglican, of a delicate and scrupulous type. His temper was academic, his life solitary; rhetoric left him unmoved, and violence of statement caused him to shiver. To make the State religious was his dearest wish. But he did not forget that to accomplish it you must keep the Church reasonable. A deep, though generally silent enthusiasm for the Anglican *Via Media* possessed him; and, like the Newman of Oriel, he was inclined to look upon the appearance of Antichrist as coincident with the Council of Trent. In England it seemed to him that persecution of the Church was gratuitous and inexcusable; for the Church had never wronged the State. In Italy, on the contrary, supposing the State had been violent, it could plead the earlier violences of the Church. He did not see how the ugly facts could be denied; nor did a candid unveiling of them displease his Anglican taste.

'You should have made a study--and you have written a pamphlet,' he would say, with that slow shake of the head which showed him inexorable. 'Why have you given yourself to the Jesuits? You were an Englishman and an outsider--enormous advantages! Why have you thrown them away?'

'One must have information!--I merely went to headquarters.'

'You have paid for it too dear. Your book is a plea for superstition!'

Whereupon a flame in Manisty's black eyes, and a burst in honour of superstition, which set the garden paths echoing.

But Neal pushed quietly on; untiring, unappeasable; pointing to a misstatement here, an exaggeration there, till Manisty was in a roar of argument, furious half with his friend, half with himself.

Meanwhile if the writer bore attack hardly, the man of piety found it still harder to endure the praise of piety. When Manisty denounced irresponsible science and free thought, as the enemies of the State, which must live, and can only live by religion; when he asked with disdain 'what reasonable man would nowadays weigh the membership of the Catholic church against an opinion in geology or exegesis'; when he dwelt on the *easiness* of faith,--which had nothing whatever to do with knowledge, and had, therefore, no quarrel with knowledge; or upon the incomparable social power of religion;--his friend grew restive. And while Manisty, intoxicated with his own phrases, and fluencies, was alternately smoking and declaiming, Neal with his grey hair, his tall spare form, and his air of old-fashioned punctilium, would sit near, fixing the speaker with his pale-blue eyes,--a little threateningly; always ready to shatter an exuberance, to check an oratorical flow by some quick double-edged word that would make Manisty trip and stammer; showing, too, all the time, by his evident shrinking, by certain impregnable reserves, or by the banter that hid a feeling too keen to show itself, how great is the gulf between a literary and a practical Christianity.

Nevertheless, from the whole wrestle two facts emerged:--the pleasure which these very dissimilar men took in each other's society; and that strange ultimate pliancy of Manisty which lay hidden somewhere under all the surge and froth of his vivacious rhetoric. Both were equally surprising to Lucy Foster. How had Manisty ever attached himself to Vanbrugh Neal? For Neal had a large share of the weaknesses of the student and recluse; the failings, that is to say, of a man who had lived much alone, and found himself driven to an old-maidish care of health and nerves, if a delicate physique was to do its work. He had fads; and his fads were often unexpected and disconcerting. One day he would not walk; another day he would not eat; driving was out of the question, and the sun must be avoided like the plague. Then again it was the turn of exercise, cold baths, and hearty fare. It was all done with a grace that made his whims more agreeable than other men's sense. But one might have supposed that such claims on a friend's part would have annoyed a man of Manisty's equally marked but very different peculiarities. Not at all. He was patience and good temper itself on these occasions.

'Isn't he **bon enfant**?' Mr. Neal said once to Mrs. Burgoyne in Lucy's presence, with a sudden accent of affection and emotion--on some occasion when Manisty had borne the upsetting of a cherished plan for the afternoon with quite remarkable patience.

'He has learnt how to spoil *you*!' said Eleanor, with a fluttering smile, and an immediate change of subject. Lucy looking up, felt a little pang.

For nothing could he more curious than the change in Manisty's manner towards the most constant of companions and secretaries. He had given up all continuous work at his book; he talked now of indefinite postponement; and it seemed as if with the change of plan Mrs. Burgoyne had dropped out of the matter altogether. He scarcely consulted her indeed; he consulted Mr. Neal. Mr. Neal often, moved by a secret chivalry, would insist upon bringing her in to their counsels; Manisty immediately became unmanageable, silent, and embarrassed. And how characteristic and significant was that embarrassment of his! It was as though he had a grievance against her; which however he could neither formulate for himself nor express to her.

On the other hand--perhaps inevitably--he began to take much more notice of Lucy Foster, and to find talking with her an escape. He presently found it amusing to 'draw' her; and subjects presented themselves in plenty. She was now much less shy; and her secret disapproval gave her tongue. His challenges and her replies became a feature of the day; Miss Manisty and Mr. Neal began to listen with half-checked smiles, to relish the girl's crisp frankness, and the quick sense of fun that dared to show itself now that she was more at home.

'And how improved she is! That's like all the Americans--they're so adaptable,'--Miss Manisty would think, as she watched her nephew in the evenings teasing, sparring, or arguing with Lucy Foster--she so adorably young and fresh, the new and graceful lines of the *coiffure* that Eleanor had forced upon her, defining the clear oval of the face and framing the large eyes and pure brow. Her hands, perhaps, would be lightly clasped on her white lap, their long fingers playing with some flower she had taken from her belt. The lines of the girlish figure would be full of dignity and strength. She might have been herself the young America, arguing, probing, deciding for herself--refusing to be overawed or brow-beaten by the old Europe.

Eleanor meanwhile was unfailingly gracious both to Lucy and the others, though perhaps the grace had in it sometimes a new note of distance, of that delicate *hauteur*, which every woman of the world has at command. She gave as much attention as ever--more than ever--to the fashioning of Lucy's dresses; the girl was constantly pricked with compunction and shame on the subject. Who was she, that Mrs. Burgoyne--so elegant and distinguished a person--should waste so much time and thought upon her? But sometimes she could not help seeing that Mrs. Burgoyne was glad of the occupation. Her days had been full to the brim; they were now empty. She said nothing; she took up the new books; she talked to and instructed the maids; but Lucy divined a secret suffering.

                    *   *   *   *   *

One evening, about a week after Mr. Neal's arrival at the Villa, Manisty was
more depressed than usual. He had been making some attempts to rearrange a certain section of his book which had fallen especially under the ban of Neal's criticism. He had not been successful; and in the process his discontent with one chapter had spread to several. In talking about the matter to Vanbrugh Neal in the salon
after dinner he broke out into some expression of disgust as to the waste of time
involved in much of his work of the winter. The two friends were in a corner of the
vast room; and Manisty spoke in an undertone. But his voice had the carrying and
penetrating power of his personality.

Presently Eleanor Burgoyne rose, and softly approached Miss Manisty. 'Dear
Aunt Pattie--don't move'--she said, bending over her--'I am tired and will go to
bed.'

Manisty, who had turned at her movement, sprang up, and came to her.

'Eleanor! did we walk you too far this afternoon?'

She smiled, but hardly replied. He busied himself with gathering up her posses-
sions, and lit her candle at the side-table.

As she passed by him to the door, he looked at her furtively for a moment,--
hanging his head. Then he pressed her hand, and said so that only she could hear--

'I should have kept my regrets to myself!'

She shook her head, with faint mockery.

'It would be the first time.'

Her hand dropped from his, and she passed out of sight. Manisty walked back
to his seat discomfited. He could not defend himself against the charges of secret
tyranny and abominable ill-humour that his conscience was pricking him with. He
was sorry--he would have liked to tell her so. And yet somehow her very weakness
and sweetness, her delicate uncomplainingness seemed only to develope his own
small egotisms and pugnacities.

*   *   *   *   *

That night--a night of rain and scirocco--Eleanor wrote in her journal--'Will he ever finish the book? Very possibly it has been all a mistake. Yet when he began it, he was in the depths. Whatever happens, it has been his salvation.

'--Surely he will finish it? He cannot forego the effect he is almost sure it will produce. But he will finish it with impatience and disgust; he is out of love with it and all its associations. All that he was talking of to-night represents what I had most share in,--the chapters which brought us most closely together. How happy we were over them! And now, how different!

'It is curious--the animation with which he has begun to talk to Lucy Foster. Pretty child! I like to feel that I have been the fairy god-mother, dressing her for the ball. How little she knows what it means to be talked to by him, to receive courtesies from him,--how many women would like to be in her place. Yet now she is not shy; she has no alarms; she treats him like an equal. If it were not ridiculous, one could be angry.

'She dislikes and criticises him, and he can have no possible understanding of or sympathy with her. But she is a way out of embarrassment. How fastidious and proud he is with women!--malicious too, and wilful. Often I have wished him more generous--more kind.

'... In three weeks the anniversary will be here--the ninth. Why am I still alive? How often have I asked myself that! Where is my place?--who needs me?--My babe, if he still exists, is alone--there. And I still here. If I had only had the courage to rejoin him! The doctors deceived me. They made me think it could not be long. And now I am better--much better. If I were happy I should be quite well.

'How weary seems this Italian spring!--the restlessness of this eternal wind--the hot clouds that roll up from the Campagna. "Que vivre est difficile, o mon coeur fatigue!"'

CHAPTER VII

I think it's lovely,' said Lucy in an embarrassed voice. 'And I just don't know how to thank you--indeed I don't.'

She was standing inside the door of Mrs. Burgoyne's room, arrayed in the white crepe gown with the touches of pale green and vivid black that Eleanor had designed for her. Its flowing elegance made her positively a stranger to herself. The two maids moreover who had attired her had been intent upon a complete, an indisputable perfection. Her hat had been carried off and retrimmed, her white gloves, her dainty parasol, the bunch of roses at her belt--everything had been thought for; she had been allowed a voice in nothing. And the result was extraordinary. The day before she had been still a mere fresh-cheeked illustration of those 'moeurs de province' which are to be found all over the world, in Burgundy and Yorkshire no less and no more than in Vermont; to-day she had become what others copy, the best of its kind--the 'fleeting flower' that 'blooms for one day at the summit'--as the maids would no doubt have expressed themselves, had they been acquainted with the works of Mr. Clough.

And thanks to that pliancy of her race, which Miss Manisty had discovered, although she was shy in these new trappings, she was not awkward. She was assimilating her new frocks, as she had already assimilated so many other things, during her weeks at the villa--points of manner, of speech, of mental perspective. Unconsciously she copied Mrs. Burgoyne's movements and voice; she was learning to understand Manisty's paradoxes, and Aunt Pattie's small weaknesses. She was less raw, evidently; yet not less individual. Her provincialisms were dropping away; her character, perhaps, was only emerging.

'Are you pleased with it?' she said timidly, as Mrs. Burgoyne bade her come in, and she advanced towards that lady, who was putting on her own hat before the glass.

Eleanor, with uplifted arms, turned and smiled.--

'Charming! You do one credit!--Is Aunt Pattie better?'

Lucy was conscious of a momentary chill. Mrs. Burgoyne had been so kind and friendly during the whole planning and making of this dress, the girl, perhaps, had inevitably expected a keener interest in its completion.

She answered in some discomfort:--

'I am afraid Miss Manisty's not coming. I saw Benson just now. Her headache is still so bad.'

'Ah!'--said Eleanor, absently, rummaging among her gloves; 'this scirocco weather doesn't suit her.'

Lucy fidgetted a little as she stood by the dressing-table, took up one knick-knack after another and put it down. At last she said--

'Do you mind my asking you a question?'

Mrs. Burgoyne turned in surprise.

'By all means!--What can I do?'

'Do you mind telling me whether you think I ought to stay on here? Miss Manisty is so kind--she wants me to stay till you leave, and then go to Vallombrosa with you--next month. But--'

'Why "but"?'--said Mrs. Burgoyne, briskly, still in quest of rings, handkerchief, and fan,--'unless you are quite tired of us.'

The girl smiled. 'I couldn't be that. But--I think you'll be tired of me! And I've heard from the Porters of a quiet pension in Florence, where some friends of theirs will be staying till the middle of June. They would let me join them, till the Porters are ready for me.'

There was just a moment's pause before Eleanor said--

'Aunt Pattie would be very sorry. I know she counts on your going with her to Vallombrosa. I must go home by the beginning of June, and I believe Mr. Manisty goes to Paris.'

'And the book?' Lucy could not help saying, and then wished vehemently that she had left the question alone.

'I don't understand'--said Mrs. Burgoyne, stooping to look for her walking-shoes.

'I didn't--I didn't know whether it was still to be finished by the summer?'

'No one knows,--certainly not the author! But it doesn't concern me in the least.'

'How can it be finished without you?' said Lucy wondering. Again she could not restrain the spirit of eager championship which had arisen in her mind of late; though she was tremulously uncertain as to how far she might express it.

Certainly Mrs. Burgoyne showed a slight stiffening of manner.

'It will have to get finished without me, I'm afraid. Luckily I'm not wanted; but if I were, I shall have no time for anything but my father this summer.'

Lucy was silent. Mrs. Burgoyne finished tying her shoes, then rose, and said lightly--

'Besides--poor book! It wanted a change badly. So did I.--Now Mr. Neal will see it through.'

*   *   *   *   *

Lucy went to say good-bye to Aunt Pattie before starting. Eleanor, left alone, stood a moment, thoughtful, beside the dressing-table.

'She is sorry for me!' she said to herself, with a sudden, passionate movement.

This was the Nemi day--the day of festival, planned a fortnight before, to celebrate the end, the happy end of the book. It was to have been Eleanor's special day--the sign and seal of that good fortune she had brought her cousin and his work.

And now?--Why were they going? Eleanor hardly knew. She had tried to stop it. But Reggie Brooklyn had been asked, and the Ambassador's daughter. And Vanbrugh Neal had a fancy to see Nemi. Manisty, who had forgotten all that the day was once to signify, had resigned himself to the expedition--he who hated expeditions!--' because Neal wanted it.' There had not been a word said about it during the last few days that had not brought gall and wound to Eleanor. She, who thought she knew all that male selfishness was capable of, was yet surprised and pricked anew, hour after hour, by Manisty's casual sayings and assumptions.

It was like some gourd-growth in the night--the rise of this entangling barrier between herself and him. She knew that some of it came from those secret superstitions and fancies about himself and his work which she had often detected in him.

If a companion or a place, even a particular table or pen had brought him luck, he would recur to them and repeat them with eagerness. But once prove to him the contrary, and she had seen him drop friend and pen with equal decision.

And as far as she could gather--as far as he would discuss the matter at all--it was precisely with regard to those portions of the book where her influence upon it had been strongest, that the difficulties put forward by Mr. Neal had arisen.

Her lip quivered. She had little or no personal conceit. Very likely Mr. Neal's criticisms were altogether just, and she had counselled wrongly. When she thought of the old days of happy consultation, of that vibrating sympathy of thought which had arisen between them, glorifying the winter days in Rome, of the thousand signs in him of a deep, personal gratitude and affection--

Vanished!--vanished! The soreness of heart she carried about with her, proudly concealed, had the gnawing constancy of physical pain. While he!--Nothing seemed to her more amazing than the lapses in mere gentlemanliness that Manisty could allow himself. He was capable on occasion of all that was most refined and tender in feeling. But once jar that central egotism of his, and he could behave incredibly! Through the small actions and omissions of every day, he could express, if he chose, a hardness of soul before which the woman shuddered.

Did he in truth mean her to understand, not only that she had been an intruder, and an unlucky one, upon his work and his intellectual life, but that any dearer hopes she might have based upon their comradeship were to be once for all abandoned? She stood there, lost in a sudden tumult of passionate pride and misery, which was crossed every now and then by a strange and bitter wonder.

Each of us carries about with him a certain mental image of himself--typical, characteristic--as we suppose; draped at any rate to our fancy; round which we group the incidents of life. Eleanor saw herself always as the proud woman; it is a guise in which we are none of us loth to masquerade. Haughtily dumb and patient during her married years; proud morally, socially, intellectually; finding in this stiffening of the self her only defence against the ugly realities of daily life. Proud too in her loneliness and grief--proud of her very grief, of her very capacity for suffering, of all the delicate shades of thought and sorrow which furnished the matter of her secret life, lived without a sign beside the old father whose coarser and commoner pride took such small account of hers!

And now--she seemed to herself to be already drinking humiliation, and fore-seeing ever deeper draughts of it to come. She, who had never begged for anything, was in the mood to see her whole existence as a refused petition, a rejected gift. She had offered Edward Manisty her all of sympathy and intelligence, and he was throwing it back lightly, inexorably upon her hands. Her thin cheek burnt; but it was the truth. She annoyed and wearied him; and he had shaken her off; her, Elea-nor Burgoyne! She did not know herself. Her inmost sense of identity was shaken.

She leant her head an instant against the frame of the open window, closing her tired eyes upon the great Campagna below her. A surge of rebellious will passed through her. Always submission, patience, silence,--till now! But there are mo-ments when a woman must rouse herself, and fight--must not accept, but make, her fate.

Jealous! Was that last heat and ignominy of the soul to be hers too? She was to find it a threat and offence that he should spend some of the evenings that now went so heavily, talking with this girl,--this nice simple girl, whom she had her-self bade him cultivate, whom she had herself brought into notice, rubbing off her angles,--drilling her into beauty? The very notion was madness and absurdity. It degraded her in her own eyes. It was the measure of her own self-ignorance. She--resign him at the first threat of another claim! The passionate life of her own heart amazed and stunned her.

The clock in the salon struck. She started, and went to straighten her veil at the glass. What would the afternoon bring her? Something it should bring her. The Nemi days of the winter were shrined in memory--each with its halo. Let her put out her full strength again, and now, before it was too late--before he had slipped too far away from her.

The poor heart beat hotly against the lace of her dress. What did she intend or hope for? She only knew that this might be one of her last chances with him--that the days were running out--and the moment of separation approached. Her whole nature was athirst, desperately athirst for she knew not what. Yet something told her that among these ups and downs of daily temper and fortune there lay strewn for her the last chances of her life.

'Please, ma'am, will you go in for a moment to Miss Manisty?'

The voice was Benson's, who had waylaid Mrs. Burgoyne in the salon.

Eleanor obeyed.

From the shadows of her dark room Aunt Pattie raised a wan face.

'Eleanor!--what do you think?'--

Eleanor ran to her. Miss Manisty handed her a telegram which read as follows--

'Your letter arrived too late to alter arrangements. Coming to-morrow--two or three nights--discuss plans.--ALICE.'

Eleanor let her hand drop, and the two ladies looked at each other in dismay.

'But you told her you couldn't receive her here?'

'Several times over. Edward will be in despair. How are we to have her here with Miss Foster? Her behaviour the last two months has been too extraordinary.'

Aunt Pattie fell back a languid little heap upon her pillows. Eleanor looked almost equally disconcerted.

'Have you told Edward?'

'No,' said Aunt Pattie miserably, raising a hand to her aching head, as though to excuse her lack of courage.

'Shall I tell him?'

'It's too bad to put such things on you.'

'No, not at all. But I won't tell him now. It would spoil the day. Some time before the evening.'

Aunt Pattie showed an aspect of relief.

'Do whatever you think best. It's very good of you--'

'Not at all. Dear Aunt Pattie!--lie still. By the way--has she anyone with her?'

'Only her maid--the one person who can manage her at all. That poor lady, you know, who tried to be companion, gave it up some time ago. Where shall we put her?'

'There are the two east rooms. Shall I tell Andreina to get them ready?'

Aunt Pattie acquiesced, with a sound rather like a groan.

'There is no chance still of stopping her?' said Eleanor, moving away.

'Then we must be prepared. Don't fret--dear Aunt Pattie!--we'll help you through.'

Eleanor stood a moment in the salon, thinking.

Unlucky! Manisty's eccentric and unmanageable sister had been for many years the secret burden of his life and Aunt Pattie's. Eleanor had been a witness of the annoyance and depression with which he had learnt during the winter that she was in Italy. She knew something of the efforts that had been made to keep her away from the villa.--

He would be furiously helpless and miserable under the infliction.--Somehow, her spirits rose.--

She went to the door of the salon, and heard the carriage drive up that was to take them to Nemi. Across Manisty's room, she saw himself on the balcony lounging and smoking till the ladies should appear. The blue lake with its green shores sparkled beyond him. The day was brightening. Certainly--let the bad news wait!

*   *   *   *   *

As they drove along the Galleria di Sotto, Manisty seemed to be preoccupied. The carriage had interrupted him in the midst of reading a long letter which he still held crumpled in his hand.

At last he said abruptly to Eleanor--'Benecke's last chance is up. He is summoned to submit next week at latest.'

'He tells you so?'

'Yes. He writes me a heart-broken letter.'

'Poor, poor fellow! It's all the Jesuits' doing. Mr. Neal told me the whole story.'

'Oh! it's tyranny of course. And the book's only a fraction of the truth,--a little Darwinian yeast leavening a lump of theology. But they're quite right. They can't help it.'

Eleanor looked at Lucy Foster and laughed.

'Dangerous to say those things before Miss Foster.'

'Does Miss Foster know anything about it?'--he said coolly.

Lucy hastily disclaimed any knowledge of Father Benecke and his affairs.

'They're very simple'--said Manisty. 'Father Benecke is a priest, but also a Professor. He published last year a rather Liberal book--very mildly liberal--some evolution--some Biblical criticism--just a touch! And a good deal of protest against the way in which the Jesuits are ruining Catholic University education in Germany. Lord! more than enough. They put his book on the Index within a month; he has had a year's grace to submit in; and now, if the submission is not made within a week or so, he will be first suspended, and then--excommunicated.'

'Who's "they"? 'said Lucy.

'Oh! the Congregation of the Index--or the people who set them on.'

'Is the book a bad book?'

'Quite the contrary.'

'And you're pleased?'

'I think the Papacy is keeping up discipline--and is not likely to go under just yet.'

He turned to her with his teasing laugh and was suddenly conscious of her new elegance. Where was the 'Sunday school teacher'? Transformed!--in five weeks--into this vision that was sitting opposite to him? Really, women were too wonderful! His male sense felt a kind of scorn for the plasticity of the sex.

'He has asked your opinion?' said Lucy, pursuing the subject.

'Yes. I told him the book was excellent--and his condemnation certain.'

Lucy bit her lip.

'Who did it?'

'The Jesuits--probably.'

'And you defend them?'

'Of course!--They're the only gentlemen in Europe who thoroughly understand their own business.'

'What a business!' said Lucy, breathing quick.--'To rush on every little bit of truth they see and stamp it out!'

'Like any other dangerous firework,--your simile is excellent.'

'Dangerous!' She threw back her head.--'To the blind and the cripples.'

'Who are the larger half of mankind. Precisely.'

She hesitated, then could not restrain herself.

'But *you're* not concerned?'

'I? Oh dear no. I can be trusted with fireworks. Besides I'm not a Catholic.'

'Is that fair?--to stand outside slavery--and praise it?'

'Why not?--if it suits my purpose?'

The girl was silent. Manisty glanced at Eleanor; she caught the mischievous laugh in his eyes, and lightly returned it. It was his old comrade's look, come back. A warmer, more vital life stirred suddenly through all her veins; the slight and languid figure drew itself erect; her senses told her, hurriedly, for the first time that the May sun, the rapidly freshening air, and the quick movement of the carriage were all physically delightful.

How fast, indeed, the spring was conquering the hills! As they passed over the great viaduct at Aricia, the thick Chigi woods to the left masked the deep ravine in torrents of lightest foamiest green; and over the vast plain to the right, stretching to Ardea, Lanuvium and the sea, the power of the reawakening earth, like a shuttle in the loom, was weaving day by day its web of colour and growth, the ever brightening pattern of crop, and grass and vine. The beggars tormented them on the approach to Genzano, as they tormented of old Horace and Maecenas; and presently the long falling street of the town, with its multitudes of short, wiry, brown-faced folk, its clatter of children and mules, its barbers and wine shops, brought them in sight again of the emerald-green Campagna, and the shiny hazes over the sea. In front rose the tower-topped hill of Monte Giove, marking the site of Corioli; and just as they turned towards Nemi the Appian Way ran across their path. Overhead, a marvellous sky with scudding veils of white cloud. The blur and blight of the scirocco had vanished without rain, under a change of wind. An all-blessing, all-penetrating sun poured upon the stirring earth. Everywhere fragments and ruins--ghosts of the great past--yet engulfed, as it were, and engarlanded by the active and fertile present.

And now they were to follow the high ridge above the deep-sunk lake, toward Nemi on its farther side--Nemi with its Orsini tower, grim and tall, rising on its fortress rock, high over the lake and what was once the thick grove or 'Nemus' of the Goddess, mantling the proud white of her inviolate temple.

'Look!'--slid Eleanor, touching Lucy's hand. 'There's the niched wall--and the platform of the temple.'

And Lucy, bending eager brows, saw across the lake a line of great recesses, overgrown and shadowy against the steep slopes or cliffs of the crater, and in front of them a flat space, with one farm-shed upon it.

In the crater-wall, just behind and above the temple-site, was a black vertical cleft. Eleanor pointed it out to Manisty.

'Do you remember we never explored it? But the spring must be there?--Egeria's spring?'

Manisty lazily said he didn't know.

'Don't imagine you will be let off,' said Eleanor, laughing. 'We have settled every other point at Nemi. This is left for to-day. It will make a scramble after tea.'

'You will find it further than you think,' said Manisty, measuring the distance.

'So it was somewhere on that terrace he died--poor priest!'--said Lucy, musing.

Manisty, who was walking beside the carriage, turned towards her. Her little speech flattered him. But he laughed.

'I wonder how much it was worth--that place--in hard cash,' he said, drily. 'No doubt that was the secret of it.'

Lucy smiled--unwillingly. They were mounting a charming road high above the lake. Stretching between them and the lake were steep olive gardens and vineyards; above them light half-fledged woods climbed to the sky. In the vineyards the fresh red-brown earth shone amid the endless regiments of vines, just breaking into leaf; daisies glittered under the olives; and below, on a mid-way crag, a great wild-cherry, sun-touched, flung its boughs and blossoms, a dazzling pearly glory, over the dark blue hollow of the lake.

And on the farther side, the high, scooped-out wall of the crater rose rich and dark above the temple-site. How white--*white*--it must have shone!--thought Lucy. Her imagination had been caught by the priest's story. She saw Nemi for the first time as one who had seen it before. Timidly she looked at the man walking beside the carriage. Strange! She no longer disliked him as she had done, no longer felt it impossible that he should have written the earlier book which had been so dear to her. Was it that she had seen him chastened and depressed of late--had realised the comparative harmlessness of his vanity, the kindness and docility he could show to a friend? Ah no!--if he had been kind for one friend, he had been difficult and ungrateful for another. The thinness of Eleanor's cheek, the hollowness of her blue eye accused him. But even here the girl's inner mind had begun to doubt and de-mur. After all did she know much--or anything--of their real relation?

Certainly this afternoon he was a delightful companion. That phrase which Vanbrugh Neal had applied to him in Lucy's hearing, which had seemed to her so absurd, began after all to fit. He was **bon enfant** both to Eleanor and to her on this golden afternoon. He remembered Eleanor's love for broom and brought her bunches of it from the steep banks; he made affectionate mock of Neal's old-maidish ways; he threw himself with ejaculations, joyous, paradoxical, violent, on the unfolding beauty of the lake and the spring; and throughout he made them feel his presence as something warmly strong and human, for all his provoking defects, and that element of the uncommunicated and unexplained which was always to be felt in him. Eleanor began to look happier and younger than she had looked for days. And Lucy wondered why the long ascent to Nemi was so delightful; why the scirocco seemed to have gone from the air, leaving so purpureal and divine a light on mountain and lake and distance.

*   *   *   *   *

When they arrived at Nemi, Manisty as usual showed that he knew nothing of the practical arrangements of the day, which were always made for him by other people.

'*What* am I to do with these?' he said, throwing his hands in despair towards the tea-baskets in the carriage.--'We can't drive beyond this--And how are we to meet the others?--when do they come?--why aren't they here?'

He turned with peremptory impatience to Eleanor. She laid a calming hand upon his arm, pointing to the crowd of peasant folk from the little town that had already gathered round the carriage.

'Get two of those boys to carry the baskets. We are to meet the others at the temple. They come by the path from Genzano.'

Manisty's brow cleared at once like a child's. He went into the crowd, chattering his easy Italian, and laid hands on two boys, one of whom was straight and lithe and handsome as a young Bacchus, and bore the noble name of Aristodemo. Then, followed by a horde of begging children which had to be shaken off by degrees, they began the descent of the steep cliff on which Nemi stands. The path zig-zagged downwards, and as they followed it, they came upon files of peasant women ascending, all bearing on their kerchiefed heads great flat baskets of those small wood-strawberries, or *fragole*, which are the chief crop of Nemi and its fields.

The handsome women, the splendid red of the fruit and the scent which it shed along the path, the rich May light upon the fertile earth and its spray of leaf and blossom, the sense of growth and ferment and pushing life everywhere--these things made Lucy's spirits dance within her. She hung back with the two boys, shyly practising her Italian upon them, while Eleanor and Manisty walked ahead.

But Manisty did not forget her. Half-way down the path, he turned back to look at her, and saw that she was carrying a light waterproof, which aunt Pattie had forced upon her lest the scirocco should end in rain. He stopped and demanded it. Lucy resisted.

'I *can* carry that,' he urged impatiently; 'it isn't baskets.'

'You *could* carry those,' she said laughing.

'Not in a world that grows boys and sixpences. But I want that cloak. Please!'

The tone was imperious and she yielded. He hurried on to join Eleanor, carrying the cloak with his usual awkwardness, and often trailing it in the dust. Lucy, who was very neat and precise in all her personal ways, suffered at the sight, and wished she had stood firm. But to be waited on and remembered by him was not a disagreeable experience; perhaps because it was still such a new and surprising one.

Presently they were on the level of the lake, and their boys guided them through a narrow and stony by-path, to the site of the temple, or as the peasant calls it the 'Giardino del Lago.'

It is a flat oblong space, with a two-storied farm building--part of it showing brickwork of the early Empire--standing upon it. To north and east runs the niched wall in which, deep under accumulations of soil, Lord Savile found the great Tiberi-us, and those lost portrait busts which had been waiting there through the centuries till the pick and spade of an Englishman should release them. As to the temple walls which the English lord uncovered, the trenches that he dug, and the sacrificial altar that he laid bare--the land, their best guardian, has taken them back into itself. The strawberries grow all over them; only strange billows and depressions in the soil make the visitor pause and wonder. The earth seems to say to him--'Here indeed are secrets and treasures--but not for you! I have been robbed enough. The dead are mine. Leave them in my breast. And you!--go your ways in the sun!'

They made their way across the strawberry fields, looking for the friends who were to join them--Reggie Brooklyn, Mr. Neal, and the two ladies. There was no sign of them whatever. Yet, according to time and trains, they should have been on the spot, waiting.

'Annoying!' said Manisty, with his ready irritability. 'Reggie might really have managed better.--Who's this fellow?'

It was the padrone or tenant of the Giardino, who came up and parleyed with them. Yes, 'Vostra Eccellenza' might put down their baskets and make their tea. He pointed to a bench behind the shed. The *forestieri* came every day; he turned away in indifference.

Meanwhile the girls and women gathering among the strawberries, raised themselves to look at the party, flashing their white teeth at Aristodemo, who was evidently a wit among them. They flung him gibes as he passed, to which he replied disdainfully. A group of girls who had been singing together, turned round upon him, 'chaffing' him with shrill voices and outstretched necks, like a flock of young cackling geese, while he, holding himself erect, threw them back flinty words and glances, hitting at every stroke, striding past them with the port of a young king. Then they broke into a song which they could hardly sing for laughing--about a lover who had been jilted by his mistress. Aristodemo turned a deaf ear, but the mocking song, sung by the harsh Italian voices, seemed to fill the hollow of the lake and echoed from the steep side of the crater. The afternoon sun, striking from the ridge of Genzano, filled the rich tangled cup, and threw its shafts into the hollows of the temple wall. Lucy standing still under the heat and looking round her, felt herself steeped and bathed in Italy. Her New England reserve betrayed almost nothing; but underneath, there was a young passionate heart, thrilling to nature and the spring, conscious too of a sort of fate in these delicious hours, that were so much sharper and full of meaning than any her small experience had yet known.

She walked on to look at the niched wall, while Manisty and Eleanor parleyed with Aristodemo as to the guardianship of the tea. Presently she heard their steps behind her, and she turned back to them eagerly.

'The boy was in that tree!'--she said to Manisty, pointing to a great olive that flung its branches over a mass of ruin, which must once have formed part of an outer enclosure wall beyond the statued recesses.

'Was he?' said Manisty, surprised into a smile. 'You know best.--You are very kind to that nonsense.'

She hesitated.

'Perhaps--perhaps you don't know why I liked it so particularly. It reminded me of things in your other book.'

'The "Letters from Palestine"?' said Manisty, half amused, half astonished.

'I suppose you wonder I should have seen it? But we read a great deal in my country! All sorts of people read--men and women who do the roughest work with their hands, and never spend a cent on themselves they can help. Uncle Ben gave it me. There was a review of it in the "Springfield Republican"--I guess they will have sent it you. But'--her voice took a shy note--'do you remember that piece about the wedding feast at Cana--where you imagined the people going home afterwards over the hill paths--how they talked, and what they felt?'

'I remember something of the sort,' said Manisty--I wrote it at Nazareth--in the spring. I'm sure it was bad!'

'I don't know why you say that?' She knit her brows a little. 'If I shut my eyes, I seemed to be walking with them. And so with your goat-herd. I'm certain it was that tree!' she said, pointing to the tree, her bright smile breaking. 'And the grove was here.--And the people came running down from the village on the cliff,'--she turned her hand towards Nemi.

Manisty was flattered again, all the more because the girl had evidently no intention of flattery whatever, but was simply following the pleasure of her own thought. He strolled on beside her, poking into the niches, and talking, as the whim took him, pouring out upon her indeed some of the many thoughts and fancies which had been generated in him by those winter visits to Nemi that he and Eleanor had made together.

Eleanor loitered behind, looking at the strawberry gatherers.

'The next train should bring them here in about an hour,' she thought to herself in great flatness of spirit. 'How stupid of Reggie!'

Then as she lifted her eyes, they fell upon Manisty and Lucy, strolling along the wall together, he talking, she turning her brilliant young face towards him, her white dress shining in the sun.

A thought--a perception--thrust itself like a lance-point through Eleanor's mind.--She gave an inward cry--a cry of misery. The lake seemed to swim before her.

CHAPTER VIII

They made their tea under the shadow of the farm-building, which consisted of a loft above, and a large dark room on the ground floor, which was filled with the flat strawberry-baskets, full and ready for market.

Lucy found the little festa delightful, though all that the ladies had to do was to make an audience for Aristodemo and Manisty. The handsome dare-devil lad began to talk, drawn out by the Englishman, and lo! instead of a mere peasant they had got hold of an artist and a connoisseur! Did he know anything of the excavations and the ruins? Why, he knew everything! He chattered to them, with astonishing knowledge and shrewdness, for half an hour. Complete composure, complete good-humour, complete good manners--he possessed them all. Easy to see that he was the son of an old race, moulded by long centuries of urbane and civilised living!

A little boastful, perhaps. He too had found the head of a statue, digging in his father's orchard. Man or woman?--asked Mrs. Burgoyne. A woman. And handsome? The handsomest lady ever seen. And perfect? Quite perfect. Had she a nose, for instance? He shook his young head in scorn. Naturally she had a nose! Did the ladies suppose he would have picked up a creature without one?

Then he rose and beckoned smiling to Eleanor and Lucy. They followed him through the cool lower room, where the strawberries gleamed red through the dark, up the creaking stairs to the loft. And there on the ground was an old box and in the box, a few score of heads and other fragments--little terracottas, such as the peasants turn up every winter as they plough or dig among the olives.. Delicate little hooded women, heads of Artemis with the crown of Cybele, winged heads, or heads covered with the Phrygian cap, portrait-heads of girls or children, with their sharp profiles still perfect, and the last dab of the clay under the thumb of the artist, as clear and clean as when it was laid there some twenty-two centuries ago.

Lucy bent over them in a passion of pleasure, turning over the little things quite silently, but with sparkling looks.

'Would you like them?' said Manisty, who had followed them, and stood over her, cigarette in hand.

'Oh no!' said Lucy, rising in confusion. 'Don't get them for me.'

'Come away,' said Eleanor, laughing. 'Never interfere between a man and a bargain.'

The *padrone* indeed appeared at the moment. Manisty sent the ladies downstairs, and the bargaining began.

When he came downstairs ten minutes later a small basket was in his hand. He offered it to Lucy, while he held out his other hand to Eleanor. The hand contained two fragments only, but of exquisite quality, one a fine Artemis head with the Cybele crown, the other merely the mask or shell of a face, from brow to chin,--a gem of the purest and loveliest Greek work.

Eleanor took them with a critical delight. Her comments were the comments of taste and knowledge. They were lightly given, without the smallest pedantry, but Manisty hardly answered them. He walked eagerly to Lucy Foster, whose shy intense gratitude, covering an inward fear that he had spent far, far too much money upon her, and that she had indecorously provoked his bounty, was evidently attractive to him. He told her that he had got them for a mere nothing, and they sat down on the bench behind the house together, turning them over, he holding forth, and now and then discovering through her modest or eager replies, that she had been somehow remarkably well educated by that old Calvinist uncle of hers. The tincture of Greek and Latin, which had looked so repellent from a distance, presented itself differently now that it enabled him to give his talk rein, and was partly the source in her of these responsive grateful looks which became her so well. After all perhaps her Puritan stiffness was only on the surface. How much it had yielded already to Eleanor's lessons! He really felt inclined to continue them on his own account; to test for himself this far famed pliancy of the American woman.

Meanwhile Eleanor moved away, watching the path from Genzano which wound downwards from the Sforza Cesarini villa to the 'Giardino,' and was now visible, now hidden by the folds of the shore.

Presently Manisty and Lucy heard her exclamation.

'At last!--What has Reggie been about?'

'Coming?' said Manisty.

'Yes--thank goodness! Evidently they missed that first train. But now there are four people coming down the hill--two men and two ladies. I'm sure one's Reggie.'

'Well, for the practical man he hasn't distinguished himself,' said Manisty, taking out another cigarette.

'I can't see them now--they're hidden behind that bend. They'll be ten minutes more, I should think, before they arrive. Edward!'

'Yes?--Don't be energetic!'

'There's just time to explore that ravine--while they're having tea. Then we shall have seen it all--done the last, last thing! Who knows--dear Nemi!--if we shall ever see it again?'

Her tone was quite gay, yet, involuntarily, there was a touching note in it. Lucy looked down guiltily, wishing herself away. But Manisty resisted.

'You'll be very tired, Eleanor--it's much further than you think--and it's very hot.'

'Oh no, it's not far--and the sun's going down fast. You wouldn't be afraid? They'll be here directly,' she said, turning to Lucy. 'I'm sure it was they.'

'Don't mind me, please!' said Lucy. 'I shall be perfectly right. I'll boil the kettle again, and be ready for them. Aristodemo will look after me.'

Eleanor turned to Manisty.

'Come!' she said.

This time she rather commanded than entreated. There was a delicate stateliness in her attitude, her half-mourning dress of grey and black, her shadowy hat, the gesture of her hand, that spoke a hundred subtle things--all those points of age and breeding, of social distinction and experience, that marked her out from Lucy--from the girl's charming immaturity.

Manisty rose ungraciously. As he followed his cousin along the narrow path among the strawberry beds his expression was not agreeable. Eleanor's heart--if she had looked back--might have failed her. But she hurried on.

*   *   *   *   *

Lucy, left to herself, set the stove under the kettle alight and prepared some fresh tea, while Aristodemo and the other boy leant against the wall in the shade chattering to each other.

The voices of Eleanor and Manisty had vanished out of hearing in the wood behind the Giardino. But the voices from Genzano began to come nearer. A quarter to six.--There would be only a short time for them to rest and have their tea in, before they must all start home for the villa, where Miss Manisty was expecting the whole party for dinner at eight. Was that Mr. Brooklyn's voice? She could not see them, but she could hear them talking in the narrow overgrown lane leading from the lake to the ruins.

How *very* strange! The four persons approaching entered the Giardino still noisily laughing and talking--and Lucy knew none of them! The two men, of whom one certainly resembled Mr. Brooklyn in height and build, were quite strangers to her; and she felt certain that the two ladies, who were stout and elderly, had nothing to do either with Mrs. Elliott, Mr. Reggie's married sister, or with the Ambassador's daughter.

She watched them with astonishment. They were English, tourists apparently from Frascati, to judge from their conversation. And they were in a great hurry. The walk had taken them longer than they expected, and they had only a short time to stay. They looked carelessly at the niched wall, and the shed with the strawberry baskets, remarking that there was 'precious little to see, now you'd done it.' Then they walked past Lucy, throwing many curious glances at the solitary English girl with the tea-things before her, the gentlemen raising their hats. And finally they hurried away, and all sounds of them were soon lost in the quiet of the May evening.

Lucy was left, feeling a little forlorn and disconcerted. Presently she noticed that all the women working on the Giardino land were going home. Aristodemo and his companion ran after some of the girls, and their discordant shouts and laughs could be heard in the distance, mingled with the 'Ave Maria' sung by groups of woman and girls who were mounting the zigzag path towards Nemi, their arms linked together.

The evening stillness came flooding into the great hollow like a soft resistless wave. Every now and then the voices of peasants going home rippled up from unseen paths, then sank again into the earth. On the high windows of Nemi the sunset light from the Campagna struck and flamed, '***Ave Maria--gratia plena.***' How softened now, how thinly, delicately far! The singers must be nearing their homes in the little hill town.

Lucy looked around her. No one on the Giardino, no one in the fields near, no one on the Genzano road. She seemed to be absolutely alone. Her two companions indeed could not be far away, and the boys no doubt would come back for the baskets. But meanwhile she could see and hear no one.

The sun disappeared behind the Genzano ridge, and it grew cold all in a moment. She felt the chill, together with a sudden consciousness of fatigue. Was there fever in this hollow of the lake? Certainly the dwellings were all placed on the heights, save for the fisherman's cottage half-way to Genzano. She got up and began to move about, wishing for her cloak. But Mr. Manisty had carried it off, absently, on his arm.

Then she packed up the tea-things. What had happened to the party from Rome?

Surely more than an hour had passed. Had it taken them longer to climb to the spring's source than they supposed? How fast the light was failing, the rich Italian light, impatient to be gone, claiming all or nothing!

The girl began to be a little shaken with vague discomforts and terrors. She had been accustomed to wander about the lake of Albano by herself, and to make friends with the peasants. But after all the roads would not be so closely patrolled by *carabinieri* if all was quite as safe as in Vermont or Middlesex; and there were plenty of disquieting stories current among the English visitors, even among the people themselves. Was it not only a month since a carriage containing some German royalties had been stopped and robbed by masked peasants on the Rocca di Papa road? Had not an old resident in Rome told her, only the day before, that when he walked about these lake paths he always filled his pockets with cigars and divested them of money, in order that the charcoal-burners might love him without robbing him? Had not friends of theirs going to Cori and Ninfa been followed by mounted police all the way?

These things weighed little with her as she wandered in broad daylight about the roads near the villa. But now she was quite alone, the night was coming, and the place seemed very desolate.

But of course they would be back directly! Why not walk to meet them? It was the heat and slackness of the day which had unnerved her. Perhaps, too, unknown to herself!--the stir of new emotions and excitements in a deep and steadfast nature.

She had marked the path they took, and she made her way to it. It proved to be very steep, dark, and stony under meeting trees. She climbed it laboriously, calling at intervals.

Presently--a sound of steps and hoofs. Looking up she could just distinguish a couple of led mules with two big lads picking their way down the rocky lane. There was no turning aside. She passed them with as much dispatch as possible.

They stopped, however, and stared at her,--the elegant lady in her white dress all alone. Then they passed, and she could not but be conscious of relief, especially as she had neither money nor cigars.

Suddenly there was a clatter of steps behind her, and she turned to see one of the boys, holding out his hand--

'Signora!--un soldino!'

She walked fast, shaking her head.

'Non ho niente--niente.'

He followed her, still begging, his whining note passing into something more insolent. She hurried on. Presently there was a silence; the steps ceased; she supposed he was tired of the pursuit, and had dropped back to the point where his companion was waiting with the mules.

But there was a sudden movement in the lane behind. She put up her hand with a little cry. Her cheek was struck,--again!--another stone struck her wrist. The blood flowed over her hand. She began to run, stumbling up the path, wondering how she could defend herself if the two lads came back and attacked her together.

Luckily the path turned; her white dress could no longer offer them a mark. She fled on, and presently found a gap in the low wall of the lane, and a group of fig-trees just beyond it, amid which she crouched. The shock, the loneliness, the pang of the boys' brutality, had brought a sob into her throat. Why had her companions left her?--it was not kind!--till they were sure that the people coming were their expected guests. Her cheek seemed to be merely grazed, but her wrist was deeply cut. She wrapped her handkerchief tightly round it, but it soon began to drip again upon her pretty dress. Then she tore off some of the large young fig-leaves beside her, not knowing what else to do, and held them to it.

*   *   *   *   *

A few minutes later, Manisty and Eleanor descended the same path in haste. They had found the ascent longer and more intricate than even he had expected, and had lost count of time in a conversation beside Egeria's spring--a conversation that brought them back to Lucy changed beings, in a changed relation. What was the meaning of Manisty's moody, embarrassed look? and of that white and smiling composure that made a still frailer ghost of Eleanor than before?

'Did you hear that call?' said Manisty, stopping.

It was repeated, and they both recognised Lucy Foster's voice, coming from somewhere close to them on the richly grown hillside. Manisty exclaimed, ran on--paused--listened again--shouted--and there, beside the path, propping herself against the stones of the wall, was a white and tremulous girl holding a swathed arm stiffly in front of her so that the blood dripping from it should not fall upon her dress.

Manisty came up to her in utter consternation. 'What has happened? How are you here? Where are the others?'

She answered dizzily, then said, faintly trying to smile, 'If you could provide me with--something to tie round it?'

'Eleanor!' Manisty's voice rang up the path. Then he searched his own pockets in despair--remembering that he had wrapped his handkerchief round Eleanor's precious terracottas just before they started, that the little parcel was on the top of the basket he had given to Miss Foster, and that both were probably waiting with the tea-things below.

Eleanor came up.

'Why did we leave her?' cried Manisty, turning vehemently upon his cousin--'That was *not* Reggie and his party! What a horrible mistake! She has been attacked by some of these peasant brutes. Just look at this bleeding!'

Something in his voice roused a generous discomfort in Lucy even through her faintness.

'It is nothing,' she said. 'How could you help it? It is so silly!--I am so strong--and yet any cut, or prick even, makes me feel faint. If only we could make it stop--I should be all right.'

Eleanor stooped and looked at the wound, so far as the light would serve, touching the wrist with her ice-cold fingers. Manisty watched her anxiously. He valued her skill in nursing matters.

'It will soon stop,' she said. 'We must bind it tightly.'

And with a spare handkerchief, and the long muslin scarf from her own neck, she presently made as good a bandage as was possible.

'My poor frock!' said Lucy, half laughing, half miserable,--'what will Benson say to me?'

Mrs. Burgoyne did not seem to hear.

'We must have a sling,' she was saying to herself, and she took off the light silk shawl she wore round her own shoulders.

'Oh no! Don't, please!' said Lucy. 'It has grown so cold.'

And then they both perceived that she was trembling from head to foot.

'Good Heavens!' cried Manisty, looking at something on his own arm. 'And I carried off her cloak! There it's been all the time! What a pretty sort of care to take of you!'

Eleanor meanwhile was turning her shawl into a sling in spite of Lucy's remonstrances. Manisty made none.

When the arm was safely supported, Lucy pulled herself together with a great effort of will, and declared that she could now walk quite well.

'But all that way round the lake to Genzano!'--said Manisty; 'or up that steep hill to Nemi? Eleanor! how can she possibly manage it?'

'Let her try,' said Eleanor quietly. 'It is the best. Now let her take your arm.'

Lucy looked up at Mrs. Burgoyne, smiling tremulously. 'Thank you!--thank you! What a trouble I am!'

She put out her free hand, but Mrs. Burgoyne seemed to have moved away. It was taken by Manisty, who drew it within his arm.

They descended slowly, and just as they were emerging from the heavy shadow of the lane into the mingled sunset and moonlight of the open 'Giardino, sounds reached them that made them pause in astonishment.

'Reggie!' said Manisty--'and Neal! Listen! Good gracious!--there they are!'

And sure enough, there in the dim light behind the farm-building, gathered in a group round the tea-baskets, laughing, and talking eagerly with each other, or with Aristodemo, was the whole lost party--the two ladies and the two men. And beside the group, held by another peasant, was a white horse with a side-saddle.

Manisty called. The new-comers turned, looked, then shouted exultant.

'Well!'--said Reggie, throwing up his arms at sight of Manisty, and skimming over the strawberry furrows towards them. 'Of all the muddles! I give you this blessed country. I'll never say a word for it again. Everything on this beastly line altered for May--no notice to anybody!--all the old trains printed as usual, and a wretched flyleaf tucked in somewhere that nobody saw or was likely to see. Station full of people for the 2.45. Train taken off--nothing till 4.45. Never saw such a confusion!--and the *Capo-stazione* as rude as he could be. I *say*!--what's the matter?'

He drew up sharp in front of them.

'We'll tell you presently, my dear fellow,' said Manisty peremptorily. 'But now just help us to get Miss Foster home. What a mercy you thought of bringing a horse!'

'Why!--I brought it for--for Mrs. Burgoyne,' said the young man, astonished, looking round for his cousin. 'We found the carriage waiting at the Sforza Cesarini gate, and the man told us you were an hour behind your time. So I thought Eleanor would be dead-tired, and I went to that man--you remember?--we got a horse from before--'

But Manisty had hurried Lucy on without listening to a word; and she herself was now too dizzy with fatigue and loss of blood to grasp what was being said around her.

Reggie fell back in despair on Mrs. Burgoyne.

'Eleanor!--what have you been doing to yourselves! What a nightmare of an afternoon! How on earth are you going to walk back all this way? What's wrong with Miss Foster?'

'Some rough boys threw stones at her, and her arm is badly cut. Edward will take her on to Genzano, find a doctor and then bring her home.--We'll go on first, and send back another carriage for them. You angel, Reggie, to think of that horse!'

'But I thought of it for you, Eleanor,' said the young man, looking in distress at the delicate woman for whom he had so frank and constant an affection. 'Miss Foster's as strong as Samson!--or ought to be. What follies has she been up to?'

'*Please*, Reggie--hold your tongue! You shall talk as much nonsense as you please when once we have started the poor child off.'

And Eleanor too ran forward. Manisty had just put together a rough mounting block from some timber in the farm-building. Meanwhile the other two ladies had been helpful and kind. Mrs. Elliott had wrapped a white Chudda shawl round Lucy's shivering frame. A flask containing some brandy had been extracted from Mr. Neal's pocket, more handkerchiefs and a better sling found for the arm. Finally Lucy, all her New England pride outraged by the fuss that was being made about her, must needs submit to be almost lifted on the horse by Manisty and Mr. Brooklyn. When she found herself in the saddle, she looked round bewildered. 'But this must have been meant for Mrs. Burgoyne! Oh how tired she will be!'

'Don't trouble yourself about me! I am as fresh as paint,' said Eleanor's laughing voice beside her.

'Eleanor! will you take them all on ahead?' said Manisty impatiently; 'we shall have to lead her carefully to avoid rough places.'

Eleanor carried off the rest of the party. Manisty established himself at Lucy's side. The man from Genzano led the horse.

After a quarter of an hour's walking, mixed with the give and take of explanations on both sides as to the confusion of the afternoon, Eleanor paused to recover breath an instant on a rising ground. Looking back, she saw through the blue hazes of the evening the two distant figures--the white form on the horse, the protecting nearness of the man.

She stifled a moan, drawn deep from founts of covetous and passionate agony. Then she turned and hurried up the stony path with an energy, a useless haste that evoked loud protests from Reggie Brooklyn. Eleanor did not answer him. There was beating within her veins a violence that appalled herself. Whither was she going? What change had already passed on all the gentle tendernesses and humanities of her being?

*   *   *   *   *

Meanwhile Lucy was reviving in the cool freshness of the evening air. She seemed to be travelling through a world of opal colour, arched by skies of pale green, melting into rose above, and daffodil gold below. All about her, blue and purple shadows were rising, like waves interfused with moonlight, flooding over the land. Where did the lake end and the shore begin? All was drowned in the same dim wash of blue--the olives and figs, the reddish earth, the white of the cherries, the pale pink of the almonds. In front the lights of Genzano gleamed upon the tall cliff. But in this lonely path all was silence and woody fragrance; the honeysuckles threw breaths across their path; tall orchises, white and stately, broke here and there from the darkness of the banks. In spite of pain and weakness her senses seemed to be flooded with beauty. A strange peace and docility overcame her.

'You are better?' said Manisty's voice beside her. The tones of it were grave and musical; they expressed an enwrapping kindness, a 'human softness' that still further moved her.

'So much better! The bleeding has almost stopped. I--I suppose it would have been better, if I had waited for you?--if I had not ventured on those paths alone?'

There was in her scrupulous mind a great penitence about the whole matter. How much trouble she was giving!--how her imprudence had spoilt the little festa! And poor Mrs. Burgoyne!--forced to walk up this long, long way.

'Yes--perhaps it would have been better'--said Manisty. 'One never quite knows about this population. After all, for an Italian lady to walk about some English country lanes alone, might not be quite safe--and one ruffian is enough. But the point is--we should not have left you.'

She was too feeble to protest. Manisty spoke to the man leading the horse, bidding him draw on one side, so as to avoid a stony bit of path. Then the reins fell from her stiff right hand, which seemed to be still trembling with cold. Instantly Manisty gathered them up, and replaced them in the chill fingers. As he did so he realised with a curious pleasure that the hand and wrist, though not small, were still beautiful, with a fine shapely strength.

Presently, as they mounted the steep ascent towards the Sforza Cesarini woods, he made her rest half way.

'How those stones must have jarred you!'--he said frowning, as he turned the horse, so that she sat easily, without strain.

'No! It was nothing. Oh--glorious!'

For she found herself looking towards the woods of the south-eastern ridge of the lake, over which the moon had now fully risen. The lake was half shade, half light; the fleecy forests on the breast of Monte Cavo rose soft as a cloud into the infinite blue of the night-heaven. Below, a silver shaft struck the fisherman's hut beside the shore, where, deep in the water's breast, lie the wrecked ships of Caligula,--the treasure ships--whereof for seventy generations the peasants of Nemi have gone dreaming.

As they passed the hut,--half an hour before--Manisty had drawn her attention, in the dim light, to the great beams from the side of the nearer ship, which had been recently recovered by the divers, and were lying at the water's edge. And he had told her,--with a kindling eye--how he himself, within the last few months, had seen fresh trophies recovered from the water,--a bronze Medusa above all, fiercely lovely, the work of a most noble and most passionate art, not Greek though taught by Greece, fresh, full-blooded, and strong, the art of the Empire in its eagle-youth.

'Who destroyed the ships, and why?' he said, as they paused, looking down upon the lake. 'There is not a shred of evidence. One can only dream. They were a madman's whim; incredibly rich in marble, and metal, and terra-cotta, paid for, no doubt, from the sweat and blood of this country-side. Then the young monster who built and furnished them was murdered on the Palatine. Can't you see the rush of an avenging mob down this steep lane?--the havoc and the blows--the peasants hacking at the statues and the bronzes--loading their ox-carts perhaps with the plunder--and finally letting in the lake upon the wreck! Well!--somehow like that it must have happened. The lake swallowed them; and, in spite of all the efforts of the Renaissance people, who sent down divers, the lake has kept them, substantially, till now. Not a line about them in any known document! History knows nothing. But the peasants handed down the story from father to son. Not a fisherman on this lake, for eighteen hundred years, but has tried to reach the ships. They all believed--they still believe--that they hold incredible treasures. But the lake is jealous--they lie deep!'

Lucy bent forward, peering into the blue darkness of the lake, trying to see with his eyes, to catch the same ghostly signals from the past. The romance of the story and the moment, Manisty's low, rushing speech, the sparkle of his poet's look--the girl's fancy yielded to the spell of them; her breath came quick and soft. Through all their outer difference, Manisty suddenly felt the response of her temperament to his. It was delightful to be there with her--delightful to be talking to her.

'I was on the shore,' he continued, 'watching the divers at work, on the day they drew up the Medusa. I helped the man who drew her up to clean the slime and mud from them, and the vixen glared at me all the time, as though she thirsted to take vengeance upon us all. She had had time to think about it,--for she sank perhaps ten years after the Crucifixion,--while Mary still lived in the house of John!'

His voice dropped to the note of reverie, and a thrill passed through Lucy. He turned the horse's head towards Genzano, and they journeyed on in silence. She indeed was too weak for many words; but enwrapped as it were by the influences around her,--of the place, the evening beauty, the personality of the man beside her,--she seemed to be passing through a many-coloured dream, of which the interest and the pleasure never ceased.

Presently they passed a little wayside shrine. Within its penthouse eave an oil-lamp flickered before the frescoed Madonna and Child; the shelf in front of the picture was heaped with flowers just beginning to fade. Manisty stayed the horse a moment; pointed first to the shrine, then to the bit of road beneath their feet.

'Do you see this travertine--these blocks? This is a bit of the old road to the temple. I was with the exploring party when they carried up the Medusa and some other of their finds along here past the shrine. It was nearly dark--they did not want to be observed. But I was an old friend of the man in command, and he and I were walking together. The bearers of the heavy bronze things got tired. They put down their load just here, and lounged away. My friend stepped up to the sort of wooden bier they were carrying, to see that all was right. He uncovered the Medusa, and turned her to the light of the lamp before the shrine. You never saw so strange and wild a thing!--the looks she threw at the Madonna and Child. "Ah! Madam," I said to her--"the world was yours when you went down--but now it's theirs! Tame your insolence!" And I thought of hanging her here, at night, just outside, under the lamp against the wall of the shrine--and how one might come in the dark upon the fierce head with the snakes--and watch her gazing at the Christ.'

Lucy shuddered and smiled.

'I'm glad she wasn't yours!'

'Why? The peasants would soon have made a saint of her, and invented a legend to fit. The snakes, for them, would have been the instruments of martyrdom--turned into a martyr's crown. Italy and Catholicism absorb--assimilate--everything. "*Santa Medusa!*"--I assure you, she would be quite in order.'

There was a pause. Then she heard him say under his breath--'Marvellous, marvellous Italy!'

She started and gave a slight cry--unsteady, involuntary.

'But you don't love her!--you are ungrateful to her!'

He looked up surprised--then laughed--a frank, pugnacious laugh.

'There is Italy--and Italy.'

'There is only one Italy!--Aristodemo's Italy--the Italy the peasants work in.'

She turned to him, breathing quicker, the colour returning to her pale cheek.

'The Italy that has just sent seven thousand of her sons to butchery in a wretched colony, because her hungry politicians must have glory and keep themselves in office? You expect me to love that Italy?'

Within the kind new sweetness of his tone--a sweetness no man could use more subtly--there had risen the fiery accustomed note. But so restrained, so tempered to her weakness, her momentary dependence upon him!

'You might be generous to her--just, at least!--for the sake of the old.'

She trembled a little from the mere exertion of speaking, and he saw it.

'No controversy to-night!' he said smiling. 'Wait till you are fit for it, and I will overwhelm you. Do you suppose I don't know all about the partisan literature you have been devouring?'

'One had to hear the other side.'

'Was I such a bore with the right side?'

They both laughed. Then he said, shrugging his shoulders with sudden emphasis:

'What a nation of revolutionists you are in America! What does it feel like, I wonder, to be a people without a past, without traditions?'

Lucy exclaimed: 'Why, we are made of traditions!'

'Traditions of revolt and self-will are no traditions,' he said provokingly. 'The submission of the individual to the whole--that's what you know nothing of.'

'We shall know it when we want it! But it will be a free submission--given willingly.'

'No priests allowed? Oh! you will get your priests. You are getting them. No modern nation can hold together without them.'

They sparred a little longer. Then Lucy's momentary spirit of fight departed. She looked wistfully to see how near they were to Genzano. Manisty approached her more closely.

'Did my nonsense cheer you--or tire you?' he said in a different voice. 'I only meant it to amuse you, Hark!--did you hear that sound?'

They stopped. Above them, to the right, they saw through the dusk a small farm in a patch of vineyard. A dark figure suddenly hurled itself down a steep path towards them. Other figures followed it--seemed to wrestle with it; there was a confused wailing and crying--the piteous shrill lamenting of a woman's voice.

'Oh, what is it?' cried Lucy, clasping her hands.

Manisty spoke a few sharp words to the man leading the horse. The man stood still and checked his beast. Manisty ran towards the sounds and the dim struggle on the slope above them.

Such a cry! It rent and desolated the evening peace. It seemed to Lucy the voice of an old woman, crossed by other voices--rough, chiding voices of men. Oh, were they ill-treating her? The girl said hurriedly to the man beside her that she would dismount.

'No, no, signorina,' said the man, placidly, raising his hand. 'The signor will be here directly. It happens often, often.'

And almost at the same moment Manisty was beside her again, and the gruesome sounds above were dying away.

'Were you frightened?' he said, with anxiety. 'There was no need. How strange that it should have happened just now! It's a score that *your* Italy must settle--*mine* washes her hands of it!' and he explained that what she had heard were the cries of a poor hysterical woman, a small farmer's wife, who had lost both her sons in the Abyssinian war, in the frightful retreat of Adowa, and had never been in her right mind since the news arrived. With the smallest lapse in the vigilance of those about her, she would rush down to the road, and throw herself upon any passer-by, imploring them to intercede for her with the Government--that they should give her back her sons--Nino, at least!--Nino, her youngest, and darling. It was impossible that they should both be dead--impossible! The Holy Virgin would never have suffered it.

'Poor soul!--she tried to cling round my knees--wailing out the candles and prayers she had offered--shrieking something about the "Governo." I helped the sons to carry her in. They were quite gentle to her.'

Lucy turned away her head; and they resumed their march. She governed herself with all her power; but her normal self-control was weakened, and that cry of anguish still haunted her. Some quiet tears fell--she hoped, she believed that they were unseen.

But Manisty perceived them. He gave not the smallest direct sign; he began at once to talk of other things in a quite other vein. But underlying his characteristic whims and sallies she was presently conscious of a new and exquisite gentleness. It seemed to address itself both to her physical fatigue, and to the painful impression of the incident which had just passed. Her sudden tears--the tears of a tired child--and his delicate feeling--there arose out of them, as out of their whole journey, a relation, a bond, of which both were conscious, to which she yielded herself in a kind of vague and timid pleasure.

For Manisty--as she sat there, high above him, yet leaning a little towards him--there was something in the general freshness and purity of her presence, both physical and moral, that began most singularly to steal upon his emotions. Certain barriers seemed to be falling, certain secret sympathies emerging, drawn from regions far below their differences of age and race, of national and intellectual habit. How was it she had liked his Palestine book so much? He almost felt as though in some mysterious way he had been talking to her, and she listening, for years,--since first, perhaps, her sweet crude youth began.

Then even his egotism felt the prick of humour. Five weeks had she been with them at the villa?--and in a fortnight their party was to break up. How profitably indeed he had used his time with her! How civil--how kind--how discerning he had shown himself!

Yet soreness of this kind was soon lost in the surge of this new and unexpected impulse, which brought his youth exultantly back upon him. A beautiful woman rode beside him, through the Italian evening. With impatience, with an inward and passionate repudiation of all other bonds and claims, he threw himself into that mingled process--at once exploring and revealing--which makes the thrill of all the higher relations between men and women, and ends invariably either in love--or tragedy.

*   *   *   *   *

They found a carriage waiting for them near the Sforza-Cesarini gate, and in it Mrs. Elliott, Reggie Brooklyn's kind sister. Lucy was taken to a doctor, and the hurt was dressed. By nine o'clock she was once more under the villa-roof. Miss Manisty received her with lamentations and enquiries, that the tottering Lucy was too weary even to hear aright. Amid what seemed to her a babel of tongues and lights and kind concern, she was taken to bed and sleep.

Mrs. Burgoyne did not attend her. She waited in Manisty's library, and when Manisty entered the room she came forward--

'Edward, I have some disagreeable news'--

He stopped abruptly.

'Your sister Alice will be here to-morrow.'

'My sister--Alice?'--he repeated incredulously.

'She telegraphed this morning that she must see you. Aunt Pattie consulted me. The telegram gave no address--merely said that she would come to-morrow for two or three nights.'

Manisty first stared in dismay, then, thrusting his hands into his pockets, began to walk hurriedly to and fro.

'When did this news arrive?'

'This morning, before we started.'

'Eleanor!-- *Why* was I not told?'

'I wanted to save the day,'--the words were spoken in Eleanor's most charming, most musical voice. 'There was no address. You could not have stopped her.'

'I would have managed somehow,'--said Manisty striking his hand on the table beside him in his annoyance and impatience.

Eleanor did not defend herself. She tried to soothe him, to promise him as usual that the dreaded visit should be made easy to him. But he paid little heed. He sat moodily brooding in his chair; and when Eleanor's persuasions ceased, he broke out--

'That poor child!--After to-day's experiences,--to have Alice let loose upon her!--I would have given anything--anything!--that it should not have happened.'

'Miss Foster?' said Eleanor lightly--'oh! she will bear up.'

'There it is!'--said Manisty, in a sudden fury. 'We have all been misjudging her in the most extraordinary way! She is the most sensitive, tender-natured creature--I would not put an ounce more strain upon her for the world.'

His aunt called him, and he went stormily away. Eleanor's smile as she stood looking after him--how pale and strange it was!

CHAPTER IX

'Miss Foster is not getting up? How is she?'

'I believe Aunt Pattie only persuaded her to rest till after breakfast, and that was hard work. Aunt Pattie thought her rather shaken still.'

The speakers were Manisty and Mrs. Burgoyne. Eleanor was sitting in the deep shade of the avenue that ran along the outer edge of the garden. Through the gnarled trunks to her right shone the blazing stretches of the Campagna, melting into the hot shimmer of the Mediterranean. A new volume of French memoirs, whereof not a page had yet been cut, was lying upon her knee.

Manisty, who had come out to consult with her, leant against the tree beside her. Presently he broke out impetuously:

'Eleanor! we must protect that girl. You know what I mean? You'll help me?'

'What are you afraid of?'

'Good heavens!--I hardly know. But we must keep Alice away from Miss Foster. She mustn't walk with her, or sit with her, or be allowed to worry her in any way. I should be beside myself with alarm if Alice were to take a fancy to her.'

Eleanor hesitated a moment. The slightest flush rose to her cheek, unnoticed in the shadow of her hat.

'You know--if you are in any real anxiety--Miss Foster could go to Florence. She told me yesterday that the Porters have friends there whom she could join.'

Manisty fidgeted.

'Well, I hardly think that's necessary. It's a great pity she should miss Vallombrosa. I hoped I might settle her and Aunt Pattie there by about the middle of June.'

Eleanor made so sudden a movement that her book fell to the ground.

'You are going to Vallombrosa? I thought you were due at home, the beginning of June?'

'That was when I thought the book was coming out before the end of the month. But now--

'Now that it isn't coming out at all, you feel there's no hurry?'

Manisty looked annoyed.

'I don't think that's a fair shot. Of course the book's coming out! But if it isn't June, it must be October. So there's no hurry.'

The little cold laugh with which Eleanor had spoken her last words subsided. But she gave him no sign of assent. He pulled a stalk of grass, and nibbled at it uncomfortably.

'You think I'm a person easily discouraged?' he said presently.

'You take advice so oddly,' she said, smiling; 'sometimes so ill--sometimes so desperately well.'

'I can't help it. I am made like that. When a man begins to criticise my work, I first hate him--then I'm all of his opinion--only more so.'

'I know,' said Eleanor impatiently. 'It's this dreadful modern humility--the abominable power we all have of seeing the other side. But an author is no good till he has thrown his critics out of window.'

'Poor Neal!' said Manisty, with his broad sudden smile, 'he would fall hard. However, to return to Miss Foster. There's no need to drive her away if we look after her. You'll help us, won't you, Eleanor?'

He sat down on a stone bench beside her. The momentary cloud had cleared away. He was his most charming, most handsome self. A shiver ran through Eleanor. Her thought flew to yesterday--compared the kind radiance of the face beside her, its look of brotherly confidence and appeal, with the look of yesterday, the hard evasiveness with which he had met all her poor woman's attempts to renew the old intimacy, reknit the old bond. She thought of the solitary, sleepless misery of the night she had just passed through. And here they were, sitting in cousinly talk, as though nothing else were between them but this polite anxiety for Miss Foster's peace of mind! What was behind that apparently frank brow--those sparkling grey-blue eyes? Manisty could always be a mystery when he chose, even to those who knew him best.

She drew a long inward breath, feeling the old inexorable compulsion that lies upon the decent woman, who can only play the game as the man chooses to set it.

'I don't know what I can do--' she said slowly. 'You think Alice is no better?'

Manisty shook his head. He looked at her sharply and doubtfully, as though measuring her--and then said, lowering his voice:

'I believe--I know I can trust you with this--I have some reason to suppose that there was an attempt at suicide at Venice. Her maid prevented it, and gave me the hint. I am in communication with the maid--though Alice has no idea of it.

'Ought she to come here at all?' said Eleanor after a pause.

'I have thought of that--of meeting all the trains and turning her back. But you know her obstinacy. As long as she is in Rome and we here, we can't protect ourselves and the villa. There are a thousand ways of invading us. Better let her come--find out what she wants--pacify her if possible--and send her away. I am not afraid for ourselves, you included, Eleanor! She would do us no harm. A short annoyance--and it would be over. But Miss Foster is the weak point.'

Eleanor looked at him inquiringly.

'It is one of the strongest signs of her unsound state,' said Manisty, frowning--'her wild fancies that she takes for girls much younger than herself. There have been all sorts of difficulties in hotels. She will be absolutely silent with older people--or with you and me, for instance--but if she can captivate any quite young creature, she will pour herself out to her, follow her, write to her, tease her.--Poor, poor Alice!'

Manisty's voice had become almost a groan. His look betrayed a true and manly feeling.

'One must always remember,' he resumed, 'that she has still the power to attract a stranger. Her mind is in ruins--but they are the ruins of what was once fine and noble. But it is all so wild, and strange, and desperate. A girl is first fascinated--and then terrified. She begins by listening, and pitying--then Alice pursues her, swears her to secrecy, talks to her of enemies and persecutors, of persons who wish her death, who open her letters, and dog her footsteps--till the girl can't sleep at nights, and her own nerve begins to fail her. There was a case of this at Florence last year. Dalgetty, that's the maid, had to carry Alice off by main force. The parents of the girl threatened to set the doctors in motion--to get Alice sent to an asylum.'

'But surely, surely,' cried Mrs. Burgoyne, 'that would be the right course!'

Manisty shook his head.

'Impossible!' he said with energy. 'Don't imagine that my lawyers and I haven't looked into everything. Unless the disease has made much progress since I last saw her, Alice will always baffle any attempts to put her in restraint. She is queer--eccentric--melancholy; she envelopes the people she victimises with a kind of moral poison; but you can't **prove**--so far, at least--that she is dangerous to herself or others. The evidence always falls short.' He paused; then added with cautious emphasis: 'I don't speak without book. It has been tried.'

'But the attempt at Venice?'

'No good. The maid's letter convinced me of two things--first, that she had attempted her life, and next, that there is no proof of it.'

Eleanor bent forward.

'And the suitor--the man?'

'Dalgetty tells me there have been two interviews. The first at Venice--probably connected with the attempt we know of. The second some weeks ago at Padua. I believe the man to be a reputable person, though no doubt not insensible to the fact that Alice has some money. You know who he is?--a French artist she came across in Venice. He is melancholy and lonely like herself. I believe he is genuinely attached to her. But after the last scene at Padua she told Dalgetty that she would never make him miserable by marrying him.'

'What do you suppose she is coming here for?'

'Very likely to get me to do something for this man. She won't be his wife, but she likes to be his Providence: I shall promise anything, in return for her going quickly back to Venice--or Switzerland--where she often spends the summer. So long as she and Miss Foster are under one roof, I shall not have a moment free from anxiety.'

Eleanor sank back in her chair. She was silent; but her eye betrayed the bitter animation of the thoughts passing behind them, thoughts evoked not so much by what Manisty had said, as by what he had **not** said. All alarm, all consideration to be concentrated on one point?--nothing, and no one else, to matter?

But again she fought down the rising agony, refused to be mastered by it, or to believe her own terrors. Another wave of feeling rose. It was so natural to her to love and help him!

'Well, of course I shall do what you tell me! I generally do--don't I? What are your commands?'

He brought his head nearer to hers, his brilliant eyes bent upon her intently:

'Never let her be alone with Miss Foster! Watch her. If you see any sign of persecution--if you can't check it--let me know at once. I shall keep Alice in play of course. One day we can send Miss Foster into Rome--perhaps two. Ah! hush!--here she comes!'

Eleanor looked round. Lucy had just appeared in the cool darkness of the avenue. She walked slowly and with a languid grace, trailing her white skirts. The shy rusticity, the frank robustness of her earlier aspect were now either gone, or temporarily merged in something more exquisite and more appealing. Her youth too had never been so apparent. She had been too strong too self-reliant. The touch of physical delicacy seemed to have brought back the child.

Then, turning back to her companion, Eleanor saw the sudden softness in Manisty's face--the alert expectancy of his attitude.

'What a wonderful oval of the head and cheek!' he said under his breath, half to himself, half to her. 'Do you know, Eleanor, what she reminds me of?'

Eleanor shook her head.

'Of that little head--little face rather--that I gave you at Nemi. Don't you see it?'

'I always said she was like your Greek bust,' said Eleanor slowly.

'Ah, that was in her first archaic stage. But now that she's more at ease with us--you see?--there's the purity of line just the same--but subtilised--humanised--somehow! It's the change from marble to terra-cotta, isn't it?'

His fancy pleased him, and his smile turned to hers for sympathy. Then, springing up, he went to meet Lucy.

'Oh, there can be nothing in his mind! He could not speak--look--smile--like that to *me*,' thought Eleanor with passionate relief.

Then as they approached, she rose, and with kind solicitude forced Lucy to take her chair, on the plea that she herself was going back to the villa.

Lucy touched her hand with timid gratitude. 'I don't know what's happened to me,' she said, half wistful, half smiling; 'I never stayed in bed to breakfast in my life before. At Greyridge, they'd think I had gone out of my mind.'

Eleanor inquired if it was an invariable sign of lunacy in America to take your breakfast in bed. Lucy couldn't say. All she knew was that nobody ever took it so in Greyridge, Vermont, unless they were on the point of death.

'I should never be any good, any more,' she said, with an energy that brought the red back to her cheeks,--'if they were to spoil me at home, as you spoil me here.'

Eleanor waved her hand, smiled, and went her way.

As she moved further and further away from them down the long avenue, she saw them all the time, though she never once looked back--saw the eager inquiries of the man, the modest responsiveness of the girl. She was leaving them to themselves--at the bidding of her own pride--and they had the May morning before them. According to a telegram just received, Alice Manisty was not expected till after lunch.

*   *   *   *   *

Meanwhile Manisty was talking of his sister to Lucy, With coolness, and as much frankness as he thought necessary.

'She is very odd--and very depressing. She is now very little with us. There is no company she likes as well as her own. But in early days, she and I were great friends. We were brought up in an old Yorkshire house together, and a queer pair we were. I was never sent to school, and I got the better of most of my tutors. Alice was unmanageable too, and we spent most of our time rambling and reading as we pleased. Both of us dreamed awake half our time. I had shooting and fishing to take me out of myself; but Alice, after my mother's death, lived with her own fancies and got less like other people every day. There was a sort of garden house in the park,--a lonely, overgrown kind of place. We put our books there, and used practically to live there for weeks together. That was just after I came into the place, before I went abroad. Alice was sixteen. I can see her now sitting in the doorway of the little house, hour after hour, staring into the woods like a somnambulist, one arm behind her head. One day I said to her: "Alice, what are you thinking of?" "Myself!" she said. So then I laughed at her, and teased her. And she answered quite quietly, "I know it is a pity--but I can't help it."'

Lucy's eyes were wide with wonder. 'But you ought to have given her something to do--or to learn: couldn't she have gone to school, or found some friends?'

'Oh! I dare say I ought to have done a thousand things,' said Manisty impatiently. 'I was never a model brother, or a model anything! I grew up for myself and by myself, and I supposed Alice would do the same. You disapprove?'

He turned his sharp, compelling eyes upon her, so that Lucy flinched a little. 'I shouldn't dare,' she said laughing. 'I don't know enough about it. But it's plain, isn't it, that girls of sixteen shouldn't sit on doorsteps and think about themselves?'

'What did you think about at sixteen?'

Her look changed.

'I had mother then,'--she said simply.

'Ah! then--I'm afraid you've no right to sit in judgment upon us. Alice and I had no mother--no one but ourselves. Of course all our relations and friends disapproved of us. But that somehow has never made much difference to either of us. Does it make much difference to you? Do you mind if people praise or blame you? What does it matter what anybody thinks? Who can know anything about you but yourself?--Eh?'

He poured out his questions in a hurry, one tumbling over the other. And he had already begun to bite the inevitable stalk of grass. Lucy as usual was conscious both of intimidation and attraction--she felt him at once absurd and magnetic.

'I'm sure we're meant to care what people think,' she said, with spirit. 'It helps us. It keeps us straight.'

His eyes flashed.

'You think so? Then we disagree entirely--absolutely--and *in toto*! I don't want to be approved--outside my literary work any way--I want to be happy. It never enters my head to judge other people--why should they judge me?'

'But--but'--Then she laughed out, remembering his book, and his political escapade, 'Aren't you *always* judging other people?'

'Fighting them--yes! That's another matter. But I don't give myself superior airs. I don't judge--I just love--and hate.'

Her attention followed the bronzed expressive face, so bold in outline, so delicate in detail, with a growing fascination.

'It seems to me you hate more than you love.'

He considered it.

'Quite possible. It isn't an engaging world. But I don't hate readily--I hate slowly and by degrees. If anybody offends me, for instance, at first I hardly feel it,--it doesn't seem to matter at all. Then it grows in my mind gradually, it becomes a weight--a burning fire--and drives everything else out. I hate the men, for instance, that I hated last year in England, much worse now than I did then!'

She bit her lip, but could not help the broadening smile, to which his own responded.

'Do you take any interest, Miss Foster, in what happened to me last year?'

'I often wonder whether you regret it,' she said, rather shyly. 'Wasn't it--a great pity?'

'Not at all,' he said peremptorily; 'I shall recover all I let slip.'

She did not reply. But the smile still trembled on her lips, while she copied his favourite trick in stripping the leaves from a spray of box.

'You don't believe that?'

'Does one ever recover all one lets slip--especially in politics?'

'Goodness--you are a pessimist! Why should one not recover it?'

Her charming mouth curved still more gaily.

'I have often heard my uncle say that the man who "resigns" is lost.'

'Ah!--never regret--never resign--never apologise? We know that creed. Your uncle must be a man of trenchant opinions. Do you agree with him?'

She tried to be serious.

'I suppose one should count the cost before--'

'Before one joins a ministry? Yes, that's a fair stroke. I wish to heaven I had never joined it. But when I began to think that this particular Ministry was taking English society to perdition, it was as well--wasn't it?--that I should leave it?'

Her face suddenly calmed itself to a sweet gravity.

'Oh yes--yes!--if it was as bad as that.'

'I'm not likely to confess, anyway, that it wasn't as bad as that!--But I will confess that I generally incline to hate my own side,--and to love my adversaries. English Liberals moreover hold the ridiculous opinion that the world is to be governed by intelligence. I couldn't have believed it of any sane men. When I discovered it, I left them. My foreign experience had given the lie to all that. And when I left them, the temptation to throw a paradox in their faces was irresistible.'

She said nothing, but her expression spoke for her.

'You think me mad?'

She turned aside--dumb--plucking at a root of cyclamen beside her.

'Insincere?'

'No. But you like to startle people--to make them talk about you!'

Her eyes were visible again; and he perceived at once her courage and her diffidence.

'Perhaps! English political life runs so smooth, that to throw in a stone and make a splash was amusing.'

'But was it fair?' she said, flushing.

'What do you mean?'

'Other people were in earnest; and you--'

'Were not? Charge home. I am prepared,' he said, smiling.

'You talk now--as though you were a Catholic--and you are not, you don't believe,' she said suddenly, in a deep, low voice.

He looked at her for a moment in a smiling silence. His lips were ready to launch a reckless sentence or two; but they refrained. Her attitude meanwhile betrayed an unconscious dread--like a child that fears a blow.

'You charming saint!'--he thought; surprised at his own feeling of pleasure. Pleasure in what?--in the fact that however she might judge his opinions, she was clearly interested in the holder of them?

'What does one's own point of view matter?' he said gently. 'I believe what I can,--and as long as I can--sometimes for a whole twenty-four hours! Then a big doubt comes along, and sends me floundering. But that has nothing to do with it. The case is quite simple. The world can't get on without morals; and Catholicism, Anglicanism too--the religions of authority in short--are the great guardians of morals. They are the binding forces--the forces making for solidarity and continuity. Your cocksure, peering Protestant is the dissolvent--the force making for ruin. What's his private judgment to me, or mine to him? But for the sake of it, he'll make everything mud and puddle! Of course you may say to me--it is perfectly open to you to say'--he looked away from her, half-forgetting her, addressing with animation and pugnacity an imaginary opponent--'what do morals matter?--how do you know that the present moral judgments of the world represent any ultimate truth? Ah! well'--he shrugged his shoulders--'I can't follow you there. Black may be really white--and white black; but I'm not going to admit it. It would make me too much of a dupe. I take my stand on morals. And if you give me morals, you must give me the only force that can guarantee them,--Catholicism, more or less:--and dogma,--and ritual,--and superstition,--and all the foolish ineffable things that bind mankind together, and send them to "face the music" in this world and the next!'

She sat silent, with twitching lips, excited, yet passionately scornful and an- tagonistic. Thoughts of her home, of that Puritan piety amid which she had been brought up, flashed thick and fast through her mind. Suddenly she covered her face with her hands, to hide a fit of laughter that had overtaken her.

'All that amuses you?'--said Manisty, breathing a little faster.

'No--oh! no. But--I was thinking of my uncle--of the people in our village at home. What you said of Protestants seemed to me, all at once, so odd--so ridicu- lous!'

'Did it? Tell me then about the people in your valley at home.'

And turning on his elbows beside her, he put her through a catechism as to her village, her uncle, her friends. She resisted a little, for the brusque assurance of his tone still sounded oddly in her American ear. But he was not easy to resist; and when she had yielded she soon discovered that to talk to him was a no less breath- less and absorbing business than to listen to him. He pounced on the new, the char- acteristic, the local; he drew out of her what he wanted to know; he made her see her own trees and fields, the figures of her home, with new sharpness, so quick, so dramatic, so voracious, one might almost say, were his own perceptions.

Especially did he make her tell him of the New England winter; of the long pauses of its snow-bound life; its whirling winds and drifts; its snapping, crackling frosts; the lonely farms, and the deep sleigh-tracks amid the white wilderness, that still in the winter silence bind these homesteads to each other and the nation; the strange gleams of moonrise and sunset on the cold hills; the strong dark armies of the pines; the grace of the stripped birches. Above all, must she talk to him of the people in these farms, the frugal, or silent, or brooding people of the hills; honourable, hard, knotted, prejudiced, believing folk, whose lives and fates, whose spiritual visions and madnesses, were entwined with her own young memories and deepest affections.

Figure after figure, story after story, did he draw from her,--warm from the hidden fire of her own strenuous, loving life. Once or twice she spoke of her mother--like one drawing a veil for an instant from a holy of holies. He felt and saw the burning of a sacred fire; then the veil dropped, nor would it lift again for any word of his. And every now and then, a phrase that startled him by its quality,--its suggestions. Presently he was staring at her with his dark absent eyes.

'Heavens!'--he was thinking--'what a woman there is in her!--what a nature!'

The artist--the poet--the lover of things significant and moving,--all these were stirred in him as he listened to her, as he watched her young and noble beauty.

*   *   *   *   *

But, in the end, he would not grant her much, argumentatively.

'You make me see strange things--magnificent things, if you like! But your old New England saints and dreamers are not your last word in America. They tell me your ancestral Protestantisms are fast breaking down. Your churches are turning into concert and lecture rooms. Catholicism is growing among you,--science gaining on the quack-medicines! But there--there--I'll not prate. Forgive me. This has been a fascinating half-hour. Only, take care! I have seen you a Catholic once, for three minutes!'

'When?'

'In St. Peter's.'

His look, smiling, provocative, drove home his shaft.

'I saw you overthrown. The great tradition swept upon you. You bowed to it,--you felt!'

She made no reply. Far within she was conscious of a kind of tremor. The personality beside her seemed to be laying an intimate, encroaching hand upon her own, and her maidenliness shrank before it.

She threw herself hastily upon other subjects. Presently, he found to his surprise that she was speaking to him of his book.

'It would be so sad if it were not finished,' she said timidly. 'Mrs. Burgoyne would feel it so.'

His expression changed.

'You think Mrs. Burgoyne cares about it so much?'

'But she worked so hard for it!'--cried Lucy, indignant with something in his manner, though she could not have defined what. Her mind, indeed, was full of vague and generous misgivings on the subject of Mrs. Burgoyne. First she had been angry with Mr. Manisty for what had seemed to her neglect and ingratitude. Now she was somehow dissatisfied with herself too.

'She worked too hard,' said Manisty gravely. 'It is a good thing the pressure has been taken off. Have you found out yet, Miss Foster, what a remarkable woman my cousin is?'

He turned to her with a sharp look of inquiry.

'I admire her all day long,' cried Lucy, warmly.

'That's right,' said Manisty slowly--'that's right. Do you know her history?'

'Mr. Brooklyn told me--

'He doesn't know very much,--shall I tell it you?'

'If you ought--if Mrs. Burgoyne would like it,' said Lucy, hesitating. There was a chivalrous feeling in the girl's mind that she was too new an acquaintance, that she had no right to the secrets of this friendship, and Manisty no right to speak of them.

But Manisty took no notice. With half-shut eyes, like a man looking into the past, he began to describe his cousin; first as a girl in her father's home; then in her married life, silent, unhappy, gentle; afterwards in the dumb years of her irreparable grief; and finally in this last phase of intellectual and spiritual energy, which had been such an amazement to himself, which had first revealed to him indeed the true Eleanor.

He spoke slowly, with a singular and scrupulous choice of words; building up the image of Mrs. Burgoyne's life and mind with an insight and a delicacy which presently held his listener spell-bound. Several times Lucy felt herself flooded with hot colour.

'Does he guess so much about--about us all?' she asked herself with a secret excitement.

Suddenly Manisty said, with an entire change of tone, springing to his feet as he did so:

'In short, Miss Foster--my cousin Eleanor is one of the ablest and dearest of women--and she and I have been completely wasting each other's time this winter!'

Lucy stared at him in astonishment.

'Shall I tell you why? We have been too kind to each other!'

He waited, studying his companion's face with a hard, whimsical look.

'Eleanor gave my book too much sympathy. It wanted brutality. I have worn her out--and my book is in a mess. The best thing I could do for us both--was to cut it short.'

Lucy was uncomfortably silent.

'There's no use in talking about it,' Manisty went on, impatiently, with a shake of his great shoulders; 'I am not meant to work in partnership. A word of blame depresses me; and I am made a fool by praise. It was all a mistake. If only Eleanor could understand--that it's my own fault--and I know it's my own fault--and not think me unjust and unkind. Miss Foster--'

Lucy looked up. In the glance she encountered, the vigorous and wilful personality beside her seemed to bring all its force to bear upon herself--

'--if Eleanor talks to you--

'She never does!' cried Lucy.

'She might,' said Manisty, coolly. 'She might. If she does, persuade her of my admiration, my gratitude! Tell her that I know very well that I am not worth her help. Her inspiration would have led any other man to success. It only failed because I was I. I hate to seem to discourage and disavow what I once accepted so eagerly.--But a man must find out his own mistakes--and thrash his own blunders. She was too kind to thrash them--so I have appointed Neal to the office. Do you understand?'

She rose, full of wavering approvals and disapprovals, seized by him,--and feeling with Mrs. Burgoyne.

'I understand only a very little,' she said, lifting her clear eyes to his; 'except that I never saw anyone I--I cared for so much, in so short a time--as Mrs. Burgoyne.'

'Ah! care for her!' he said, in another voice, with another aspect. 'Go on caring for her! She needs it.'

They walked on together towards the villa, for Alfredo was on the balcony signalling to them that the twelve o'clock breakfast was ready.

On the way Manisty turned upon her.

'Now, you are to be obedient! You are not to pay any attention to my sister. She is not a happy person--but you are not to be sorry for her. You can't understand her; and I beg you will not try. You are, please, to leave her alone. Can I trust you?'

'Hadn't you better send me into Rome?' said Lucy, laughing and embarrassed.

'I always intended to do so,' said Manisty shortly.

*   *   *   *   *

Towards five o'clock, Alice Manisty arrived, accompanied by an elderly maid. Lucy, before she escaped into the garden, was aware of a very tall woman, possessing a harshly handsome face, black eyes, and a thin long-limbed frame. These black eyes, uneasily bright, searched the salon, as she entered it, only to fasten, with a kind of grip, in which there was no joy, upon her brother. Lucy saw her kiss him with a cold perfunctoriness, bowed herself, as her name was nervously pronounced by Miss Manisty, and then withdrew. Mrs. Burgoyne was in Rome for the afternoon.

But at dinner they all met, and Lucy could satisfy some of the curiosity that burnt in her very feminine mind. Alice Manisty was dressed in black lace and satin, and carried herself with stateliness. Her hair, black like her brother's, though with a fine line of grey here and there, was of enormous abundance, and she wore it heavily coiled round her head in a mode which gave particular relief to the fire and restlessness of the eyes which flashed beneath it. Beside her, Eleanor Burgoyne, though she too was rather tall than short, suffered a curious eclipse. The plaintive distinction that made the charm of Eleanor's expression and movements seemed for the moment to mean and say nothing, beside the tragic splendour of Alice Manisty.

The dinner was not agreeable. Manisty was clearly ill at ease, and seething with inward annoyance; Miss Manisty had the air of a frightened mouse; Alice Manisty talked not at all, and ate nothing except some poached eggs that she had apparently ordered for herself before dinner; and Eleanor--chattering of her afternoon in Rome--had to carry through the business as best she could, with occasional help from Lucy.

From the first it was unpleasantly evident to Manisty that his sister took notice of Miss Foster. Almost her only words at table were addressed to the girl sitting opposite to her; and her roving eyes returned again and again to Lucy's fresh young face and quiet brow.

After dinner Manisty followed the ladies into the salon, and asked his aunt's leave to smoke his cigarette with them.

Lucy wondered what had passed between him and his sister before dinner. He was polite to her; and yet she fancied that their relations were already strained.

Presently, as Lucy was busy with some embroidery on one of the settees against the wall of the salon, she was conscious of Alice Manisty's approach. The new-comer sat down beside her, bent over her work, asked her a few low, deep-voiced questions. Those strange eyes fastened upon her,--stared at her indeed.

But instantly Manisty was there, cigarette in hand, standing between them. He distracted his sister's attention, and at the same moment Eleanor called to Lucy from the piano.

'Won't you turn over for me? I can't play them by heart.'

Lucy wondered at the scantiness of Mrs. Burgoyne's musical memory that night. She, who could play by the hour without note, on most occasions, showed herself, on this, tied and bound to the printed page; and that page must be turned for her by Lucy, and Lucy only.

Meanwhile Manisty sat beside his sister smoking, throwing first the left leg over the right, then the right leg over the left, and making attempts at conversation with her, that Eleanor positively must not see, lest music and decorum both break down in a wreck of nervous laughter.

Alice Manisty scarcely responded; she sat motionless, her wild black head bent like that of a Maenad at watch, her gaze fixed, her long thin hands grasping the arm of her chair with unconscious force.

'What is she thinking of?' thought Lucy once, with a momentary shiver. 'Her-self?'

When bedtime came, Manisty gave the ladies their candles. As he bade good-night to Lucy, he said in her ear: 'You said you wished to see the Lateran Museum. My aunt will send Benson with you to-morrow.'

His tone did not ask whether she wished for the arrangement, but simply imposed it.

Then, as Eleanor approached him, he raised his shoulders with a gesture that only she saw, and led her a few steps apart in the dimly lighted ante-room, where the candles were placed.

'She wants the most impossible things, my dear lady,' he said in low-voiced despair--'things I can no more do than fly over the moon!'

'Edward!'--said his sister from the open door of the salon--'I should like some further conversation with you before I go to bed.'

Manisty with the worst grace in the world saw his aunt and Eleanor to their rooms, and then went back to surrender himself to Alice. He was a man who took family relations hardly, impatient of the slightest bond that was not of his own choosing. Yet it was Eleanor's judgment that, considering his temperament, he had not been a bad brother to this wild sister. He had spent both heart and thought upon her case; and at the root of his relation to her, a deep and painful pity was easily to be divined.

Vast as the villa-apartment was, the rooms were all on one floor, and the doors fitted badly. Lucy's sleep was haunted for long by a distant sound of voices, generally low and restrained, but at moments rising and sharpening as though their owners forgot the hour and the night. In the morning it seemed to her that she had been last conscious of a burst of weeping, far distant--then of a sudden silence ...

*   *   *   *   *

The following day, Lucy in Benson's charge paid her duty to the Sophocles of the Lateran Museum, and, armed with certain books lent her by Manisty, went wandering among the art and inscriptions of Christian Rome. She came home, inexplicably tired, through a glorious Campagna, splashed with poppies, embroidered with marigold and vetch; she climbed the Alban slopes from the heat below, and rejoiced in the keener air of the hills, and the freshness of the *ponente*, as she drove from the station to the villa.

Mrs. Burgoyne was leaning over the balcony looking out for her. Lucy ran up to her, astonished at her own eagerness of foot, at the breath of home which seemed to issue from the great sun-beaten house.

Eleanor looked pale and tired, but she took the girl's hand kindly.

'Oh! you must keep all your gossip for dinner!' said Eleanor, as they greeted. 'It will help us through. It has been rather a hard day.'

Lucy's face showed her sympathy, and the question she did not like to put into words.

'Oh, it has been a wrestle all day,' said Eleanor wearily. 'She wants Mr. Manisty to do certain things with her property, that as her trustee he *cannot* do. She has the maddest ideas--she *is* mad. And when she is crossed, she is terrible.'

At dinner Lucy did her best to lighten the atmosphere, being indeed most truly sorry for her poor friends and their dilemma. But her pleasant girlish talk seemed to float above an abyss of trouble and discomfort, which threatened constantly to swallow it up.

Alice Manisty indeed responded. She threw off her silence, and talked of Rome, exclusively to Lucy and with Lucy, showing in her talk a great deal of knowledge and a great deal of fine taste, mingled with occasional violence and extravagance. Her eyes indeed were wilder than ever. They shone with a miserable intensity, that became a positive glare once or twice, when Manisty addressed her. Her whole aspect breathed a tragic determination, crossed with an anger she was hardly able to restrain. Lucy noticed that she never spoke to or answered her brother if she could help it.

After dinner Lucy found herself the object of various embarrassing overtures on the part of the new-comer. But on each occasion Manisty interposed at first adroitly, then roughly. On the last occasion Alice Manisty sprang to her feet, went to the side table where the candles were placed, disappeared and did not return. Manisty, his aunt, and Mrs. Burgoyne, drew together in a corner of the salon discussing the events of the day in low anxious voices. Lucy thought herself in the way, and went to bed.

*   *   *   *   *

After some hours of sleep, Lucy awoke, conscious of movement somewhere near her. With the advent of the hot weather she had been moved to a room on the eastern side of the villa, in one of two small wings jutting out from the facade. She had locked her door, but the side window of her room, which overlooked the balcony towards the lake, was open, and slight sounds came from the balcony. Springing up she crept softly towards the window. The wooden shutters had been drawn forward, but both they and the casements were ajar.

Through the chink she saw a strange sight. On the step leading from the house to the terrace of the balcony sat Alice Manisty. Her head was thrown back against the wall of the villa, and her hands were clasped upon her knee. Her marvellous hair fell round her shoulders, and a strange illumination, in which a first gleam of dawn mingled with the moonlight, struck upon the white face and white hands emerging from the darkness of her hair and of her loose black dress.

Was she asleep? Lucy, holding back so as not to be seen, peered with held breath. No!--the large eyes were wide open, though it seemed to Lucy that they saw nothing. Minute after minute passed. The figure on the terrace sat motionless. There were two statues on either side of her, a pair of battered round-limbed nymphs, glorified by the moonlight into a grace and poetry not theirs by day. They seemed to be looking down upon the woman at their feet in a soft bewilderment--wondering at a creature so little like themselves; while from the terrace came up the scent of the garden, heavy with roses and bedrenched with dew.

Suddenly it seemed to Lucy as though that white face, those intolerable eyes, awoke--turned towards herself, penetrated her room, pursued her. The figure moved, and there was a low sound of words. Her window was in truth inaccessible from the terrace; but in a panic fear, Lucy threw herself on the casement and the shutters, closed them and drew the bolts; as noiselessly as: she could, still not without some noise. Then hurrying to her bed, she threw herself upon it, panting--in a terror she could neither explain nor compose.

CHAPTER X

M y dear lady--there's nothing to be done with her whatever. She will not yield one inch--and I cannot. But one thing at last is clear to me. The mischief has made progress--I fear, great progress.'

Manisty had drawn his cousin into the garden, and they were pacing the avenue. With his last words he turned upon her a grave significant look.

The cause of Alice Manisty's visit, indeed, had turned out to be precisely what Manisty supposed. The sister had come to Marinata in order to persuade her brother, as one of the trustees of her property, to co-operate with her in bestowing some of her money on the French artist, Monsieur Octave Vacherot, to whom, as she calmly avowed, her affections were indissolubly attached, though she did not ever intend to marry him, nor indeed to see much of him in the future. 'I shall never do him the disservice of becoming his wife'--she announced, with her melancholy eyes full upon her brother--'But money is of no use to me. He is young and can employ it.' Manisty inquired whether the gentleman in question was aware of what she proposed. Alice replied that if money were finally settled upon him he would accept it; whereas his pride did not allow him to receive perpetual small sums at her hands. 'But if I settle a definite sum upon him, he will take it as an endowment of his genius. It would be giving to the public, not to him. His great ideas would get their chance.'

Manisty, in his way as excitable as she, had evidently found it difficult to restrain himself when M. Octave Vacherot's views as to his own value were thus explained to him. Nevertheless he seemed to have shown on the whole a creditable patience, to have argued with his sister, to have even offered her money of his own, for the temporary supply of M. Vacherot's necessities. But all to no avail; and in the end it had come of course to his flatly refusing any help of his to such a scheme, and without it the scheme fell. For their father had been perfectly well aware of his daughter's eccentricities, and had placed her portion, by his will, in the hands of two trustees, of whom her brother was one, without whose consent she could not touch the capital.

'It always seemed to her a monstrous arrangement,' said Manisty, 'and I can see now it galls her to the quick to have to apply to me, in this way. I don't wonder--but I can't help it. The duty's there--worse luck!--and I've got to face it, for my father's sake. Besides, if I were to consent, the other fellow--an old cousin of ours--would never dream of doing it. So what's the good? All the same, it makes me desperately anxious, to see the effect that this opposition of mine produces upon her.'

'I saw yesterday that she must have been crying in the night'--said Eleanor.

Her words evoked some emotion in Manisty.

'She cried in my presence, and I believe she cried most of the night afterwards,'--he said in hasty pain. 'That beast Vacherot!'

'Why doesn't she marry him?'

'For the noblest of reasons!--She knows that her brain is clouded, and she won't let him run the risk.'

Their eyes met in a quick sympathy. She saw that his poetic susceptibility, the romantic and dramatic elements in him were all alive to his sister's case. How critically, sharply perceptive he was--or could be--with regard apparently to everybody in the world--save one! Often--as they talked--her heart stirred in this way, far out of sight, like a fluttering and wounded thing.

'It is the strangest madness'--said Manisty presently--'Many people would say it was only extravagance of imagination unless they knew--what I know. She told me last night, that she was not one person but two--and the other self was a brother!--not the least like me--who constantly told her what to do, and what not to do. She calls him quite calmly "my brother John"--"my heavenly brother." She says that he often does strange things, things that she does not understand; but that he tells her the most wonderful secrets; and that he is a greater poet than any now living. She says that the first time she perceived him as separate from herself was one day in Venice, when a friend came for her to the hotel. She went out with the friend, or seemed to go out with her--and then suddenly she perceived that she was lying on her bed, and that the other Alice--had been John! He looks just like herself--but for the eyes. The weirdness of her look as she tells these things! But she expresses herself often with an extraordinary poetry. I envy her the words, and the phrases!--It seemed to me once or twice, that she had all sorts of things I wished to have. If one could only be a little mad--one might write good books!'

He turned upon his companion, with a wild brilliance in his own blue eyes, that, taken together with the subject of their conversation and his many points of physical likeness to his sister, sent an uncomfortable thrill through Eleanor. Nevertheless, as she knew well, at the very bottom of Manisty's being, there lay a remarkable fund of ordinary capacity, an invincible sanity in short, which had always so far rescued him in the long run from that element which was extravagance in him, and madness in his sister.

And certainly nothing could have been more reasonable, strong and kind, than his further talk about his sister. He confided to his cousin that his whole opinion of Alice's state had changed; that certain symptoms for which he had been warned to be on the watch had in his judgment appeared; that he had accordingly written to a specialist in Rome, asking him to come and see Alice, without warning, on the following day; and that he hoped to be able to persuade her without too much conflict to accept medical watching and treatment for a time.

'I feel that it is plotting against her,' he said, not without feeling, 'but it has gone too far--she is not safe for herself or others. One of the most anxious things is this night-wandering, which has taken possession of her. Did you hear her last night?'

'Last night?'--said Eleanor, startled.

'I had been warned by Dalgetty,' said Manisty. 'And between three and four I thought I heard sounds somewhere in the direction of the Albano balcony. So I crept out through the salon into the library. And there, sitting on the step of the glass passage--was Alice--looking as though she were turned to marble--and staring at Miss Foster's room! To my infinite relief I saw that Miss Foster's shutters and windows were fast closed. But I felt I could not leave Alice there. I made a little noise in the library to warn her, and then I came out upon her. She showed no surprise--nor did I. I asked her to come and look at the sunrise striking over the Campagna. She made no objection, and I took her through my room and the salon to the salon balcony. The sight was marvellous; and first, it gave her pleasure--she said a few things about it with her old grace and power. Then--in a minute--a veil

seemed to fall over her eyes. The possessed, miserable look came back. She remembered that she hated me--that I had thwarted her. Yet I was able to persuade her to
go back to her room. I promised that we would have more talk to-day. And when
she had safely shut her own door--you know that tiled ante-room, that leads to her
room?--I found the key of it, and locked it safely from outside. That's one access to
her. The other is through the room in which Dalgetty was sleeping. I'd have given
a good deal to warn Dalgetty, but I dared not risk it. She had not heard Alice go
out by the ante-room, but she told me the other day the smallest sound in her own
room woke her. So I felt tolerably safe, and I went to bed.--Eleanor! do you think
that child saw or knew anything of it?'

'Lucy Foster? I noticed nothing.'

The name, even on her own lips, struck Eleanor's aching sense like a sound of
fate. It seemed now as if through every conversation she foresaw it--that all talk led
up to it.

'She looks unlike herself still, this morning--don't you think?' said Manisty, in
disquiet.

'Very possibly she got some chill at Nemi--some slight poison--which will pass
off.'

'Well, now'--he said, after a pause--'how shall we get through the day? I shall
have another scene with Alice, I suppose. I don't see how it is to be avoided. Mean-
while--will you keep Miss Foster here?'--he pointed to the garden--'out of the way?'

'I must think of Aunt Pattie, remember,' said Eleanor quickly.

'Ah! dear Aunt Pattie!--but bring her too.--I see perfectly well that Alice has
already marked Miss Foster. She has asked me many questions about her. She feels
her innocence and freshness like a magnet, drawing out her own sorrows and griev-
ances. My poor Alice--what a wreck! Could I have done more?--could I?'

He walked on absently, his hands behind his back, his face working painfully.

Eleanor was touched. She did her best to help him throw off his misgivings;
she defended him from himself; she promised him her help, not with the old effusion, but still with a cousinly kindness. And his mercurial nature soon passed into
another mood--a mood of hopefulness that the doctor would set everything right,
that Alice would consent to place herself under proper care, that the crisis would
end well--and in twenty-four hours.

'Meanwhile for this afternoon?' said Eleanor.

'Oh! we must be guided by circumstances. We understand each other.--Eleanor!--what a prop, what a help you are!'

She shrank into herself. It was true indeed that she had passed through a good many disagreeable hours since Alice Manisty arrived, on her own account; for she had been left in charge several times; and she had a secret terror of madness. Manisty had not given her much thanks till now. His facile gratitude seemed to her a little tardy. She smiled and put it aside.

*   *   *   *   *

Manisty wrestled with his sister again that morning, while the other three ladies, all of them silent and perturbed, worked and read in the garden. Lucy debated with herself whether she should describe what she had seen the night before. But her instinct was always to make no unnecessary fuss. What harm was there in sitting out of doors, on an Italian night in May? She would not add to the others' anxieties. Moreover she felt a curious slackness and shrinking from exertion--even the exertion of talking. As Eleanor had divined, she had caught a slight chill at Nemi, and the effects of it were malarious, in the Italian way. She was conscious of a little shiveriness and languor, and of a wish to lie or sit quite still. But Aunt Pattie was administering quinine, and keeping a motherly eye upon her. There was nothing, according to her, to be alarmed about.

At the end of a couple of hours, Manisty came out from his study much discomposed. Alice Manisty shut herself up in her room, and Manisty summoned Eleanor to walk up and down a distant path with him.

When luncheon came Alice Manisty did not appear. Dalgetty brought a message excusing her, to which Manisty listened in silence.

Aunt Pattie slipped out to see that the visitor had everything she required. But she returned almost instantly, her little parchment face quivering with nervousness.

'Alice would not see me,' she said to Manisty.

'We must leave her alone,' he said quickly. 'Dalgetty will look after her.'

The meal passed under a cloud of anxiety. For once Manisty exerted himself to make talk, but not with much success.

As the ladies left the dining-room, he detained Lucy.

'Would it be too hot for you in the garden now? Would you mind returning there?'

Lucy fetched her hat. There was only one short stretch of sun-beaten path to cross, and then, beyond, one entered upon the deep shade of the ilexes, already penetrated, at the turn of the day, by the first breaths of the sea-wind from the west. Manisty carried her books, and arranged a chair for her. Then he looked round to see if any one was near. Yes. Two gardeners were cutting the grass in the central zone of the garden--well within call.

'My aunt, or Mrs. Burgoyne will follow you very shortly,' he said 'You do not mind being alone?'

'Please, don't think of me!' cried Lucy. 'I am afraid I am in your way.'

'It will be all right to-morrow,' he said, following his own thoughts. 'May I ask that you will stay here for the present?'

Lucy promised, and he went.

She was left to think first, to think many times, of the constant courtesy and kindness which had now wholly driven from her mind the memory of his first manner to her; then to ponder, with a growing fascination which her own state of slight fever and the sultry heat of the day seemed to make it impossible for her to throw off, on Alice Manisty, on the incident of the night before, and on the meaning of the poor lady's state and behaviour. She had taken Mrs. Burgoyne's word of 'mad' in a general sense, as meaning eccentricity and temper. But surely they were gravely anxious--and everything was most strange and mysterious. The memory of the white staring face under the moonlight appalled her. She tried not to think of it; but it haunted her.

Her nerves were not in their normal state; and as she sat there in the cool, dark, vague, paralysing fears swept across her, of which she was ashamed, One minute she longed to go back to them, and help them. The next, she recognised that the best help she could give was to stay where she was. She saw very well that she was a responsibility and a care to them.

'If it lasts, I must go away'--she said to herself firmly. 'Certainly I must go.'

But at the thought of going, the tears came into her eyes. At most, there was little more than a fortnight before the party broke up, and she went with Aunt Pattie to Vallombrosa.

She took up the book upon her knee. It was a fine poem in Roman dialect, on the immortal retreat of Garibaldi after '49. But after a few lines, she let it drop again, listlessly. One of the motives which had entered into her reading of these things--a constant heat of antagonism and of protest--seemed to have gone out of her.

*   *   *   *   *

Meanwhile Aunt Pattie, Eleanor and Manisty held conclave in Aunt Pattie's sitting-room, which was a little room at the south-western corner of the apartment. It opened out of the salon, and overlooked the Campagna.

On the north-eastern side, Dalgetty, Alice Manisty's maid, sat sewing in a passage-room, which commanded the entrance to the glass passage--her own door--the door of the ante-room that Manisty had spoken of to Eleanor, and close beside her a third door--which was half open--communicating with Manisty's library. The glass passage, or conservatory, led directly to the staircase and the garden, past the French windows of the library.

Dalgetty was a person of middle age, a strongly made Scotchwoman with a high forehead and fashionable rolls of sandy hair. Her face was thin and freckled, and one might have questioned whether its expression was shrewd, or self-important. She was clearly thinking of other matters than needlework. Her eyes travelled constantly to one or other of the doors in sight; and her lips had the pinched tension that shows preoccupation.

Her mind indeed harboured a good many disagreeable thoughts. In the first place she was pondering the qualities of a certain drug lately recommended as a sedative to her mistress. It seemed to Dalgetty that its effect had not been good, but evil; or rather that it acted capriciously, exciting as often as it soothed. Yet Miss Alice would take it. On coming to her room after her interview with her brother, she had fallen first into a long fit of weeping, and then, after much restless pacing to and fro, she had put her hands to her head in a kind of despair, and had bidden Dalgetty give her the new medicine. 'I must lie down and sleep--*sleep!*'--she had said, 'or--'

And then she had paused, looking at Dalgetty with an aspect so piteous and wild that the maid's heart had quaked within her. Nevertheless she had tried to keep the new medicine away from her mistress. But Miss Alice had shown such uncontrollable anger on being crossed, that there was nothing for it but to yield. And as all was quiet in her room, Dalgetty hoped that this time the medicine would prove to be a friend, and not a foe, and that the poor lady would wake up calmer and less distraught.

She was certainly worse--much worse. The maid guessed at Mr. Manisty's opinion; she divined the approach of some important step. Very likely she would soon be separated from her mistress; and the thought depressed her. Not only because she had an affection for her poor charge; but also because she was a rather lazy and self-indulgent woman. Miss Alice had been very trying certainly; but she was not exacting in the way of late hours and needlework; she had plenty of money, and she liked moving about. All these qualities suited the tastes of the maid, who knew that she would not easily obtain another post so much to her mind.

The electric bell on the outer landing rang. Alfredo admitted the caller, and Dalgetty presently perceived a tall priest standing in the library. He was an old man with beautiful blue eyes, and he seemed to Dalgetty to have a nervous timid air.

Alfredo had gone to ask Mr. Manisty whether he could receive this gentleman--and meanwhile the stranger stood there twisting his long bony hands, and glancing about him with the shyness of a bird.

Presently Alfredo came back, and conducted the priest to the salon.

He had not been gone five minutes before Mr. Manisty appeared. He came through the library, and stood in the doorway of the passage room where she sat.

'All right, Dalgetty?' he said, stooping to her, and speaking in a whisper.

'I think and hope she's asleep, sir,' said the maid, in his ear--'I have heard nothing this half-hour.'

Manisty looked relieved, repeated his injunctions to be watchful, and went back to the salon. Dalgetty presently heard his voice in the distance, mingling with those of the priest and Mrs. Burgoyne.

Now she had nothing left to amuse her but the view through the glass passage to the balcony and the lake. It was hot, and she was tired of her sewing. The balcony however was in deep shade, and a breath of cool air came up from the lake. Dalgetty could not resist it. She glanced at her mistress's door and listened a moment. All silence.

She put down her work and slipped through the glass passage on to the broad stone balcony.

There her ears were suddenly greeted with a sound of riotous shouting and singing on the road, and Alfredo ran out from the dining-room to join her.

'*Festa!*'--he said, nodding to her in a kindly patronage, and speaking as he might have spoken to a child--'*Festa!*'

And Dalgetty began to see a number of carts adorned with green boughs and filled with singing people, coming along the road. Each cart had a band of girls dressed alike--red, white, orange, blue, and so forth.

Alfredo endeavoured to explain that these were Romans who after visiting the church of the 'Madonna del Divino Amore' in the plain were now bound to an evening of merriment at Albano. According to him it was not so much a case of 'divino amore' as of 'amore di vino,' and he was very anxious that the English maid should understand his pun. She laughed--pretended--showed off her few words of Italian. She thought Alfredo a funny, handsome little man, a sort of toy wound up, of which she could not understand the works. But after all he was a man; and the time slipped by.

After ten minutes, she remembered her duties with a start, and hastily crossing the glass passage, she returned to her post. All was just as she had left it. She listened at Miss Alice's door. Not a sound was to be heard; and she resumed her sewing.

*   *   *   *   *

Meanwhile Manisty and Eleanor were busy with Father Benecke. The poor priest had come full of a painful emotion, which broke its bounds as soon as he had Manisty's hand in his.

'You got my letter?' he said. 'That told you my hopes were dead--that the sands for me were running out?--Ah! my kind friend--there is worse to tell you!'

He stood clinging unconsciously to Manisty's hand, his eyes fixed upon the Englishman's face.

'I had submitted. The pressure upon me broke me down. I had given way. They brought me a message from the Holy Father which wrung my heart. Next week they were to publish the official withdrawal--"*librum reprobavit, et se laudabili-ter subjecit*"--you know the formula? But meanwhile they asked more of me. His Eminence entreated of me a private letter that he might send it to the Holy Father. So I made a condition. I would write,--but they must promise, on their part, that nothing should be published beyond the formal submission,--that my letter should be for his eyes alone, and for the Pope. They promised,--oh! not in writing--I have nothing written!--so I wrote. I placed myself, like a son, in the hands of the Holy Father.--Now, this morning there is my letter--the whole of it--in the ***Osservatore Romano***! To-morrow!--I came to tell you--I withdraw it. I withdraw my submission!'

He drew himself up, his blue eyes shining. Yet they were swollen with fatigue and sleeplessness, and over the whole man a blighting breath of age and pain had passed since the day in St. Peter's.

Manisty looked at him in silence a moment. Then he said--

'I'm sorry--heartily, heartily sorry!'

At this Eleanor, thinking that the two men would prefer to be alone, turned to leave the room. The priest perceived it.

'Don't leave us, madame, on my account. I have no secrets, and I know that you are acquainted with some at least of my poor history. But perhaps I am intruding; I am in your way?'

He looked round him in bewilderment. It was evident to Eleanor that he had come to Manisty in a condition almost as unconscious of outward surroundings as that of the sleep-walker. And she and Manisty, on their side, as they stood looking at him, lost the impression of the bodily man in the overwhelming impression of a wounded spirit, struggling with mortal hurt.

'Come and sit down,' she said to him gently, and she led him to a chair. Then she went into the next room, poured out and brought him a cup of coffee. He took it with an unsteady hand and put it down beside him untouched. Then he looked at Manisty and began in detail the story of all that had happened to him since the letter in which he had communicated to his English friend the certainty of his con-demnation.

Nothing could have been more touching than his absorption in his own case; his entire unconsciousness of anything in Manisty's mind that could conflict with it. Eleanor turning from his tragic simplicity to Manisty's ill-concealed worry and impatience, pitied both. That poor Father Benecke should have brought his grief to Manisty, on this afternoon of all afternoons!

It had been impossible to refuse to see him. He had come a pilgrimage from Rome and could not be turned away. But she knew well that Manisty's ear was listening all the time for every sound in the direction of his sister's room; his anxieties indeed betrayed themselves in every restless movement as he sat with averted head--listening.

Presently he got up, and with a hurried 'Excuse me an instant'--he left the room.

Father Benecke ceased to speak, his lips trembling. To find himself alone with Mrs. Burgoyne embarrassed him. He sat, folding his soutane upon his knee, answering in monosyllables to the questions that she put him. But her sympathy perhaps did more to help him unpack his heart than he knew; for when Manisty returned, he began to talk rapidly and well, a natural eloquence returning to him. He was a South German, but he spoke a fine literary English, of which the very stumbles and occasional naivetes had a peculiar charm; like the faults which reveal a pure spirit even more plainly than its virtues.

He reached his climax, in a flash of emotion--

'My submission, you see--the bare fact of it--left my cause intact. It was the soldier falling by the wall. But my letter must necessarily be misunderstood--my letter betrays the cause. And for that I have no right. You understand? I thought of the Pope--the old man. They told me he was distressed--that the Holy Father had suffered--had lost sleep--through me! So I wrote out of my heart--like a son. And the paper this morning!--See--I have brought it you--the ***Osservatore Romano***. It is insolent--brutal--but not to me! No, it is all honey to me! But to the truth--to our ideas.--No!--I cannot suffer it. I take it back!--I bear the consequences.'

And with trembling fingers, he took a draft letter from his pocket, and handed it, with the newspaper, to Manisty.

Manisty read the letter, and returned it, frowning.

'Yes--you have been abominably treated--no doubt of that. But have you counted the cost? You know my point of view! It's one episode, for me, in a world-wide struggle. Intellectually I am all with you--strategically, all with them. They can't give way! The smallest breach lets in the flood. And then, chaos!'

'But the flood is truth!' said the old man, gazing at Manisty. There was a spot of red on each wasted cheek.

Manisty shrugged his shoulders, then dropped his eyes upon the ground, and sat pondering awhile in a moody silence. Eleanor looked at him in some astonishment. It was as though for the first time his habitual paradox hurt him in the wielding--or rather as though he shrank from using what was a conception of the intellect upon the flesh and blood before him. She had never yet seen him visited by a like compunction.

It was curious indeed to see that Father Benecke himself was not affected by Manisty's attitude. From the beginning he had always instinctively appealed from the pamphleteer to the man. Manisty had been frank, brutal even. But notwithstanding, the sensitive yet strong intelligence of the priest had gone straight for some core of thought in the Englishman that it seemed only he divined. And it was clear that his own utter selflessness--his poetic and passionate detachment from all the objects of sense and ambition--made him a marvel to Manisty's more turbid and ambiguous nature. There had been a mystical attraction between them from the first; so that Manisty, even when he was most pugnacious, had yet a filial air and way towards the old man.

Eleanor too had often felt the spell. Yet to-day there were both in herself and Manisty hidden forces of fever and unrest which made the pure idealism, the intellectual tragedy of the priest almost unbearable. Neither--for different and hidden reasons--could respond; and it was an infinite relief to both when the old man at last rose to take his leave.

They accompanied him through the library to the glass passage.

'Keep me informed,' said Manisty, wringing him by the hand; 'and tell me if there is anything I can do.'

Eleanor said some parting words of sympathy. The priest bowed to her with a grave courtesy in reply.

'It will be as God wills,' he said gently; and then went his way in a sad abstraction.

Eleanor was left a moment alone. She put her hands over her heart, and pressed them there. 'He suffers from such high things!'--she said to herself in a sudden passion of misery--'and I?'

*   *   *   *   *

Manisty came hurrying back from the staircase, and crossed the library to the passage-room beyond. When he saw Dalgetty there, still peacefully sewing, his look of anxiety cleared again.

'All right?' he said to her.

'She hasn't moved, sir. Miss Manisty's just been to ask, but I told her it's the best sleep Miss Alice has had this many a day. After all, that stuff do seem to have done her good.'

'Well, Eleanor--shall we go and look after Miss Foster?'--he said, returning to her.

They entered the garden with cheered countenances. The secret terror of immediate and violent outbreak which had possessed Manisty since the morning subsided; and he drew in the *ponente* with delight.

Suddenly, however, as they turned into the avenue adorned by the battered bust of Domitian, Manisty's hand went up to his eyes. He stopped; he gave a cry.

'Good God!'--he said--'She is there!'

And halfway down the shadowy space, Eleanor saw two figures, one white, the other dark, close together.

She caught Manisty by the arm.

'Don't hurry!--don't excite her!'

As they came nearer, they saw that Lucy was still in the same low chair where Manisty had left her. Her head was thrown back against the cushions, and her face shone deathly white from the rich sun-warmed darkness shed by the over-arching trees. And kneeling beside her, holding both her helpless wrists, bending over her in a kind of passionate, triumphant possession, was Alice Manisty.

At the sound of the steps on the gravel she looked round; and at the sight of her brother, she slowly let fall the hands she held--she slowly rose to her feet. Her tall emaciated form held itself defiantly erect; her eyes flashed hatred.

'Alice!'--said Manisty, approaching her--'I have something important to say to you. I have reconsidered our conversation of this morning, and I came to tell you so.

Come back with me to the library--and let us go into matters again.'

He spoke with gentleness, controlling her with a kind look. She shivered and hesitated; her eyes wavered. Then she began to say a number of rapid, incoherent things, in an under-voice. Manisty drew her hand within his arm.

'Come,' he said, and turned to the house.

She pulled herself angrily away.

'You are deceiving me,' she said. 'I won't go with you.'

But Manisty captured her again.

'Yes--we must have our talk,' he said, with firm cheerfulness; 'there will be no time to-night.'

She broke into some passionate reproach, speaking in a thick low voice almost inaudible.

He answered it, and she replied. It was a quick dialogue, soothing on his side, wild on hers. Lucy, who had dragged herself from her attitude of mortal languor, sat with both hands grasping her chair, staring at the brother and sister. Eleanor had eyes for none but Manisty. Never had she seen him so adequate, so finely master of himself.

He conquered. Alice dropped her head sullenly, and let herself be led away. Then Eleanor turned to Lucy, and the girl, with a great sob, leant against her dress, and burst into uncontrollable tears.

'Has she been long here?' said Eleanor, caressing the black hair.

'Very nearly an hour, I think. It seemed interminable. She has been telling me of her enemies--her unhappiness--how all her letters are opened--how everybody hates her--especially Mr. Manisty. She was followed at Venice by people who wished to kill her. One night, she says, she got into her gondola, in a dark canal, and found there a man with a dagger who attacked her. She only just escaped. There were many other things,--so--so--horrible!'--said Lucy, covering her eyes. But the next moment she raised them. 'Surely,' she said imploringly, 'surely she is insane?'

Eleanor looked down upon her, mutely nodding.

'There is a doctor coming to-morrow,' she said, almost in a whisper.

Lucy shuddered.

'But we have to get through the night,' said Eleanor.

'Oh! at night'--said Lucy--'if one found her there--beside one--one would die of it! I tried to shake her off just now, several times; but it was impossible.'

She tried to control herself, to complain no more, but she trembled from head to foot. It was evident that she was under some overmastering impression, some overthrow of her own will-power which had unnerved and disorganised her. Eleanor comforted her as best she could.

'Dalgetty and Edward will take care of her to-night,'--she said. 'And to-morrow, she will be sent to some special care. How she escaped from her room this afternoon I cannot imagine. We were all three on the watch.'

Lucy said nothing. She clung to Eleanor's hand, while long shuddering breaths, gradually subsiding, passed through her; like the slow departure of some invading force.

CHAPTER XI

After Manisty had carried off his sister, Eleanor and Lucy sat together in the garden, talking sometimes, but more often silent, till the sun began to drop towards Ostia and the Mediterranean.

'You must come in,' said Eleanor, laying her hand on the girl's. 'The chill is beginning.'

Lucy rose, conscious again of the slight giddiness of fever, and they walked towards the house. Half way, Lucy said with sudden, shy energy--

'I do *wish* I were quite myself! It is I who ought to be helping you through this--and I am just nothing but a worry!'

Eleanor smiled.

'You distract our thoughts,' she said. 'Nothing could have made this visit of Alice's other than a trial.'

She spoke kindly, but with that subtle lack of response to Lucy's sympathy which had seemed to spring first into existence on the day of Nemi. Lucy had never felt at ease with her since then, and her heart, in truth, was a little sore. She only knew that something intangible and dividing had arisen between them; and that she felt herself once more the awkward, ignorant girl beside this delicate and high-bred woman, on whose confidence and friendship she had of course no claim whatever. Already she was conscious of a certain touch of shame when she thought of her new dresses and of Mrs. Burgoyne's share in them. Had she been after all the mere troublesome intruder? Her swimming head and languid spirits left her the prey of these misgivings.

Aunt Pattie met them at the head of the long flight of stone stairs which led from the garden to the first floor. Her finger was on her lip.

'Will you come through my room?' she said under her breath. 'Edward and

Alice are in the library.'

So they made a round--every room almost in the apartment communicating with every other--and thus reached Aunt Pattie's sitting-room and the salon. Lucy sat shivering beside the wood-fire in Aunt Pattie's room, which Miss Manisty had lit as soon as she set eyes upon her; while the two other ladies murmured to each other in the salon.

The rich wild light from the Campagna flooded the room; the day sank rapidly and a strange hush crept through the apartment. The women working among the olives below had gone home; there were no sounds from the Marinata road; and the crackling of the fire alone broke upon the stillness--except for a sound which emerged steadily as the silence grew. It seemed to be a man's voice reading. Once it was interrupted by a laugh out of all scale--an ugly, miserable laugh--and Lucy shuddered afresh.

Meanwhile Aunt Pattie was whispering to Eleanor.

'He was wonderful--quite wonderful! I did not think he could--'

'He can do anything he pleases. He seems to be reading aloud?'

'He is reading some poems, my dear, that she wrote at Venice. She gave them to him to look at the day she came. I daresay they're quite mad, but he's reading and discussing them as though they were the most important things, and it pleases her,--poor, poor Alice! First, you know, he quieted her very much about the money. I listened at the door sometimes, before you came in. She seems quite reconciled to him.'

'All the same, I wish this night were over and the doctor here!' said Eleanor, and Miss Manisty, lifting her hands, assented with all the energy her small person could throw into the gesture.

*   *   *   *   *

Lucy, in the course of dressing for dinner, decided that to sit through a meal was beyond her powers, and that she would be least in the way if she went to bed. So she sent a message to Miss Manisty, and was soon lying at ease, with the window opposite her bed opened wide to Monte Cavo and the moonlit lake. The window on her left hand, which looked on the balcony, she herself had closed and fastened with all possible care. And she had satisfied herself that her key was in her door. As soon as Miss Manisty and Eleanor had paid her their good-night visit, she meant to secure herself.

And presently Aunt Pattie came in, to see that she had her soup and had taken her quinine. The little old lady did not talk to Lucy of her niece, nor of the adventure of the afternoon, though she had heard all from Eleanor. Her family pride, as secret as it was intense, could hardly endure this revelation of the family trouble and difficulty to a comparative stranger, much as she liked the stranger. Nevertheless her compunctions on the subject showed visibly. No cares and attentions could be too much for the girl in her charge, who had suffered annoyance at the hands of a Manisty, while her own natural protectors were far away.

'Benson, my dear, will come and look after you the last thing,' said the old lady, not without a certain stateliness. 'You will lock your door--and I hope you will have a very good night.'

Half an hour later came Mrs. Burgoyne. Lucy's candle was out. A wick floating on oil gave a faint light in one corner of the room. Across the open window a muslin curtain had been drawn, to keep out bats and moths. But the moonlight streamed through, and lay in patches on the brick floor. And in this uncertain illumination Lucy could just see the dark pits of Eleanor's eyes, the sharp slightness of her form, the dim wreath of hair.

'You may be quite happy,' said Eleanor bending over her, and speaking almost in a whisper. 'She is much quieter. They have given her a stronger sleeping draught and locked all the doors--except the door into Dalgetty's room. And that is safe, for Dalgetty has drawn her bed right across it. If Alice tries to come through, she must wake her, and Dalgetty is quite strong enough to control her. Besides, Manisty would be there in a moment. So you may be quite, quite at ease.'

Lucy thanked her.

'And you?' she said wistfully, feeling for Eleanor's hand.

Eleanor yielded it for an instant, then withdrew it, and herself.--'Oh, thank you--I shall sleep excellently. Alice takes no interest, alas! in me! You are sure there is nothing else we can do for you?' She spoke in a light, guarded voice, that seemed to Lucy to come from a person miles away.

'Thank you--I have everything.'

'Benson will bring you milk and lemonade. I shall send Marie the first thing for news of you. You know she sleeps just beyond you, and you have only to cross the dining room to find me. Good-night. Sleep well.'

As Eleanor closed the door behind her, Lucy was conscious of a peculiar sinking of heart. Mrs. Burgoyne had once made all the advances in their friendship. Lucy thought of two or three kisses that formerly had greeted her cheek, to which she had been too shy and startled to respond. Now it seemed to her difficult to imagine that Mrs. Burgoyne had ever caressed her, had ever shown herself so sweet and gay and friendly as in those first weeks when all Lucy's pleasure at the villa depended upon her. What was wrong?--what had she done?

She lay drooping, her hot face pressed upon her hands, pondering the last few weeks, thoughts and images passing through her brain with a rapidity and an occasional incoherence that was the result of her feverish state. How much she had seen and learnt in these flying days!--it often seemed to her as though her old self had been put off along with her old clothes. She was carried back to the early time when she had just patiently adapted herself to Mr. Manisty's indifference and neglect, as she might have adapted herself to any other condition of life at the villa. She had made no efforts. It had seemed to her mere good manners to assume that he did not want the trouble of her acquaintance, and be done with it. To her natural American feeling indeed, as the girl of the party, it was strange and disconcerting that her host should not make much of her. But she had soon reconciled herself. After all, what was he to her or she to him?

Then, of a sudden, a whole swarm of incidents and impressions rushed upon memory. The semi-darkness of her room was broken by images, brilliant or tormenting--Mr. Manisty's mocking look in the Piazza of St. Peter's--his unkindness to his cousin--his sweetness to his friend--the aspect, now petulant, even childish, and now gracious and commanding beyond any other she had ever known, which he had worn at Nemi. His face, upturned beside her, as she and her horse climbed the steep path; the extraordinary significance, fulness, warmth of the nature behind it; the gradual unveiling of the man's personality, most human, faulty, self-willed, yet perpetually interesting and challenging, whether to the love or hate of the bystander:--these feelings or judgments about her host pulsed through the girl's mind with an energy that she was powerless to arrest. They did not make her happy, but they seemed to quicken and intensify all the acts of thinking and living.

At last, however, she succeeded in recapturing herself, in beating back the thoughts which, like troops over-rash on a doubtful field, appeared to be carrying her into the ambushes and strongholds of an enemy. She was impatient and scornful of them. For, crossing all these memories of things, new or exciting, there was a constant sense of something untoward, something infinitely tragic, accompanying them, developing beside them. In this feverish silence it became a nightmare presence filling the room.

What was the truth about Mr. Manisty and his cousin? Lucy searched her own innocent mind and all its new awakening perceptions in vain. The intimacy of the friendship, as she had first seen it; the tone used by Mr. Manisty that afternoon in speaking of Mrs. Burgoyne; the hundred small signs of a deep distress in her, of a new detachment in him--Lucy wandered in darkness as she thought of them, and yet with vague pangs and jarring vibrations of the heart.

Her troubled dream was suddenly broken by a sound. She sprang up trembling. Was it an angry, distant voice? Did it come from the room across the balcony? No!-- it was the loud talking of a group of men on the road outside. She shook all over, unable to restrain herself. 'What would Uncle Ben think of me?' she said to herself in despair. For Uncle Ben loved calm and self-control in women, and had often praised her for not being flighty and foolish, as he in his bachelor solitude conceived most other young women to be.

She looked down at her bandaged wrist. The wound still ached and burned from the pressure of that wild grip which she had not been able to ward off from it. Lucy herself had the strength of healthy youth, but she had felt her strength as nothing in Alice Manisty's hands. And the tyranny of those black eyes!--so like her brother's, without the human placable spark--and the horror of those fierce possessing miseries that lived in them!

Perhaps after all Uncle Ben would not have thought her so cowardly! As she sat up in bed, her hands round her knees, a pitiful home-sickness invaded her. A May scent of roses coming from the wall below the open window recalled to her the spring scents at home--not these strong Italian scents, but thin northern perfumes of lilac and lavender, of pine-needles and fresh grass. It seemed to her that she was on the slope behind Uncle Ben's house, with the scattered farms below--and the maple green in the hollow--and the grassy hillsides folded one upon another--and the gleam of a lake among them--and on the furthest verge of the kind familiar scene, the blue and shrouded heads of mountain peaks. She dropped her head on her knees, and could hear the lowing of cattle and the clucking of hens; she saw the meeting-house roof among the trees, and groups scattered through the lanes on the way to the prayer meeting, the older women in their stuff dresses and straw bonnets, the lean, bronzed men.

Benson's knock dispelled the mirage. The maid brought lemonade and milk, brushed Lucy's long hair and made all straight and comfortable.

When her tendance was over she looked at the door and then at Lucy. 'Miss Manisty said, Miss, I was to see you had your key handy. It's there all right--but it is the door that's wrong. Never saw such flimsy things as the doors in all this place.'

And Benson examined the two flaps of the door, filled with that frank contempt for the foreigner's powers and intelligence which makes the English race so beloved of Europe.

'Why, the floor-bolts'll scarcely hold, neither of them; and the lock's that loose, it's a disgrace. But I shouldn't think the people that own this place had spent a shilling on it since I was born. When you go to lay hold on things they're just tumbling to bits.'

'Oh! never mind, Benson,' said Lucy--shrinking. 'I'm sure it'll be all right. Thank you--and good-night.'

She and Benson avoided looking at each other; and the maid was far too highly trained to betray any knowledge she was not asked for. But when she had taken her departure Lucy slipped out of bed, turned the key, and tightened the bolts herself. It was true that their sockets in the brick floor were almost worn away; and the lock-case seemed scarcely to hold upon the rotten wood. The wood-work, indeed, throughout the whole villa was not only old and worm-eaten, but it had been originally of the rudest description, meant for summer uses, and a villeggiatura existence in which privacy was of small account. The Malestrini who had reared the villa above the Campagna in the late seventeenth century had no money to waste on the superfluities of doors that fitted and windows that shut; he had spent all he had, and more, on the sprawling *putti* and fruit wreaths of the ceilings, and the arabesques of the walls. And now doors, windows, and shutters alike, shrunken and scorched and blistered by the heat of two hundred summers, were dropping into ruin.

The handling of this rotten lock and its rickety accompaniments suddenly brought back a panic fear on Lucy. What if Alice Manisty and the wind, which was already rising, should burst in upon her together? She looked down upon her nightgown and her bare feet. Well, at least she would not be taken quite unawares! She opened her cupboard and brought from it a white wrapper of a thin woollen stuff which she put on. She thrust her feet into her slippers, and so stood a moment listening, her long hair dropping about her. Nothing! She lay down, and drew a shawl over her. 'I won't--won't--sleep,' she said to herself.

And the last sound she was conscious of was the cry of the little downy owl--so near that it seemed to be almost at her window.

*   *   *   *   *

'You are unhappy,' said a voice beside her.

Lucy started. The self in her seemed to wrestle its way upward from black and troubled depths of sleep. She opened her eyes. Someone was bending over her. She felt an ineffable horror, but not the smallest astonishment. Her dreams had prophesied; and she saw what she foreknew.

In the wavering light she perceived a stooping form, and again she noticed a whiteness of hands and face set in a black frame.

'Yes!' she said, lifting herself on her elbow. 'Yes!--what do you want?'

'You have been sobbing in your sleep,' said the voice. 'I know why you are unhappy. My brother is beginning to love you--you might love him. But there is some one between you--and there always will be. There is no hope for you--unless I show you the way out.'

'Miss Manisty!--you oughtn't to be here,' said Lucy, raising herself higher in bed and trying to speak with absolute self-command. 'Won't you go back to bed--won't you let me take you?'

And she made a movement. Instantly a hand was put out. It seized her arm first gently, then irresistibly.

'Don't, don't do that,' said the voice. 'It makes me angry--and--that hurts.'

Alice Manisty raised her other hand to her head, with a strange piteous gesture.

Lucy was struck with the movement of the hand. It was shut over something that it concealed.

'I don't want to make you angry,' she said, trying to speak gently and keep down the physical tumult of the heart; 'but it is not good for you to be up like this. You are not strong--you ought to have rest.'

The grip upon her arm relaxed.

'I don't rest now'--a miserable sigh came out of the darkness. 'I sleep some-times--but I don't rest. And it used all to be so happy once--whether I was awake or asleep. I was extraordinarily happy, all the winter, at Venice. One day Octave and I had a quarrel. He said I was mad--he seemed to be sorry for me--he held my arms and I saw him crying. But it was quite a mistake--I wasn't unhappy then. My brother John was always with me, and he told me the most wonderful things--secrets that no one else knows. Octave could never see him--and it was so strange--I saw him so plain. And my mother and father were there too--there was nothing between me and any dead person. I could see them and speak to them whenever I wished. People speak of separation from those who die. But there is none--they are always there. And when you talk to them, you know that you are immortal as they are--only you are not like them. You remember this world still--you know you have to go back to it. One night John took me--we seemed to go through the clouds--through little waves of white fire--and I saw a city of light, full of spirits--the most beautiful people, men and women--with their souls showing like flames through their frail bodies. They were quite kind--they smiled and talked to me. But I cried bitterly--because I knew I couldn't stay with them--in their dear strange world--I must come back--back to all I hated--all that strangled and hindered me.'

The voice paused a moment. Through Lucy's mind certain incredible words which it had spoken echoed and re-echoed. Consciousness did not master them; but they made a murmur within it through which other sounds hardly penetrated. Yet she struggled with herself--she remembered that only clearness of brain could save her.

She raised herself higher on her pillows that she might bring herself more on a level with her unbidden guest.

'And these ideas gave you pleasure?' she said, almost with calm.

'The intensest happiness,' said the low, dragging tones. 'Others pity me.--"Poor creature--she's mad"--I heard them say. And it made me smile. For I had powers they knew nothing of; I could pass from one world to another; one place to another. I could see in a living person the soul of another dead long ago. And everything spoke to me--the movement of leaves on a tree--the eyes of an animal--all kinds of numbers and arrangements that come across one in the day. Other people noticed nothing. To me it was all alive--everything was alive. Sometimes I was so happy, so ecstatic, I could hardly breathe. The people who pitied me seemed to me dull and crawling beings. If they had only known! But now--'

A long breath came from the darkness--a breath of pain. And again the figure raised its hand to its head.

'Now--somehow, it is all different. When John comes, he is cold and unkind-- he won't open to me the old sights. He shows me things instead that shake me with misery--that kill me. My brain is darkening--its powers are dying out. That means that I must let this life go--I must pass into another. Some other soul must give me room. Do you understand?'

Closer came the form. Lucy perceived the white face and the dimly burning eyes, she felt herself suffocating, but she dared make no sudden move for fear of that closed hand and what it held.

'No--I don't understand,' she said faintly; 'but I am sure--no good can come to you--from another's harm.'

'What harm would it be? You are beginning to love--and your love will never make you happy. My brother is like me. He is not mad--but he has a being apart. If you cling to him, he puts you from him--if you love him he tires. He has never loved but for his own pleasure--to complete his life. How could you complete his life? What have you that he wants? His mind now is full of you--his senses, his feeling are touched--but in three weeks he would weary of and despise you. Besides-- you know--you know well--that is not all. There is another woman--whose life you must trample on--and you are not made of stuff strong enough for that. No, there is no hope for you, in this existence--this body. But there is no death; death is only a change from one form of being to another. Give up your life, then--as I will give up mine. We will escape together. I can guide you--I know the way. We shall find endless joy--endless power! I shall be with Octave then, as and when I please--and you with Edward. Come!'

The face bent nearer, and the iron hold closed again stealthily on the girl's wrist. Lucy lay with her own face turned away and her eyes shut. She scarcely breathed. A word of prayer passed through her mind--an image of her white-haired uncle, her second father left alone and desolate.

Suddenly there was a quick movement beside her. Her heart fluttered wildly. Then she opened her eyes. Alice Manisty had sprung up, had gone to the window, and flung back the muslin curtains. Lucy could see her now quite plainly in the moonlight--the haggard energy of look and movement, the wild dishevelled hair.

'I knew the end was come--this afternoon,' said the hurrying voice. 'When I came out to you, as I walked along the terrace--the sun went out! I saw it turn black above the Campagna--all in a moment--and I said to myself, "What will the world do without the sun?--how will it live?" And now--do you see?'--she raised her arm, and Lucy saw it for an instant as a black bar against the window, caught the terrible dignity of gesture,--'there is not one moon--but many! Look at them! How they hurry through the clouds--one after the other! Do you understand what that means? Perhaps not--for your sight is not like mine. But I know. It means that the earth has left its orbit--that we are wandering--wandering in space--like a dis-masted vessel! We are tossed this way and that, sometimes nearer to the stars--and sometimes further away. That is why they are first smaller--and then larger. But the crash must come at last--death for the world--death for us all--'

Her hands fell to her side, the left hand always tightly closed--her head drooped; her voice, which had been till now hoarse and parched as though it came from a throat burnt with fever, took a deep dirge-like note. Noiselessly Lucy raised herself--she measured the distance between herself and the door--between the mad woman and the door. Oh God!--was the door locked? Her eyes strained through the darkness. How deep her sleep must have been that she had heard no sound of its yielding! Her hand was ready to throw off the shawl that covered her, when she was startled by a laugh--a laugh vile and cruel that seemed to come from a new presence--another being. Alice Manisty rapidly came back to her, stood between her bed and the wall, and Lucy felt instinctively that some hideous change had passed.

'Dalgetty thought that all was safe, so did Edward. And indeed the locks were safe--the only doors that hold in all the villa--I tried *yours* in the afternoon while

Manisty and the priest were talking! But mine held. So I had to deal with Dalgetty.' She stooped, and whispered:--'I got it in Venice one day--the chemist near the Rialto. She might have found it--but she never did--she is very stupid. I did her no harm--I think. But if it kills her, death is nothing!--nothing!--only the gate of life. Come!--come! prove it!'

A hand darted and fell, like a snake striking. Lucy just threw herself aside in time--she sprang up--she rushed--she tore at the door--pulling at it with a frantic strength. It yielded with a crash, for the lock was already broken. Should she turn left or right?--to the room of Mrs. Burgoyne's maid, or to Mr. Manisty's library? She chose the right and fled on. She had perhaps ten seconds start, since the bed had been between her enemy and the door. But if any other door interposed between her and succour, all was over!--for she heard a horrible cry behind her, and knew that she was pursued. On she dashed, across the landing at the head of the stairs. Ah! the dining-room door was open! She passed it, and then turned, holding it desperately against her pursuer.

'Mr. Manisty! help!'

The agonised voice rang through the silent rooms. Suddenly--a sound from the library--a chair overturned--a cry--a door flung open. Manisty stood in the light.

He bounded to her side. His strength released hers. The upper part of the door was glass, and that dark gasping form on the other side of it was visible to them both, in a pale dawn light from the glass passage.

'Go!'--he said--'Go through my room--find Eleanor!'

She fled. But as she entered the room, she tottered--she fell upon the chair that Manisty had just quitted,--and with a long shudder that relaxed all her young limbs, her senses left her.

Meanwhile the whole apartment was alarmed. The first to arrive upon the scene was the strong housemaid, who found Alice Manisty stretched upon the floor of the glass passage, and her brother kneeling beside her, his clothes and hands torn in the struggle with her delirious violence. Alfredo appeared immediately afterwards; and then Manisty was conscious of the flash of a hand-lamp, and the soft, hurrying step of Eleanor Burgoyne.

She stood in horror at the entrance of the glass passage. Manisty gave his sister into Alfredo's keeping as he rose and went towards her.

'For God's sake'--he said under his breath--'go and see what has happened to Dalgetty.'

He took for granted that Lucy had taken refuge with her, and Eleanor stayed to ask no questions, but fled on to Dalgetty's room. As she opened the door the fumes of chloroform assailed her, and there on the bed lay the unfortunate maid, just beginning to moan herself back to consciousness from beneath the chloroformed handkerchief that had reduced her to impotence.

Her state demanded every care. While Manisty and the housemaid Andreina conveyed Alice Manisty, now in a state of helpless exhaustion, to her room, and secured her there, Alfredo ran for the Marinata doctor. Eleanor and Aunt Pattie forced brandy through the maid's teeth, and did what they could to bring back warmth and circulation.

They were still busy with their task when the elderly Italian arrived who was the communal doctor and chemist of the village. The smell of the room, the sight of the woman, was enough. The man was efficient and discreet, and he threw himself into his work without more questions than were absolutely necessary. In the midst of their efforts Manisty reappeared, panting.

'Ought he not to see Miss Foster too?' he said anxiously to Eleanor Burgoyne.

Eleanor looked at him in astonishment.

A smothered exclamation broke from him. He rushed away, back to the library which he had seen Lucy enter.

The cool clear light was mounting. It penetrated the wooden shutters of the library and mingled with the dying light of the lamp which had served him to read with through the night, beside which, in spite of his utmost efforts, he had fallen asleep at the approach of dawn. There, in the dream-like illumination, he saw Lucy lying within his deep arm-chair. Her face was turned away from him and hidden against the cushion; her black hair streamed over the white folds of her wrapper: one arm was beneath her, the other hung helplessly over her knee.

He went up to her and called her name in an agony.

She moved slightly, made an effort to rouse herself and raised her hand. But the hand fell again, and the word half-formed upon her lips died away. Nothing could be more piteous, more disarmed. Yet even her disarray and helplessness were lovely; she was noble in her defeat; her very abandonment breathed youth and purity; the man's wildly surging thoughts sank abashed.

But words escaped him--words giving irrevocable shape to feeling. For he saw that she could not hear.

'Lucy!--Lucy--dear, beautiful Lucy!'

He hung over her in an ardent silence, his eyes breathing a respect that was the very soul of passion, his hand not daring to touch even a fold of her dress. Meanwhile the door leading to the little passage-room opened noiselessly. Eleanor Burgoyne entered. Manisty was not aware of it. He bent above Lucy in a tender absorption speaking to her as he might have spoken to a child, calling to her, comforting and rousing her. His deep voice had an enchanter's sweetness; and gradually it wooed her back to life. She did not know what he was saying to her, but she responded. Her lids fluttered; she moved in her chair, a deep sigh lifted her breast.

At that moment the door in Eleanor's hand escaped her and swung to. Manisty started back and looked round him.

'Eleanor!--is that you?'

In the barred and ghostly light Eleanor came slowly forward. She looked first at Lucy--then at Manisty. Their eyes met.

Manisty was the first to move uneasily.

'Look at her, Eleanor!--poor child!--Alice must have attacked her in her room. She escaped by a marvel. When I wrestled with Alice, I found this in her hand. One second more, and she would have used it on Miss Foster.'

He took from his pocket a small surgical knife, and looked, shuddering, at its sharpness and its curved point.

Eleanor too shuddered. She laid her hand on Lucy's shoulder, while Manisty withdrew into the shadows of the room.

Lucy raised herself by a great effort. Her first half-conscious impulse was to throw herself into the arms of the woman standing by her. Then as she perceived Eleanor clearly, as her reason came back, and her gaze steadied, the impulse died.

'Will you help me?' she said, simply--holding out her hand and tottering to her feet.

A sudden gleam of natural feeling lit up the frozen whiteness of Eleanor's face. She threw her arm round Lucy's waist, guiding her. And so, closely entwined, the two passed from Manisty's sight.

CHAPTER XII

The sun had already deserted the eastern side of the villa when, on the morning following these events, Lucy woke from a fitful sleep to find Benson standing beside her. Benson had slept in her room since the dawn; and, thanks to exhaustion and the natural powers of youth, Lucy came back to consciousness, weak but refreshed, almost free from fever and in full possession of herself. Nevertheless, as she raised herself in bed to drink the tea that Benson offered her--as she caught a glimpse through the open window of the convent-crowned summit and wooded breast of Monte Cavo, flooded with a broad white sunlight--she had that strange sense of change, of a yesterday irrevocably parted from to-day, that marks the entry into another room of life. The young soul at such times trembles before a power unknown, yet tyrannously felt. All in a moment without our knowledge or co-operation something has happened. Life will never be again as it was last week. 'How?--or why?' the soul cries. 'I knew nothing--willed nothing.' And then dimly, through the dark of its own tumult, the veiled Destiny appears.

Benson was not at all anxious that Lucy should throw off the invalid.

'And indeed, Miss, if I may say so, you'll be least in the way where you are. They're expecting the doctor from Rome directly.'

The maid looked at her curiously. All that the household knew was that Miss Alice Manisty had escaped from her room in the night, after pinioning Dalgetty's arms and throwing a chloroformed handkerchief over her face. Miss Foster, it seemed, had been aroused and alarmed, and Mr. Manisty coming to the rescue had overpowered his sister by the help of the stout *cameriera*, Andreina. This was all that was certainly known.

Nor did Lucy shew herself communicative. As the maid threw back all the shutters and looped the curtains, the girl watched the summer light conquer the room with a shiver of reminiscence.

'And Mrs. Burgoyne?' she asked eagerly.

The maid hesitated.

'She's up long ago, Miss. But she looks that ill, it's a pity to see her. She and Mr. Manisty had their coffee together an hour ago--and she's been helping him with the arrangements. I am sure it'll be a blessing when the poor lady's put away. It would soon kill all the rest of you.'

'Will she go to-day, Benson?' said Lucy, in a low voice.

The maid replied that she believed that was Mr. Manisty's decision, that he had been ordering a carriage, and that it was supposed two nurses were coming with the doctor. Then she enquired whether she might carry good news of Lucy to Miss Manisty and the master.

Lucy hurriedly begged they might be told that she was quite well, and nobody was to take the smallest trouble about her any more. Benson threw a sceptical look at the girl's blanched cheek, shook her head a little, and departed.

A few minutes afterwards there was a light tap at the door and Eleanor Burgoyne entered.

'You have slept?--you are better,' she said, standing at Lucy's bedside.

'I am only ashamed you should give me a thought,' the girl protested. 'I should be up now but for Benson. She said I should be out of the way.'

'Yes,' said Eleanor quietly. 'That is so.' She hesitated a moment, and then resumed--'If you should hear anything disagreeable don't be alarmed. There will be a doctor and nurses. But she is quite quiet this morning--quite broken--poor soul! My cousins are going into Rome with her. The home where she will be placed is on Monte Mario. Edward wishes to assure himself that it is all suitable and well managed. And Aunt Pattie will go with him.'

Through the girl's mind flashed the thought--'Then *we* shall be alone together all day,'--and her heart sank. She dared not look into Mrs. Burgoyne's tired eyes. The memory of words spoken to her in the darkness--of that expression she had surprised on Mrs. Burgoyne's face as she woke from her swoon in the library, suddenly renewed the nightmare in which she had been living. Once more she felt herself walking among snares and shadows, with a trembling pulse.

Yet the feeling which rose to sight was nothing more than a stronger form of that remorseful tenderness which had been slowly invading her during many days. She took Eleanor's hand in hers and kissed it shyly.

'Then *I* shall look after *you*,' she said trying to smile. 'I'll have my way this time!'

'Wasn't that a carriage?' said Eleanor hurriedly. She listened a moment. Yes--a carriage had drawn up. She hastened away.

Lucy, left alone, could hear the passage of feet through the glass passage, and the sound of strange voices, representing apparently two men, and neither of them Mr. Manisty.

She took a book from her table and tried not to listen. But she could not distract her mind from the whole scene which she imagined must be going on,--the consultation of the doctors, the attitude of the brother.

How had Mr. Manisty dealt with his sister the night before? What weapon was in Alice Manisty's hand? Lucy remembered no more after that moment at the door, when Manisty had rushed to her relief, bidding her go to Mrs. Burgoyne. He himself had not been hurt, or Mrs. Burgoyne would have told her. Ah!--he had surely been kind, though strong. Her eyes filled. She thought of the new light in which he had appeared to her during these terrible days with his sister; the curb put on his irritable, exacting temper; his care of Alice, his chivalry towards herself. In another man such conduct would have been a matter of course. In Manisty it touched and captured, because it could not have been reckoned on. She had done him injustice, and--unknowing--he had revenged himself.

The first carriage apparently drove away; and after an interval another replaced it. Nearly an hour passed:--then sudden sounds of trampling feet and opening doors broke the silence which had settled over the villa. Voices and steps approached, entered the glass passage. Lucy sprang up. Benson had flung the window looking on the balcony and the passage open, but had fastened across it the outside sunshutters. Lucy, securely hidden herself, could see freely through the wooden strips of the shutter.

Ah!--sad procession! Manisty came first through the passage, the sides of which were open to the balcony. His sister was on his arm, veiled and in black. She moved feebly, sometimes hesitating and pausing, and Lucy distinguished the wild eyes, glancing from side to side. But Manisty bent his fine head to her; his left hand secured hers upon his arm; he spoke to her gently and cheerfully. Behind walked Aunt Pattie, very small and nervously pale, followed by a nurse. Then two men-- Lucy recognised one as the Marinata doctor--and another nurse; then Alfredo, with luggage.

They passed rapidly out of her sight. But the front door was immediately below the balcony, and her ear could more or less follow the departure. And there was Mrs. Burgoyne, leaning over the balcony. Mr. Manisty spoke to her from below. Lucy fancied she caught her own name, and drew back indignant with herself for listening.

Then a sound of wheels--the opening of the iron gate--the driving up of an- other carriage--some shouting between Alfredo and Andreina--and it was all over. The villa was at peace again.

Lucy drew herself to her full height, in a fierce rigidity of self-contempt. What was she still listening for--still hungering for? What seemed to have gone suddenly out of heaven and earth, with the cessation of one voice?

She fell on her knees beside her bed. It was natural to her to pray, to throw herself on a sustaining and strengthening power. Such prayer in such a nature is not the specific asking of a definite boon. It is rather a wordless aspiration towards a Will not our own--a passionate longing, in the old phrase, to be 'right with God,' whatever happens, and through all the storms of personal impulse.

*   *   *   *   *

An hour later Lucy entered the salon just as Alfredo, coming up behind her, announced that the midday breakfast was ready. Mrs. Burgoyne was sitting near the western window with her sketching things about her. Some western clouds had come up from the sea to veil the scorching heat with which the day had opened. Eleanor had thrown the sun-shutters hack, and was finishing and correcting one of the Nemi sketches she had made during the winter.

She rose at sight of Lucy.

'Such a relief to throw oneself into a bit of drawing!' She looked down at her work. 'What hobby do you fly to?'

'I mend the house-linen, and I tie down the jam,' said Lucy, laughing. 'You have heard me play--so you know I don't do that well! And I can't draw a hay-stack.'

'You play very well,' said Eleanor embarrassed, as they moved towards the dining-room.

'Just well enough to send Uncle Ben to sleep when he's tired! I learnt it for that. Will you play to me afterwards?'

'With pleasure,' said Eleanor, a little formally.

How long the luncheon seemed! Eleanor, a white shadow in her black transparent dress, toyed with her food, eat nothing, and complained of the waits between the courses.

Lucy reminded her that there were fifty steps between the kitchen and their apartment. Eleanor did not seem to hear her; she had apparently forgotten her own remark, and was staring absently before her. When she spoke next it was about London, and the June season. She had promised to take a young cousin, just 'come out,' to some balls. Her talk about her plans was careless and languid, but it showed the woman naturally at home in the fashionable world, with connections in half the great families, and access to all doors. The effect of it was to make Lucy shrink into herself. Mrs. Burgoyne had spoken formerly of their meeting in London. She said nothing of it to-day, and Lucy felt that she could never venture to remind her.

From Eleanor's disjointed talk, also, there flowed another subtle impression. Lucy realised what kinship means to the English wealthy and well-born class--what a freemasonry it establishes, what opportunities it confers. The Manistys and Eleanor Burgoyne were part of a great clan with innumerable memories and traditions. They said nothing of them; they merely took them for granted with all that they implied, the social position, the 'consideration,' the effect on others.

The American girl is not easily overawed. The smallest touch of English assumption in her new acquaintances would have been enough, six weeks before, to make Lucy Foster open her dark eyes in astonishment or contempt. That is not the way in which women of her type understand life.

But to-day the frank forces of the girl's nature felt themselves harassed and crippled. She sat with downcast eyes, constrainedly listening and sometimes replying. No--it was very true. Mr. Manisty was not of her world. He had relations, friendships, affairs, infinitely remote from hers--none of which could mean anything to her. Whereas his cousin's links with him were the natural inevitable links of blood and class. He might be unsatisfactory or uncivil; but she had innumerable ways of recovering him, not to be understood even, by those outside.

When the two women returned to the salon, a kind of moral distance had established itself between them. Lucy was silent; Eleanor restless.

Alfredo brought the coffee. Mrs. Burgoyne looked at her watch as he retired.

'Half past one,' she said in a reflective voice. 'By now they have made all arrangements.'

'They will be back by tea-time?'

'Hardly,--but before dinner. Poor Aunt Pattie! She will be half dead.'

'Was she disturbed last night?' asked Lucy in a low voice.

'Just at the end. Mercifully she heard nothing till Alice was safe in her room.'

Then Eleanor's eyes dwelt broodingly on Lucy. She had never yet questioned the girl as to her experiences. Now she said with a certain abruptness--

'I suppose she forced your door?'

'I suppose so.--But I was asleep.'

'Were you terribly frightened when you found her there?'

As she spoke Eleanor said to herself that in all probability Lucy knew nothing of Manisty's discovery of the weapon in Alice's hand. While she was helping the girl to bed, Lucy, in her dazed and shivering submission, was true to her natural soberness and reserve. Instead of exaggerating, she had minimised what had happened. Miss Alice Manisty had come to her room,--had behaved strangely,--and Lucy, running to summon assistance, had roused Mr. Manisty in the library. No doubt she might have managed better, both then and in the afternoon. And so, with a resolute repression of all excited talk, she had turned her blanched face from the light, and set herself to go to sleep, as the only means of inducing Mrs. Burgoyne also to leave her and rest.

Eleanor's present question, however, set the girl's self-control fluttering, so sharply did it recall the horror of the night. She curbed herself visibly before replying.

'Yes,--I was frightened. But I don't think she could have hurt me. I should have been stronger when it came to the point.'

'Thank God Edward was there!' cried Eleanor.

'Where did he come to you?'

'At the dining-room door. I could not have held it much longer. Then he told me to go to you. And I tried to. But I only just managed to get to that chair in the library.'

'Mr. Manisty found you quite unconscious.'

A sudden red dyed Lucy's cheek.

'Mr. Manisty!--was he there? I hoped he knew nothing about it. I only saw you.'

Eleanor's thought drew certain inferences. But they gave her little comfort. She turned away abruptly, complaining of the heat, and went to the piano.

Lucy sat listening, with a book on her knee. Everything seemed to have grown strangely unreal in this hot silence of the villa--the high room with its painted walls--the marvellous prospect outside, just visible in sections through the half-closed shutters--herself and her companion. Mrs. Burgoyne played snatches of Brahms and Chopin; but her fingers stumbled more than usual. Her attention seemed to wander.

Inevitably the girl's memory went back to the wild things which Alice Manisty had said to her. In vain she rebuked herself. The fancies of a mad-woman were best forgotten,--so common-sense told her. But over the unrest of her own heart, over the electrical tension and dumb hostility that had somehow arisen between her and Eleanor Burgoyne, common-sense had small power. She could only say to herself with growing steadiness of purpose that it would be best for her not to go to Vallombrosa, but to make arrangements as soon as possible to join the Porters' friends at Florence, and go on with them to Switzerland.

To distract herself, she presently drew towards her the open portfolio of Eleanor's sketches, which was lying on the table. Most of them she had seen before, and Mrs. Burgoyne had often bade her turn them over as she pleased.

She looked at them, now listlessly, now with sudden stirs of feeling. Here was the niched wall of the Nemi temple; the arched recesses overgrown with ilex and fig and bramble; in front the strawberry pickers stooping to their work. Here, an impressionist study of the lake at evening, with the wooded height of Genzano breaking the sunset; here a sketch from memory of Aristodemo teasing the girls. Below this drawing, lay another drawing of figures. Lucy drew it out, and looked at it in bewilderment.

At the foot of it was written--'The Slayer and the Slain.' Her thoughts rushed back to her first evening at the villa--to the legend of the priest. The sketch indeed contained two figures--one erect and triumphant, the other crouching on the ground. The prostrate figure was wrapped in a cloak which was drawn over the head and face. The young victor, sword in hand, stood above his conquered enemy.

Or--Was it a man?

Lucy looked closer, her cold hand shaking on the paper. The vague classical dress told nothing. But the face--whose was it?--and the long black hair? She raised her eyes towards an old mirror on the wall in front, then dropped them to the drawing again, in a sudden horror of recognition. And the piteous figure on the ground, with the delicate woman's hand?--Lucy caught her breath. It was as though the blow at her heart, which Manisty had averted the night before, had fallen.

Then she became aware that Eleanor had turned round upon her seat at the piano, and was watching her.

'I was looking at this strange drawing,' she said. Her face had turned a sudden crimson. She pushed the drawing from her and tried to smile.

Eleanor rose and came towards her.

'I thought you would see it,' she said. 'I wished you to see it.'

Her voice was hoarse and shaking. She stood opposite to Lucy, supporting herself by a marble table that stood near.

Lucy's colour disappeared, she became as pale as Eleanor.

'Is this meant for me?'

She pointed to the figure of the victorious priest. Eleanor nodded.

'I drew it the night after our Nemi walk,' she said with a fluttering breath. 'A vision came to me so--of you--and me.'

Lucy started. Then she put her arms on the table and dropped her face into her arms. Her voice became a low and thrilling murmur that just reached Eleanor's ears.

'I wish--oh! how I wish--that I had never come here!'

Eleanor wavered a moment, then she said with gentleness, even with sweetness:

'You have nothing to blame yourself for. Nor has anyone. That picture accuses no one. It draws the future--which no one can stop or change--but you.'

'In the first place,' said Lucy, still hiding her eyes and the bitter tears that dimmed them--'what does it mean? Why am I the slayer?--and--and--you the slain? What have I done? How have I deserved such a thing?'

Her voice failed her. Eleanor drew a little nearer.

'It is not you--but fate. You have taken from me--or you are about to take from me--the last thing left to me on this earth! I have had one chance of happiness, and only one, in all my life, till now. My boy is dead--he has been dead eight years. And at last I had found another chance--and after seven weeks, you--you--are dashing it from me!'

Lucy drew back from the table, like one that shrinks from an enemy.

'Mrs. Burgoyne!'

'You don't know it!' said Eleanor calmly. 'Oh! I understand that. You are too good--too loyal. That's why I am talking like this. One could only dare it with some one whose heart one knew. Oh! I have had such gusts of feeling towards you--such mean, poor feeling. And then, as I sat playing there, I said to myself, "I'll tell her! She will find that drawing, and--I'll tell her! She has a great, true nature--she'll understand. Why shouldn't one try to save oneself? It's the natural law. There's only the one life."'

She covered her eyes with her hand an instant, choking down the sob which interrupted her. Then she moved a little nearer to Lucy.

'You see,' she said, appealing,--'you were very sweet and tender to me one day. It's very easy to pretend to mourn with other people--because one thinks one ought--or because it makes one liked. I am always pretending in that way--I can't help it. But you--no: you don't say what you don't feel, and you've the gift to feel. It's so rare--and you'll suffer from it. You'll find other people doing what I'm doing now--throwing themselves upon you--taking advantage--trusting to you. You pitied mo because I had lost my boy. But you didn't know--you couldn't guess how bare my life has been always--but for him. And then--this winter--' her voice changed and broke--'the sun rose again for me. I have been hungry and starving for years, and it seemed as though I--even I!--might still feast and be satisfied.

'It would not have taken much to satisfy me. I am not young, like you--I don't ask much. Just to be his friend, his secretary, his companion--in time--perhaps--his wife--when he began to feel the need of home, and peace--and to realise that no one else was so dear or so familiar to him as I. I understood him--he me--our minds touched. There was no need for "falling in love." One had only to go on from day to day--entering into each other's lives--I ministering to him and he growing accustomed to the atmosphere I could surround him with, and the sympathy I could give him--till the habit had grown so deep into heart and flesh that it could not be wrenched away. His hand would have dropped into mine, almost without his willing or knowing it.... And I should have made him happy. I could have lessened his faults--stimulated his powers. That was my dream all these later months--and every week it seemed to grow more reasonable, more possible. Then you came--'

She dropped into a chair beside Lucy, resting her delicate hands on the back of it. In the mingled abandonment and energy of her attitude, there was the power that belongs to all elemental human emotion, made frankly visible and active. All her plaintive clinging charm had disappeared. It was the fierceness of the dove--the egotism of the weak. Every line and nerve of the fragile form betrayed the exasperation of suffering and a tension of the will, unnatural and irresistible. Lucy bowed to the storm. She lay with her eyes hidden, conscious only of this accusing voice close to her,--and of the song of two nightingales without, rivalling each other among the chestnut trees above the lower road. Eleanor resumed after a momentary pause--a momentary closing of the tired eyes, as though in search of calm and recollection.

'You came. He took no notice of you. He was rude and careless--he complained that our work would be interrupted. It teased him that you should be here--and that you represented something so different from his thoughts and theories. That is like him. He has no real tolerance. He wants to fight, to overbear, to crush, directly he feels opposition. Among women especially, he is accustomed to be the centre--to be the master always. And you resisted--silently. That provoked and attracted him. Then came the difficulties with the book--and Mr. Neal's visit. He has the strangest superstitions. It was ill-luck, and I was mixed up with it. He began to cool to me--to avoid me. You were here; you didn't remind him of failure. He found relief in talking to you. His ill-humour would all have passed away like a child's sulkiness, but that--Ah! well!--' She raised her hand with a long, painful sigh, and let it drop.

'Don't imagine I blame anyone. You were so fresh and young--it was all so natural. Yet somehow I never really feared--after the first evening I felt quite at ease. I found myself drawn to like--to love--you. And what could you and he have in common? Then on the Nemi day I dared to reproach him--to appeal to the old times--to show him the depth of my own wound--to make him explain himself. Oh! but all those words are far, far too strong for what I did? Who could ever suppose it to their advantage to make a scene with him--to weary or disgust him? It was only a word--a phrase or two here and there. But he understood,--and he gave me my answer. Oh! what humiliations we women can suffer from a sentence--a smile--and show nothing--nothing!'

Her face had begun to burn. She lifted her handkerchief to brush away two slow tears that had forced their way. Lucy's eyes had been drawn to her from their hiding-place. The girl's brow was furrowed, her lips parted; there was a touch of fear--unconscious, yet visible--in her silence.

'It was that day, while you and he were walking about the ruins, that a flash of light came to me. I suppose I had seen it before. I know I had been unhappy long before! But as long as one can hide things from oneself--it seems to make them not true,--as though one's own will still controlled them. But that day--after our walk--when we came back and found you on the hill-side! How was it your fault? Yet I could almost have believed that you had invented the boys and the stone! Certainly he spared me nothing. He had eyes and ears only for you. After he brought you home all his thoughts were for you. Nobody else's fatigues and discomforts mattered anything. And it was the same with Alice. His only terrors were for you. When he heard that she was coming, he had no alarms for Aunt Pattie or for me. But you must be shielded--you must be saved from everything repulsive or shocking. He sat up last night to protect you--and even in his sleep--he heard you.'

Her voice dropped. Eleanor sat staring before her into the golden shadows of the room, afraid of what she had said, instinctively waiting for its effect on Lucy.

And Lucy crouched no longer. She had drawn herself erect.

'Mrs. Burgoyne, is it kind--is it **bearable**--that you should say these things to me? I have not deserved them! No! no!--I have **not**. What right have you? I can't protect myself--I can't escape you--but--'

Her voice shook. There was in it a passion of anger, pain, loneliness, and yet something else--the note of something new-born and transforming.

'What right?' repeated Eleanor, in low tones--tones almost of astonishment. She turned to her companion. 'The right of hunger--the right of poverty--the right of one pleading for a last possession!--a last hope!'

Lucy was silenced. The passion of the older woman bore her down, made the protest of her young modesty seem a mere trifling and impertinence. Eleanor had slid to her knees. Her face had grown tremulous and sweet. A strange dignity quivered in the smile that transformed her mouth as she caught the girl's reluctant hands and drew them against her breast.

'Is it forbidden to cry out when grief--and loss--go beyond a certain point? No!--I think not. I couldn't struggle with you--or plot against you--or hate you. Those things are not in my power. I was not made so. But what forbids mo to come to you and say?--"I have suffered terribly. I had a dreary home. I married, ignorantly, a man who made me miserable. But when my boy came, that made up for all. I never grumbled. I never envied other people after that. It seemed to me I had all I deserved--and so much, much more than many! Afterwards, when I woke up without him that day in Switzerland, there was only one thing that made it endurable. I overheard the Swiss doctor say to my maid--he was a kind old man and very sorry for me--that my own health was so fragile that I shouldn't live long to pine for the child. But oh!--what we can bear and not die! I came back to my father, and for eight years I never slept without crying--without the ghost of the boy's head against my breast. Again and again I used to wake up in an ecstasy, feeling it there--feeling the curls across my mouth."' A deep sob choked her. Lucy, in a madness of pity, struggled to release herself that she might throw her arms round the kneeling figure. But Eleanor's grasp only tightened. She hurried on.

'But last year, I began to hope. Everybody thought badly of me; the doctors spoke very strongly; and even Papa made no objection when Aunt Pattie asked me to come to Rome. I came to Rome in a strange state--as one looks at things and loves them, for the last time, before a journey. And then--well, then it all began!--new life for me, new health. The only happiness--except for the child--that had ever come my way. I know--oh! I don't deceive myself--I know it was not the same to Edward as to me. But I don't ask much. I knew he had given the best of his heart to other women--long ago--long before this. But the old loves were all dead, and I could almost be thankful for them. They had kept him for me, I thought,--tamed and exhausted him, so that I--so colourless and weak compared to those others!--might just slip into his heart and find the way open--that he might just take me in, and be glad, for sheer weariness.'

She dropped Lucy's hands, and rising, she locked her own, and began to walk to and fro in the great room; her head thrown back, her senses turned as it were inward upon the sights and sounds of memory.

Lucy gazed upon her in bewilderment. Then she too rose and approached Mrs. Burgoyne.

'When shall I go?' she said simply. 'You must help me to arrange it with Miss Manisty. It might be to-morrow--it would be easy to find some excuse.'

Eleanor looked at her with a convulsed face.

'That would help nothing,' she said--'nothing! He would guess what I had done.'

Lucy was silent a moment. Then she broke out piteously.

'What can I do?'

'What claim have I that you should do anything?' said Eleanor despairingly. 'I don't know what I wanted, when I began this scene.'

She moved on, her eyes bent upon the ground--Lucy beside her.

The girl had drawn Mrs. Burgoyne's arm through her own. The tears were on her check, but she was thinking, and quite calm.

'I believe,' she said at last, in a voice that was almost steady--'that all your fears are quite, quite vain. Mr. Manisty feels for me nothing but a little kindness--he could feel nothing else. It will all come back to you--and it was not I that took it away. But--whatever you tell me--whatever you ask, I will do.'

With a catching breath Eleanor turned and threw her arm round the girl's neck. 'Stay,' she breathed--'stay for a few days. Let there be no shock--nothing to challenge him. Then slip away--don't let him know where--and there is one woman in the world who will hold you in her inmost heart, who will pray for you with her secretest, sacredest prayers, as long as you live!'

The two fell into each other's embrace. Lucy, with the maternal tenderness that should have been Eleanor's, pressed her lips on the hot brow that lay upon her breast, murmuring words of promise, of consolation, of self-reproach, feeling her whole being passing out to Eleanor's in a great tide of passionate will and pity.

CHAPTER XIII

They were all going down to the midday train for Rome.

At last the Ambassador--who had been passing through a series of political and domestic difficulties, culminating in the mutiny of his Neapolitan cook--had been able to carry out his whim. A luncheon had been arranged for the young American girl who had taken his fancy. At the head of his house for the time being was his married daughter, Lady Mary, who had come from India for the winter to look after her babies and her father. When she was told to write the notes for this luncheon, she lifted her eyebrows in good-humoured astonishment.

'My dear,' said the Ambassador, 'we have been doing our duty for six months--and I find it pall!'

He had been entertaining Royalties and Cabinet Ministers in heavy succession, and his daughter understood. There was an element of insubordination in her father, which she knew better than to provoke.

So the notes were sent.

'Find her some types, my dear,' said the Ambassador;--'and little of everything.'

Lady Mary did her best. She invited an Italian Marchesa whom she had heard her father describe as 'the ablest woman in Rome,' while she herself knew her as one of the most graceful and popular; a young Lombard landowner formerly in the Navy, now much connected with the Court, whose blue eyes moreover were among the famous things of the day; a Danish professor and savant who was also a rich man, collector of flints and torques, and other matters of importance to primitive man; an artist or two; an American Monsignore blessed with some Irish wit and much influence; Reggie Brooklyn, of course, and his sister; Madame Variani, who would prevent Mr. Manisty from talking too much nonsense; and a dull English Admiral and his wife, official guests, whom the Ambassador admitted at the last moment with a groan, as still representing the cold tyranny of duty invading his snatch of pleasure.

'And Mr. Bellasis, papa?' said Lady Mary, pausing, pen in hand, like Fortitude prepared for all extremities.

'Heavens, no!' said the Ambassador, hastily. 'I have put him off twice. This time I should have to read him.'

* * * * *

Manisty accordingly was smoking on the balcony of the villa while he waited for the ladies to appear. Miss Manisty, who was already suffering from the heat, was not going. The fact did not improve Manisty's temper. Three is no company--that we all know.

If Lady Mary, indeed, had only planned this luncheon because she must, Manisty was going to it under a far more impatient sense of compulsion. It would be a sickening waste of time. Nothing now had any attraction for him, nothing seemed to him desirable or important, but that conversation with Lucy Foster which he was bent on securing, and she apparently was bent on refusing him.

His mind was full of the sense of injury. During all the day before, while he had been making the arrangements for his unhappy sister--during the journeys backward and forward to Rome--a delicious image had filled all the background of his thoughts, the image of the white Lucy, helpless and lovely, lying unconscious in his chair.

In the evening he could hardly command his eagerness sufficiently to help his tired little aunt up the steps of the station, and put her safely in her cab, before hurrying himself up the steep short-cut to the villa. Should he find her perhaps on the balcony, conscious of his step on the path below, weak and shaken, yet ready to lift those pure, tender eyes of hers to his in a shy gratitude?

He had found no one on the balcony, and the evening of that trying day had been one of baffling disappointment. Eleanor was in her room, apparently tired out by the adventures of the night before; and although Miss Foster appeared at dinner she had withdrawn immediately afterwards, and there had been no chance for anything but the most perfunctory conversation.

She had said of course all the proper things, so far as they could be said. 'I trust you have been able to make the arrangements you wished. Mrs. Burgoyne and I have been so sorry! Poor Miss Manisty must have had a very tiring day--'

Bah!--he could not have believed that a girl could speak so formally, so trivially to a man who within twenty-four hours had saved her from the attack of a mad-woman. For that was what it came to--plainly. Did she know what had happened? Had her swoon blotted it all out? If so, was he justified in revealing it. There was an uneasy feeling that it would be more chivalrous towards her, and kinder towards his sister, if he left the veil drawn, seeing that she seemed to wish it so--if he said no more about her fright, her danger, her faint. But Manisty was not accustomed to let himself be governed by the scruples of men more precise or more timid. He wished passionately to force a conversation with her more intimate, more personal than any one had yet allowed him; to break down at a stroke most if not all of the barriers that separate acquaintance from--

From what? He stood, cigarette in hand, staring blindly at the garden, lost in an intense questioning of himself.

Suddenly he found himself back again, as it were, among the feelings and sensations of Lucy Foster's first Sunday at the villa; his repugnance towards any notion of marriage; his wonder that anybody should suppose that he had any immediate purpose of marrying Eleanor Burgoyne; the mood, half lazy, half scornful, in which he had watched Lucy, in her prim Sunday dress, walking along the avenue.

What had attracted him to this girl so different from himself, so unacquainted with his world?

There was her beauty of course. But he had passed the period when mere beauty is enough. He was extremely captious and difficult to please where the ordinary pretty woman was concerned. Her arts left him now quite unmoved. Of self-conscious vanity and love of effect he had himself enough and to spare. He could not mend himself; but he was often weary of his own weaknesses, and detested them in other people. If Lucy Foster had been merely a beauty, aware of her own value, and bent upon making him aware of it also, he would probably have been as careless of her now in the eighth week of their acquaintance as he had been in the first.

But it was a beauty so innocent, so interfused with suggestion, with an enchanting thrill of prophecy! It was not only what she said and looked, but what a man might divine in her--the 'white fire' of a nature most pure, most passionate, that somehow flashed through her maiden life and aspect, fighting with the restraints imposed upon it, and constantly transforming what might otherwise have been a cold seemliness into a soft and delicate majesty.

In short, there was a mystery in Lucy, for all her simplicity;--a mystery of feeling, which piqued and held the fastidious taste of Manisty. It was this which made her loveliness tell. Her sincerity was so rich and full, that it became dramatic,--a thing to watch, for the mere joy of the fresh, unfolding spectacle. She was quite unconscious of this significance of hers. Rather she was clearly and always conscious of weakness, ignorance, inexperience. And it was this lingering childishness, compared with the rarity, the strength, the tenderness of the nature just emerging from the sheath of first youth, that made her at this moment so exquisitely attractive to Manisty.

In the presence of such a creature marriage began to look differently. Like many men with an aristocratic family tradition, who have lived for a time as though they despised it, there were in him deep stores of things inherited and conventional which re-emerged at the fitting moment. Manisty disliked and had thrown aside the role of country gentleman; because, in truth, he had not money enough to play it magnificently, and he had set himself against marriage; because no woman had yet appeared to make the probable boredoms of it worth while.

But now, as he walked up and down the balcony, plunged in meditation, he began to think with a new tolerance of the English *cadre* and the English life. He remembered all those illustrious or comely husbands and wives, his forebears, whose portraits hung on the walls of his neglected house. For the first time it thrilled him to imagine a new mistress of the house--young, graceful, noble--moving about below them. And even--for the first time--there gleamed from out the future the dim features of a son, and he did not recoil. He caressed the whole dream with a new and strange complacency. What if after all the beaten roads are best?

To the old paths, my soul!

Then he paused, in a sudden chill of realisation. His thoughts might rove as they please. But Lucy Foster had given them little warrant. To all her growing spell upon him, there was added indeed the charm of difficulty foreseen, and delighted in. He was perfectly aware that he puzzled and attracted her. And he was perfectly aware also of his own power with women, often cynically aware of it. But he could not flatter himself that so far he had any hold over the senses or the heart of Lucy Foster. He thought of her eager praise of his Palestine letters--of the Nemi tale. She was franker, more enthusiastic than an English girl would have been--and at the same time more remote, infinitely more incalculable!

His mind filled with a delicious mingling of desire and doubt. He foresaw the sweet approach of new emotions,--of spells to make 'the colours freshen on this threadbare world.' All his life he had been an epicurean, in search of pleasures beyond the ken of the crowd. It was pleasure of this kind that beckoned to him now,--in the wooing, the conquering, the developing of Lucy.

A voice struck on his ear. It was Eleanor calling to Lucy from the salon.

Ah!--Eleanor? A rush of feeling--half generous, half audacious--came upon him. He knew that he had given her pain at Nemi. He had been a brute, an ungrateful brute! Women like Eleanor have very exalted and sensitive ideals of friendship. He understood that he had pulled down Eleanor's ideal, that he had wounded her sorely. What did she expect of him? Not any of the things which the ignorant or vulgar bystander expected of him--that he was certain. But still her claim had wearied him; and he had brushed it aside. His sulkiness about the book had been odious, indefensible. And yet--perhaps from another point of view--it had not been a bad thing for either of them. It had broken through habits which had become, surely, an embarrassment to both.

But now, let him make amends; select fresh ground; and from it rebuild their friendship. His mind ran forward hazily to some bold confidence or other, some dramatic appeal to Eleanor for sympathy and help.

The affection between her and Miss Foster seemed to be growing closer. He thought of it uncomfortably, and with vague plannings of counter-strokes. It did not suit him--nay, it presented itself somehow as an obstacle in his path. For he had a half remorseful, half humorous feeling that Eleanor knew him too well.

*   *   *   *   *

'Ah! my dear lady,' said the Ambassador--'how few things in this world one does to please oneself! This is one of them.'

Lucy flushed with a young and natural pleasure. She was on the Ambassador's left, and he had just laid his wrinkled hand for an instant on hers, with a charming and paternal freedom.

'Have you enjoyed yourself?--Have you lost your heart to Italy?' said her host, stooping to her. He was amused to see the transformation in her, the pretty dress, the developed beauty.

'I have been in fairy-land,' said Lucy, shyly, opening her blue eyes upon him. 'Nothing can ever be like it again.'

'No--because one can never be twenty again,' said the old man, sighing. 'Twenty years hence you will wonder where the magic came from. Never mind--just now, anyway, the world's your oyster.'

Then he looked at her a little more closely. And it seemed to him that, though she was handsomer, she was not so happy. He missed some of that quiver of youth and enjoyment he had felt in her before, and there were some very dark lines under the beautiful eyes. What was wrong? Had she met the man--the appointed one?

He began to talk to her with a kindness that was at once simple and stately.

'We must all have our ups and downs,' he said to her presently. 'Let me just give you a word of advice. It'll carry you through most of them. Remember you are very young, and I shall soon be very old.'

He stopped and surveyed her. His kind humorous eyes blinked through their blanched lashes. Lucy dropped her fork and looked back at him with smiling expectancy.

'*Learn Persian!*' said the old man in an urgent whisper--'and get the dictionary by heart!'

Lucy still looked--wondering.

'I finished it this morning,' said the Ambassador, in her ear. 'To-morrow I shall begin it again. My daughter hates the sight of the thing. She says I over-tire myself, and that when old people have done their work they should take a nap. But I know that if it weren't for my dictionary, I should have given up long ago. When too many tiresome people dine here in the evening--or when they worry me from home--I take a column. But generally half a column's enough--good tough Persian roots, and no nonsense. Oh! of course I can read Hafiz and Omar Khayyam, and all that kind of thing. But that's the whipped cream. That don't count. What one wants is something to set one's teeth in. Latin verse will do. Last year I put half Tommy Moore into hendecasyllables. But my youngest boy who's at Oxford, said he wouldn't be responsible for them--so I had to desist. And I suppose the mathematicians have always something handy. But, one way or another, one must learn one's dictionary. It comes next to cultivating one's garden. Now Mr. Manisty--how is he provided in that way?'

His sudden question took Lucy by surprise, and the quick rise of colour in the clear cheeks did not escape him.

'Well--I suppose he has his book?' she said, smiling.

'Oh! no use at all! He can do what he likes with his book. But you can't do what you like with the dictionary. You must take it or leave it. That's what makes it so reposeful. Now if I were asked, I could soon find some Persian roots for Mr. Manisty--to be taken every day!'

Lucy glanced across the table. Her eyes fell, and she said in the low full voice that delighted the old man's ears:

'I suppose you would send him home?'

The Ambassador nodded.

'Tenants, turnips, and Petty Sessions! Persian's pleasanter--but those would serve.'

He paused a moment, then said seriously, under the cover of a loud buzz of talk, 'He's wasting his time, dear lady--there's no doubt of that.'

Lucy still looked down, but her attitude changed imperceptibly. 'The subject interests her!' thought the old man. 'It's a thousand pities,' he resumed, with the caution, masked by the ease, of the diplomat, 'he came out here in a fit of pique. He saw false--and as far as I can hear, the book's a mistake. Yet it was not a bad subject. Italy *is* just now an object lesson and a warning. But our friend there could not have taken it more perversely. He has chosen to attack not the violence of the

Church--but the weakness of the State. And meanwhile--if I may be allowed to say so--his own position is something of an offence. Religion is too big a pawn for any man's personal game. Don't you agree? Often I feel inclined to apply to him the saying about Benjamin Constant and liberty--"Grand homme devant la religion--*s'il y croyait!*" I compare with him a poor old persecuted priest I know--Manisty knows too.--Ah! well, I hear the book is very brilliant--and venomous to a degree. It will be read of course. He has the power to be read. But it is a blunder--if not a crime. And meanwhile he is throwing away all his chances. I knew his father. I don't like to see him beating the air. If you have any influence with him'--the old man smiled--'send him home! Or Mrs. Burgoyne there. He used to listen to her.'

A great pang gripped Lucy's heart.

'I should think he always took his own way,' she said, with difficulty. 'Mr. Neal sometimes advises him.'

The Ambassador's shrewd glance rested upon her for a moment. Then without another word he turned away. 'Reggie!' he said, addressing young Brooklyn, 'you seem to be ill-treating Madame Variani. Must I interpose?'

Reggie and his companion, who were in a full tide of 'chaff' and laughter, turned towards him.

'Sir,' said Brooklyn, 'Madame Variani is attacking my best friend.'

'Many of us find that agreeable,' said the Ambassador.

'Ah! but she makes it so personal,' said Reggie, dallying with his banana. 'She abuses him because he's not married--and calls him a selfish fop. Now *I'm* not married--and I object to these wholesale classifications. Besides, my friend has the most conclusive answer.'

'I wait for it,' said Madame Variani.

Reggie delicately unsheathed his banana.

'Well, some of us once enquired what he meant by it, and he said: "My dear fellow, I've asked all the beautiful women I know to marry me, and they won't! Now!--I'd be content with cleanliness and conduct."'

There was a general laugh, in the midst of which Reggie remarked:

'I thought it the most touching situation. But Madame Variani has the heart of a stone.'

Madame Variani looked down upon him unmoved. She and the charming lad were fast friends.

'I will wager you he never asked,' she said quietly.

Reggie protested.

'No--he never asked. Englishmen don't ask ladies to marry them any more.'

'Let Madame Variani prove her point,' said the Ambassador, raising one white hand above the hubbub, while he hollowed the other round his deaf ear. 'This is a most interesting discussion.'

'But it is known to all that Englishmen don't get married any more!' cried Madame Variani. 'I read in an English novel the other day that it is spoiling your English society, that the charming girls wait and wait--and nobody marries them.'

'Well, there are no English young ladies present,' said the Ambassador, looking round the table; 'so we may proceed. How do you account for this phenomenon, Madame?'

'Oh! you have now too many French cooks in England!' said Madame Variani, shrugging her plump shoulders.

'What in the world has that got to do with it?' cried the Ambassador.

'Your young men are too comfortable,' said the lady, with a calm wave of the hand towards Reggie Brooklyn. 'That's what I am told. I ask an English lady, who knows both France and England--and she tells me--your young men get now such good cooking at their clubs, and at the messes of their regiments--and their sports amuse them so well, and cost so much money--they don't want any wives!--they are not interested any more in the girls. That is the difference between them and the Frenchman. The Frenchman is still interested in the ladies. After dinner the Frenchman wants to go and sit with the ladies--the Englishman, no! That is why the French are still agreeable.'

The small black eyes of the speaker sparkled, but otherwise she looked round with challenging serenity on the English and Americans around her. Madame Variani--stout, clever, middle-aged, and disinterested--had a position of her own in Rome. She was the correspondent of a leading French paper; she had many English friends; and she and the Marchesa Fazzoleni, at the Ambassador's right hand, had just been doing wonders for the relief of the Italian sick and wounded after the miserable campaign of Adowa.

'Oh! I hide my diminished head!' said the old Ambassador, taking his white locks in both hands. 'All I know is, I have sent twenty wedding presents already this year--and that the state of my banking account is wholly inconsistent with these theories.'

'Ah! you are exceptional,' said the lady. 'Only this morning I get an account of an English gentleman of my acquaintance. He is nearly forty--he possesses a large estate--his mother and sisters are on their knees to him to marry--it will all go to a cousin, and the cousin has forged--or something. And he--not he! He don't care what happens to the estate. He has only got the one life, he says--and he won't spoil it. And of course it does your women harm! Women are always dull when the men don't court them!'

The table laughed. Lucy, looking down it, caught first the face of Eleanor Burgoyne, and in the distance Manisty's black head and absent smile. The girl's young mind was captured by a sudden ghastly sense of the human realities underlying the gay aspects and talk of the luncheon-table. It seemed to her she still heard that heart-rending voice of Mrs. Burgoyne: 'Oh! I never dreamed it could be the same for him as for me. I didn't ask much.'

She dreaded to let herself think. It seemed to her that Mrs. Burgoyne's suffering must reveal itself to all the world, and the girl had moments of hot shame, as though for herself. To her eyes, the change in aspect and expression, visible through all the elegance and care of dress, was already terrible.

Oh! why had she come to Rome? What had changed the world so? Some wounded writhing thing seemed to be struggling in her own breast--while she was holding it down, trying to thrust it out of sight and hearing.

She had written to Uncle Ben, and to the Porters. To-morrow she must break it to Aunt Pattie that she could not go to Vallombrosa, and must hurry back to England. The girl's pure conscience was tortured already by the thought of the excuses she would have to invent. And not a word, till Mr. Manisty was safely started on his way to that function at the Vatican which he was already grumbling over, which he would certainly shirk if he could. But, thank Heaven, it was not possible for him to shirk it.

Again her eyes crossed those of Manisty. He was now discussing the strength of parties in the recent Roman municipal elections with the American Monsignore, talking with all his usual vehemence. Nevertheless, through it all, it seemed to her, that she was watched, that in some continuous and subtle way he held her in sight.

How cold and ungrateful he must have thought her the night before! To-day, at breakfast, and in the train, he had hardly spoken to her.

Yet--mysteriously--Lucy felt herself threatened, hard pressed. Alice Manisty's talk in that wild night haunted her ear. Her hand, cold and tremulous, shook on her knee. Even the voice of the Ambassador startled her.

After luncheon the Ambassador's guests fell into groups on the large shady lawn of the Embassy garden.

The Ambassador introduced Lucy to the blue-eyed Lombard, Fioravanti, while he, pricked with a rueful sense of duty, devoted himself for a time to the wife of the English Admiral who had been Lady Mary's neighbour at luncheon. The Ambassador examined her through his half-closed eyes, as he meekly offered to escort her indoors to see his pictures. She was an elegant and fashionable woman with very white and regular false teeth. Her looks were conventional and mild. In reality the Ambassador knew her to be a Tartar. He walked languidly beside her; his hands were lightly crossed before him; his white head drooped under the old wideawake that he was accustomed to wear in the garden.

Meanwhile the gallant and be-whiskered Admiral would have liked to secure Manisty's attention. To get hold of a politician, or something near a politician, and explain to them a new method of fusing metals in which he believed, represented for him the main object of all social functions.

But Manisty peremptorily shook him off. Eleanor, the American Monsignore, and Reggie Brooklyn were strolling near. He retreated upon them. Eleanor addressed some question to him, but he scarcely answered her. He seemed to be in a brown study, and walked on beside her in silence.

Reggie fell back a few paces, and watched them.

'What a bear he can be when he chooses!' the boy said to himself indignantly. 'And how depressed Eleanor looks! Some fresh worry I suppose--and all his fault. Now look at that!'

For another group--Lucy, her new acquaintance the Count, and Madame Variani--had crossed the path of the first. And Manisty had left Eleanor's side to approach Miss Foster. All trace of abstraction was gone. He looked ill at ease, and yet excited; his eyes were fixed upon the girl. He stooped towards her, speaking in a low voice.

'There's something up'--thought Brooklyn. 'And if that girl's any hand in it she ought to be cut! I thought she was a nice girl.'

His blue eyes stared fiercely at the little scene. Since the day at Nemi, the boy had understood half at least of the situation. He had perceived then that Eleanor was miserably unhappy. No doubt Manisty was disappointing and tormenting her. What else could she expect?

But really--that she should be forsaken and neglected for this chit of a girl--this interloping American--it was too much! Reggie's wrath glowed within him.

Meanwhile Manisty addressed Lucy.

'I have something I very much wish to say to you. There is a seat by the fountain, quite in shade. Will you try it?'

She glanced hurriedly at her companions.

'Thank you--I think we were going to look at the rose-walk.'

Manisty gave an angry laugh, said something inaudible, and walked impetuously away; only to be captured however by the Danish Professor, Doctor Jensen, who took no account of bad manners in an Englishman, holding them as natural as daylight. The flaxen-haired savant therefore was soon happily engaged in pouring out upon his impatient companion the whole of the latest **Boletino** of the Accademia.

Meanwhile Lucy, seeing nothing, it is to be feared, of the beauty of the Embassy garden, followed her two companions and soon found herself sitting with them on a stone seat beneath a spreading ilex. In front was a tangled mass of roses; beyond, an old bit of wall with Roman foundations; and in the hot blue sky above the wall, between two black cypresses, a slender brown Campanile--furthest of all a glimpse of Sabine mountains. The air was heavy with the scent of the roses, with the heat that announced the coming June, with that indefinable meaning and magic, which is Rome.

Lucy drooped and was silent. The young Count Fioravanti however was not the person either to divine oppression in another or to feel it for himself. He sat with his hat on the back of his head, smoking and twisting his cane, displaying to the fullest advantage those china-blue eyes, under the blackest of curls, which made him so popular in Rome. His irregular and most animated face was full of talent and wilfulness. He liked Madame Variani, and thought the American girl handsome. But it mattered very little to him with whom he talked; he could have chattered to a tree-stump. He was over-flowing with the mere interest and jollity of life.

'Have you known Mr. Manisty long?' he asked of Lucy, while his gay look followed the Professor and his captive.

'I have been staying with them for six weeks at Marinata.'

'What--to finish the book?' he said, laughing.

'Mr. Manisty hoped to finish it.'

The Count laughed again, more loudly and good-humouredly, and shook his head.

'Oh! he won't finish it. It's a folly! And I know, for I made him read some of it to me and my sister. No; it is a strange case--is Manisty's. Most Englishmen have two sides to their brain--while we Latins have only one. But Manisty is like a Latin--he has only one. He takes a whim, and then he must cut and carve the world to it. But the world is tough--*et ca ne marche pas*! We can't go to ruin to please him. Italy is not falling to pieces--not at all. This war has been a horror--but we shall get through. And there will be no revolution. The people in the streets won't cheer the King and Queen for a little bit--but next year, you will see, the House of Savoy will be there all the same. And he thinks that our priests will destroy us. Nothing of the sort. We can manage our priests!'

Madame Variani made a gesture of dissent. Her heavy, handsome face was turned upon him rather sleepily, as though the heat oppressed her. But her slight frown betrayed, to anyone who knew her, alert attention.

'We can, I say!' cried the Count, striking his knee. 'Besides, the battle is not ranged as Manisty sees it. There are priests, and priests. Up in my part of the world the older priests are all right. We landowners who go with the monarchy can get on with them perfectly. Our old Bishop is a dear: but it is the young priests, fresh from the seminaries--I grant you, they're a nuisance! They swarm over us like locusts, ready for any bit of mischief against the Government. But the Government will win!--Italy will win! Manisty first of all takes the thing too tragically. He doesn't see the farce in it. We do. We Italians understand each other. Why, the Vatican raves and scolds--and all the while, as the Prefect of Police told me only the other day, there is a whole code of signals ready between the police headquarters and a certain

lightly.

'Dear, foolish, old man! he was telling me how he had gone back to the Hermitage Library at St. Petersburg the other day to read, after thirty years. And there in a book that had not been taken down since he had used it last he found a leaf of paper and some pencil words scribbled on it by him when he was a youth--"my own darling." "And if I only knew now *vich* darling!" he said, looking at me and slapping his knee. "Vich darling"!' Eleanor repeated, laughing extravagantly. Then suddenly she wavered. Lucy instinctively caught her by the arm, and Eleanor lent heavily upon her.

'Dear Mrs. Burgoyne--you are not well,' cried the girl, terrified. 'Let us go to a hotel where you can rest till the train goes--or to some friend.'

Eleanor's face set in the effort to control herself--she drew her hand across her eyes. 'No, no, I am well,' she said, hurriedly. 'It is the sun--and I could not eat at luncheon. The Ambassador's new cook did not tempt me. And besides'--she suddenly threw a look at Lucy before which Lucy shrank--'I am out of love with myself. There is one hour yesterday which I wish to cancel--to take back. I give up everything--everything.'

They were advancing across a wide lawn. The Ambassador and Mrs. Swetenham were coming to meet them. The Ambassador, weary of his companion, was looking with pleasure at the two approaching figures, at the sweep of Eleanor's white dress upon the grass, and the frame made by her black lace parasol for the delicacy of her head and neck.

Meanwhile Eleanor and Lucy saw only each other. The girl coloured proudly. She drew herself erect.

'You cannot give up--what would not be taken--what is not desired,' she said fiercely. Then, in another voice: 'But please, please let me take care of you! Don't let us go to the Villa Borghese!'

She felt her hand pressed passionately, then dropped.

'I am all right,' said Eleanor, almost in her usual voice. '*Eccellenza*! we must bid you good-bye--have you seen our gentleman?'

'*Ecco*,' said the Ambassador, pointing to Manisty, who, in company with the American Monsignore, was now approaching them. 'Let him take you out of the sun at once--you look as though it were too much for you.'

Manisty, however, came up slowly, in talk with his companion. The frowning impatience of his aspect attracted the attention of the group round the Ambassador. As he reached them, he said to the priest beside him--

'You know that he has withdrawn his recantation?'

'Ah! yes'--said the Monsignore, raising his eyebrows, 'poor fellow!'--

The mingled indifference and compassion of the tone made the words bite. Manisty flushed.

'I hear he was promised consideration,' he said quickly.

'Then he got it,' was the priest's smiling reply.

'He was told that his letter was not for publication. Next morning it appeared in the **Osservatore Romano**.'

'Oh no!--impossible! Your facts are incorrect.'

The Monsignore laughed, in unperturbed good humour. But after the laugh, the face reappeared, hard and a little menacing, like a rock that has been masked by a wave. He watched Manisty for a moment silently.

'Where is he?' said Manisty abruptly.

'Are you talking of Father Benecke'?' said the Ambassador. 'I heard of him yesterday. He has gone into the country, but he gave me no address. He wished to be undisturbed.'

'A wise resolve'--said the Monsignore, holding out his hand. 'Your Excellency must excuse me. I have an audience of his Holiness at three o'clock.'

He made his farewells to the ladies with Irish effusion, and departed. The Ambassador looked curiously at Manisty. Then he fell back with Lucy.

'It will be a column to-night,' he said with depression. 'Why didn't you stand by me? I showed Mrs. Swetenham my pictures--my beauties--my ewe-lambs--that I have been gathering for twenty years--that the National Gallery shall have, when I'm gone, if it behaves itself. And she asked me if they were originals, and took my Luini for a Raphael! Yes! it will be a column,' said the Ambassador pensively. Then, with a brisk change, he looked up and took the hand that Lucy offered him.

'Good-bye--good-bye! You won't forget my prescription?--nor me?' said the old man, smiling and patting her hand kindly. 'And remember!'--he bent towards her, dropping his voice with an air in which authority and sweetness mingled--'send Mr. Manisty home!'

He felt the sudden start in the girl's hand before he dropped it. Then he turned to Manisty himself.

'Ah! Manisty, here you are. Your ladies want to leave us.'

Manisty made his farewells, and carried Lucy off. But as they walked towards the house he said not a word, and Lucy, venturing a look at him, saw the storm on his brow, the stiffness of the lips.

'We are going to the Villa Borghese, are we not?' she said timidly--'if Mrs. Burgoyne ought to go?'

'We must go somewhere, I suppose,' he said, stalking on before her. 'We can't sit in the street.'

CHAPTER XIV

The party returning to Marinata had two hours to spend in the gallery and garden of the Villa Borghese. Of the pictures and statues of the palace, of the green undulations, the stone pines, the *tempietti* of the garden, Lucy afterwards had no recollection. All that she remembered was flight on her part, pursuit on Manisty's, and finally a man triumphant and a girl brought to bay.

It was in a shady corner of the vast garden, where hedges of some fragrant yellow shrub shut in the basin of a fountain, surrounded by a ring of languid nymphs, that Lucy at last found herself face to face with Manisty, and knew that she must submit.

'I do not understand how I have missed Mrs. Burgoyne,' she said hastily, looking round for her companion Mrs. Elliot, who had just left her to overtake her brother and go home; while Lucy was to meet Eleanor and Mr. Neal at this rendezvous.

Manisty looked at her with his most sparkling, most determined air.

'You have missed her—because I have misled her.' Then, as Lucy drew back, he hurried on,—'I cannot understand, Miss Foster, why it is that you have constantly refused all yesterday evening—all to-day—to give me the opportunity I desired! But I, too, have a will,—and it has been roused!

'I don't understand,' said Lucy, growing white.

'Let me explain, then,' said Manisty, coolly. 'Miss Foster, two nights ago you were attacked,—in danger—under my roof, in my care. As your host, you owe it to me, to let me account and apologise for such things—if I can. But you avoid me. You give me no chance of telling you what I had done to protect you—of expressing my infinite sorrow and regret. I can only imagine that you resent our negligence too deeply even to speak of it—that you cannot forgive us!'

'Forgive!' cried Lucy, fairly taken aback. 'What could I have to forgive, Mr. Manisty?--what can you mean?'

'Explain to me then,' said he, unflinching, 'why you have never had a kind word for me, or a kind look, since this happened. Please sit down, Miss Foster'--he pointed to a marble bench close beside her--'I will stand here. The others are far away. Ten minutes you owe me--ten minutes I claim.'

Lucy sat down, struggling to maintain her dignity and presence of mind.

'I am afraid I have given you very wrong ideas of me,' she said, throwing him a timid smile. 'I of course have nothing to forgive anybody--far, far the contrary. I know that you took all possible pains that no harm should happen to me. And through you--no harm did happen to me.'

She turned away her head, speaking with difficulty. To both that moment of frenzied struggle at the dining-room door was almost too horrible for remembrance. And through both minds there swept once more the thrill of her call to him--of his rush to her aid.

'You knew'--he said eagerly, coming closer.

'I knew--I was in danger--that but for you--perhaps--your poor sister--'

'Oh! don't speak of it,' he said, shuddering.

And leaning over the edge of one of the nymphs' pedestals, beside her, he stared silently into the cool green water.

'There,' said Lucy tremulously, 'you don't want to speak of it. And that was my feeling. Why should we speak of it any more? It must be such a horrible grief to you. And I can't do anything to help you and Miss Manisty. It would be so different if I could.'

'You can,--you must--let me tell you what I had done for your safety that night,' he said firmly, interrupting her. 'I had made such arrangements with Dalgetty--who is a strong woman physically--I had so imprisoned my poor sister, that I could not imagine any harm coming to you or any other of our party. When my aunt said to me that night before she went to bed that she was afraid your door was unsafe, I laughed--"That doesn't matter!" I said to her. I felt quite confident. I sat up all night,--but I was not anxious,--and I suppose it was that which at last betrayed me into sleep. Of course, the fatal thing was that we none of us knew of the chloroform she had hidden away.'

Lucy fidgetted in distress.

'Please--please--don't talk as though anyone were to blame--as though there were anything to make excuses for--'.

'How should there not be? You were disturbed--attacked--frightened. You might--'

He drew in his breath. Then he bent over her.

'Tell me,' he said in a low voice, 'did she attack you in your room?'

Lucy hesitated. 'Why will you talk about it?' she said despairingly.

'I have a right to know.'

His urgent imperious look left her no choice. She felt his will, and yielded. In very simple words, faltering yet restrained, she told the whole story. Manisty followed every word with breathless attention.

'My God!' he said, when she paused, 'my God!' And he hid his eyes with his hand a moment. Then--

'You knew she had a weapon?' he said.

'I supposed so,' she said quietly. 'All the time she was in my room, she kept her poor hand closed on something.'

'Her poor hand!'--the little phrase seemed to Manisty extraordinarily touching. There was a moment's pause--then he broke out:

'Upon my word, this has been a fine ending to the whole business. Miss Foster, when you came out to stay with us, you imagined, I suppose, that you were coming to stay with friends? You didn't know much of us; but after the kindness my aunt and I had experienced from your friends and kinsfolk in Boston--to put it in the crudest way--you might have expected at least that we should welcome you warmly--do all we could for you--take you everywhere--show you everything?'

Lucy coloured--then laughed.

'I don't know in the least what you mean, Mr. Manisty! I knew you would be kind to me; and of course--of course--you have been!'

She looked in distress first at the little path leading from the fountain, by which he barred her exit, and then at him. She seemed to implore, either that he would let her go, or that he would talk of something else.

'Not I,' he said with decision. 'I admit that since Alice appeared on the scene you have been my chief anxiety. But before that, I treated you, Miss Foster, with a discourtesy, a forgetfulness, that you can't, that you oughtn't to forget; I made no plans for your amusement; I gave you none of my time. On your first visit to Rome, I let you mope away day after day in that stifling garden, without taking a single thought for you. I even grudged it when Mrs. Burgoyne looked after you. To be quite, quite frank, I grudged your coming to us at all. Yet I was your host--you were in my care--I had invited you. If there ever was an ungentlemanly boor, it was I. There! Miss Foster, there is my confession. Can you forgive it? Will you give me another chance?'

He stood over her, his broad chest heaving with an agitation that, do what she would, communicated itself to her. She could not help it. She put out her hand, with a sweet look, half smiling, half appealing--and he took it. Then, as she hurriedly withdrew it, she repeated:

'There is nothing--nothing--to forgive. You have *all* been good to me. And as for Mrs. Burgoyne and Aunt Pattie, they have been just angels!'

Manisty laughed.

'I don't grudge them their wings. But I should like to grow a pair of my own. You have a fortnight more with us--isn't it so?' Lucy started and looked down. 'Well, in a fortnight, Miss Foster, I could yet redeem myself; I could make your visit really worth while. It is hot, but we could get round the heat. I have many opportunities here--friends who have the keys of things not generally seen. Trust yourself to me. Take me for a guide, a professor, a courier! At last I will give you a good time!'

He smiled upon her eagerly, impetuously. It was like him, this plan for mending all past errors in a moment, for a summary and energetic repentance. She could hardly help laughing; yet far within her heart made a leap towards him--beaten back at once by its own sad knowledge.

She turned away from him--away from his handsome face, and that touch in him of the 'imperishable child,' which moved and pleased her so. Playing with some flowers on her lap, she said shyly--

'Shall I tell you what you ought to do with this fortnight?'

'Tell me,' said Manisty, stooping towards her. It was well for her that she could not see his expression, as he took in with covetous delight her maidenly simpleness and sweetness.

'Oughtn't you--to finish the book? You could--couldn't you? And Mrs. Burgoyne has been so disappointed. It makes one sad to see her.'

Her words gave her courage. She looked at him again with a grave, friendly air.

Manisty drew himself suddenly erect. After a pause, he said in another voice: 'I thought I had explained to you before that the book and I had reached a *cul de sac*--that I no longer saw my way with it.'

Lucy thought of the criticisms upon it she had heard at the Embassy, and was uncomfortably silent.

'Miss Foster!' said Manisty suddenly, with determination.

Lucy's heart stood still.

'I believe I see the thought in your mind. Dismiss it! There have been rumours in Rome--in which even perhaps my aunt has believed. They are unjust--both to Eleanor and to me. She would be the first to tell you so.'

'Of course,' said Lucy hurriedly, 'of course,'--and then did not know what to say, torn as she was between her Puritan dread of falsehood, her natural woman's terror of betraying Eleanor, and her burning consciousness of the man and the personality beside her.

'No!--you still doubt. You have heard some gossip and you believe it.'

He threw away the cigarette with which he had been playing, and came to sit down on the curving marble bench beside her.

'I think you must listen to me,' he said, with a quiet and manly force that became him. 'The friendship between my cousin and me has been unusual, I know. It has been of a kind that French people, rather than English, understand; because for French people literature and conversation are serious matters, not trifles that don't count, as they are with us. She has been all sweetness and kindness to me, and I suppose that she, like a good many other people, has found me an unsatisfactory and disappointing person to work with!'

'She is so ill and tired,' said Lucy, in a low voice.

'Is she?' said Manisty, concerned. 'But she never can stand heat. She will pick up when she gets to England.--But now suppose we grant all my enormities. Then please tell me what I am to do? How am I to appease Eleanor?--and either transform the book, to satisfy Neal,--or else bury it decently? Beastly thing!--as if it were worth one tithe of the trouble it has cost her and me. Yet there are some uncommon good things in it too!' he said, with a change of tone.

'Well, if you did bury it,' said Lucy, half laughing, yet trying to pluck up courage to obey the Ambassador,--'what would you do? Go back to England?--and--and to your property?'

'What! has that dear old man been talking to you?' he said with amusement. 'I thought as much. He has snubbed my views and me two or three times lately. I don't mind. He is one of the privileged. So the Ambassador thinks I should go home?'

He threw one arm over the back of the seat, and threw her a brilliant hectoring look which led her on.

'Don't people in England think so too?'

'Yes--some of them,' he said considering. 'I have been bombarded with letters lately as to politics, and the situation, and a possible new constituency. A candid friend says to me this morning, "Hang the Italians!--what do you know about them,--and what do they matter? English people can only be frightened by their own bogies. Come home, for God's sake! There's a glorious fight coming, and if you're not in it, you'll be a precious fool."'

'I daren't be as candid as that!' said Lucy, her face quivering with suppressed fun.

Their eyes met in a common flash of laughter. Then Manisty fell heavily back against the seat.

'What have I got to go home for?' he said abruptly, his countenance darkening.

Lucy's aspect changed too, instantly. She waited.

Manisty's lower jaw dropped a little. A sombre bitterness veiled the eyes fixed upon the distant vistas of the garden.

'I hate my old house,' he said slowly. 'Its memories are intolerable. My father was a very eminent person, and had many friends. His children saw nothing of him, and had not much reason to love him. My mother died there--of an illness it is appalling to think of. No, no--not Alice's illness!--not that. And now, Alice,--I should see her ghost at every corner!'

Lucy watched him with fascination. Every note of the singular voice, every movement of the picturesque ungainly form, already spoke to her, poor child, with a significance that bit these passing moments into memory, as an etcher's acid bites upon his plate.

'Oh! she will recover!' she said, softly, leaning towards him unconsciously.

'No!--she will never recover,--never! And if she did, she and I have long ceased to be companions and friends. No, Miss Foster, there is nothing to call me home,--except politics. I may set up a lodging in London, of course. But as for playing the country squire--' He laughed, and shrugged his shoulders. 'No,--I shall let the place as soon as I can. Anyway, I shall never return to it--alone!'

He turned upon her suddenly. The tone in which the last word was spoken, the steady ardent look with which it was accompanied, thrilled the hot May air.

A sickening sense of peril, of swift intolerable remorse, rushed upon Lucy. It gave her strength.

She changed her position, and spoke with perfect self-possession, gathering up her parasol and gloves.

'We really must find the others, Mr. Manisty. They will wonder what has become of us.'

She rose as she spoke. Manisty drew a long breath as he still sat observing her. Her light, cool dignity showed him that he was either not understood--or too well understood. In either case he was checked. He took back his move; not without a secret pleasure that she was not too yielding--too much of the *ingenue*!

'We shall soon discover them,' he said carelessly, relighting his cigarette. 'By the way, I saw what company you were in after lunch! You didn't hear any good of the book or me--there!'

'I liked them all,' she said with spirit. 'They love their country, and they believe in her. Where, Mr. Manisty, did you leave Mr. Neal and Mrs. Burgoyne?'

'I will show you,' he said, unwillingly. 'They are in a part of the garden you don't know.'

Her eye was bright, a little hostile. She moved resolutely forward, and Manisty followed her. Both were conscious of a hidden amazement. But a minute, since he had spoken that word, looked that look? How strange a thing is human life! He would not let himself think,--talked of he hardly knew what.

'They love their country, you say? Well, I grant you that particular group has pure hands, and isn't plundering their country's vitals like the rest--as far as I know. A set of amiable dreamers, however, they appear to me; fiddling at small reforms, while the foundations are sinking from under them. However, you liked them,-

-that's enough. Now then, when and how shall we begin our campaign? Where will you go?--what will you see? The crypt of St. Peter's?--that wants a Cardinal's order. The Villa Albani?--closed to the public since the Government laid hands on the Borghese pictures,--but it shall open to you. The great function at the Austrian Embassy next week with all the Cardinals? Give me your orders,--it will be hard if I can't compass them!'

But she was silent, and he saw that she still hurried, that her look sought the distance, that her cheek was flushed. Why? What new thing had he said to press--to disturb her? A spark of emotion passed through him. He approached her gently, persuasively, as one might approach a sweet, resisting child--

You'll come? You'll let me make amends?'

'I thought,' said Lucy, uncertainly, 'that you were going home directly--at the beginning of June. Oh! please, Mr. Manisty, will you look? Is that Mrs. Burgoyne?'

Manisty frowned.

'They are not in that direction.--As to my going home, Miss Foster, I have no engagements that I cannot break.'

The wounded feeling in the voice was unmistakable. It hurt her ear.

'I should love to see all those things,' she said vaguely, still trying, as it seemed to him, to outstrip him, to search the figures in the distance; 'but--but--plans are so difficult. Oh! that is--that is Mr. Neal!'

She began to run towards the approaching figure, and presently Manisty could hear her asking breathlessly for Mrs. Burgoyne.

Manisty stood still. Then as they approached him, he said--

'Neal!--well met! Will you take these ladies to the station, or, at any rate, put them in their cab? It is time for their train. I dine in Rome.'

He raised his hat formally to Lucy, turned, and went his way.

*　　　*　　　*　　　*　　　*

It was night at the villa.

Eleanor was in her room, the western room overlooking the olive-ground and the Campagna, which Lucy had occupied for a short time on her first arrival.

It was about half an hour since Eleanor had heard Manisty's cab arrive, and his voice in the library giving his orders to Alfredo. She and Lucy Foster and Aunt Pattie had already dispersed to their rooms. It was strange that he should have dined in town. It had been expressly arranged on their way to Rome that he should bring them back.

Eleanor was sitting in a low chair beside a table that carried a paraffin lamp. At her back was the window, which was open save for the sun-shutter outside, and the curtains, both of which had been drawn close. A manuscript diary lay on Eleanor's lap, and she was listlessly turning it over, with eyes that saw nothing, and hands that hardly knew what they touched. Her head, with its aureole of loosened hair, was thrown back against the chair, and the crude lamplight revealed each sharpened feature with a merciless plainness. She was a woman no longer young-- ill--and alone.

By the help of the entries before her she had been living the winter over again.

How near and vivid it was,--how incredibly, tangibly near!--and yet as dead as the Caesars on the Palatine.

For instance:--

'November 22. To-day we worked well. Three hours this morning--nearly three this afternoon. The survey of the financial history since 1870 is nearly finished. I could not have held out so long, but for his eagerness, for my head ached, and last night it seemed to me that Rome was all bells, and that the clocks never ceased striking.

'But how his eagerness carries one through, and his frank and generous recognition of all that one does for him! Sometimes I copy and arrange; sometimes he dictates; sometimes I just let him talk till he has got a page or section into shape. Even in this handling of finance, you feel the flame that makes life with him so exciting. It is absurd to say, as his enemies do, that he has no steadiness of purpose. I have seen him go through the most tremendous drudgery the last few weeks,--and then throw it all into shape with the most astonishing ease and rapidity. And he is delightful to work with. He weighs all I say. But no false politeness! If he doesn't like it, he frowns and bites his lip, and tears me to pieces. But very often I prevail, and no one can yield with a better grace. People here talk of his vanity. I don't deny it--perhaps I think it part of his charm.

'He thinks too much of me, far, far too much.

'December 16. A luncheon at the Marchesa's. The Fioravantis were there, and some Liberal Catholics. Manisty was attacked on all sides. At first he was silent and rather sulky--it is not always easy to draw him. Then he fired up,--and it was wonderful how he met them all in an Italian almost as quick as their own. I think they were amazed: certainly I was.

'Of course I sometimes wish that it were conviction with him and not policy. My heart aches, hungers sometimes--for another note. If instead of this praise from outside, this cool praise of religion as the great policeman of the world, if only his voice, his dear voice, spoke for one moment the language of faith!--all barren tension and grief and doubt would be gone then for me, at a breath. But it never, never does. And I remind myself--painfully--that his argument holds whether the arguer believe or no. "Somehow or other you must get conduct out of the masses or society goes to pieces. But you can only do this through religion. What folly, then, for nations like Italy and France to quarrel with the only organisation which can ever get conduct out of the ignorant!--in the way they understand!"--It is all so true. I know it by heart--there is no answering it. But if instead he once said to me--"Eleanor, there is a God!--and it is He that has brought us together in this life and work,--He that will comfort you, and open new ways for me"--Ah then--then!--

*   *   *   *   *

'Christmas Day. We went last night to the midnight mass at Santa Maria Maggiore. Edward is always incalculable at these functions; sometimes bored to death, sometimes all enthusiasm and sympathy. Last night the crowd jarred him, and I wished we had not come. But as we walked home through the moonlit streets, full of people hurrying in and out of the churches, of the pifferari with their cloaks and pipes--black and white nuns--brown monks--lines of scarlet seminarists, and the like, he suddenly broke out with the prayer of the First Christmas Mass--I must give it in English, for I have forgotten the Latin:

'"*O God, who didst cause this most holy Night to be illumined by the rising of the true Light, we beseech Thee that we who know on earth the secret shining of His splendour may win in Heaven His eternal joys.*"

'We were passing through Monte Cavallo, beside the Two Divine Horsemen who saved Rome of old. The light shone on the fountains--it seemed as if the two godlike figures were just about to leap, in fierce young strength, upon their horses.

'Edward stopped to look at them.

'"And we say that the world lives by Science! Fools! when has it lived by anything else than Dreams--at Athens, at Rome, or Jerusalem?"

'We stayed by the fountains talking. And as we moved away, I said: "How strange at my age to be enjoying Christmas for the first time!" And he looked at me as though I had given him pleasure, and said with his most delightful smile--"Who else should enjoy life if not you--kind, kind Eleanor?"

'When I got home, and to my room, I opened my windows wide. Our apartment is at the end of the Via Sistina, and has a marvellous view over Rome. It was a gorgeous moon--St. Peter's, the hills, every dome and tower radiantly clear. And at last it seemed to me that I was not a rebel and an outlaw--that beauty and I were reconciled.

'Such peace in the night! It opened and took me in. Oh! my little, little son!--I have had such strange visions of you all these last days. That horror of the whirling river--and the tiny body--tossed and torn. Oh! my God! my God!--has it not filled all my days and nights for eight years? And now I see him so no more. I see him always carried in the arms of dim majestic forms--wrapped close and warm. Sometimes the face that bends over him is that of some great Giotto angel--sometimes, so dim and faint! the pure Mother herself--sometimes the Hands that fold him in are marred. Is it the associations of Rome--the images with which this work with Edward fills my mind? Perhaps.

'But at least I am strangely comforted--some kind hand seems to be drawing the smart from the deep deep wound. Little golden-head! you lie soft and safe, but often you seem to me to turn your dear eyes--the baby-eyes that still know all--to look out over the bar of heaven--to search for me--to bid me be at peace, *at last*.

'February 20. How delicious is the first breath of the spring! The almond trees are pink in the Campagna. The snow on the Sabine peaks is going. The Piazza di Spagna is heaped with flowers--anemones and narcissus and roses. And for the first time in my life I too feel the "Sehnsucht"--the longing of the spring! At twenty-nine!'

'March 24, Easter week. I went to a wedding at the English church to-day.

Some barrier seems to have fallen between me and life. The bride--a dear girl who has often been my little companion this winter--kissed me as she was going up to take off her dress. And I threw my arms round her with such a rush of joy. Other women have felt all these things ten years earlier perhaps than I. But they are not less heavenly when they come late--into a heart seared with grief.

'March 26. It is my birthday. From the window looking on the Piazza, I have just seen Edward bargaining with the flower woman. Those lilacs and pinks are for me--I know it! Already he has given me the little engraved emerald I wear at my watch-chain. A little genius with a torch is cut upon it. He said I was to take it as the genius of our friendship.

'I changed the orders for my dress to-day. I have discovered that black is positively disagreeable to him. So Mathilda will have to devise something else.

'April 5. He is away at Florence, and I am working at some difficult points for him--about some suppressed monasteries. I have asked Count B--, who knows all about such things, to help me, and am working very hard. He comes back in four days.

'April 9. He came back to-day. Such a gay and happy evening. When he saw what I had done, he took both my hands, and kissed them impetuously. "Eleanor, my queen of cousins!" And now we shall be at the villa directly. And there will be no interruption. There is one visitor coming. But Aunt Pattie will look after her. I think the book should be out in June. Of course there are some doubtful things. But it must, it will have a great effect.--How wonderfully well I have been lately! The doctor last week looked at me in astonishment. He thought that the Shadow and I were to be soon acquainted, when he saw me first!

'I hope that Edward will get as much inspiration from the hills as from Rome. Every little change makes me anxious. Why should we change? Dear beloved, golden Rome!--even to be going fourteen miles away from you somehow tears my heart.'

* * * * *

Yes, there they were, those entries,--mocking, ineffaceable, for ever.

As she had read them, driving through all the memories they suggested, like a keen and bitter wind that kills and blights the spring bloom, there had pressed upon her the last memory of all,--the memory of this forlorn, this intolerable day. Had Manisty ever yet forgotten her so completely--abandoned her so utterly? She had simply dropped out of his thoughts. She had become as much of a stranger to him again, as on her first arrival at Rome. Nay, more! For when two people are first brought into a true contact, there is the secret delightful sense on either side of possibilities, of the unexplored. But when the possibilities are all known, and all exhausted?

What had happened between him and Lucy Foster? Of course she understood that he had deliberately contrived their interview. But as Lucy and she came home together they had said almost nothing to each other. She had a vision of their two silent figures in the railway-carriage side by side,--her hand in Lucy's. And Lucy--so sad and white herself!--with the furrowed brow that betrayed the inner stress of thought.

Had the crisis arrived?--and had she refused him? Eleanor had not dared to ask.

Suddenly she rose from her chair. She clasped her hands above her head, and began to walk tempestuously up and down the bare floor of her room. In this creature so soft, so loving, so compact of feeling and of tears, there had gradually arisen an intensity of personal claim, a hardness, almost a ferocity of determination, which was stiffening and transforming the whole soul. She could waver still--as she had wavered in that despairing, anguished moment with Lucy in the Embassy garden. But the wavering would soon be over. A jealousy so overpowering that nothing could make itself heard against it was closing upon her like a demoniacal possession. Was it the last effort of self-preservation?--the last protest of the living thing against its own annihilation?

He was not to be hers--but this treachery, this wrong should be prevented.

She thought of Lucy in Manisty's arms--of that fresh young life against his breast--and the thought maddened her. She was conscious of a certain terror of herself--of this fury in the veins, so strange, so alien, so debasing. But it did not affect her will.

Was Lucy's own heart touched? Over that question Eleanor had been racking herself for days past. But if so it could be only a passing fancy. It made it only the more a duty to protect her from Manisty. Manisty--the soul of caprice and wilfulness--could never make a woman like Lucy happy. He would tire of her and neglect her. And what would be left for Lucy--Lucy the upright, simple, profound--but heartbreak?

Eleanor paused absently in front of the glass, and then looked at herself with a start of horror. That face--to fight with Lucy's!

On the dressing-table there were still lying the two terra-cotta heads from Nemi, the Artemis, and the Greek fragment with the clear brow and nobly parted hair, in which Manisty had seen and pointed out the likeness to Lucy. Eleanor recalled his words in the garden--his smiling, absorbed look as the girl approached.

Yes!--it was like her. There was the same sweetness in strength, the same adorable roundness and youth.

And that was the beauty that Eleanor had herself developed and made doubly visible--as a man may free a diamond from the clay.

A mad impulse swept through her--that touch of kinship with the criminal and the murderer that may reveal itself in the kindest and the noblest.

She took up the little mask, and, reaching to the window, she tore back the curtains and pushed open the sun-shutters outside.

The night burst in upon her, the starry night hanging above the immensity of the Campagna, and the sea. There was still a faint glow in the western heaven. On the plain were a few scattered lights, fires lit, perhaps, by wandering herdsmen against malaria. On the far edge of the land to the south-west, a revolving light flashed its message to the Mediterranean and the passing ships. Otherwise, not a sign of life. Below, a vast abyss of shadow swallowed up the olive-garden, the road, and the lower slopes of the hills.

Eleanor felt herself leaning out above the world, alone with her agony and the balmy peace which mocked it. She lifted her arm, and, stretching forward, she flung the little face violently into the gulf beneath. The villa rose high above the olive-ground, and the olive-ground itself sank rapidly towards the road. The fragment had far to fall. It seemed to Eleanor that in the deep stillness she heard a sound like the striking of a stone among thick branches. Her mind followed with a wild triumph the breaking of the terra-cotta,--the shivering of the delicate features--their burial in the stony earth.

With a long breath she tottered from the window and sank into her chair. A horrible feeling of illness overtook her, and she found herself gasping for breath. 'If I could only reach that medicine on my table!' she thought. But she could not reach it. She lay helpless.

The door opened.

Was it a dream? She seemed to struggle through rushing waters back to land.

There was a low cry. A light step hurried across the room. Lucy Foster sank on her knees beside her and threw her arms about her.

'Give me--those drops--on the table,' said Eleanor, with difficulty.

Lucy said not a word. Quietly, with steady hands, she brought and measured the medicine. It was a strong heart-stimulant, and it did its work. But while her strength came back, Lucy saw that she was shivering with cold, and closed the window.

Then, silently, Lucy looked down upon the figure in the chair. She was almost as white as Eleanor. Her eyes showed traces of tears. Her forehead was still drawn with thought as it had been in the train.

Presently she sank again beside Eleanor.

'I came to see you, because I could not sleep, and I wanted to suggest a plan to you. I had no idea you were ill. You should have called me before.'

Eleanor put out a feeble hand. Lucy took it tenderly, and laid it against her cheek. She could not understand why Eleanor looked, at her with this horror and wildness,--how it was that she came to be up, by this open window, in this state of illness and collapse. But the discovery only served an antecedent process--a struggle from darkness to light--which had brought her to Eleanor's room.

She bent forward and said some words in Eleanor's ear.

Gradually Eleanor understood and responded. She raised herself piteously in her chair. The two women sat together, hand locked in hand, their faces near to each other, the murmur of their voices flowing on brokenly, for nearly an hour.

Once Lucy rose to get a guide book that lay on Eleanor's table. And on another occasion, she opened a drawer by Eleanor's direction, took out a leather pocket-book and counted some Italian notes that it contained. Finally she insisted on Eleanor's going to bed, and on helping her to undress.

Eleanor had just sunk into her pillows, when a noise from the library startled them. Eleanor looked up with strained eyes.

'It must be Mr. Manisty,' said Lucy hurriedly. 'He was out when I came through the glass passage. The doors were all open, and his lamp burning.' I am nearly sure that I heard him unbar the front door. I must wait now till he is gone.'

They waited--Eleanor staring into the darkness of the room--till there had been much opening and shutting of doors, and all was quiet again.

Then the two women clung to each other in a strange and pitiful embrace--offered with passion on Lucy's side, accepted with a miserable shame on Eleanor's--and Lucy slipped away.

'He was out?--in the garden?' said Eleanor to herself bewildered. And with those questions on her lips, and a mingled remorse and fever in her blood, she lay sleepless waiting for the morning.

*   *   *   *   *

Manisty indeed had also been under the night, bathing passion and doubt in its cool purity.

Again and again had he wandered up and down the terrace in the starlight, proving and examining his own heart, raised by the growth of love to a more manly and more noble temper than had been his for years.

What was in his way? His conduct towards his cousin? He divined what seemed to him the scruple in the girl's sensitive and tender mind. He could only meet it by truth and generosity--by throwing himself on Eleanor's mercy. ***She*** knew what their relations had been--she would not refuse him this boon of life and death--the explanation of them to Lucy.

Unless! There came a moment when his restless walk was tormented with the prickly rise of a whole new swarm of fears. He recalled that moment in the library after the struggle with Alice, when Lucy was just awakening from unconsciousness--when Eleanor came in upon them. Had she heard? He remembered that the possibility of it had crossed his mind. Was she in truth working against him--avenging his neglect--establishing a fatal influence over Lucy?

His soul cried out in fierce and cruel protest. Here at last was the great passion of his life. Come what would, Eleanor should not be allowed to strangle it.

Absently he wandered down a little path leading from the terrace to the *podere* below, and soon found himself pacing the dim grass walks among the olives. The old villa rose above him, dark and fortress-like. That was no longer her room-- that western corner? No--he had good cause to remember that she had been moved, to the eastern side, beyond his library, beyond the glass passage! Those were now Eleanor's windows, he believed.

Ah!--what was that sudden light? He threw his head back in astonishment. One of the windows at which he had been looking was flung open, and in the bright lamplight a figure appeared. It stooped forward. Eleanor! Something fell close beside him. He heard the breaking of a branch from one of the olives.

In his astonishment, he stood motionless, watching the window. It remained open for a while. Then again some one appeared--not the same figure as at first. A thrill of delight and trouble ran through him. He sent his salutation, his homage through the night.

But the window shut--the light went out. All was once more still and dark.

Then he struck a match and groped under the tree close by him. Yes, there was the fallen branch. But what had broken it? He lit match after match, holding the light with his left hand while he turned over the dry ground with his knife. Presently he brought up a handful of stones and earth, and laid them on a bit of ruined wall close by. Stooping over them with his dim, sputtering lights, he presently discovered some terra-cotta fragments. His eye, practised in such things, detected them at once. They were the fragments of a head, which had measured about three inches from brow to chin.

The head, or rather the face, which he had given Eleanor at Nemi! The parting of the hair above the brow was intact--so was the beautiful curve of the cheek.

He knew it--and the likeness to Lucy. He remembered his words to Eleanor in the garden. Holding the pieces in his hand, he went slowly back towards the terrace.

Thrown out?--flung out into the night--by Eleanor? But why? He thought--

and thought. A black sense of entanglement and fate grew upon him in the darkness, as he thought of the two women together, in the midnight silence, while he was pacing thus, alone. He met it with the defiance of newborn passion--with the resolute planning of a man who feels himself obscurely threatened, and realises that his chief menace lies, not in the power of any outside enemy, but in the very goodness of the woman he loves.

PART II.

'Alas! there is no instinct like the heart--

The heart--which may be broken: happy they!
Thrice fortunate! who of that fragile mould,
The precious porcelain of human clay,
Break with the first fall: they can ne'er behold
The long year linked with heavy clay on day,
And all which must be borne, and never told.'

CHAPTER XV

Can you stand this heat?' said Lucy, anxiously.

'Oh, it will soon be cooler,' was Eleanor's languid reply.

She and Lucy sat side by side in a large and ancient landau; Mrs. Burgoyne's maid, Marie Vefour, was placed opposite to them, a little sulky and silent. On the box, beside the driver of the lean brown horses, was a bright-eyed, neatly-dressed youth who was going with the ladies to Torre Amiata.

They had just left the hill-town of Orvieto, had descended rapidly into the valley lying to the south-west of its crested heights, and were now mounting again on the further side. As they climbed higher and higher Lucy, whose attention had been for a time entirely absorbed by the weariness of the frail woman beside her, began to realise that they were passing through a scene of extraordinary beauty. Her eyes, which had been drawn and anxious, relaxed. She looked round her with a natural and rising joy.

To their left, as the road turned in zig-zag to the east, was the marvellous town which the traveller who has seen Palestine likens to Jerusalem, so steep and high and straight is the crest of warm brown and orange precipice on which it stands, so deep the valleys round it, so strange and complete the fusion between the city and the rock, so conspicuous the place of the great cathedral, which is Orvieto, as the Temple was Zion.

It was the sixth of June, and the day had been very hot. The road was deep in thick white dust. The fig-trees and vines above the growing crops were almost at a full leafiness; scarlet poppies grew thick among the corn; and at the dusty edges of the road, wild roses of a colour singularly vivid and deep, the blue flowers of love-in-a-mist, and some spikes of wine-coloured gladiolus struck strangely on a northern eye.

Then as the road turned back again--behold! a great valley, opening out westward, beyond Orvieto,--the valley of the Paglia; a valley with wooded hills on either side, of a bluish-green colour, chequered with hill-towns and slim campaniles and winding roads; and binding it all in one, the loops and reaches of a full brown river. Heat everywhere!--on the blinding walls of the buildings, on the young green of the vineyards, on the yellowing corn, on the beautiful ragged children running barefoot and bareheaded beside the carriage, on the peasants working among the vines, on the drooping heads of the horses, on the brick-red face of the driver.

'If Madame had only stayed at Orvieto!' murmured Marie the maid, looking back at the city and then at her mistress.

Eleanor smiled faintly and tapped the girl's hand.

'*Rassure-toi*, Marie! Remember how soon we made ourselves comfortable at the villa.'

Marie shook her much be-curled head. Because it had taken them three months to make the Marinata villa decently habitable, was that any reason for tempting the wilderness again?

Lucy, too, had her misgivings. Nominally she was travelling, she supposed, under Eleanor Burgoyne's chaperonage. Really she was the guardian of the whole party, and she was conscious of a tender and anxious responsibility. Already they had been delayed a whole week in Orvieto by Eleanor's prostrate state. She had not been dangerously ill; but it had been clearly impossible to leave doctor and chemist behind and plunge into the wilds. So they had hidden themselves in a little Italian inn in a back street, and the days had passed somehow.

*   *   *   *   *

Surely this hot evening and their shabby carriage and the dusty unfamiliar road were all dream-stuff--an illusion from which she was to wake directly and find herself once more in her room at Marinata, looking out on Monte Cavo?

Yet as this passed across Lucy's mind, she felt again upon her face the cool morning wind, as she and Eleanor fled down the Marinata hill in the early sunlight, between six and seven o'clock,--through the streets of Albano, already full and busy,--along the edge of that strange green crater of Aricia, looking up to Pio Nono's great viaduct, and so to Cecchina, the railway station in the plain.

An escape!--nothing else; planned the night before when Lucy's strong commonsense had told her that the only chance for her own peace and Eleanor's was to go at once, to stop any further development of the situation, and avoid any fresh scene with Mr. Manisty.

She thought of the details--the message left for Aunt Pattie that they had gone into Rome to shop before the heat; then the telegram 'Urgente,' despatched to the villa after they were sure that Mr. Manisty must have safely left it for that important field day of his clerical and Ultramontane friends in Rome, in which he was pledged to take part; then the arrival of the startled and bewildered Aunt Pattie at the small hotel where they were in hiding--her conferences--first with Eleanor, then with Lucy.

Strange little lady, Aunt Pattie! How much had she guessed? What had passed between her and Mrs. Burgoyne? When at last she and Lucy stood together hand in hand, the girl's sensitive spirit had divined in her a certain stiffening, a certain diminution of that constant kindness which she had always shown her guest. Did Aunt Pattie blame her? Had she cherished her own views and secret hopes for her nephew and Mrs. Burgoyne? Did she feel that Lucy had in some way unwarrantably and ambitiously interfered with them?

At any rate, Lucy had divined the unspoken inference 'You must have given him encouragement!' and behind it--perhaps?--the secret ineradicable pride of family and position that held her no fitting match for Edward Manisty. Lucy's inmost mind was still sore and shrinking from this half-hour's encounter with Aunt Pattie.

But she had not shown it. And at the end of it Aunt Pattie had kissed her ruefully with tears--'It's *very* good of you! You'll take care of Eleanor!'

Lucy could hear her own answer--'Indeed, indeed, I will!'--and Aunt Pattie's puzzled cry, 'If only someone would tell me what I'm to do with *him*!'

And then she recalled her own pause of wonder as Aunt Pattie left her--beside the hotel window, looking into the narrow side street. Why was it 'very good of her'?--and why, nevertheless, was this dislocation of all their plans felt to be somehow her fault and responsibility?--even by herself? There was a sudden helpless inclination to laugh over the topsy-turviness of it all.

And then her heart had fluttered in her breast, stabbed by the memory of Eleanor's cry the night before. 'It is of no use to say that you know nothing--that he has said nothing. *I* know. If you stay, he will give you no peace--his will is indomitable. But if you go, he will guess my part in it. I shall not have the physical strength to conceal it--and he can be a hard man when he is resisted! What am I to do? I would go home at once--but--I might die on the way. Why not?'

And then--in painful gasps--the physical situation had been revealed to her--the return of old symptoms and the reappearance of arrested disease. The fear of the physical organism alternating with the despair of the lonely and abandoned soul,--never could Lucy forget the horror of that hour's talk, outwardly so quiet, as she sat holding Eleanor's hands in hers, and the floodgates of personality and of grief were opened before her.

*   *   *   *   *

Meanwhile the patient, sweating horses climbed and climbed. Soon they were at the brow of the hill, and looking back for their last sight of Orvieto. And now they were on a broad tableland, a bare, sun-baked region where huge flocks of sheep, of white, black, and brown goats wandered with ragged shepherds over acres of burnt and thirsty pasture. Here and there were patches of arable land and groups of tilling peasants in the wide untidy expanse; once or twice too an *osteria*, with its bush or its wine-stained tables under the shadow of its northern wall. But scarcely a farmhouse. Once indeed a great building like a factory or a workhouse, in the midst of wide sun-beaten fields. 'Ecco! la fattoria,' said the driver, pointing to it. And once a strange group of underground dwellings, their chimneys level with the surrounding land, whence wild swarms of troglodyte children rushed up from the bowels of the earth to see the carriage pass and shriek for *soldi*.

But the beauty of the sun-scorched upland was its broom! Sometimes they were in deep tufa lanes; like English lanes, save for their walls and canopies of gold; sometimes they journeyed through wide barren stretches, where only broom held the soil against all comers, spreading in sheets of gold beneath the dazzling sky. Large hawks circled overhead; in the rare woods the nightingales were loud and merry; and goldfinches were everywhere. A hot, lonely, thirsty land--the heart of Italy--where the rocks are honeycombed with the tombs of that mysterious Etruscan race, the Melchisedek of the nations, coming no one knows whence, 'without father and without mother'--a land which has to the west of it the fever-stricken Maremma and the heights of the Amiata range, and to the south the forest country of Viterbo.

Eleanor looked out upon the road and the fields with eyes that faintly remembered, and a heart held now, as always, in the grip of that *tempo felice* which was dead.

It was she who had proposed this journey. Once in late November she and Aunt Pattie and Manisty had spent two or three days at Orvieto with some Italian friends. They had made the journey back to Rome, partly by *vetturino*, driving from Orvieto to Bolsena and Viterbo, and spending a night on the way at a place of remote and enchanting beauty which had left a deep mark on Eleanor's imagination. They owed the experience to their Italian friends, acquaintances of the great proprietor whose agent gave the whole party hospitality for the night; and as they jogged on through this June heat she recalled with bitter longing the bright November day, the changing leaves, the upland air, and Manisty's delight in the strange unfamiliar country, in the vast oak woods above the Paglia, and the marvellous church at Monte Fiascone.

But it was not the agent's house, the scene of their former stay, to which she was now guiding Lucy. When she and Manisty, hurrying out for an early walk before the carriage started, had explored a corner of the dense oak woods below the **palazzo** on the hill, they had come across a deserted convent, with a conta-dino's family in one corner of it, and a ruinous chapel with a couple of dim frescoes attributed to Pinturicchio.

How well she remembered Manisty's rage over the spoliation of the convent and the ruin of the chapel! He had gone stalking over the deserted place, raving against 'those brigands from Savoy,' and calculating how much it would cost to buy back the place from the rascally Municipio of Orvieto, to whom it now belonged, and return it to its former Carmelite owners.

Meanwhile Eleanor had gossiped with the **massaja**, or farmer's wife, and had found out that there were a few habitable rooms in the convent still, roughly fur-nished, and that in summer, people of a humble sort came there sometimes from Orvieto for coolness and change--the plateau being 3,000 feet above the sea. Elea-nor had inquired if English people ever came.

'*Inglesi! no!--mai Inglesi*,' said the woman in astonishment.

The family were, however, in some sort of connection with an hotel propri-etor at Orvieto, through whom they got their lodgers. Eleanor had taken down the name and all particulars in a fit of enthusiasm for the beauty and loneliness of the place. 'Suppose some day we came here to write?' Manisty had said vaguely, looking round him with regret as they drove away. The mere suggestion had made the name of Torre Amiata sweet to Eleanor thenceforward.

Was it likely that he would remember?--that he would track them? Hardly. He would surely think that in this heat they would go northward. He would not dream of looking for them in Italy.

She too was thinking of nothing--nothing!--but the last scenes at the villa and in Rome, as the carriage moved along. The phrases of her letter to Manisty ran through her mind. Had they made him her lasting enemy? The thought was like a wound draining blood and strength. But in her present state of jealous passion it was more tolerable than that other thought which was its alternative--the thought of Lucy surrendered, Lucy in her place.

'Lucy Foster is with me,' she had written. 'We wish to be together for a while before she goes back to America. And that we may be quite alone, we prefer to give no address for a few weeks. I have written to Papa to say that I am going away for a time with a friend, to rest and recruit. You and Aunt Pattie could easily arrange that there should be no talk and no gossip about the matter. I hope and think you will. Of course if we are in any strait or difficulty we shall communicate at once with our friends.'

How had he received it? Sometimes she thought of his anger and disappointment with terror, sometimes with a vindictive excitement that poisoned all her being. Gentleness turned to hate and violence,--was it of that in truth, and not of that heart mischief to which doctors gave long names, that Eleanor Burgoyne was dying?

*   *   *   *   *

They had turned into a wide open space crossed by a few wire fences at vast intervals. The land was mostly rough pasture, or mere sandy rock and scrub. In the glowing west, towards which they journeyed, rose far purple peaks peering over the edge of the great tableland. To the east and south vast woods closed in the horizon.

The carriage left the main road and entered an ill-defined track leading apparently through private property.

'Ah! I remember!' cried Eleanor, starting up. 'There is the *palazzo*--and the village.'

In front of them, indeed, rose an old villa of the Renaissance, with its long flat roofs, its fine *loggia*, and terraced vineyards. A rude village of grey stone, part, it seemed, of the tufa rocks from which it sprang, pressed round the villa, invaded its olive-gardens, crept up to its very walls. Meanwhile the earth grew kinder and more fertile. The vines and figs stood thick again among the green corn and flowering lucerne. Peasants streaming home from work, the men on donkeys, the women carrying their babies, met the carriage and stopped to stare after it, and talk.

Suddenly from the ditches of the roadside sprang up two martial figures.

'Carabinieri!' cried Lucy in delight.

She had made friends with several members of this fine corps on the closely guarded roads about the Alban lake, and to see them here gave her a sense of protection.

Bending over the side of the carriage, she nodded to the two handsome brown-skinned fellows, who smiled back at her.

'How far,' she said, 'to Santa Trinita?'

'*Un miglio grasso* (a good mile), Signorina. ***E tutto***. But you are late. They expected you half an hour ago.'

The driver took this for reproach, and with a shrill burst of defence pointed to his smoking horses. The Carabinieri laughed, and diving into the field, one on either side, they kept up with the carriage as it neared the village.

'Why, it is like coming home!' said Lucy, wondering. And indeed they were now surrounded by the whole village population, just returned from the fields--pointing, chattering, laughing, shouting friendly directions to the driver. 'Santa Trinita!' 'Ecco!--Santa Trinita!' sounded on all sides, amid a forest of gesticulating hands.

'How could they know?' said Eleanor, looking at the small crowd with startled eyes. Lucy spoke a word to the young man on the box.

'They knew, he says, as soon as the carriage was ordered yesterday. Look! there are the telegraph wires! The whole countryside knows! They are greatly excited by the coming of *forestieri*--especially at this time of year.'

'Oh! we can't stay!' said Eleanor with a little moan, wringing her hands.

'It's only the country people,' said Lucy tenderly, taking one of the hands in hers. 'Did you see the Contessa when you were here before?'

And she glanced up at the great yellow mass of the *palazzo* towering above the little town, the sunset light flaming on its long western face.

'No. She was away. And the *fattore* who took us in left in January. There is a new man.'

'Then it's quite safe!' said Lucy in French. And her kind deep eyes looked steadily into Eleanor's, as though mutely cheering and supporting her.

Eleanor unconsciously pressed her hand upon her breast. She was looking round her in a sudden anguish of memory. For, now they were through the village, they were descending--they were in the woods. Ah! the white walls of the convent--the vacant windows in its ruined end--and at the gate of the rough farmyard that surrounded it the stalwart *capoccia*, the grinning, harsh-featured wife that she remembered.

   She stepped feebly down upon the dusty road. When her feet last pressed it, Manisty was beside her, and the renewing force of love and joy was filling all the sources of her being.

CHAPTER XVI

Can you bear it? Can you be comfortable?' said Lucy, in some dismay. They were in one of the four or five bare rooms that had been given up to them. A bed with a straw palliasse, one or two broken chairs, and bits of worm-eaten furniture filled what had formerly been one of a row of cells running along an upper corridor. The floor was of brick and very dirty. Against the wall a tattered canvas, a daub of St. Laurence and his gridiron, still recalled the former uses of the room.

They had given orders for a few comforts to be sent out from Orvieto, but the cart conveying them had not yet arrived. Meanwhile Marie was crying in the next room, and the *contadina* was looking on astonished and a little sulky. The people who came from Orvieto never complained. What was wrong with the ladies?

Eleanor looked round her with a faint smile.

'It doesn't matter,' she said under her breath. Then she looked at Lucy.

'What care we take of you! How well we look after you!'

And she dropped her head on her hands in a fit of hysterical laughter--very near to sobs.

'I!' cried Lucy. 'As if I couldn't sleep anywhere, and eat anything! But you-- that's another business. When the cart comes, we can fix you up a little better--but to-night!'

She looked, frowning, round the empty room.

'There is nothing to do anything with--or I'd set to work right away.'

'Ecco, Signora!' said the farmer's wife. She carried triumphantly in her hands a shaky carpet-chair, the only article of luxury apparently that the convent provided.

Eleanor thanked her, and the woman stood with her hands on her hips, surveying them. She frowned, but only because she was thinking hard how she could somehow propitiate these strange beings, so well provided, as it seemed, with superfluous *lire*.

'Ah!' she cried suddenly; 'but the ladies have not seen our *bella vista*!--our *loggia*! Santa Madonna! but I have lost my senses! Signorina! *venga--venga lei*.'

And beckoning to Lucy she pulled open a door that had remained unnoticed in the corner of the room.

Lucy and Eleanor followed.

Even Eleanor joined her cry of delight to Lucy's.

'Ecco!' said the *massaja* proudly, as though the whole landscape were her chattel,--'Monte Amiata! Selvapendente--the Paglia--does the Signora see the bridge down there?--*veda lei*, under Selvapendente? Those forests on the mountain there--they belong all to the Casa Guerrini--*tutto, tutto*! as far as the Signorina can see! And that little house there, on the hill--that *casa di caccia*--that was poor Don Emilio's, that was killed in the war.'

And she chattered on, in a *patois* not always intelligible, even to Eleanor's trained ear, about the widowed Contessa, her daughter, and her son; about the new roads that Don Emilio had made through the woods; of the repairs and rebuilding at the Villa Guerrini--all stopped since his death; of the Sindaco of Selvapendente, who often came up to Torre Amiata for the summer; of the nuns in the new convent just built there under the hill, and their *fattore*,--whose son was with Don Emilio after he was wounded, when the poor young man implored his own men to shoot him and put him out of his pain--who had stayed with him till he died, and had brought his watch and pocket-book back to the Contessa--

'Is the Contessa here?' said Eleanor, looking at the woman with the strained and startled air that was becoming habitual to her, as though each morsel of passing news only served somehow to make life's burden heavier.

But certainly the Contessa was here! She and Donna Teresa were always at the Villa. Once they used to go to Rome and Florence part of the year, but now--no more!

A sudden uproar arose from below--of crying children and barking dogs. The woman threw up her hands. 'What are they doing to me with the baby?' she cried, and disappeared.

Lucy went back to fetch the carpet-chair. She caught up also a couple of Florentine silk blankets that were among their wraps. She laid them on the bricks of the *loggia*, found a rickety table in Eleanor's room, her travelling-bag, and a shawl.

'Don't take such trouble about me!' said Eleanor, almost piteously, as Lucy established her comfortably in the chair, with a shawl over her knees and a book or two beside her.

Lucy with a soft little laugh stooped and kissed her.

'Now I must go and dry Marie's tears. Then I shall dive downstairs and discover the kitchen. They say they've got a cook, and the dinner'll soon be ready. Isn't that lovely? And I'm sure the cart'll be here directly. It's the most beautiful place I ever saw in my life!' said Lucy, clasping her hands a moment in a gesture familiar to her, and turning towards the great prospect of mountain, wood, and river. 'And it's so strange--so strange! It's like another Italy! Why, these woods--they might be just in a part of Maine I know. You can't see a vineyard--not one. And the air--isn't it fresh? Isn't it lovely? Wouldn't you guess you were three thousand feet up? I just know this--we're going to make you comfortable. I'm going right down now to send that cart back to Orvieto for a lot of things. And you're going to get ever, ever so much better, aren't you? Say you will!'

The girl fell on her knees beside Eleanor, and took the other's thin hands into her own. Her face, thrown back, had lost its gaiety; her mouth quivered.

Eleanor met the girl's tender movement dry-eyed. For the hundredth time that day she asked herself the feverish, torturing question--'Does she love him?'

'Of course I shall get better,' she said lightly, stroking the girl's hair; 'or if not--what matter?'

Lucy shook her head.

'You must get better,' she said in a low, determined voice. 'And it must all come right.'

Eleanor was silent. In her own heart she knew more finally, more irrevocably every hour that for her it would never come right. But how say to Lucy that her whole being hung now--not on any hope for herself, but on the fierce resolve that there should be none for Manisty?

Lucy gave a long sigh, rose to her feet, and went off to household duties.

Eleanor was left alone. Her eyes, bright with fever, fixed themselves, unseeing, on the sunset sky, and the blue, unfamiliar peaks beneath it.

Cheerful sounds of rioting children and loud-voiced housewives came from below. Presently there was a distant sound of wheels, and the *carro* from Orvieto appeared, escorted by the whole village, who watched its unpacking with copious comment on each article, and a perpetual scuffling for places in the front line of observation. Even the *padre parroco* and the doctor paused as they passed along the road, and Lucy as she flitted about caught sight of the smiling young priest, in his flat broad-brimmed hat and caped soutane, side by side with the meditative and gloomy countenance of the doctor, who stood with his legs apart, smoking like a chimney.

But Lucy had no time to watch the crowd. She was directing the men with the *carro* where to place the cooking-stove that had been brought from Orvieto, in the dark and half-ruinous kitchen on the lower floor of the convent; marvelling the while at the *risotto* and the *pollo* that the local artist, their new cook, the sister of the farmer's wife, was engaged in producing, out of apparently nothing in the way either of fire or tools. She was conferring with Cecco the little manservant, who, with less polish than Alfredo, but with a like good-will, was running hither and thither, intent only on pleasing his ladies, and on somehow finding enough spoons and forks to lay a dinner-table with; or she was alternately comforting and laughing at Marie, who was for the moment convinced that Italy was pure and simple Hades, and Torre Amiata the lowest gulf thereof.

Thus--under the soft, fresh evening--the whole forlorn and ruinous building was once more alive with noise and gaiety, with the tread of men carrying packages, with the fun of skirmishing children, with the cries of the cook and Cecco, with Lucy's stumbling yet sweet Italian.

Eleanor only was alone--but how terribly alone!

She sat where Lucy had left her--motionless--her hands hanging listlessly. She had been always thin, but in the last few weeks she had become a shadow. Her dress had lost its old perfection, though its carelessness was still the carelessness of instinctive grace, of a woman who could not throw on a shawl or a garden-hat without a natural trick of hand, that held even through despair and grief. The delicacy and emaciation of the face had now gone far beyond the bounds of beauty. It spoke of disease, and drew the pity of the passer-by.

Her loneliness grew upon her--penetrated and pursued her. She could not resign herself to it. She was always struggling with it, beating it away, as a frightened child might struggle with the wave that overwhelms it on the beach. A few weeks ago she had been so happy, so rich in friends--the world had been so warm and kind!

And now it seemed to her that she had no friends; no one to whom she could turn; no one she wished to see, except this girl--this girl she had known barely a couple of months--by whom she had been made desolate!

She thought of those winter gatherings in Rome which she had enjoyed with so keen a pleasure; the women she had liked, who had liked her in return, to whom her eager wish to love and be loved had made her delightful. But beneath her outward sweetness she carried a proud and often unsuspected reserve. She had made a *confidante* of no one. That her relation to Manisty was accepted and understood in Rome; that it was regarded as a romance, with which it was not so much ill-natured as ridiculous to associate a breath of scandal--a romance which all kind hearts hoped might end as most of such things should end--all this she knew. She had been proud of her place beside him, proud of Rome's tacit recognition of her claim upon him. But she had told her heart to nobody. Her wild scene with Lucy stood out unique, unparalleled in the story of her life.

And now there was no one she craved to see--not one. With the instinct of the stricken animal she turned from her kind. Her father? What had he ever been to her? Aunt Pattie? Her very sympathy and pity made Eleanor thankful to be parted from her. Other kith and kin? No! Happy, she could have loved them; miserable, she cared for none of them. Her unlucky marriage had numbed and silenced her for years. From that frost the waters of life had been loosened, only to fail now at their very source.

Her whole nature was one wound. At the moment when, standing spell-bound in the shadow, she had seen Manisty stooping over the unconscious Lucy, and had heard his tender breathless words, the sword had fallen, dividing the very roots of being.

And now--strange irony!--the only heart on which she leant, the only hand to which she clung, were the heart and the hand of Lucy!

'Why, why are we here?' she cried to herself with a sudden change of position and of anguish.

Was not their flight a mere absurdity?--humiliation for herself, since it revealed what no woman should reveal--but useless, ridiculous as any check on Manisty! Would he give up Lucy because she might succeed in hiding her for a few weeks? Was that passionate will likely to resign itself to the momentary defeat she had inflicted on it? Supposing she succeeded in despatching Lucy to America without any further interview between them; are there no steamers and trains to take impatient lovers to their goal? What childish folly was the whole proceeding!

And would she even succeed so far? Might he not even now be on their track? How possible that he should remember this place--its isolation--and her pleasure in it! She started in her chair. It seemed to her that she already heard his feet upon the road.

Then her thought rebounded in a fierce triumph, an exultation that shook the feeble frame. She was secure! She was entrenched, so to speak, in Lucy's heart. Never would that nature grasp its own joy at the cost of another's agony. No! no!--she is not in love with him!--the poor hurrying brain insisted. She has been interested, excited, touched. That, he can always achieve with any woman, if he pleases. But time and change soon wear down these first fancies of youth. There is no real congruity between them--there never, never could be.

But supposing it were not so--supposing Lucy could be reached and affected by Manisty's pursuit, still Eleanor was safe. She knew well what had been the effect, what would now be the increasing effect of her weakness and misery on Lucy's tender heart. By the mere living in Lucy's sight she would gain her end. From the first she had realised the inmost quality of the girl's strong and diffident personality. What Manisty feared she counted on.

Sometimes, just for a moment, as one may lean over the edge of a precipice, she imagined herself yielding, recalling Manisty, withdrawing her own claim, and the barrier raised by her own vindictive agony. The mind sped along the details that might follow--the girl's loyal resistance--Manisty's ardour--Manisty's fascination--the homage and the seduction, the quarrels and the impatience with which he would surround her--the scenes in which Lucy's reserve mingling with her beauty would but evoke on the man's side all the ingenuity, all the delicacy of which he was capable--and the final softening of that sweet austerity which hid Lucy's heart of gold.--

No!--Lucy had no passion!--she would tell herself with a feverish, an angry vehemence. How would she ever bear with Manisty, with the alternate excess and defect of his temperament?

And suddenly, amid the shadows of the past winter Eleanor would see herself writing, and Manisty stooping over her,--his hand taking her pen, his shoulder touching hers. His hand was strong, nervous, restless like himself. Her romantic imagination that was half natural, half literary, delighted to trace in it both caprice and power. When it touched her own slender fingers, it seemed to her they could but just restrain themselves from nestling into his. She would draw herself back in haste, lest some involuntary movement should betray her. But not before the lightning thought had burnt its way through her--'What if one just fell back against his breast--and all was said--all ventured in a moment! Afterwards--ecstasy, or despair--what matter!'--

When would Lucy have dared even such a dream? Eleanor's wild jealousy would secretly revenge itself on the girl's maidenly coldness, on the young stiffness, Manisty had once mocked at. How incredible that she should have attracted him!--how, impossible that she should continue to attract him! All Lucy's immaturities and defects passed through Eleanor's analysing thought.

For a moment she saw her coldly, odiously, as an enemy might see her.

And then!--quick revulsion--a sudden loathing of herself--a sudden terror of these new meannesses and bitterness that were invading her, stealing from her her very self, robbing her of the character that unconsciously she had loved in herself, as other people loved it--knowing that in deed and truth she was what others thought her to be, kind, and gentle, and sweet-natured.

And last of all--poor soul!--an abject tenderness and repentance towards Lucy, which yet brought no relief, because it never affected for an instant the fierce tension of will beneath.

A silvery night stole upon the sunset, absorbed, transmuted all the golds and crimsons of the west into its own dimly shining blue.

Eleanor was in bed; Lucy's clever hands had worked wonders with her room; and now Eleanor had been giving quick remorseful directions to Marie to concern herself a little with Miss Foster's comfort and Miss Foster's luggage.

Lucy escaped from the rooms littered with trunks and clothes. She took her hat and a light cape, and stole out into the broad passage, on either side of which opened the long series of small rooms which had once been Carmelite cells. Only the four or five rooms at the western end, the bare 'apartment' which they occupied, were still whole and water-tight. Half-way down the passage, as Lucy had already discovered, you came to rooms where the windows had no glass and the plaster had dropped from the walls, and the ceilings hung down in great gaps and rags of ruin. There was a bay window at the eastern end of the passage, which had been lately glazed for the summer tenants' sake. The rising moon streamed through on the desolation of the damp-stained walls and floors. And a fresh upland wind was beginning to blow and whistle through the empty and windowless cells. Even Lucy shivered a little. It was perhaps not wonderful that the French maid should be in revolt.

Then she went softly down an old stone staircase to the lower floor. Here was the same long passage with rooms on either side, but in even worse condition. At the far end was a glow of light and a hum of voices, coming from the corner of the building occupied by the *contadino*, and their own kitchen. But between the heavy front door, that Lucy was about to open, and the distant light, was an earthen floor full of holes and gaps, and on either side--caverns of desolation--the old wine and oil stores, the kitchens and wood cellars of the convent, now black dens avoided by the cautious, and dark even at midday because of the rough boarding-up of the windows. There was a stable smell in the passage, and Lucy already knew that one of the further dens held the *contadino's* donkey and mule.

'*Can* we stay here?' she said to herself, half laughing, half doubtful.

Then she lifted the heavy iron bar that closed the old double door, and stepped out into the courtyard that surrounded the convent, half of which was below the road as it rapidly descended from the village, and half above it.

She took a few steps to the right.

Exquisite!

There opened out before her a little cloister, with double shafts carrying Romanesque arches; and at the back of the court, the chapel, and a tiny bell-tower. The moon shone down on every line and moulding. Under its light, stucco and brick turned to ivory and silver. There was an absolute silence, an absolute purity of air; and over all the magic of beauty and of night. Lucy thought of the ruined frescoes in the disused chapel, of the faces of saints and angels looking out into the stillness.

Then she mounted some steps to the road, and turned downwards towards the forest that crept up round them on all sides.

Ah! was there yet another portion of the convent?--a wing running at right angles to the main building in which they were established, and containing some habitable rooms? In the furthest window of all was a light, and a figure moving across it. A tall black figure--surely a priest? Yes!--as the form came nearer to the window, seen from the back, Lucy perceived distinctly the tonsured head and the soutane.

How strange! She had heard nothing from the *massaja* of any other tenant. And this tall gaunt figure had nothing in common with the little smiling *parroco* she had seen in the crowd.

She moved on, wondering.

Oh, those woods! How they sank, like great resting clouds below her, to the shining line of the river, and rose again on the further side! They were oak woods, and spoke strangely to Lucy of the American and English north. Yet, as she came nearer, the moon shone upon delicate undergrowth of heath and arbutus, that chid her fancy back to the 'Saturnian land.'

And beyond all, the blue mountains, aetherially light, like dreams on the horizon; and above all, the radiant serenity of the sky.

Ah! there spoke the nightingales, and that same melancholy note of the little brown owl which used to haunt the olive grounds of Marinata. Lucy held her breath. The tears rushed into her eyes--tears of memory, tears of longing.

But she drove them back. Standing on a little cleared space beside the road that commanded the whole night scene, she threw herself into the emotion and poetry which could be yielded to without remorse, without any unnerving of the will. How far, far she was from Uncle Ben, and that shingled house in Vermont! It was near midsummer, and all the English and Americans had fled from this Southern Italy. Italy was at home, and at ease in her own house, living her own rich immemorial life, knowing and thinking nothing of the foreigner. Nor indeed on those uplands and in those woods had she ever thought of him; though below in the valley ran the old coach road from Florence to Rome, on which Goethe and

Winckelmann had journeyed to the Eternal City. Lucy felt as though, but yesterday a tourist and stranger, she had now crept like a child into the family circle. Nay, she had raised a corner of Italy's mantle, and drawn close to the warm breast of one of the great mother-lands of the world.

Ah! but feeling sweeps fast and far, do what we will. Soon she was struggling out of her depth. These weeks of rushing experience had been loosening soul and tongue. To-night how she could have talked of these things to one now parted from her, perhaps for ever! How he would have listened to her--impatiently often! How he would have mocked and rent her! But then the quick softening--and the beautiful kindling eye--the dogmatism at once imperative and sweet--the tyranny that a woman might both fight and love!

Yet how painful was the thought of Manisty! She was ashamed--humiliated. Their flight assumed as a certainty what after all, let Eleanor say what she would, he had never, never said to her--what she had no clear authority to believe. Where was he? What was he thinking? For a moment, her heart fluttered towards him like a homing bird.

Then in a sharp and stern reaction she rebuked, she chastened herself. Standing there in the night, above the forests, looking over to the dim white cliffs on the side of Monte Amiata, she felt herself, in this strange and beautiful land, brought face to face with calls of the spirit, with deep voices of admonition and pity that rose from her own inmost being.

With a long sigh, like one that lifts a weight she raised her young arms above her head, and then brought her hands down slowly upon her eyes, shutting out sight and sense. There was a murmur--

'Mother!--darling mother!--if you were just here--for one hour--'

She gathered up the forces of the soul.

'So help me God!' she said. And then she started, perceiving into what formula she had slipped, unwittingly.

* * * * *

She moved on a few paces down the road, meaning just to peep into the woods and their scented loneliness. The night was so lovely she was loth to leave it.

Suddenly she became aware of a point of light in front, and the smell of tobacco.

A man rose from the wayside. Lucy stayed her foot, and was about to retreat swiftly when she heard a cheerful--

'Buona sera, Signorina!' She recognised a voice of the afternoon. It was the handsome carabiniere. Lucy advanced with alacrity.

'I came out because it was so fine,' she said. 'Are you on duty still? Where is your companion?'

He smiled, and pointed to the wood. 'We have a hut there. First Ruggieri sleeps--then I sleep. We don't often come this way; but when there are *forestieri*, then we must look out.'

'But there are no brigands here?'

He showed his white teeth. 'I shot two once with this gun,' he said, producing it.

'But not here?' she said, startled.

'No--but beyond the mountains--over there--in Maremma.' He waved his hand vaguely towards the west. Then he shook his head. 'Bad country--bad people--in Maremma.'

'Oh yes, I know,' said Lucy, laughing. 'If there is anything bad here, you say it comes from Maremma. When our harness broke this afternoon our driver said, "*Che vuole?* It was made in Maremma!"--Tell me--who lives in that part of the convent--over there?'

And, turning back, she pointed to the distant window and the light.

The man spat upon the road without replying. After replenishing his pipe he said slowly: 'That, Signorina, is a *forestiere*, too.'

'A priest--isn't it?'

'A priest--and not a priest,' said the man after another pause.

Then he laughed, with the sudden *insouciance* of the Italian.

'A priest that doesn't say his Mass!--that's a queer sort of priest--isn't it?'

'I don't understand,' said Lucy.

'*Per Dio!* what does it matter?' said the man, laughing. 'The people here wouldn't trouble their heads, only--But you understand, Signorina'--he dropped his voice a little--'the priests have much power--*molto, molto*! Don Teodoro, the *parroco* there,--it was he founded the *cassa rurale*. If a *contadino* wants some money for his seed-corn--or to marry his daughter--or to buy himself a new team of oxen--he must go to the *parroco*. Since these new banks began, it is the priests that have the money--*capisce?* If you want it you must ask them! So you understand, Signorina, it doesn't profit to fall out with them. You must love their friends, and--' His grin and gesture finished the sentence.

'But what's the matter?' said Lucy, wondering. 'Has he committed any crime?' And she looked curiously at the figure in the convent window.

'*E un prete spretato, Signorina.*'

'*Spretato?*' (unpriested--unfrocked). The word was unfamiliar to her. She frowned over it.

'*Scomunicato!*' said the *carabiniere*, with a laugh.

'Excommunicated?' She felt a thrill of pity, mingled with a vague horror.

'Why?--what has he done?'

The *carabiniere* laughed again. The laugh was odious, but she was already acquainted with that strange instinct of the lower-class Italian which leads him to make mock of calamity. He has passion, but no sentiment; he instinctively hates the pathetic.

'*Chi sa, Signorina?* He seems a quiet old man. We keep a sharp eye on him; he won't do any harm. He used to give the children *confetti*, but the mothers have forbidden them to take them. Gianni there'--he pointed to the convent, and Lucy understood that he referred to the *contadino*--'Gianni went to Don Teodoro, and asked if he should turn him out. But Don Teodoro wouldn't say Yes or No. He pays well, but the village want him to go. They say he will bring them ill-luck with their harvest.'

'And the *Padre parroco*? Does he not speak to him?'

Antonio laughed.

'When Don Teodoro passes him on the road he doesn't see him--*capisce*, Signorina? And so with all the other priests. When he comes by they have no eyes. The Bishop sent the word.'

'And everybody here does what the priests tell them?'

Lucy's tone expressed that instinctive resentment which the Puritan feels against a ruling and dominant Catholicism.

Antonio laughed again, but a little stupidly. It was the laugh of a man who knows that it is not worth while even to begin to explain certain matters to a stranger.

'They understand their business--*i preti!*'--was all he would say. Then--'*Ma!*--they are rich--the priests! All these last years--so many banks--so many *casse*--so many *societa*! That holds the people better than prayers.'

* * * * *

When Lucy turned homewards she found herself watching the light in the far window with an eager attention. A priest in disgrace?--and a foreigner? What could he be hiding here for?--in this remote corner of a district which, as they had been already told at Orvieto, was Catholic, *fino al fanatismo*?

* * * * *

The morning rose, fresh and glorious, over mountain and forest.

Eleanor watched the streaks of light that penetrated through the wooden sun-shutters grow brighter and brighter on the white-washed wall. She was weary of herself, weary of the night. The old building was full of strange sounds--of murmurs and resonances, of slight creepings and patterings, that tried the nerves. Her room communicated with Lucy's, and their doors were provided with bolts, the newness of which, perhaps, testified to the fears of other summer tenants before them. Nevertheless, Eleanor had been a prey to starts and terrors, and her night had passed in a bitter mingling of moral strife and physical discomfort.

Seven o'clock striking from the village church. She slipped to her feet. Ready to her hand lay one of the soft and elegant wrappers--fresh, not long ago, from Paris--as to which Lucy had often silently wondered how anyone could think it right to spend so much money on such things.

Eleanor, of course, was not conscious of the smallest reproach in the matter. Dainty and costly dress was second nature to her; she never thought about it. But this morning as she first took up the elaborate silken thing, to which pale girls in hot Parisian workrooms had given so much labour of hand and head, and then caught sight of her own face and shoulders in the cracked glass upon the wall, she was seized with certain ghastly perceptions that held her there motionless in the semi-darkness, shivering amid the delicate lace and muslin which enwrapped her. Finished!--for her--all the small feminine joys. Was there one of her dresses that did not in some way speak to her of Manisty?--that had not been secretly planned with a view to tastes and preferences she had come to know hardly less intimately than her own?

She thought of the face of the Orvieto doctor, of certain words that she had stopped on his lips because she was afraid to hear them. A sudden terror of death,--of the desolate, desolate end swept upon her. To die, with this cry of the heart unspent, untold for ever! Unloved, unsatisfied, unrewarded--she whose whole nature gave itself--gave itself perpetually, as a wave breaks upon a barren shore. How can any God send human beings into the world for such a lot? There can be no God. But how is the riddle easier, for thinking Him away?

When at last she rose, it was to make quietly for the door opening on the *loggia*.

Still there, this radiant marvel of the world!--this pageant of rock and stream and forest, this pomp of shining cloud, this silky shimmer of the wheat, this sparkle of flowers in the grass; while human hearts break, and human lives fail, and the graveyard on the hill yonder packs closer and closer its rows of metal crosses and wreaths!

Suddenly, from a patch of hayfield on the further side of the road, she heard a voice singing. A young man, tall and well made, was mowing in a corner of the field. The swathes fell fast before him: every movement spoke of an assured rejoicing strength. He sang with the sharp stridency which is the rule in Italy--the words clear, the sounds nasal.

Gradually Eleanor made out that the song was the farewell of a maiden to her lover who is going for winter work to the Maremma.

The labourers go to Maremma--
Oh! 'tis long till the days of June,
And my heart is all in a flutter
Alone here, under the moon.
 O moon!--all this anguish and sorrow!
Thou know'st why I suffer so--
Oh! send him me back from Maremma,
Where he goes, and I must not go!

The man sang the little song carelessly, commonly, without a thought of the words, interrupting himself every now and then to sharpen his scythe, and then beginning again. To Eleanor it seemed the natural voice of the morning; one more, echo of the cry of universal parting, now for a day, now for a season, now for ever--which fills the world.

*   *   *   *   *

She was too restless to enjoy the *loggia* and the view, too restless to go back to bed. She pushed back the door between her and Lucy, only to see that Lucy was still fast asleep. But there were voices and stops downstairs. The farm-people had been abroad for hours.

She made a preliminary toilette, took her hat, and stole downstairs. As she opened the outer door the children caught sight of her and came crowding round, large-eyed, their fingers in their mouths. She turned towards the chapel and the little cloister that she remembered. The children gave a shout and swooped back into the convent. And when she reached the chapel door, there they were on her skirts again, a big boy brandishing the key.

Eleanor took it and parleyed with them. They were to go away and leave her alone--quite alone. Then when she came back they should have *soldi*. The children nodded shrewdly, withdrew in a swarm to the corner of the cloister, and watched events.

Eleanor entered. From some high lunette windows the cool early sunlight came creeping and playing into the little whitewashed place. On either hand two cinque-cento frescoes had been rescued from the whitewash. They shone like delicate flowers on the rough, yellowish-white of the walls; on one side a martyrdom of St. Catharine, on the other a Crucifixion. Their pale blues and lilacs, their sharp pure greens and thin crimsons, made subtle harmony with the general lightness and cleanness of the abandoned chapel. A poor little altar with a few tawdry furnishings at the further end, a confessional box falling to pieces with age, and a few chairs-- these were all that it contained besides.

Eleanor sank kneeling beside one of the chairs. As she looked round her, physical weakness and the concentration of all thought on one subject and one person made her for the moment the victim of an illusion so strong that it was almost an 'apparition of the living.'

Manisty stood before her, in the rough tweed suit he had worn in November, one hand, holding his hat, upon his hip, his curly head thrown back, his eyes just turning from the picture to meet hers; eyes always eagerly confident, whether their owner pronounced on the affinities of a picture or the fate of a country.

'School of Pinturicchio certainly!--but local work. Same hand--don't you think so?--as in that smaller chapel in the cathedral. Eleanor! you remember?'

She gave a gasp, and hid her face, shaking. Was this haunting of eye and ear to pursue her now henceforward? Was the passage of Manisty's being through the world to be--for her--ineffaceable?--so that earth and air retained the impress of his form and voice, and only her tortured heart and sense were needed to make the phantom live and walk and speak again?

She began to pray--brokenly and desperately, as she had often prayed during the last few weeks. It was a passionate throwing of the will against a fate, cruel, unjust, intolerable; a means not to self-renunciation, but to a self-assertion which was in her like madness, so foreign was it to all the habits of the soul.

'That he should make use of me to the last moment, then fling me to the winds- -that I should just make room, and help him to his goal--and then die meekly--out of the way--No! He too shall suffer!--and he shall know that it is Eleanor who exacts it!--Eleanor who bars the way!'

And in the very depths of consciousness there emerged the strange and bitter recognition that from the beginning she had allowed him to hold her cheaply; that she had been content, far, far too content, with what he chose to give; that if she had claimed more, been less delicate, less exquisite in loving, he might have feared and regarded her more.

She heard the chapel door open. But at the same moment she became aware that her face was bathed in tears, and she did not dare to look round. She drew down her veil, and composed herself as she best could.

The person behind, apparently, also knelt down. The tread and movements were those of a heavy man--some countryman, she supposed.

But his neighbourhood was unwelcome, and the chapel ceased to be a place of refuge where feeling might have its way. In a few minutes she rose and turned towards the door.

She gave a little cry. The man kneeling at the back of the chapel rose in astonishment and came towards her.

'Madame!'

'Father Benecke! *you* here,' said Eleanor, leaning against the wall for support-- so weak was she, and so startling was this sudden apparition of the man whom she had last seen on the threshold of the glass passage at Marinata, barely a fortnight before.

'I fear, Madame, that I intrude upon you,' said the old priest, staring at her with embarrassment. 'I will retire.'

'No, no,' said Eleanor, putting out her hand, with some recovery of her normal voice and smile. 'It was only so--surprising; so--unexpected. Who could have thought of finding you here, Father?'

The priest did not reply. They left the chapel together. The knot of waiting children in the cloister, as soon as they saw Eleanor, raised a shout of glee, and began to run towards her. But the moment they perceived her companion, they stopped dead.

Their little faces darkened, stiffened, their black eyes shone with malice. Then suddenly the boys swooped on the pebbles of the courtyard, and with cries of '*Bestia!--bestia!*' they flung them at the priest over their shoulders, as they all fled helter-skelter, the brothers dragging off the sisters, the big ones the little ones, out of sight.

'Horrid little imps!' cried Eleanor in indignation. 'What is the matter with them? I promised them some *soldi*. Did they hit you, Father?'

She paused, arrested by the priest's face.

'They?' he said hoarsely. 'Did you mean the children? Oh! no, they did no harm?'

What had happened to him since they met last at the villa? No doubt he had been in conflict with his superiors and his Church. Was he already suspended?--excommunicate? But he still wore the soutane?

Then panic for herself swept in upon and silenced all else. All was over with their plans. Father Benecke either was, or might at any moment be, in communication with Manisty. Alas, alas!--what ill-luck!

They walked together to the road--Eleanor first imagining, then rejecting one sentence after another. At last she said, a little piteously:

'It is so strange, Father--that you should be here!'

The priest did not answer immediately. He walked with a curiously uncertain gait. Eleanor noticed that his soutane was dusty and torn, and that he was unshaven. The peculiar and touching charm that had once arisen from the contrast between the large-limbed strength which he inherited from a race of Suabian peasants, and an extraordinary delicacy of feature and skin, a childish brightness and sweetness in the eyes, had suffered eclipse. He was dulled and broken. One might have said almost that he had become a mere ungainly, ill-kept old man, red-eyed for lack of sleep, and disorganised by some bitter distress.

'You remember--what I told you and Mr. Manisty, at Marinata?' he said at last, with difficulty.

'Perfectly. You withdrew your letter?'

'I withdrew it. Then I came down here. I have an old friend--a Canon of Orvieto. He told me once of this place.'

Eleanor looked at him with a sudden return of all her natural kindness and compassion.

'I am afraid you have gone through a great deal, Father,' she said, gravely.

The priest stood still. His hand shook upon his stick.

'I must not detain you, Madame,' he said suddenly, with a kind of tremulous formality. 'You will be wishing to return to your apartment I heard that two English ladies were expected--but I never thought--'

'How could you?' said Eleanor hurriedly. 'I am not in any hurry. It is very early still. Will you not tell me more of what has happened to you? You would'--she turned away her head--'you would have told Mr. Manisty?'

'Ah! Mr. Manisty!' said the priest, with a long, startled sigh. 'I trust he is well, Madame?'

Eleanor flushed.

'I believe so. He and Miss Manisty are still at Marinata. Father Benecke!'

'Madame?'

Eleanor turned aside, poking at the stones on the road with her parasol.

'You would do me a kindness if for the present you would not mention my being here to any of your friends in Rome, to--to anybody, in fact. Last autumn I happened to pass by this place, and thought it very beautiful. It was a sudden determination on my part and Miss Foster's--you remember the American lady who was staying with us?--to come here. The villa was getting very hot, and--and there were other reasons. And now we wish to be quite alone for a little while--to be in retirement even from our friends. You will, I am sure, respect our wish?'

She looked up, breathing quickly. All her sudden colour had gone. Her anxiety and discomposure were very evident. The priest bowed.

'I will be discreet, Madame,' he said, with the natural dignity of his calling. 'May I ask you to excuse me? I have to walk into Selvapendente to fetch a letter.'

He took off his flat beaver hat, bowed low and departed, swinging along at a great pace. Eleanor felt herself repulsed. She hurried back to the convent. The children were waiting for her at the door, and when they saw that she was alone they took their *soldi*, though with a touch of sulkiness.

And the door was opened to her by Lucy.

'Truant!' said the girl reproachfully, throwing her arm round Eleanor. 'As if you ought to go out without your coffee! But it's all ready for you on the *loggia*. Where have you been? And why!--what's the matter?'

Eleanor told the news as they mounted to their rooms.

'Ah! *that* was the priest I saw last night!' cried Lucy. 'I was just going to tell you of my adventure. Father Benecke! How very, very strange! And how very tiresome! It's made you look so tired.'

And before she would hear a word more Lucy had put the elder woman into her chair in the deep shade of the *loggia*, had brought coffee and bread and fruit from the little table she herself had helped Cecco to arrange, and had hovered round till Eleanor had taken at least a cup of coffee and a fraction of roll. Then she brought her own coffee, and sat down on the rug at Eleanor's feet.

'I know what you're thinking about!' she said, looking up with her sweet, sudden smile. 'You want to go--right away!'

'Can we trust him?' said Eleanor, miserably. 'Edward doesn't know where he is,--but he could write of course to Edward at any moment.'

She turned away her face from Lucy. Any mention of Manisty's name dyed it with painful colour--the shame of the suppliant living on the mercy of the conqueror.

'He might,' said Lucy, thinking. 'But if you asked him? No; I don't believe he would. I am sure his soul is beautiful--like his face.'

'His poor face! You don't know how changed he is.'

'Ah! the *carabiniere* told me last night. He is excommunicated,' said Lucy, under her breath.

And she repeated her conversation with the handsome Antonio. Eleanor capped it with the tale of the children.

'It's his book,' said Lucy, frowning. 'What a tyranny!'

They were both silent. Lucy was thinking of the drive to Nemi, of Manisty's words and looks; Eleanor recalled the priest's last visit to the villa and that secret storm of feeling which had overtaken her as she bade him good-bye.

But when Lucy speculated on what might have happened, Eleanor hardly responded. She fell into a dreamy silence from which it was difficult to rouse her. It was very evident to Lucy that Father Benecke's personal plight interested her but little. Her mind could not give it room. What absorbed her was the feverish question: Were they safe any longer at Torre Amiata, or must they strike camp and go further?

CHAPTER XVII

The day grew very hot, and Eleanor suffered visibly, even though the quality of the air remained throughout pure and fresh, and Lucy in the shelter of the broad *loggia* felt nothing but a keen physical enjoyment of the glow and blaze that held the outer world.

After their midday meal Lucy was sitting idly on the outer wall of the *loggia* which commanded the bit of road just outside the convent, when she perceived a figure mounting the hill.

'Father Benecke!' she said to Eleanor. 'What a climb for him in this heat! Did you say he had gone to Selvapendente? Poor old man!--how hot and tired he looks!--and with that heavy parcel too!'

And withdrawing herself a little out of sight she watched the priest. He had just paused in a last patch of shade to take breath after the long ascent. Depositing the bundle he had been carrying on a wayside stone, he took out his large coloured handkerchief and mopped the perspiration from his face with long sighs of exhaustion. Then with his hands on his sides he looked round him. Opposite to him was a little shrine, with the usual rude fresco and enthroned Madonna behind a grating. The priest walked over to it, and knelt down.

In a few minutes he returned and took up his parcel. As he entered the outer gate of the convent, Lucy could see him glancing nervously from side to side. But it was the hour of siesta and of quiet. His tormentors of the morning were all under cover.

The parcel that he carried had partly broken out of its wrappings during the long walk, and Lucy could see that it contained clothes of some kind.

'Poor Father!' she said again to Eleanor. 'Couldn't he have got some boy to carry that for him? How I should like to rest him and give him some coffee? Shall I send Cecco to ask him to come here?'

Eleanor shook her head.

'Better not. He wouldn't come. We shall have to tame him like a bird.'

The hours passed on. At last the western sun began to creep round into the **loggia**. The empty cells on the eastern side were now cool, but they looked upon the inner cloistered court which was alive with playing children, and all the farm life. Eleanor shrank both from noise and spectators. Yet she grew visibly more tired and restless, and Lucy went out to reconnoitre. She came back recommending a descent into the forest.

So they braved a few yards of sun-scorched road and plunged into a little right-hand track, which led downward through a thick undergrowth of heath and arbutus towards what seemed the cool heart of the woods.

Presently they came to a small gate, and beyond appeared a broad, well-kept path, winding in zig-zags along the forest-covered side of the hill.

'This must be private,' said Eleanor, looking at the gate in some doubt. 'And there you see is the Palazzo Guerrini.'

She pointed. Above them through a gap in the trees showed the great yellow pile on the edge of the plateau, the forest stretching steeply up to it and enveloping it from below.

'There is nothing to stop us,' said Lucy. 'They won't turn us out, if it is theirs. I can't have you go through that sun again.'

And she pressed on, looking for shade and rest.

But soon she stopped, with a little cry, and they both stood looking in astonishment at the strange and lovely thing upon which they had stumbled unawares.

'I know!' cried Lucy. 'The woman at the convent tried to tell me--and I couldn't understand. She said we must see the "Sassetto"--that it was a wonder--and all the strangers thought so. And it *is* a wonder! And so cool!'

Down from the very brow of the hill, in an age before man was born, the giant force of some primeval convulsion had flung a lava torrent of molten rock to the bed of the Paglia. And there still was the torrent--a rock-stream composed of huge blocks of basalt--flowing in one vast steep fall, a couple of hundred yards wide, through the forest from top to bottom of the hill.

And very grim and stern would that rock-river have been but for Italy, and the powers of the Italian soil. But the forest and its lovely undergrowths, its heaths and creepers, its ferns and periwinkles, its lichen and mosses had thrown themselves on the frozen lava, had decked and softened its wild shapes, had reared oaks and pines amid the clefts of basalt, and planted all the crannies below with lighter, featherier green, till in the dim forest light all that had once been terror had softened into grace, and Nature herself had turned her freak to poetry.

And throughout the 'Sassetto' there reigned a peculiar and delicious coolness--the blended breath of mountain and forest. The smooth path that Eleanor and Lucy had been following wound in and out among the strange rock-masses, bearing the signs of having been made at great cost and difficulty. Soon, also, benches of grey stone began to mark the course of it at frequent intervals.

'We must live here!' cried Lucy in enchantment. 'Let me spread the shawl for you--there!--just in front of that glimpse of the river.'

They had turned a corner of the path. Lucy, whose gaze was fixed upon the blue distance towards Orvieto, heard a hurried word from Eleanor, looked round, and saw Father Benecke just rising from a seat in front.

A shock ran through her. The priest stood hesitating and miserable before them, a hot colour suffusing his hollow cheeks. Lucy saw that he was no longer in clerical dress. He wore a grey alpaca suit, and a hat of fine Leghorn straw with a broad black ribbon. Both ladies almost feared to speak to him.

Then Lucy ran forward, her cheeks too a bright red, her eyes wet and sparkling. 'How do you do, Father Benecke? You won't remember me, but I was just introduced to you that day at luncheon--don't you remember--on the Aventine?'

The priest took her offered hand, and looked at her in astonishment.

'Yes--I remember--you were with Miss Manisty.'

'I wish you had asked me to come with you this morning,' cried the girl suddenly. 'I'd have helped you carry that parcel up the hill. It was too much for you in the heat.'

Her face expressed the sweetest, most passionate sympathy, the indignant homage of youth to old age unjustly wounded and forsaken. Eleanor was no less surprised than Father Benecke. Was this the stiff, the reticent Lucy?

The priest struggled for composure, and smiled as he withdrew his hand.

'You would have found it a long way, Signorina. I tried to get a boy at Selvapendente, but no one would serve me.'

He paused a moment, then resumed speaking with a sort of passionate reluctance, his eyes upon the ground.

'I am a suspended priest--and the Bishop of Orvieto has notified the fact to his clergy. The news was soon known through the whole district. And now it seems the people hate me. They will do nothing for me. Nay, if they could, they would willingly do me an injury.'

The flush had died out of the old cheeks. He stood bareheaded before them, the tonsure showing plainly amid his still thick white locks--the delicate face and hair, like a study in ivory and silver, thrown out against the deep shadows of the Sassetto.

'Father, won't you sit down and tell me about it all?' said Eleanor gently. 'You didn't send me away, you know--the other day--at the villa.'

The priest sighed and hesitated. 'I don't know, Madame, why I should trouble you with my poor story.

'It would not trouble me. Besides, I know so much of it already.'

She pointed to the bench he had just left.

'And I,' said Lucy, 'will go and fetch a book I left in the *loggia*. Father Benecke, Mrs. Burgoyne is not strong. She has walked more than enough. Will you kindly make her rest while I am gone?'

She fixed upon him her kind beseeching eyes. The sympathy, the homage of the two women enveloped the old man. His brow cleared a little.

She sped down the winding path, aglow with anger and pity. The priest's crushed strength and humiliated age--what a testimony to the power of that tradition for which Mr. Manisty was working--its unmerciful and tyrannous power!

Why such a penalty for a 'mildly Liberal' book?--'a fraction of the truth'? She could hear Manisty's ironic voice on that bygone drive to Nemi. If he saw his friend now, would he still excuse--defend?--

Her thoughts wrestled with him hotly--then withdrew themselves in haste, and fled the field.

*   *   *   *   *

Meanwhile Father Benecke's reserve had gradually yielded. He gave Eleanor a long troubled look, and said at last, very simply--

'Madame, you see a man broken hearted--'

He stopped, staring desolately at the ground. Eleanor threw in a few gentle words and phrases, and presently he again mustered courage to speak:

'You remember, Madame, that my letter was sent to the ***Osservatore Romano*** after a pledge had been given to me that only the bare fact of my submission, the mere formula that attends the withdrawal of any book that has been placed upon the Index, should be given to the public. Then my letter appeared. And suddenly it all became clear to me. I cannot explain it. It was with me as it was with St. Paul: "Placuit Domino ut revelaret filium suum in me!" My heart rose up and said: "Thou hast betrayed the truth"--"***Tradidisti Sanctum et Justum!***" After I left you that day I wrote withdrawing my letter and my submission. And I sent a copy to one of the Liberal papers. Then my heart smote me. One of the Cardinals of the Holy Office had treated me with much kindness. I wrote to him--I tried to explain what I had done. I wrote to several other persons at the Vatican, complaining of the manner in which I had been dealt with. No answer--not one. All were silent--as though I were already a dead man. Then I tried to see one or two of my old friends. But no one would receive me; one and all turned me from their doors. So then I left Rome. But I could not make up my mind to go home till I knew the worst. You understand, Madame, that I have been a Professor of Theology; that my Faculty can remove me--that my Faculty obeys the Bishops, and the Bishops obey the Holy See. I remembered this place--I left my address in Rome--and I came down here to wait. Ah! it was not long!'

He drew himself up, smiling bitterly.

'Two days after I arrived here I received two letters simultaneously--one from my Bishop, the other from the Council of my Faculty--suspending me both from my priestly and my academical functions. By the next post arrived a communication from the Bishop of this diocese, forbidding me the Sacraments.'

He paused. The mere recital of his case had brought him again into the bewilderment of that mental anguish he had gone through. Eleanor made a murmur of sympathy. He faced her with a sudden ardour.

'I had expected it, Madame; but when it came I was stunned--I was bowed to the earth. A few days later, I received an anonymous letter--from Orvieto, I think--reminding me that a priest suspended *a divinis* has no right to the soutane. "Let the traitor," it said, "give up the uniform he has disgraced--let him at least have the decency to do that." In my trouble I had not thought of it. So I wrote to a friend in Rome to send me clothes.'

Eleanor's eyes filled with tears. She thought of the old man staggering alone up the dusty hill under his unwelcome burden.

He himself was looking down at his new clothes in a kind of confusion. Suddenly he said under his breath, 'And for what?--because I said what every educated man in Europe knows to be true?'

'Father,' said Eleanor, longing to express some poor word of comfort and respect, 'you have suffered greatly--you will suffer--but it is not for yourself.'

He shook his head.

'Madame, you see a man dying of hunger and thirst! He cannot cheat himself with fine words. He starves!'

She stared at him, startled--partly understanding.

'For forty-two years,' he said, in a low, pathetic voice, 'have I received my Lord--day after day--without a break. And now "they have taken Him away--and I know not where they have laid Him!"'

Nothing could be more desolate than tone and look. Eleanor understood. She had seen this hunger before. She remembered a convent in Rome where on Good Fridays some of the nuns were often ill with restlessness and longing, because for twenty-four hours the Sacrament was not upon the altar.

Under the protection of her reverent and pitying silence he gradually recovered himself. With great delicacy, with fine and chosen words, she began to try and comfort him, dwelling on his comradeship with all the martyrs of the world, on the help and support that would certainly gather round him, on the new friends that would replace the old. And as she talked there grew up in her mind an envy of him so passionate, so intense, that she could have thrown herself at his feet there and then and opened her own wretched heart to him.

He, tortured by the martyrdom of thought, by the loss of Christian fellowship!--She, scorched and consumed by a passion that was perfectly ready to feed itself on the pain and injury of the beloved, or the innocent, as soon as its own selfish satisfaction was denied it! There was a moment when she felt herself unworthy to breathe the same air with him.

She stared at him, frowning and pale, her hand clasping her breast, lest he should hear the beating of her heart.

$$* \qquad * \qquad * \qquad * \qquad *$$

Then the hand dropped. The inner tumult passed. And at the same moment the sound of steps was heard approaching.

Round the further corner of the path came two ladies, descending towards them. They were both dressed in deep mourning. The first was an old woman, powerfully and substantially built. Her grey hair, raised in a sort of toupe under her plain black bonnet, framed a broad and noticeable brow, black eyes, and other features that were both benevolent and strong. She was very pale, and her face expressed a haunting and prevailing sorrow. Eleanor noticed that she was walking alone, some distance ahead of her companion, and that she had gathered up her black skirts in an ungloved hand, with an absent disregard of appearances. Behind her came a younger lady, a sallow and pinched woman of about thirty, very slight and tall.

As they passed Eleanor and her companion, the elder woman threw a lingering glance at the strangers. The scrutiny of it was perhaps somewhat imperious. The younger lady walked past stiffly with her eyes on the ground.

Eleanor and Father Benecke were naturally silent as they passed. Eleanor had just begun to speak again when she heard herself suddenly addressed in French.

She looked up in astonishment and saw that the old lady had returned and was standing before her.

'Madame--you allow me to address you?'

Eleanor bowed.

'You are staying at Santa Trinita, I believe!'

'*Oui, Madame*. We arrived yesterday.'

The Contessa's examining eye, whereof the keenness was but just duly chastened by courtesy, took note of that delicate and frail refinement which belonged both to Eleanor's person and dress.

'I fear, Madame, you are but roughly housed at the Trinita. They are not accustomed to English ladies. If my daughter and I, who are residents here, can be of any service to you, I beg that you will command us.'

Eleanor felt nothing but an angry impatience. Could even this remote place give them no privacy? She answered however with her usual grace.

'You are very good, Madame. I suppose that I am speaking to the Contessa Guerrini?'

The other lady made a sign of assent.

'We brought a few things from Orvieto--my friend and I,' Eleanor continued. 'We shall only stay a few weeks. I think we have all that is necessary. But I am very grateful to you for your courtesy.'

Her manner, however, expressed no effusion, hardly even adequate response. The Contessa understood. She talked for a few moments, gave a few directions as to paths and points of view, pointed out a drive beyond Selvapendente on the mountain side, bowed and departed.

Her bow did not include the priest. But he was not conscious of it. While the ladies talked, he had stood apart, holding the hat that seemed to burn him, in his finger-tips, his eyes, with their vague and troubled intensity, expressing only that inward vision which is at once the paradise and the torment of the prophet.

* * * * *

Three weeks passed away. Eleanor had said no more of further travelling. For some days she lived in terror, startled by the least sound upon the road. Then, as it seemed to Lucy, she resigned herself to trust in Father Benecke's discretion, influenced also no doubt by the sense of her own physical weakness, and piteous need of rest.

And now--in these first days of July--their risk was no doubt much less than it had been. Manisty had not remembered Torre Amiata--another thorn in Eleanor's heart! He must have left Italy. As each fresh morning dawned, she assured herself drearily that they were safe enough.

As for the heat, the sun indeed was lord and master of this central Italy. Yet on the high tableland of Torre Amiata the temperature was seldom oppressive. Lucy, indeed, soon found out from her friend the Carabiniere that while malaria haunted the valley, and scourged the region of Bolsena to the south, the characteristic disease of their upland was pneumonia, caused by the daily ascent of the labourers from the hot slopes below to the sharp coolness of the night.

No, the heat was not overwhelming. Yet Eleanor grew paler and feebler. Lucy hovered round her in a constantly increasing anxiety. And presently she began to urge retreat, and change of plan. It was madness to stay in the south. Why not more at once to Switzerland, or the Tyrol?

Eleanor shook her head.

'But I can't have you stay here,' cried Lucy in distress.

And coming closer, she chose her favourite seat on the floor of the *loggia* and laid her head against Eleanor's arm.

'Oughtn't you to go home?' she said, in a low urgent voice, caressing Eleanor's hand. 'Send me back to Uncle Ben. I can go home any time. But you ought to be in Scotland. Let me write to Miss Manisty!'

Eleanor laid her hand on her mouth. 'You promised!' she said, with her sweet stubborn smile.

'But it isn't right that I should let you run these risks. It--it--isn't kind to me.'

'I don't run risks. I am as well here as anywhere. The Orvieto doctor saw no objection to my being here--for a month, at any rate.'

'Send me home,' murmured Lucy again, softly kissing the hand she held. 'I don't know why I ever came.'

Eleanor started. Her lips grew pinched and bitter. But she only said:

'Give me our six weeks. All I want is you--and quiet.'

She held out both her hands very piteously, and Lucy took them, conquered, though not convinced.

'If anything went really wrong,' said Eleanor, 'I am sure you could appeal to that old Contessa. She has the face of a mother in Israel.'

'The people here seem to be pretty much in her hand,' said Lucy, as she rose. 'She manages most of their affairs for them. But poor, poor thing!--did you see that account in the *Tribuna* this morning?'

The girl's voice dropped, as though it had touched a subject almost too horrible to be spoken of.

Eleanor looked up with a sign of shuddering assent. Her daily *Tribuna*, which the postman brought her, had in fact contained that morning a letter describing the burial--after three months!--of the remains of the army slain in the carnage of Adowa on March 1. For three months had those thousands of Italian dead lain a prey to the African sun and the African vultures, before Italy could get leave from her victorious foe to pay the last offices to her sons.

That fine young fellow of whom the neighbourhood talked, who seemed to have left behind him such memories of energy and goodness, his mother's idol, had his bones too lain bleaching on that field of horror? It did not bear thinking of.

Lucy went downstairs to attend to some household matters. It was about ten o'clock in the morning, and presently Eleanor heard the postman from Selvapendente knock at the outer door. Marie brought up the letters.

There were four or five for Lucy, who had never concealed her address from her uncle, though she had asked that it might be kept for a while from other people. He had accordingly forwarded some home-letters, and Marie laid them on the table. Beside them were some letters that Lucy had just written and addressed. The postman went his round through the village; then returned to pick them up.

Marie went away, and suddenly Eleanor sprang from the sofa. With a flush and a wild look she went to examine Lucy's letters.

Was all quite safe? Was Lucy not tampering with her, betraying her in any way? The letters were all for America, except one, addressed to Paris. No doubt an order to a tradesman? But Lucy had said nothing about it--and the letter filled Eleanor with a mad suspicion that her weakness could hardly repress.

'Why! by now--I am not even a lady!' she said to herself at last with set teeth, as she dragged herself from the table, and began to pace the *loggia*.

But when Lucy returned, in one way or another Eleanor managed to inform herself as to the destination of all the letters. And then she scourged and humbled herself for her doubts, and became for the rest of the morning the most winning and tender of companions.

As a rule they never spoke of Manisty. What Lucy's attitude implied was that she had in some unwitting and unwilling way brought trouble on Eleanor; that she was at Torre Amiata to repair it; and that in general she was at Eleanor's orders.

Of herself she would not allow a word. Beyond and beneath her sweetness Eleanor divined a just and indomitable pride. And beyond that Mrs. Burgoyne could not penetrate.

CHAPTER XVIII

Meanwhile Eleanor found some distraction in Father Benecke.
The poor priest was gradually recovering a certain measure of serenity. The two ladies were undoubtedly of great assistance to him. They became popular in the village, where they and their wants set flowing a stream of *lire*, more abundant by far than had hitherto attended the summer guests, even the Sindaco of Selvapendente. They were the innocent causes, indeed, of some evil. Eleanor had been ordered goats' milk by the Orvieto doctor, and the gentleman who had secured the order from the *massaja* went in fear of his life at the hands of two other gentlemen who had not been equally happy. But in general they brought prosperity, and the popular smile was granted them.

So that when it was discovered that they were already acquainted with the mysterious foreign priest, and stoutly disposed to befriend him, the village showed the paralysing effect of a conflict of interests. At the moment and for various reasons the clericals were masters. And the clericals denounced Father Benecke as a traitor and a heretic. At the same time the village could not openly assail the ladies' friend without running the risk of driving the ladies themselves from Torre Amiata. And this clearly would have been a mere wanton slight to a kind Providence. Even the children understood the situation, and Father Benecke now took his walks unmolested by anything sharper than sour looks and averted faces.

Meanwhile he was busy in revising a new edition of his book. This review of his own position calmed him. Contact with all the mass of honest and laborious knowledge of which it was a summary gave him back his dignity, raised him from the pit of humiliation into which he seemed to have fallen, and strengthened him to resist. The spiritual privations that his state brought him could be sometimes forgotten. There were moments indeed when the iron entered into his soul. When the bell of the little church rang at half-past five in the morning, he was always there in his corner by the door. The peasants brushed past him suspiciously as they went in and out. He did not see them. He was absorbed in the function, or else in a bitter envy of the officiating priest, and at such moments he suffered all that any 'Vatican-ist' could have wished him to suffer.

But when he was once more among his books, large gusts of a new and strange freedom began, as it were, to blow about him. In writing the philosophical book which had now brought him into conflict with the Church, he had written in con-straint and timidity. A perpetual dread, not only of ecclesiastical censure but of the opinion of old and valued friends; a perpetual uncertainty as to the limits of Catholic liberty; these things had held him in bondage. What ought he say? What must he leave unsaid? He understood perfectly that hypothesis must not be stated as truth. But the vast accumulation of biological fact on the one hand, and of histori-cal criticism on the other, that has become the common property of the scientific mind, how was it to be recapitulated--within Catholic limits? He wrote in fear, like one walking on the burning ploughshares of the ordeal. Religion was his life; but he had at once the keen intelligence and the mystical temperament of the Suabian. He dreaded the collision which ultimately came. Yet the mental process could not be stayed.

Now, with the final act of defiance, obscurely carried out, conditioned he knew not how, there had arrived for him a marvellous liberation of soul. Even at sixty-five he felt himself tragically new-born--naked and feeble indeed, but still with unknown possibilities of growth and new life before him.

His book, instead of being revised, must be re-written. No need now to trem-ble for a phrase! Let the truth be told. He plunged into his old studies again, and the world of thought met him with a friendlier and franker welcome. On all sides there was a rush and sparkle of new light. How far he must follow and submit, his trembling soul did not yet know. But for the moment there was an extraordi-nary though painful exhilaration--the excitement of leading-strings withdrawn and walls thrown down.

This enfranchisement brought him, however, into strange conflict with his own character. His temperament was that of the ascetic and visionary religious. His intelligence had much the same acuteness and pliancy as that of another and more pronounced doubter--a South German also, like Father Benecke,--the author of the 'Leben Jesu.' But his ***character*** was the joint product of his temperament and his habits, and was often difficult to reconcile with the quick play of his intelligence.

For instance, he was, in daily habit, an austere and most devout priest, living alone with his old sister, as silent and yet fervent as himself, and knowing almost nothing of other women, except through the Confessional. To his own astonishment he was in great request as a director. But socially he knew very little of his penitents; they were to him only 'souls,' spiritual cases which he studied with the ardour of a doctor. Otherwise the small benefice which he held in a South German town, his university class, and the travail of his own research absorbed him wholly.

Hence a great innocence and unworldliness; but also an underlying sternness towards himself and others. His wants were small, and for many years the desires of the senses had been dead within him. Towards women he felt, if the truth were known, with that strange unconscious arrogance which is a most real and very primitive element in Catholicism, notwithstanding the worship of Mary and the glories of St. Teresa and St. Catharine. The Church does not allow any woman, even a 'religious,' to wash the corporal and other linen which has been used in the Mass. There is a strain of thought implied in that prohibition which goes deep and far-- back to the dim dawn of human things. It influences the priest in a hundred ways; it affected even the tender and spiritual mind of Father Benecke. As a director of women he showed them all that impersonal sweetness which is of the essence of Catholic tradition; but they often shrank nevertheless from what they felt to be a fundamental inflexibility mingled with pity.

Thus when he found himself brought into forced contact with the two ladies who had invaded his retreat, when Lucy in a hundred pretty ways began to show him a young and filial homage, when Eleanor would ask him to coffee with them, and talk to him about his book and the subjects it discussed, the old priest was both amazed and embarrassed.

How in the world did she know anything about such things? He understood that she had been of assistance to Mr. Manisty: but that it had been the assistance of a comrade and an equal--that had never entered his head.

So that at first Mrs. Burgoyne's talk silenced and repelled him. He was conscious of the male revolt of St. Paul!--'I suffer not a woman to teach'; and for a time he hung back.

On his visit to the villa, and on her first meeting with him at Torre Amiata, he had been under the influence of a shock which had crushed the child in him and broken down his reserve. Yet that reserve was naturally strong, together with certain despotic instincts which Eleanor perceived with surprise beneath his exquisite gentleness. She sometimes despaired of taming him.

Nevertheless when Eleanor presently advised him to publish a statement of his case in a German periodical; when the few quick things she said showed a knowledge of the German situation and German current literature that filled him with astonishment; when with a few smiles, hints, demurs, she made plain to him that she perfectly understood where he had weakened his book--which lay beside her--out of deference to authority, and where it must be amended, if it was to produce any real influence upon European cultivated opinion, the old priest was at first awkward or speechless. Then slowly he rose to the bait. He began to talk; he became by degrees combative, critical, argumentative. His intelligence took the field; his character receded. Eleanor had won the day.

Presently, indeed, he began to haunt them. He brought to Eleanor each article and letter as it arrived, consulting her on every phase of a controversy, concerning him and his book, which was now sweeping through certain Catholic circles and newspapers. He was eager, forgetful, exacting even. Lucy began to dread the fatigue that he sometimes produced. While for Lucy he was still the courteous and paternal priest, for Eleanor he gradually became--like Manisty--the intellectual comrade, crossing swords often in an equal contest, where he sometimes forgot the consideration due to the woman in the provocation shown him by the critic.

And when she had tamed him, it was to Eleanor all ashes and emptiness!

'*This* is the kind of thing I can always do,' she said to herself one day, throwing out her hands in self-scorn, as he left her on the *loggia*, where he had been taking coffee with herself and Lucy.

And meanwhile what attracted her was not in the least the controversialist and the man of letters--it was the priest, the Christian, the ascetic.

Torn with passion and dread as she was, she divined in him the director; she felt towards him as the woman so often feels towards that sexless mystery, the priest. Other men are the potential lovers of herself or other women; she knows herself their match. But in this man set apart, she recognises the embodied conscience, the moral judge, who is indifferent to her as a woman, observant of her as a soul. Round this attraction she flutters, and has always fluttered since the beginning of things. It is partly a yearning for guidance and submission; partly also a secret pride that she who for other men is mere woman, is, for the priest, spirit, and immortal. She prostrates herself; but at the same time she seems to herself to enter through her submission upon a region of spiritual independence where she is the slave, not of man but of God.

What she felt also, tortured as she was by jealousy and angry will, was the sheer longing for human help that must always be felt by the lonely and the weak. Confession, judgment, direction--it was on these tremendous things that her inner mind was brooding all the time that she sat talking to Father Benecke of the Jewish influence in Bavaria, or the last number of the 'Civilta Cattolica.'

*   *   *   *   *

One evening at the beginning of July Eleanor and Lucy were caught in the woods by a thunder-shower. The temperature dropped suddenly, and as they mounted the hill towards the convent Eleanor in her thin white dress met a blast of cold wind that followed the rain.

The result was chill and fever. Lucy and Marie tended her as best they could, but her strength appeared to fail her with great rapidity, and there came an evening when Lucy fell into a panic of anxiety.

Should she summon the local doctor--a man who was paid 80*l.* a year by the Municipio of Selvapendente, and tended the Commune of Torre Amiata?

She had discovered, however, that he was not liked by the peasants. His appearance was not attractive, and she doubted whether she could persuade Eleanor to see him.

An idea struck her. Without consulting Mrs. Burgoyne, she took her hat and boldly walked up to the Palazzo on the hill. Here she inquired for the Contessa Guerrini. The Contessa, however, was out; Lucy left a little note in French asking for advice. Could they get a good doctor at Selvapendente, or must she send to Orvieto?

She had hardly reached home before an answer followed her from the Contessa, who regretted extremely that Mademoiselle Foster should not have found her at home. There was a good doctor at Selvapendente, and the Contessa would have great pleasure in sending a mounted messenger to fetch him. She regretted the illness of Madame. There was a fair *farmacia* in the village. Otherwise she was afraid that in illness the ladies would not find themselves very well placed at Torre Amiata. Would Mademoiselle kindly have her directions for the doctor ready, and the messenger would call immediately?

Lucy was sincerely grateful and perhaps a little astonished. She was obliged to tell Eleanor, and Eleanor showed some restlessness, but was too unwell to protest. The doctor came and proved to be competent. The fever was subdued, and Eleanor was soon convalescent. Meanwhile flowers, fruit, and delicacies were sent daily from the Palazzo, and twice did the Contessa descend from her little victoria at the door of the convent courtyard, to inquire for the patient.

On each occasion Lucy saw her, and received the impression of a dignified, kind, and masterful woman, bowed by recent grief, but nevertheless sensitively alive in a sort of old-fashioned stately way to the claims of strangers on the protection of the local grandee. It seemed to attract her that Lucy was American, and that Eleanor was English.

'I have twice visited England,' she said, in an English that was correct, but a little rusty. 'My husband learnt many things from England--for the estate. But I wonder, Mademoiselle, that you come to us at this time of year?'

Lucy laughed and coloured. She said it was pleasant to see Italy without the *forestieri*; that it was like surprising a bird on its nest. But she stumbled a little, and the Contessa noticed both the blush and the stumbling.

When Eleanor was able to go out, the little carriage was sent for her, and neither she nor Lucy knew how to refuse it. They drove up and down the miles of zig-zag road that Don Emilio had made through the forest on either side of the river, connecting the Palazzo Guerrini with the *casa di caccia* on the mountain opposite. The roads were deserted; grass was beginning to grow on them. The peasants scarcely ever used them. They clung to the old steep paths and tracts that had been theirs for generations. But the small smart horses, in their jingling harness, trotted briskly along; and Eleanor beside her companion, more frail and languid than ever, looked listlessly out upon a world of beauty that spoke to her no more.

And at last a note from the Contessa arrived, asking if the ladies would honour her and her daughter by taking tea with them at the Palazzo. 'We are in deep mourning and receiving no society,' said the note; 'but if Madame and her friend will visit us in this quiet way it will give us pleasure, and they will perhaps enjoy the high view from here over our beautiful country.'

Eleanor winced and accepted.

*   *   *   *   *

The Palazzo, as they climbed up through the village towards it, showed itself to be an imposing pile of the later seventeenth century, with heavily-barred lower windows, and, above, a series of graceful *loggie* on its northern and western fronts which gave it a delicate and habitable air. On the north-eastern side the woods, broken by the stone-fall of the Sassetto, sank sharply to the river; on the other the village and the vineyards pressed upon its very doors. The great entrance gateway opened on a squalid village street, alive with crawling babies and chatting mothers.

At this gateway, however--through which appeared a courtyard aglow with oleanders and murmurous with running water--they were received with some state. An old majordomo met them, accompanied by two footmen and a carrying-chair. Eleanor was borne up a high flight of stone stairs, and through a vast and bare 'apartment' of enormous rooms with tiled or brick floors and wide stone *cheminees*, furnished with a few old chests and cabinets, a collection of French engravings of the last century, and some indifferent pictures. A few of the rooms were frescoed with scenes of hunting or social life in a facile eighteenth-century style. Here and there was a piece of old tapestry or a Persian carpet. But as a whole, the Palazzo, in spite of its vastness, made very much the impression of an old English manor house which has belonged to people of some taste and no great wealth, and has grown threadbare and even ugly with age. Yet tradition and the family remain. So here. A frugal and antique dignity, sure of itself and needing no display, breathed in the great cool spaces.

The Contessa and her daughter were in a small and more modern *salone* looking on the river and the woods. Eleanor was placed in a low chair near the open window, and her hostess could not forbear a few curious and pitying glances at the sharp, high-bred face of the Englishwoman, the feverish lips, and the very evident emaciation, which the elegance of the loose black dress tried in vain to hide.

'I understand, Madame,' she said, after Eleanor had expressed her thanks with the pretty effusion that was natural to her, 'that you were at Torre Amiata last autumn?'

Eleanor started. The *massaja*, she supposed, had been gossiping. It was disagreeable, but good-breeding bade her be frank.

'Yes, I was here with some friends, and your agent gave us hospitality for the night.'

The Contessa looked astonished.

'Ah!' she said, 'you were here with the D----'s?'

Eleanor assented.

'And you spent the winter in Rome?'

'Part of it. Madame, you have the most glorious view in the world!' And she turned towards the great prospect at her feet.

The Contessa understood.

'How ill she is!' she thought; 'and how distinguished!'

And presently Eleanor on her side, while she was talking nervously and fast on a good many disconnected subjects, found herself observing her hostess. The Contessa's strong square face had been pale and grief-stricken when she saw it first. But she noticed now that the eyelids were swollen and red, as though from constant tears; and the little sallow daughter looked sadder and shyer than ever. Eleanor presently gathered that they were living in the strictest seclusion and saw no visitors. 'Then why'--she asked herself, wondering--'did she speak to us in the Sassetto?--and why are we admitted now? Ah! that is his portrait!'

For at the Contessa's elbow, on a table specially given up to it, she perceived a large framed photograph draped in black. It represented a tall young man in an Artillery uniform. The face was handsome, eager, and yet melancholy. It seemed to express a character at once impatient and despondent, but held in check by a strong will. With a shiver Eleanor again recalled the ghastly incidents of the war; and the story they had heard from the *massaja* of the young man's wound and despair.

Her heart, in its natural lovingness, went out to his mother. She found her tongue, and she and the Contessa talked till the twilight fell of the country and the peasants, of the improvements in Italian farming, of the old convent and its history.

Not a word of the war; and not a word, Eleanor noticed, of their fellow-lodger, Father Benecke. From various indications she gathered that the sallow daughter was *devote* and a 'black.' The mother, however, seemed to be of a different stamp. She was at any rate a person of cultivation. That, the books lying about were enough to prove. But she had also the shrewdness and sobriety, the large pleasant homeliness, of a good man of business. It was evident that she, rather than her *fattore*, managed her property, and that she perfectly understood what she was doing.

In truth, a secret and strong sympathy had arisen between the two women. During the days that followed they met often.

The Contessa asked no further questions as to the past history or future plans of the visitors. But indirectly, and without betraying her new friends, she made inquiries in Rome. One of the D---- family wrote to her:

'The English people we brought with us last year to your delicious Torre Amiata were three--a gentleman and two ladies. The gentleman was a Mr. Manisty, a former member of the English Parliament, and very conspicuous in Rome last winter for a kind of Brunetiere alliance with the Vatican and hostility to the Italian *regime*. People mostly regarded it as a pose; and as he and his aunt were rich and of old family, and Mr. Manisty was--when he chose--a most brilliant talker, they were welcome everywhere, and Rome certainly feted them a good deal. The lady staying with them was a Mrs. Burgoyne, a very graceful and charming woman whom everybody liked. It was quite plain that there was some close relation between her and Mr. Manisty. By which I mean nothing scandalous! Heavens! nobody ever thought of such a thing. But I believe that many people who knew them well felt that it would be a very natural and right thing that he should marry her. She was evidently touchingly devoted to him--acting as his secretary, and hanging on his talk. In the spring they went out to the hills, and a young American girl--quite a beauty, they say, though rather raw--went to stay with them. I heard so much of her beauty from Madame Variani that I was anxious to see her. Miss Manisty promised to bring her here before they left in June. But apparently the party broke up suddenly, and we saw no more of them.

'Now I think I have told you the chief facts about them. I wonder what makes you ask? I often think of poor Mrs. Burgoyne, and hope she may be happy some day. I can't say, however, that Mr. Manisty ever seemed to me a very desirable husband! And yet I was very sorry you were not at home in the autumn. You might have disliked him heartily, but you would have found him *piquant* and stimulating. And of all the glorious heads on man's shoulders he possesses the most glorious--the head of a god attached to a rather awkward and clumsy body.'

Happy! Well, whatever else might have happened, the English lady was not yet happy. Of that the Contessa Guerrini was tolerably certain after a first conversation with her. Amid the gnawing pressure of her own grief there was a certain distraction in the observance of this sad and delicate creature, and in the very natural speculations she aroused. Clearly Miss Foster was the young American girl. Why were they here together, in this heat, away from all their friends?

$$*\quad*\quad*\quad*\quad*$$

One day Eleanor was sitting with the Contessa on a *loggia* in the Palazzo, looking north-west towards Radicofani. It was a cool and rather cloudy evening, after a day of gasping heat. The majordomo suddenly announced; 'His reverence, Don Teodoro.'

The young *padre parroco* appeared--a slim, engaging figure, as he stood for an instant amid the curtains of the doorway, glancing at the two ladies with an expression at once shy and confiding.

He received the Contessa's greeting with effusion, bowing low over her hand. When she introduced him to the English lady, he bowed again ceremoniously. But his blue eyes lost their smile. The gesture was formal, the look constrained. Eleanor, remembering Father Benecke, understood.

In conversation with the Contessa however he recovered a boyish charm and spontaneity that seemed to be characteristic. Eleanor watched him with admiration, noticing also the subtle discernment of the Italian, which showed through all his simplicity of manner. It was impossible to mistake, for instance, that he felt himself in a house of mourning. The movements of body and voice were all at first subdued and sympathetic. Yet the mourning had passed into a second stage, and ordinary topics might now be introduced. He glided into them with the most perfect tact.

He had come for two reasons. First, to announce his appointment as Select Preacher for the coming Advent at a well-known church in Rome; secondly, to bring to the Contessa's notice a local poet--gifted, but needy--an Orvieto man, whose Muse the clergy had their own reasons for cultivating.

The Contessa congratulated him, and he bowed profoundly in a silent pleasure.

Then he took up the poet, repeating stanza after stanza with a perfect *naivete*, in his rich young voice, without a trace of display; ending at last with a little sigh, and a sudden dropping of the eyes, like a child craving pardon.

Eleanor was delighted with him, and the Contessa, who seemed more difficult to please, also smiled upon him. Teresa, the pious daughter, was with Lucy in the Sassetto. No doubt she was the little priest's particular friend. He had observed at once that she was not there, and had inquired for her.

'One or two of those lines remind me of Carducci, and that reminds me that I saw Carducci for the first time this spring,' said the Contessa, turning to Eleanor. 'It was at a meeting of the Accademia in Rome. A great affair--the King and Queen-- and a paper on Science and Religion, by Mazzoli. Perhaps you don't remember his name? He was our Minister of the Interior a few years ago.'

Eleanor did not hear. Her attention was diverted by the sudden change in the aspect of the *padre parroco*. It was the dove turned hawk. The fresh face seemed to have lost its youth in a moment, to have grown old, sharp, rancorous.

'Mazzoli!'--he said, as the Contessa paused--'*Eccellenza, e un Ebreo!*'

The Contessa frowned. Yes, Mazzoli was a Jew, but an honest man; and his address had been of great interest, as bearing witness to the revival of religious ideas in circles that had once been wholly outside religion. The *parroco's* lips quivered with scorn. He remembered the affair--a scandalous business! The King and Queen present, and a *Jew* daring before them, to plead the need of 'a new religion'--in Italy, where Catholicism, Apostolic and Roman, was guaranteed as the national religion--by the first article of the *Statuto*. The Contessa replied with some dryness that Mazzoli spoke as a philosopher. Whereupon the *parroco* insisted with heat that there could be no true philosophy outside the Church. The Contessa laughed and turned upon the young man a flashing and formidable eye.

'Let the Church add a little patriotism to her philosophy, Father,--she will find it better appreciated.'

Don Teodoro straightened to the blow. 'I am a Roman, *Eccellenza*--you also--*Scusi*!'

'I am an Italian, Father--you also. But you hate your country.'

Both speakers had grown a little pale.

'I have nothing to do with the Italy of Venti Settembre,' said the priest, twisting and untwisting his long fingers in a nervous passion. 'That Italy has three marks of distinction before Europe--by which you may know her.'

'And those--?' said the Contessa, calm and challenging.

'Debt, *Eccellenza*--hunger!--crimes of blood! *Sono il suo primato--l'unico!*'

He threw at her a look sparkling and venomous. All the grace of his youth had vanished. As he sat there, Eleanor in a flash saw in him the conspirator and the firebrand that a few more years would make of him.

'Ah!' said the Contessa, flushing. 'There were none of these things in the old Papal States?--under the Bourbons?--the Austrians? Well--we understand perfectly that you would destroy us if you could!'

'*Eccellenza*, Jesus Christ and his Vicar come before the House of Savoy!'

'Ruin us, and see what you will gain!'

'*Eccellenza*, the Lord rules.

'Well--well. Break the eggs--that's easy. But whether the omelet will be as the Jesuits please--that's another affair.'

Each combatant smiled, and drew a long breath.

'These are our old battles,' said the Contessa, shaking her head. '*Scusi!* I must go and give an order.'

And to Eleanor's alarm, she rose and left the room.

The young priest showed a momentary embarrassment at being left alone with the strange lady. But it soon passed. He sat a moment, quieting down, with his eyes dropped, his finger-tips lightly joined upon his knee. Then he said sweetly:

'You are perhaps not acquainted with the pictures in the Palazzo, Madame. May I offer you my services? I believe that I know the names of the portraits.'

Eleanor was grateful to him, and they wandered through the bare rooms, looking at the very doubtful works of art that they contained.

Presently, as they returned to the *salone* from which they had started, Eleanor caught sight of a fine old copy of the Raphael St. Cecilia at Bologna. The original has been much injured, and the excellence of the copy struck her. She was seized, too, with a stabbing memory of a day in the Bologna Gallery with Manisty!

She hurried across the room to look at the picture. The priest followed her.

'Ah! that, Madame,' he said with enthusiasm--that is a *capolavoro*. It is by Michael Angelo.'

Eleanor looked at him in astonishment. 'This one? It is a copy, Padre, of Raphael's St. Cecilia at Bologna--a very interesting and early copy.'

Don Teodoro frowned. He went up to look at it doubtfully, pushing out his lower lip.

'Oh! no, Madame,' he said, returning to her, and speaking with a soft yet obstinate complacency. 'Pardon me--but you are mistaken. That is an original work of the great Michael Angelo.'

Eleanor said no more.

When the Contessa returned, Eleanor took up a volume of French translations from the Greek Anthology that the Contessa had lent her the day before. She restored the dainty little book to its mistress, pointing to some of her favourites.

The *parroco's* face fell as he listened.

'Ah!--these are from the Greek!' he said, looking down modestly, as the Contessa handed him the book. 'I spent five years, *Eccellenza*, in learning Greek, but--!' He shrugged his shoulders gently.

Then glancing from one lady to the other, he said with a deprecating smile:

'I could tell you some things. I could explain what some of the Greek words in Italian come from--"mathematics," for instance.'

He gave the Greek word with a proud humility, emphasising each syllable.

'"Economy"--"theocracy"--"aristocracy."'

The Greek came out like a child's lesson. He was not always sure; he corrected himself once or twice; and at the end he threw back his head with a little natural pride.

But the ladies avoided looking either at him or each other.

Eleanor thought of Father Benecke; of the weight of learning on that silver head. Yet Benecke was an outcast, and this youth was already on the ladder of promotion.

When he departed the Contessa threw up her hands.

'And that man is just appointed Advent Preacher at one of the greatest church-es in Rome!'

Then she checked herself.

'At the same time, Madame,' she said, looking a little stiffly at Eleanor, 'we have learned priests--many of them.'

Eleanor hastened to assent. With what heat had Manisty schooled her during the winter to the recognition of Catholic learning, within its own self-chosen limits!

'It is this deplorable Seminary education!' sighed the Contessa. 'How is one half of the nation ever to understand the other? They speak a different language. Imag-ine all our scientific education on the one side, and this--this dangerous innocent on the other! And yet we all want religion--we all want some hope beyond this life.'

Her strong voice broke. She turned away, and Eleanor could only see the mas-sive outline of head and bust, and the coils of grey hair.

Mrs. Burgoyne drew her chair nearer to the Contessa. Silently and timidly she laid a hand upon her knee.

'I can't understand,' she said in a low voice, 'how you have had the patience to be kind to us, these last weeks!'

'Do you know why?' said the Contessa, turning round upon her, and no longer attempting to conceal the tears upon her fine old face.

'No--tell me!'

'It was because Emilio loved the English. He once spent a very happy summer in England. I--I don't know whether he was in love with anyone. But, at any rate, he looked back to it with deep feeling. He always did everything that he could for any English person--and especially in these wilds. I have known him often take trouble that seemed to me extravagant or quixotic. But he always would. And when I saw you in the *Sassetto* that day, I knew exactly what he would have done. You looked so delicate--and I remembered how rough the convent was. I had hardly spoken to anybody but Teresa since the news came, but I could not help speaking to you.'

Eleanor pressed her hand. After a pause she said gently:

'He was with General Da Bormida?'

'Yes--he was with Da Bormida. There were three columns, you remember. He was with the column that seemed for a time to be successful. I only got the full account last week from a brother-officer, who was a prisoner till the end of June. Emilio, like all the rest, thought the position was carried--that it was a victory. He raised his helmet and shouted, ***Viva il Re! Viva l'Italia!*** And then all in a moment the Scioans were on them like a flood. They were all carried away. Emilio rallied his men again and again under a hail of bullets. Several heard him say: "Courage, lads--courage! Your Captain dies with you! ***Avanti! avanti! Viva l'Italia!***" Then at last he was frightfully wounded, and perhaps you may have heard in the village'--again the mother turned her face away--' that he said to a *caporale* beside him, who came from this district, whom he knew at home--"Federigo, take your gun and finish it." He was afraid--my beloved!--of falling into the hands of the enemy. Already they had passed some wounded, horribly mutilated. The *caporale* refused. "I can't do that, ***Eccellenza***," he said; "but we will transport you or die with you!" Then again there was a gleam of victory. He thought the enemy were repulsed. A brother-officer saw him being carried along by two soldiers, and Emilio beckoned to him. "You must be my Confessor!" he said, smiling. And he gave him some messages for me and Teresa--some directions about his affairs. Then he asked: "It is victory--isn't it? We have won, after all?" And the other--who knew--couldn't bear to tell him the truth. He said, "Yes." And Emilio said, "You swear it?" "I swear." And the boy made the sign of the cross--said again, ***Viva l'Italia!***--and died.... They buried him that night under a little thicket. My God! I thank Thee that he did not lie on that accursed plain!'

She raised her handkerchief to hide her trembling lips. Eleanor said nothing. Her face was bowed upon her hands, which lay on the Contessa's knee.

'His was not a very happy temperament,' said the poor mother presently.' He was always anxious and scrupulous. I sometimes thought he had been too much influenced by Leopardi; he was always quoting him. That is the way with many of our young men. Yet Emilio was a Christian--a sincere believer. It would have been better if he had married. But he gave all his affection to me and Teresa--and to this place and the people. I was to carry on his work--but I am an old woman--and very tired. Why should the young go before their time?... Yet I have no bitterness about the war. It was a ghastly mistake--and it has humiliated us as a nation. But nations are made by their blunderings as much as by their successes. Emilio would not have grudged his life. He always thought that Italy had been "made too quick," as they say--that our day of trial and weakness was not done.... But, **Gesu mio!**--if he had not left me so much of life.'

Eleanor raised her head.

'I, too,' she said, almost in a whisper--'I, too, have lost a son. But he was a little fellow.'

The Contessa looked at her in astonishment and burst into tears.

'Then we are two miserable women!' she said, wildly.

Eleanor clung to her--but with a sharp sense of unfitness and unworthiness. She felt herself a hypocrite. In thought and imagination her boy now was but a hovering shadow compared to Manisty. It was not this sacred mother-love that was destroying her own life.

*　　*　　*　　*　　*

As they drove home through the evening freshness, Eleanor's mind pursued its endless and solitary struggle.

Lucy sat beside her. Every now and then Eleanor's furtive guilty look sought the girl's face. Sometimes a flying terror would grip her by the heart. Was Lucy graver--paler? Were there some new lines round the sweet eyes? That serene and virgin beauty--had it suffered the first withering touch since Eleanor had known it first? And if so, whose hand? whose fault?

Once or twice her heart failed within her; foreseeing a remorse that was no sooner imagined than it was denied, scouted, hurried out of sight.

That brave, large-brained woman with whom she had just been talking; there was something in the atmosphere which the Contessa's personality shed round it, that made Eleanor doubly conscious of the fever in her own blood. As in Father Benecke's case, so here; she could only feel herself humiliated and dumb before these highest griefs--the griefs that ennoble and enthrone.

That night she woke from a troubled sleep with a stifled cry of horror. In her dreams she had been wrestling with Manisty, trying to thrust him back with all the frenzied force of her weak hands. But he had wrenched himself from her hold. She saw him striding past her--aglow, triumphant. And that dim white form awaiting him--and the young arms outstretched!

'No, no! False! She doesn't--doesn't love him!' her heart cried, throwing all its fiercest life into the cry. She sat up in bed trembling and haggard. Then she stole into the next room. Lucy lay deeply, peacefully asleep. Eleanor sank down beside her, hungrily watching her. 'How could she sleep like that--if--if she cared?' asked her wild thoughts, and she comforted herself, smiling at her own remorse. Once she touched the girl's hand with her lips, feeling towards her a rush of tenderness that came like dew on the heat of the soul. Then she crept back to bed, and cried, and cried--through the golden mounting of the dawn.

CHAPTER XIX

The days passed on. Between Eleanor and Lucy there had grown up a close, intense, and yet most painful affection. Neither gave the other her full confidence, and on Eleanor's side the consciousness both of the futility and the enormity of what she had done only increased with time, embittering the resistance of a will which was still fierce and unbroken.

Meanwhile she often observed her companion with a quick and torturing curiosity. What was it that Manisty had found so irresistible, when all her own subtler arts had failed?

Lucy was in some ways very simple, primitive even, as Manisty had called her. Eleanor knew that her type was no longer common in a modern America that sends all its girls to college, and ransacks the world for an experience. But at the same time the depth and force of her nature promised rich developments in the future. She was still a daughter of New England, with many traits now fast disappearing; but for her, too, there was beginning that cosmopolitan transformation to which the women of her race lend themselves so readily.

And it was Manisty's influence that was at work! Eleanor's miserable eyes discerned it in a hundred ways. Half the interests and questions on which Manisty's mind had been fixed for so long were becoming familiar to Lucy. They got books regularly from Rome, and Eleanor had been often puzzled by Lucy's selections--till one day the key to them flashed across her.

The girl indeed was making her way, fast and silently, into quite new regions of thought and feeling. She read, and she thought. She observed the people of the village; she even frequented their humble church, though she would never go with Eleanor to Sunday Mass. There some deep, unconquerable instinct held her back.

All through, indeed, her personal beliefs and habits--Evangelical, unselfish, strong, and a little stern--seemed to be quite unchanged. But they were differently tinged, and would be in time differently presented. Nor would they ever, of themselves, divide her from Manisty. Eleanor saw that clearly enough. Lucy could hold opinion passionately, unreasonably even; but she was not of the sort that makes life depend upon opinion. Her true nature was large, tolerant, patient. The deepest forces in it were forces of feeling, and no intellectual difference would ever be able to deny them their natural outlet.

Meanwhile Lucy seemed to herself the most hopelessly backward and ignorant person, particularly in Eleanor's company.

'Oh! I am just a dunce,' she said one day to Eleanor, with a smile and sigh, after some questions as to her childhood and bringing up. 'They ought to have sent me to college. All the girls I knew went. But then Uncle Ben would have been quite alone. So I just had to get along.'

'But you know what many girls don't know.'

Lucy gave a shrug.

'I know some Latin and Greek, and other things that Uncle Ben could teach me. But oh! what a simpleton I used to feel in Boston!'

'You were behind the age?

Lucy laughed.

'I didn't seem to have anything to do with the age, or the age with me. You see, I was slow, and everybody else was quick. But an American that isn't quick's got no right to exist. You're bound to have heard the last thing, and read the last book, or people just want to know why you're there!'

'Why should people call you slow?' said Eleanor, in that voice which Lucy often found so difficult to understand, because of the strange note of hostility which, for no reason at all, would sometimes penetrate through the sweetness. 'It's absurd. How quickly you've picked up Italian--and frocks!--and a hundred things.'

She smiled, and stroked the brown head beside her.

Lucy coloured, bent over her work, and did not reply.

Generally they passed their mornings in the *loggia* reading and working. Lucy was a dexterous needle-woman, and a fine piece of embroidery had made much progress since their arrival at Torre Amiata. Secretly she wondered whether she was to finish it there. Eleanor now shrank from the least mention of change; and

Lucy, having opened her generous arms to this burden, did not know when she would be allowed to put it down. She carried it, indeed, very tenderly--with a love that was half eager remorse. Still, before long Uncle Ben must remonstrate in earnest. And the Porters, whom she had treated so strangely? They were certainly going back to America in September, if not before. And must she not go with them?

And would the heat at Torre Amiata be bearable for the sensitive Northerner after July? Already they spent many hours of the day in their shuttered and closed rooms, and Eleanor was whiter than the convolvulus which covered the new-mown hayfields.

What a darling--what a kind and chivalrous darling was Uncle Ben! She had asked him to trust her, and he had done it nobly, though it was evident from his letters that he was anxious and disturbed. 'I cannot tell you everything,' she had written, 'or I should be betraying a confidence; but I am doing what I feel to be right--what I am sure you would consent to my doing if you knew. Mrs. Burgoyne is *very* frail--and she clings to me. I can't explain to you how or why--but so it is. For the present I must look after her. This place is beautiful; the heat not yet too great; and you shall hear every week. Only, please, tell other people that I wish you to forward letters, and cannot long be certain of my address.'

And he:

'Dear child, this is very mysterious. I don't like it. It would be absurd to pretend that I did. But I haven't trusted my Lucy for fourteen years in order to begin to persecute her now because she can't tell me a secret. Only I give you warning that if you don't write to me every week, my generosity, as you call it, will break down--and I shall be for sending out a search party right away.... Do you want money? I must say that I hope July will see the end of your adventure.'

Would it? Lucy found her mind full of anxious thoughts as Eleanor read aloud to her.

Presently she discovered that a skein of silk she wanted for her work was not in her basket. She turned to look also in her old inlaid workbox, which stood on a small table beside her. But it was not there.

'Please wait a moment,' she said to her companion. 'I am afraid I must get my silk.'

She stood up hastily, and her movement upset the rickety cane table. With a crash her workbox fell to the ground, and its contents rolled all over the *loggia*. She gave a cry of dismay.

'Oh! my terra-cottas!--my poor terra-cottas!'

Eleanor started, and rose too, involuntarily, to her feet. There on the ground lay all the little Nemi fragments which Manisty had given to Lucy, and which had been stowed away, each carefully wrapped in tissue paper, in the well of her old workbox.

Eleanor assisted to pick them up, rather silently. The note of keen distress in Lucy's voice rang in her ears.

'They are not much hurt, luckily,' she said.

And indeed, thanks to the tissue paper, there were only a few small chips and bruises to bemoan when Lucy at last had gathered them all safely into her lap. Still, chips and bruises in the case of delicate Graeco-Roman terra-cottas are more than enough to make their owner smart, and Lucy bent over them with a very flushed and rueful face, examining and wrapping them up again.

'Cotton-wool would be better,' she said anxiously. 'How have you put your two away?'

Directly the words were out of her mouth she felt that they had been better unspoken.

A deep flush stained Eleanor's thin face.

'I am afraid I haven't taken much care of them,' she said hurriedly.

They were both silent for a little. But while Lucy still had her lap full of her treasures, Eleanor again stood up.

'I will go in and rest for an hour before *dejeuner*. I *think* I might go to sleep.'

She had passed a very broken night, and Lucy looked at her with tender concern. She quickly but carefully laid aside her terra-cottas, that she might go in with Eleanor and 'settle her' comfortably.

But when she was left to rest in her carefully darkened room, and Lucy had gone back to the *loggia*, Eleanor got no wink of sleep. She lay in an anguish of memory, living over again that last night at the villa--thinking of Manisty in the dark garden and her own ungovernable impulse.

Presently a slight sound reached her from the *loggia*. She turned her head quickly. A sob?--from Lucy?

Her heart stood still. Noiselessly she slipped to her feet. The door between her and the *loggia* had been left ajar for air. It was partially glazed, with shutters of plain green wood outside, and inside a muslin blind. Eleanor approached it.

Through the chink of the door she saw Lucy plainly. The girl had been sitting almost with her back to the door, but she had turned so that her profile and hands were visible.

How quiet she was! Yet never was there an attitude more eloquent. She held in her hands, which lay upon her knee, one of the little terra-cottas. Eleanor could see it perfectly. It was the head of a statuette, not unlike her own which she had destroyed,--a smaller and ruder Artemis with the Cybele crown. There flashed into her mind the memory of Manisty explaining it to the girl, sitting on the bench behind the strawberry hut; his black brows bent in the eagerness of his talk; her sweet eyes, her pure pleasure.

And now Lucy had no companion--but thought. Her face was raised, the eyes were shut, the beautiful mouth quivered in the effort to be still. She was mistress of herself, yet not for the moment wholly mistress of longing and of sorrow. A quick struggle passed over the face. There was another slight sob. Then Eleanor saw her raise the terra-cotta, bow her face upon it, press it long and lingeringly to her lips. It was like a gesture of eternal farewell; the gesture of a child expressing the heart of a woman.

Eleanor tottered back. She sat on the edge of her bed, motionless in the darkness, till the sounds of Cecco bringing up the *pranzo* in the corridor outside warned her that her time of solitude was over.

*   *   *   *   *

In the evening Eleanor was sitting in the Sassetto. Lucy with her young need of exercise had set off to walk down through the wood to the first bridge over the Paglia. Eleanor had been very weary all day, and for the first time irritable. It was almost with a secret relief that Lucy started, and Eleanor saw her depart.

Mrs. Burgoyne was left stretched on her long canvas chair, in the green shade of the Sassetto. All about her was a chaos of moss-grown rocks crowned with trees young and old; a gap in the branches showed her a distant peachy sky suffused with gold above the ethereal heights of the Amiata range; a little wind crept through the trees; the birds were silent, but the large green lizards slipped in and out, and made a friendly life in the cool shadowed place.

The Contessa was to have joined Eleanor here at six o'clock. But a note had arrived excusing her. The visit of some relations detained her.

Nevertheless a little after six a step was heard approaching along the winding path which while it was still distant Eleanor knew to be Father Benecke. For his sake, she was glad that the Contessa was not with her.

As for Donna Teresa, when she met the priest in the village or on the road she shrank out of his path as though his mere shadow brought malediction.

Her pinched face, her thin figure seemed to contract still further under an impulse of fear and repulsion. Eleanor had seen it, and wondered.

But even the Contessa would have nothing to say to him.

'*Non, Madame; c'est plus fort que moi!*' she had said to Eleanor one day that she had come across Mrs. Burgoyne and Father Benecke together in the Sassetto--in after-excuse for her behaviour to him. 'For you and me--*bien entendu!*--we think what we please. Heaven knows I am not bigoted. Teresa makes herself unhappy about me.' The stout, imperious woman stifled a sigh that betrayed much. 'I take what I want from our religion--and I don't trouble about the rest. Emilio was the same. But a priest that disobeys--that deserts--! No! that is another matter. I can't argue; it seizes me by the throat.' She made an expressive movement. 'It is an instinct--an inheritance--call it what you like. But I feel like Teresa; I could run at the sight of him.'

Certainly Father Benecke gave her no occasion to run. Since his recovery from the first shock and agitation of his suspension he had moved about the roads and tracks of Torre Amiata with the 'recollected' dignity of the pale and meditative recluse. He asked nothing; he spoke to no one, except to the ladies at the convent, and to the old woman who served him unwillingly in the little tumble-down house by the river's edge to which he had now transferred himself and his books, for greater solitude. Eleanor understood that he shrank from facing his German life and friends again till he had completed the revision of his book, and the evolution of his thought; and she had some reason to believe that he regarded his isolation and the enmity of this Italian neighbourhood as a necessary trial and testing, to be borne without a murmur.

As his step came nearer, she sat up and threw off her languor. It might have been divined, even, that she heard it with a secret excitement.

When he appeared he greeted her with the manner at once reticent and cordial that was natural to him. He had brought her an article in a German newspaper of the 'Centre' on himself and his case, the violence of which had provoked him to a reply, whereof the manuscript was also in his pocket.

Eleanor took the article and turned it over. But some inward voice told her that her *role*, of counsellor and critic was--again--played out. Suddenly Father Benecke said:

'I have submitted my reply to Mr. Manisty. I would like to show you what he says.'

Eleanor fell back in her chair. 'You know where he is?' she cried.

Her surprise was so great that she could not at once disguise her emotion. Father Benecke was also taken aback. He lifted his eyes from the papers he held.

'I wrote to him through his bankers the other day, Madame. I have always found that letters so addressed to him are forwarded.'

Then he stopped in distress and perturbation. Mrs. Burgoyne was still apparently struggling for breath and composure. His absent, seer's eyes at last took note of her as a human being. He understood, all at once, that he had before him a woman very ill, apparently very unhappy, and that what he had just said had thrown her into an anguish with which her physical weakness was hardly able to cope.

The colour rose in his own cheeks.

'Madame! let me hasten to say that I have done your bidding precisely. You were so good as to tell me that you wished no information to be given to anyone as to your stay here. I have not breathed a word of it to Mr. Manisty or to any other of my correspondents. Let me show you his letter.'

He held it out to her. Eleanor took it with uncertain fingers.

'Your mention of him took me by surprise,' she said, after a moment. 'Miss Foster and I--have been--so long--without hearing of our friends.'

Then she stooped over the letter. It seemed to her the ink was hardly dry on it--that it was still warm from Manisty's hand. The date of it was only three days old. And the place from which it came? Cosenza?--Cosenza in Calabria? Then he was still in Italy?

She put the letter back into Father Benecke's hands.

'Would you read it for me? I have rather a headache to-day.'

He read it with a somewhat embarrassed voice. She lay listening, with her eyes closed under her large hat, each hand trying to prevent the trembling of the other.

A strange pride swelled in her. It was a kind and manly letter, expressing far more personal sympathy with Benecke than Manisty had ever yet allowed himself--a letter wholly creditable indeed to the writer, and marked with a free and flowing beauty of phrase that brought home to Eleanor at every turn his voice, his movements, the ideas and sympathies of the writer.

Towards the end came the familiar Manisty-ism:

'All the same, their answer to you is still as good as ever. The system must either break up or go on. They naturally prefer that it should go on. But if it is worked by men like you, it cannot go on. Their instinct never wavers; and it is a true one.'

Then:

'I don't know how I have managed to write this letter--poor stuff as it is. My mind at this moment is busy neither with speculation nor politics. I am perched for the night on the side of a mountain thickly covered with beech woods, in a remote Calabrian hamlet, where however last year some pushing person built a small 'health resort,' to which a few visitors come from Naples and even from Rome. The woods are vast, the people savage. The brigands are gone, or going; of electric light there is plenty. I came this morning, and shall be gone to-morrow. I am a pilgrim on the face of Italy. For six weeks I have wandered like this, from the Northern Abruzzi downwards. Wherever holiday folk go to escape from the heat of the plains, I go. But my object is not theirs.... Nor is it yours, Padre. There are many quests in the world. Mine is one of the oldest that man knows. My heart pursues it, untired. And in the end I shall win to my goal.'

The old priest read the last paragraph in a hurried, unsteady voice. At every sentence he became aware of some electrical effect upon the delicate frame and face beside him; but he read on--not knowing how to save himself--lest she should think that he had omitted anything.

When he dropped the letter his hands, too, shook. There was a silence.

Slowly Eleanor dragged herself higher in her chair; she pushed her hat back from her forehead; she turned her white drawn face upon the priest.

'Father,' she said, bending towards him, 'you are a priest--and a confessor?'

His face changed. He waited an instant before replying.

'Yes, Madame--I am!' he said at last, with a firm and passionate dignity.

'Yet now you cannot act as a priest. And I am not a Catholic. Still, I am a human being--with a soul, I suppose--if there are such things!--and you are old enough to be my father, and have had great experience. I am in trouble--and probably dying. Will you hear my case--as though it were a confession--under the same seal?'

She fixed her eyes upon him. Insensibly the priest's expression had changed; the priestly caution, the priestly instinct had returned. He looked at her steadily and compassionately.

'Is there no one, Madame, to whom you might more profitably make this confession--no one who has more claim to it than I?'

'No one.'

'I cannot refuse,' he said, uneasily. 'I cannot refuse to hear anyone in trouble and--if I can--to help them. But let me remind you that this could not be in any sense a true confession. It could only be a conversation between friends.'

She drew her hand across her eyes.

'I must treat it as a confession, or I cannot speak. I shall not ask you to absolve me. That--that would do me no good,' she said, with a little wild laugh, 'What I want is direction--from some one accustomed to look at people as they are--and--and to speak the truth to them. Say "yes," Padre. You--you may have the fate of three lives in your hands.'

Her entreating eyes hung upon him. His consideration took a few moments longer. Then he dropped his own look upon the ground, and clasped his hands.

'Say, my daughter, all that you wish to say.'

The priestly phrase gave her courage.

She drew a long breath, and paused a little to collect her thoughts. When she began, it was in a low, dragging voice full of effort.

'What I want to know, Father, is--how far one may fight--how far one *should* fight--for oneself. The facts are these. I will not mention any names. Last winter, Father, I had reason to think that life had changed for me--after many years of unhappiness. I gave my whole, whole heart away.' The words came out in a gasp, as though a large part of the physical power of the speaker escaped with them. 'I thought that--in return--I was held in high value, in true affection--that--that my friend cared for me more than for anyone else--that in time he would be mine altogether. It was a great hope, you understand--I don't put it at more. But I had done much to deserve his kindness--he owed me a great deal. Not, I mean, for the miserable work I had done for him; but for all the love, the thought by day and night that I had given him.'

She bowed her head on her hands for a moment. The priest sat motionless and she resumed, torn and excited by her strange task.

'I was not alone in thinking and hoping--as I did. Other people thought it. It was not merely presumptuous or foolish on my part. But--ah! it is an old story, Padre. I don't know why I inflict it on you!'

She stopped, wringing her hands.

The priest did not raise his eyes, but sat quietly--in an attitude a little cold and stern, which seemed to rebuke her agitation. She composed herself, and resumed:

'There was of course some one else, Father--you understood that from the beginning--some one younger, and far more attractive than I. It took five weeks--hardly so much. There was no affinity of nature and mind to go upon--or I thought so. It seemed to me all done in a moment by a beautiful face. I could not be expected to bear it--to resign myself at once to the loss of everything that made life worth living--could I, Father?' she said passionately.

The priest still did not look up.

'You resisted?' he said.

'I resisted--successfully,' she said with fluttering breath. 'I separated them. The girl who supplanted me was most tender, dear, and good. She pitied me, and I worked upon her pity. I took her away from--from my friend. And why should I not? Why are we called upon perpetually to give up--give up? It seemed to me such a cruel, cold, un-human creed. I knew my own life was broken--beyond mending; but I couldn't bear the unkindness--I couldn't forgive the injury--I couldn't--couldn't! I took her away; and my power is still great enough, and will be always great enough, if I choose, to part these two from each other!'

Her hands were on her breast, as though she were trying to still the heart that threatened to silence her. When she spoke of giving up, her voice had taken a note of scorn, almost of hatred, that brought a momentary furrow to the priest's brow.

For a little while after she had ceased to speak he sat bowed, and apparently deep in thought. When he looked up she braced herself, as though she already felt the shock of judgment. But he only asked a question.

'Your girl-friend, Madame--her happiness was not involved?'

Eleanor shrank and turned away.

'I thought not--at first.' It was a mere murmur.

'But now?'

'I don't know--I suspect,' she said miserably. 'But, Father, if it were so she is young; she has all her powers and chances before her. What would kill me would only--anticipate--for her--a day that must come. She is born to be loved.'

Again she let him see her face, convulsed by the effort for composure, the eyes shining with large tears. It was like the pleading of a wilful child.

A veil descended also on the pure intense gaze of the priest, yet he bent it steadily upon her.

'Madame--God has done you a great honour.'

The words were just breathed, but they did not falter. Mutely, with parted lips, she seemed to search for his meaning.

'There are very few of whom God condescends to ask, as plainly, as generously, as He now asks of you. What does it matter, Madame, whether God speaks to us amid the thorns or the flowers? But I do not remember that He ever spoke among the flowers, but often--often, amongst deserts and wildernesses. And when He speaks--Madame! the condescension, the gift is that He should speak at all; that He, our Maker and Lord, should plead with, should as it were humble Himself to, our souls. Oh! how we should hasten to answer, how we should hurry to throw ourselves and all that we have into His hands!'

Eleanor turned away. Unconsciously she began to strip the moss from a tree beside her. The tears dropped upon her lap.

But the appeal was to religious emotion, not to the moral judgment, and she rallied her forces.

'You speak, Father, as a priest--as a Christian. I understand of course that that is the Christian language, the Christian point of view.'

'My daughter,' he said simply, 'I can speak no other language.'

There was a pause. Then he resumed: 'But consider it for a moment from an-other point of view. You say that for yourself you have renounced the expecta-tion of happiness. What, then, do you desire? Merely the pain, the humiliation of others? But is that an end that any man or woman may lawfully pursue--Pagan or Christian? It was not a Christian who said, "Men exist for the sake of one another." Yet when two other human beings--your friends--have innocently--unwittingly--done you a wrong--'

She shook her head silently.

The priest observed her.

'One at least, you said, was kind and good--showed you a compassionate spirit--and intended you no harm. Yet you will punish her--for the sake of your own pride. And she is young. You who are older, and better able to control passion, ought you not to feel towards her as a tender elder sister--a mother--rather than a rival?'

He spoke with a calm and even power, the protesting force of his own soul mounting all the time like a tide.

Eleanor rose again in revolt.

'It is no use,' she said despairingly. 'Do you understand, Father, what I said to you at first?--that I have probably not many months--a year perhaps--to live? And that to give these two to each other would embitter all my last days and hours--would make it impossible for me to believe, to hope, anything?'

'No, no, poor soul!' he said, deeply moved. 'It would be with you as with St. John: "Now we know that we have passed from death unto life, because we love the brethren."'

She shrugged her shoulders.

'I have no faith--and no hope.'

His look kindled, took a new aspect almost of command.

'You do yourself wrong. Could you have brought yourself to ask this counsel of me, if God had not been already at work in your soul--if your sin were not already half conquered?'

She recoiled as though from a blow. Her cheek burnt.

'Sin!' she repeated bitterly, with a kind of scorn, not able to bear the word.

But he did not quail.

'All selfish desire is sin--desire that defies God and wills the hurt of man. But you will cast it out. The travail is already begun in you that will form the Christ.'

'Father, creeds and dogmas mean nothing to me!'

'Perhaps,' he said calmly. 'Does religion also mean nothing to you?'

'Oh! I am a weak woman,' she said with a quivering lip. 'I throw myself on all that promises consolation. When I see the nuns from down below pass up and down this road, I often think that theirs is the only way out; that the Catholic Church and a convent are perhaps the solution to which I must come--for the little while that remains.'

'In other words,' he said after a pause, 'God offers you one discipline, and you would choose another. Well, the Lord gave the choice to David of what rod he would be scourged with; but it always has seemed to me that the choice was an added punishment. I would not have chosen. I would have left all to His Divine Majesty! This cross is not of your own making; it comes to you from God. Is it not the most signal proof of His love? He asks of you what only the strongest can bear; gives you just time to serve Him with the best. As I said before, is it not His way of honouring His creature?'

Eleanor sat without speaking, her delicate head drooping.

'And, Madame,' the priest continued with a changed voice, 'you say that creeds and dogmas mean nothing to you. How can I, who am now cast out from the Visible Church, uphold them to you--attempt to bind them on your conscience? But one thing I can do, whether as man or priest; I can bid you ask yourself whether in truth *Christ* means nothing to you--and Calvary nothing?'

He paused, staring at her with his bright and yet unseeing eyes, the wave of feeling rising within him to a force and power born of recent storm, of the personal wrestling with a personal anguish.

'Why is it'--he resumed, each word low and pleading,--'that this divine figure is enshrined, if not in all our affections--at least in all our imaginations? Why is it that at the heart of this modern world, with all its love of gold, its thirst for knowledge, its desire for pleasure, there still lives and burns '--

--He held out his two strong clenched hands, quivering, as though he held in them the vibrating heart of man--

--'this strange madness of sacrifice, this foolishness of the Cross? Why is it that in these polite and civilised races which lead the world, while creeds and Churches divide us, what still touches us most deeply, what still binds us together most sure-ly, is this story of a hideous death, which the spectators said was voluntary--which the innocent Victim embraced with joy as the ransom of His brethren--from which those who saw it received in very truth the communication of a new life--a life, a Divine Mystery, renewed amongst us now, day after day, in thousands of human beings? What does it mean, Madame? Ask yourself! How has our world of lust and iron produced such a thing? How, except as the clue to the world's secret, is man to explain it to himself? Ah! my daughter, think what you will of the nature and dignity of the Crucified--but turn your eyes to the Cross! Trouble yourself with no creeds--I speak this to your weakness--but sink yourself in the story of the Passion and its work upon the world! Then bring it to bear upon your own case. There is in you a root of evil mind--an angry desire--a ***cupido*** which keeps you from God. Lay it down before the Crucified, and rejoice--rejoice!--that you have something to give to your God--before He gives you Himself!'

The old man's voice sank and trembled.

Eleanor made no reply. Her capacity for emotion was suddenly exhausted. Nerve and brain were tired out.

After a minute or two she rose to her feet and held out her hand.

'I thank you with all my heart. Your words touch me very much, but they seem to me somehow remote--impossible. Let me think of them. I am not strong enough to talk more now.'

She bade him good-night, and left him. With her feeble step she slowly mount-ed the Sassetto path, and it was some little time before her slender form and white dress disappeared among the trees.

Father Benecke remained alone--a prey to many conflicting currents of thought.

*   *   *   *   *

For him too the hour had been strangely troubling and revolutionary. On the recognised lines of Catholic confession and direction, all that had been asked of him would have been easy to give. As it was, he had been obliged to deal with the moral emergency as he best could; by methods which, now that the crisis was over, filled him with a sudden load of scrupulous anguish.

The support of a great system had been withdrawn from him. He still felt himself neither man nor priest--wavering in the dark.

This poor woman! He was conscious that her statement of her case had roused in him a kind of anger; so passionate and unblushing had been the egotism of her manner. Even after his long experience he felt in it something monstrous. Had he been tender, patient enough?

What troubled him was this consciousness of the **woman**, as apart from the penitent, which had overtaken him; the woman with her frail physical health, possibly her terror of death, her broken heart. New perplexities and compunctions, not to be felt within the strong dykes of Catholic practice, rushed upon him as he sat thinking under the falling night. The human fate became more bewildering, more torturing. The clear landscape of Catholic thought upon which he had once looked out was wrapping itself in clouds, falling into new aspects and relations. How marvellous are the chances of human history! The outward ministry had been withdrawn; in its stead this purely spiritual ministry had been offered to him. '***Domine, in caelo misericordia tua--judicia tua abyssus multa!***'

*   *   *   *   *

Recalling what he knew of Mrs. Burgoyne's history and of Manisty's, his mind trained in the subtleties of moral divination soon reconstructed the whole story. Clearly the American lady now staying with Mrs. Burgoyne--who had showed towards himself such a young and graceful pity--was the other woman.

He felt instinctively that Mrs. Burgoyne would approach him again, coldly as she had parted from him. She had betrayed to him all the sick confusion of soul that existed beneath her intellectual competence and vigour. The situation between them, indeed, had radically changed. He laid aside deference and humility; he took up the natural mastery of the priest as the moral expert. She had no faith; and faith would save her. She was wandering in darkness, making shipwreck of herself and others. And she had appealed to him. With an extraordinary eagerness the old man threw himself into the task she had so strangely set him. He longed to conquer and heal her; to bring her to faith, to sacrifice, to God. The mingled innocence and despotism of his nature were both concerned. And was there something else?--the eagerness of the soldier who retrieves disobedience by some special and arduous service? To be allowed to attempt it is a grace; to succeed in it is pardon.

Was she dying--poor lady!--or was it a delusion on her part, one of the devices of self-pity? Yet he recalled the emaciated face and form, the cough, the trailing step, Miss Foster's anxiety, some comments overheard in the village.--

And if she died unreconciled, unhappy? Could nothing be done to help her, from outside,--to brace her to action--and in time?

He pondered the matter with all the keenness of the casuist, all the *naivete* of the recluse. In the tragical uprooting of established habit through which he was passing, even those ways of thinking and acting which become the second nature of the priest were somewhat shaken. Had Eleanor's confidence been given him in Catholic confession he might not even by word or look have ever reminded herself of what had passed between them; still less have acted upon it in any way. Nor under the weight of tradition which binds the Catholic priest, would he ever have been conscious of the remotest temptation to what his Church regards as one of the deadliest of sins.

And further. If as his penitent, yet outside confession,--in a letter or conversation--Eleanor had told him her story, his passionately scrupulous sense of the priestly function would have bound him precisely in the same way. Here, all Catholic opinion would not have agreed with him; but his own conviction would have been clear.

But now in the general shifting of his life from the standpoint of authority, to the standpoint of conscience, new aspects of the case appeared to him. He recalled certain questions of moral theology, with which as a student he was familiar. The modern discipline of the confessional 'seal' is generally more stringent than that of the middle ages. Benecke remembered that in the view of St. Thomas, it is sometimes lawful for a confessor to take account of what he hears in confession so far as to endeavour afterwards to remove some obstacle to the spiritual progress of his penitent, which has been revealed to him under the seal. The modern theologian denies altogether the legitimacy of such an act, which for him is a violation of the Sacrament.

But for Benecke, at this moment, the tender argument of St. Thomas suddenly attained a new beauty and compulsion.

He considered it long. He thought of Manisty, his friend, to whom his affectionate heart owed a debt of gratitude, wandering about Italy, in a blind quest of the girl who had been snatched away from him. He thought of the girl herself, and the love that not all Mrs. Burgoyne's jealous anguish had been able to deny. And then his mind returned to Mrs. Burgoyne, and the arid misery of her struggle.--

The darkness was falling. As he reached the last of the many windings of the road, he saw his tiny house by the riverside, with a light in the window.

He leant upon his stick, conscious of inward excitement, feeling suddenly on his old shoulders the burden of those three lives of which Mrs. Burgoyne had spoken.

'My God, give them to me!'--he cried, with a sudden leap of the heart that was at once humble and audacious. Not a word to Mr. Manisty, or to any other human being, clearly, as to Mrs. Burgoyne's presence at Torre Amiata. To that he was bound.

But--

'May I not entertain a wayfarer, a guest?'--he thought, trembling, 'like any other solitary?'

CHAPTER XX

The hot evening was passing into night. Eleanor and Lucy were on the *loggia* together.

Through the opening in the parapet wall made by the stairway to what had once been the enclosed monastery garden, Eleanor could see the fire-flies flashing against the distant trees; further, above the darkness of the forest, ethereal terraces of dimmest azure lost in the starlight; and where the mountains dropped to the south-west a heaven still fiery and streaked with threats of storm. Had she raised herself a little she could have traced far away, beyond the forest slopes, the course of those white mists that rise at night out of the wide bosom of Bolsena.

Outside, the country-folk were streaming home from their work; the men riding their donkeys or mules, the women walking, often with burdens on their heads, and children dragging at their hands; dim purplish figures, in the evening blue, charged with the eternal grace of the old Virgilian life of Italy, the life of corn and vine, of chestnut and olive. Lucy hung over the balcony, looking at the cavalcades, sometimes waving her hand to a child or a mother that she recognised through the gathering darkness. It was an evening spectacle of which she never tired. Her feeling clung to these labouring people, whom she idealised with the optimism of her clean youth. Secretly her young strength envied them their primal, necessary toils. She would not have shrunk from their hardships; their fare would have been no grievance to her. Sickness, old age, sin, cruelty, violence, death,--that these dark things entered into their lives, she knew vaguely. Her heart shrank from what her mind sometimes divined; all the more perhaps that there was in her the promise of a wide and rare human sympathy, which must some day find its appointed tasks and suffer much in the finding. Now, when she stumbled on the horrors of the world, she would cry to herself, 'God knows!'--with a catching breath, and the feeling of a child that runs from darkness to protecting arms; and so escape her pain.

Presently she came to sit by Eleanor again, trying to amuse her by the account of a talk on the roadside, with an old **spaccapietre**, or stone-breaker, who had fought at Mentana.

Eleanor listened vaguely, hardly replying. But she watched the girl in her simple white dress, her fine head, her grave and graceful movements; she noticed the voice, so expressive of an inner self-mastery through all its gaiety. And suddenly the thought flamed through her--

'If I told her!--if she knew that I had seen a letter from him this afternoon?--that he is in Italy?--that he is looking for *her*, day and night! If I just blurted it out--what would she say?--how would she take it?'

But not a word passed her lips. She began again to try and unravel the meaning of his letter. Why had he gone in search of them to the Abruzzi of all places?

Then, suddenly, she remembered.

One day at the villa, some Italian friends--a deputy and his wife--had described to them a summer spent in a wild nook of the Abruzzi. The young husband had possessed a fine gift of phrase. The mingled savagery and innocence of the people; the vast untrodden woods of chestnut and beech; the slowly advancing civilisation; the new railway line that seemed to the peasants a living and hostile thing, a kind of greedy fire-monster, carrying away their potatoes to market and their sons to the army; the contrasts of the old and new Italy; the joys of summer on the heights, of an unbroken Italian sunshine steeping a fresh and almost northern air: he had drawn it all, with the facility of the Italian, the broken, impressionist strokes of the modern. Why must Italians nowadays always rush north, to the lakes, or Switzerland or the Tyrol? Here in their own land, in the Abruzzi, and further south, in the Volscian and Calabrian mountains, were cool heights waiting to be explored, the savour of a primitive life, the traces of old cities, old strongholds, old faiths, a peasant world moreover, unknown to most Italians of the west and north, to be observed, to be made friends with.

They had all listened in fascination. Lucy especially. The thought of scenes so rarely seen, so little visited, existing so near to them, in this old old Italy, seemed to touch the girl's imagination--to mingle as it were a breath from her own New World with the land of the Caesars.

'One can ride everywhere?' she had asked, looking up at the traveller.

'Everywhere, mademoiselle.'

'I shall come,' she had said, drawing pencil circles on a bit of paper before her, with pleased intent eyes, like one planning.

And the Italian, amused by her enthusiasm, had given her a list of places where accommodation could be got, where hotels of a simple sort were beginning to develop, whence this new land that was so old could be explored by the stranger.

And Manisty had stood by, smoking and looking down at the girl's graceful head, and the charming hand that was writing down the names.

Another pang of the past recalled,--a fresh one added!

For Torre Amiata had been forgotten, while Lucy's momentary whim had furnished the clue which had sent him on his vain quest through the mountains.

*   *   *   *   *

'I do think '--said Lucy, presently, taking Eleanor's hand,--'you haven't coughed so much to-day?'

Her tone was full of anxiety, of tenderness.

Eleanor smiled. 'I am very well,' she said, dryly. But Lucy's frown did not relax. This cough was a new trouble. Eleanor made light of it. But Marie sometimes spoke of it to Lucy with expressions which terrified one who had never known illness except in her mother.

Meanwhile Eleanor was thinking--'Something will bring him here. He is writing to Father Benecke--Father Benecke to him. Some accident will happen--any day, any hour. Well--let him come!'

Her hands stiffened under her shawl that Lucy had thrown round her. A fierce consciousness of power thrilled through her weak frame. Lucy was hers! The pitiful spectacle of these six weeks had done its work. Let him come.

His letter was not unhappy!--far from it. She felt herself flooded with bitterness as she remembered the ardour that it breathed; the ardour of a lover to whom effort and pursuit are joys only second to the joys of possession.

But some day no doubt he would be unhappy--in earnest; if her will held. But it would hold.

After all, it was not much she asked. She might live till the winter; possibly a year. Not long, after all, in Lucy's life or Manisty's. Let them only wait a little.

Her hand burnt in Lucy's cool clasp. Restlessly, she asked the girl some further questions about her walk.

'I met the Sisters--the nuns--from Selvapendente, on the hill,' said Lucy. 'Such sweet faces some of them have.'

'I don't agree,' said Eleanor petulantly. 'I saw two of them yesterday. They smile at you, but they have the narrowest, stoniest eyes. Their pity would be very difficult to bear.'

A few minutes later Lucy left her for a moment, to give a message to Marie.

'These Christians are hard--*hard*!' thought Eleanor sharply, closing her tired lids.

Had Father Benecke ever truly weighed her case, her plea at all? Never! It had been the stereotyped answer of the priest and the preacher. Her secret sense resented the fact that he had been so little moved, apparently, by her physical state. It humiliated her that she should have brought so big a word as death into their debate--to no effect. Her thin cheek flushed with shame and anger.

The cracked bell which announced their meals tinkled from the sitting-room.

Eleanor dragged herself to her feet, and stood a moment by the parapet looking into the night.

'I cough less?' she thought. 'Why?--for I get worse every day. That I may make less noise in dying? Well! one would like to go without ugliness and fuss. I might as well be dead now, I am so broken--so full of suffering. How I hide it all from that child! And what is the use of it--of living a single day or hour more?'

*   *   *   *   *

She was angry with Father Benecke; but she took care to see him again.

By means of a little note about a point in the article he was just completing, she recalled him.

They met without the smallest reference to the scene which had passed between them. He asked for her literary opinion with the same simplicity, the same outward deference as before. She was once more the elegant and languid woman, no writer herself, but born to be the friend and muse of writers. She made him feel just as clearly as before the clumsiness of a phrase, the ***naivete*** of a point of view.

And yet in truth all was changed between them. Their talk ranged further, sank deeper. From the controversy of science with the Vatican, from the position of the Old Catholics, or the triumph of Ultramontanism in France, it would drop of a sudden, neither knew how, and light upon some small matter of conduct or feeling, some 'flower in the crannied wall,' charged with the profoundest things--things most intimate, most searching, concerned with the eternal passion and trouble of the human will, the 'body of this death,' the 'burden' of the 'Pilgrim's Progress.'

Then the priest's gentle insistent look would steal on hers; he would speak from his heart; he would reveal in a shrinking word or two the secrets of his own spiritual life, of that long inner discipline, which was now his only support in rebellion, the plank between him and the abyss.

She felt herself pursued; felt it with a mixture of fear and attraction. She had asked him to be her director; and then refused his advice. She had tried to persuade him that she was a sceptic and unbeliever. But he had not done with her. She divined the ardour of the Christian; perhaps the acuteness of the ecclesiastic. Often she was not strong enough to talk to him, and then he read to her--the books that she allowed him to choose. Through a number of indirect and gradual approaches he laid siege to her, and again and again did she feel her heart fluttering in his grasp, only to draw it back in fear, to stand once more on a bitter unspoken defence of herself that would not yield. Yet he recognised in her the approach of some crisis of feeling. She seemed herself to suspect it, and to be trying to ward it off, in a kind of blind anguish. Nothing meanwhile could be more touching than the love between her and Lucy. The old man looked on and wondered.

Day after day he hesitated. Then one evening, in Lucy's absence, he found her so pale, and racked with misery--so powerless either to ask help, or to help herself, so resolute not to speak again, so clearly tortured by her own coercing will, that his hesitation gave way.

He walked down the hill, in a trance of prayer. When he emerged from it his mind was made up.

*   *   *   *   *

In the days that followed he seemed to Eleanor often agitated and ill at ease. She was puzzled, too, by his manner towards Lucy. In truth, he watched Miss Foster with a timid anxiety, trying to penetrate her character, to divine how presently she might feel towards him. He was not afraid of Mrs. Burgoyne, but he was sometimes afraid of this girl with her clear, candid eyes. Her fresh youth, and many of her American ways and feelings were hard for him to understand. She showed him friendship in a hundred pretty ways; and he met her sometimes eagerly, sometimes with a kind of shame-facedness.

Soon he began to neglect his work of a morning that he might wander out to meet the postman beyond the bridge. And when the man passed him by with a short 'Non c' e niente,' the priest would turn homeward, glad almost that for one day more he was not called upon to face the judgment in Lucy Foster's face on what he had done.

*   *   *   *   *

The middle of July was past. The feast of Our Lady of Mount Carmel had come and gone, bringing processions and music, with a Madonna under a gold baldacchino, to glorify the little deserted chapel on the height.

Eleanor had watched the crowds and banners, the red-robed Compagni di Gesu, the white priests, and veiled girls, with a cold averted eye. Lucy looked back with a pang to Marinata, and to the indulgent pleasure that Eleanor had once taken in all the many-coloured show of Catholicism. Now she was always weary, and often fretful. It struck Lucy too that she was more restless than ever. She seemed to take no notice of the present--to be always living in the future--expecting, listening, waiting. The gestures and sudden looks that expressed this attitude of mind were often of the weirdest effect. Lucy could have thought her haunted by some unseen presence. Physically she was not, perhaps, substantially worse. But her state was more appealing, and the girl's mind towards her more pitiful day by day.

One thing, however, she was determined on. They would not spend August at Torre Amiata. It would need stubbornness with Eleanor to bring her to the point of change. But stubbornness there should be.

One morning, a day or two after the festa, Lucy left Eleanor on the *loggia*, while she herself ran out for a turn before their midday meal. There had been fierce rain in the morning, and the sky was still thick with thunder clouds promising more.

She escaped into a washed and cooled world. But the thirsty earth had drunk the rain at a gulp. The hill which had been running with water was almost dry, the woods had ceased to patter; on all sides could be felt the fresh restoring impulse of the storm. Nature seemed to be breathing from a deeper chest--shaking her free locks in a wilder, keener air--to a long-silent music from the quickened river below.

Lucy almost ran down the hill, so great was the physical relief of the rain and the cloudy morning. She needed it. Her spirits, too, had been uneven, her cheek paler of late.

She wore a blue cotton dress, fitting simply and closely to the young rounded form. Round her shapely throat and the lace collar that showed Eleanor's fancy and seemed to herself a little too elaborate for the morning, she wore a child's coral necklace--a gleam of red between the abundant black of her hair and the soft blue of her dress. Her hat, a large Leghorn, with a rose in it, framed the sweet gravity of her face. She was more beautiful than when she had said good-bye to Uncle Ben on the Boston platform. But it was a beauty that for his adoring old heart would have given new meaning to 'that sad word, Joy.'

She turned into the Sassetto and pushed upwards through its tumbled rocks and trees to the seat commanding the river and the mountains.

As she approached it, she was thinking of Eleanor and the future, and her eyes were absently bent on the ground.

But a scent familiar and yet strange distracted her. Suddenly, on the path in front of the seat, she saw a still burning cigarette, and on the seat a book lying.

She stopped short; then sank upon the seat, her eyes fixed upon the book.

It was a yellow-bound French novel, and on the outside was written in a hand she knew, a name that startled every pulse in her young body.

His book? And that cigarette? Father Benecke neither smoked nor did he read

French novels.

Beyond the seat the path branched, upwards to the Palazzo, and downwards to the river. She rose and looked eagerly over its steep edge into the medley of rock and tree below. She saw nothing, but it seemed to her that in the distance she heard voices talking--receding.

They had left the seat only just in time to escape her. Mr. Manisty had forgotten his book! Careless and hasty--how well she knew the trait! But he would miss it--he would come back.

She stood up and tried to collect her thoughts. If he was here, he was with Father Benecke. So the priest had betrayed the secret he had promised Mrs. Burgoyne to keep?

No, no!--that was impossible! It was chance--unkind, unfriendly chance.

And yet?--as she bit her lip in fear or bewilderment, her heart was rising like the Paglia after the storm--swelling, thundering within her.

'What shall I--what shall I do?' she cried under her breath, pressing her hands to her eyes.

Then she turned and walked swiftly homewards. Eleanor must not know--must not see him. The girl was seized with panic terror at the thought of what might be the effect of any sudden shock upon Mrs. Burgoyne.

Halfway up the hill, she stopped involuntarily, wringing her hands in front of her. It was the thought of Manisty not half a mile away, of his warm, living self so close to her that had swept upon her, like a tempest wind on a young oak.

'Oh! I mustn't--*mustn't*--be glad!'--she cried, gulping down a sob, hating, despising herself.

Then she hurried on. With every step, she grew more angry with Father Benecke. At best, he must have been careless, inconsiderate. A man of true delicacy would have done more than keep his promise, would have actively protected him.

That he had kept the letter of his promise was almost proved by the fact that Mr. Manisty had not yet descended upon the convent. For what could it mean--his lingering in Italy--but a search, a pursuit? Her cheek flamed guiltily over the certainty thus borne in upon her. But if so, what could hold back his impetuous will--but ignorance? He could not know they were there. That was clear.

So there was time--a chance. Perhaps Father Benecke was taken by surprise too--puzzled to know what to do with him? Should she write to the priest; or simply keep Eleanor indoors and watch?

At thought of her, the girl lashed herself into an indignation, an anguish that sustained her. After devotion so boundless, service so measureless--so lightly, meagrely repaid--were Mrs. Burgoyne's peace and health to be again in peril at her cousin's hands?

*   *   *   *   *

Luckily Eleanor showed that day no wish to move from her sofa. The storm had shaken her, given her a headache, and she was inclined to shiver in the cooler air.

After luncheon Lucy coaxed her to stay in one of the inner rooms, where there was a fire-place; out of sight and sound of the road. Marie made a fire on the disused hearth of what had once been an infirmary cell. The logs crackled merrily; and presently the rain streamed down again across the open window.

Lucy sat sewing and reading through the afternoon in a secret anguish of listening. Every sound in the corridor, every sound from downstairs, excited the tumult in the blood. 'What is the matter with you?' Eleanor would say, reaching out first to pinch, then to kiss the girl's cheek. 'It is all very well that thunder should set a poor wretch like me on edge--but you! Anyway it has given you back your colour. You look superbly well this afternoon.'

And then she would fall to gazing at the girl under her eyebrows with that little trick of the bitten lip, and that piteous silent look, that Lucy could hardly bear.

The rain fell fast and furious. They dined by the fire, and the night fell.

'Clearing--at last,' said Eleanor, as they pushed back their little table, and she stood by the open window, while Cecco was taking away the meal; 'but too late and too wet for me.'

An hour later indeed the storm had rolled away, and a bright and rather cold starlight shone above the woods.

'Now I understand Aunt Pattie's tales of fires at Sorrento in August,' said Eleanor, crouching over the hearth. 'This blazing Italy can touch you when she likes with the chilliest fingers. Poor peasants!--are their hearts lighter to-night? The rain was fierce, but mercifully there was no hail. Down below they say the harvest is over. Here they begin next week. The storm has been rude--but not ruinous. Last year the hail-storms in September stripped the grape; destroyed half their receipts--and pinched their whole winter. They will think it all comes of their litanies and banners the other day. If the vintage goes well too, perhaps they will give the Madonna a new frock. How simple!--how satisfying!'

She hung over the blaze, with her little pensive smile, cheered physically by the warmth, more ready to talk, more at ease than she had been for days. Lucy looked at her with a fast beating heart. How fragile she was, how lovely still, in the half light!

Suddenly Eleanor turned to her, and held out her arms. Lucy knelt down beside her, trembling lest any look or word should betray the secret in her heart. But Eleanor drew the girl to her, resting her cheek tenderly on the brown head.

'Do you miss your mother very much?' she said softly, turning her lips to kiss the girl's hair. 'I know you do. I see it in you, often.'

Lucy's eyes filled with tears. She pressed Eleanor's hand without speaking. They clung together in silence each mind full of thoughts unknown to the other. But Eleanor's features relaxed; for a little while she rested, body and mind. And as Lucy lingered in the clasp thrown round her, she seemed for the first time since the old days at the villa to be the cherished, and not the cherisher.

*   *   *   *   *

Eleanor went early to bed, and then Lucy took a warm shawl and paced up and down the ***loggia*** in a torment of indecision. Presently she was attracted by the little wooden stair which led down from the ***loggia*** to what had once been the small walled garden of the convent, where the monks of this austere order had taken their exercise in sickness, or rested in the sun, when extreme old age debarred them from the field labour of their comrades.

The garden was now a desolation, save for a tangle of oleanders and myrtle in its midst. But the high walls were still intact, and an old wooden door on the side nearest to the forest. Beneath the garden was a triangular piece of open grass land sloping down towards the entrance of the Sassetto and bounded on one side by the road.

Lucy wandered up and down, in a wild trance of feeling. Half a mile away was he sitting with Father Benecke?--winning perhaps their poor secret from the priest's incautious lips'? With what eagle-quickness could he pounce on a sign, an indication! And then the flash of those triumphant eyes, and the onslaught of his will on theirs!

Hark! She caught her breath.

Voices! Two men were descending the road. She hurried to hide her white dress, close, under the wall--she strained every sense.

The sputter of a match--the trail of its scent in the heavy air--an exclamation.

'Father!--wait a moment! Let me light up. These matches are damp. Besides I want to have another look at this old place--'

The steps diverged from the road; approached the lower wall of the garden. She pressed herself against its inner surface, trembling in every limb. Only the old door between her and them! She dared not move--but it was not only fear of discovery that held her. It was a mad uncontrollable joy, that like a wind on warm embers, kindled all her being into flame.

'One more crime--that!--of your Parliamentary Italy! What harm had the poor things done that they should be turned out? You heard what that carabiniere said?--that they farmed half the plateau. And now look at that! I feel as I do when I see a blackbird's nest on the ground, that some beastly boy has been robbing and destroying. I want to get at the boy.'

'The boy would plead perhaps that the blackbirds were too many--and the fruit too scant. Is it wise, my dear sir, to stand there in the damp?'

The voice was pitched low. Lucy detected the uneasiness of the speaker.

'One moment. You remember, I was here before in November. This summer night is a new impression. What a pure and exquisite air!'--Lucy could hear the long inhalation that followed the words. 'I recollect a vague notion of coming to read here. The *massaja* told us they took in people for the summer. Ah! There are some lights, I see, in those upper windows.'

'There are rooms in several parts of the building. Mine were in that further wing. They were hardly watertight,' said the priest hastily, and in the same subdued voice.

'It is a place that one might easily rest in--or hide in,' said Manisty with a new accent on the last words. 'To-morrow morning I will ask the woman to let me walk through it again.--And to-morrow midday, I must be off.'

'So soon? My old Francesca will owe you a grudge. She is almost reconciled to me because you eat--because you praised her omelet.'

'Ah! Francesca is an artist. But--as I told you--I am at present a wanderer and a pilgrim. We have had our talk--you and I--grasped hands, cheered each other, "passed the time of day," *undweiter noch--noch weiter--mein treuer Wanderstab*!'

The words fell from the deep voice with a rich significant note. Lucy heard the sigh, the impatient, despondent sigh, that followed.

They moved away. The whiffs of tobacco still came back to her on the light westerly wind; the sound of their voices still reached her covetous ear. Suddenly all was silent.

She spread her hands on the door in a wild groping gesture.

'Gone! gone!' she said under her breath. Then her hands dropped, and she stood motionless, with bent head, till the moment was over, and her blood tamed.

CHAPTER XXI

M aso! look here!' said Lucy, addressing a small boy, who with his brother was driving some goats along the road.

She took from a basket on her arm, first some *pasticceria*, then a square of chocolate, lastly a handful of *soldi*.

'You know the *casetta* by the river where Mamma Brigitta lives?'

'Yes.' The boy looked at her with his sharp stealthy eyes.

'Take down this letter to Mamma Brigitta. If you wait a little, she'll give you another letter in exchange, and if you bring it up to me, you shall have all those!'

And she spread out her bribes.

The boys' faces were sulky. The house by the river was unpopular, owing to its tenant. But the temptation was of a devilish force. They took the letter and scampered down the hill driving their goats before them.

Lucy also walked down some three or four of the innumerable zig-zags of the road. Presently she found a rocky knoll to the left of it. A gap in the trees opened a vision of the Amiata range, radiantly blue under a superb sky, a few shreds of moving mist still wrapped about its topmost peaks. She took her seat upon a moss-covered stone facing the road which mounted towards her. But some bushes of tall heath and straggling arbutus made a light screen in front of her. She saw, but she could hardly be seen, till the passer-by coming from the river was close upon her.

She sat there with her hands lightly crossed upon her knees, holding herself a little stiffly--waiting.

The phrases of her letter ran in her head. It had been short and simple.--'Dear Father Benecke,--I have reason to know that Mr. Manisty is here--is indeed staying with you. Mrs. Burgoyne is not aware of it and I am anxious that she should not be told. She wishes--as I think she made clear to you--to be quite alone here, and if she desired to see her cousins she would of course have written to them herself. She is too ill to be startled or troubled in any way. Will you do us a great kindness? Will you persuade Mr. Manisty to go quietly away without letting Mrs. Burgoyne know that he has been here? Please ask him to tell Miss Manisty that we shall not be here much longer, that we have a good doctor, and that as Torre Amiata is on the hills the heat is not often oppressive.'

... The minutes passed away. Presently her thoughts began to escape the control she had put upon them; and she felt herself yielding to a sense of excitement. She resolutely took a book of Italian stories from the bottom of her basket, and began to read.

At last! the patter of the goats and the shouts of the boys.

They rushed upon her with the letter. She handed over their reward and broke the seal.

'Hochgeehrtes Fraeulein,--

'It is true that Mr. Manisty is here. I too am most anxious that Mrs. Burgoyne should not be startled or disturbed. But I distrust my own diplomacy; nor have I yet mentioned your presence here to my guest. I am not at liberty to do so, having given my promise to Mrs. Burgoyne. Will you not see and speak to Mr. Manisty yourself? He talks of going up this morning to see the old convent. I cannot prevent him, without betraying what I have no right to betray. At present he is smoking in my garden. But his carriage is ordered from Selvapendente two hours hence. If he does go up the hill, it would surely be easy for you to intercept him. If not, you may be sure that he has left for Orvieto.'

Lucy read the letter with a flush and a frown. It struck her that it was not quite simple; that the priest knew more, and was more concerned in the new turn of events than he avowed.

She was well aware that he and Eleanor had had much conversation; that Eleanor was still possessed by the same morbid forces of grief and anger which, at the villa, had broken down all her natural reticence and self-control. Was it possible--?

Her cheek flamed. She felt none of that spell in the priestly office which affected Eleanor. The mere bare notion of being 'managed' by this kind old priest was enough to rouse all her young spirit and defiance.

But the danger was imminent. She saw what she must do, and prepared herself to do it--simply, without any further struggle.

The little goatherds left her, munching their cakes and looking back at her from time to time in a childish curiosity. The pretty blue lady had seated herself again as they had found her--a few paces from the roadside, under the thick shadow of an oak.

*   *   *   *   *

Meanwhile, Manisty was rejoined by Father Benecke--who had left him for a few minutes to write his letter--beside the Paglia, which was rushing down in a brown flood, after the rain of the day before. Around and above them, on either side of the river, and far up the flanks of the mountains opposite, stretched the great oak woods, which are still to-day the lineal progeny of that vast Ciminian forest where lurked the earliest enemies of Rome.

'But for the sun, it might be Wales!' said Manisty, looking round him, as he took out another cigarette.

Father Benecke made no reply. He sat on a rock by the water's side, in what seemed to be a reverie. His fine white head was uncovered. His attitude was gentle, dignified, abstracted.

'It is a marvellous country this!' Manisty resumed. 'I thought I knew it pretty well. But the last five weeks have given one's mind a new hold upon it. The forests have been wasted--but by George!--what forests there are still!--and what a superb mountain region, half of which is only known to a few peasants and shepherds. What rivers--what fertility--what a climate! And the industry of the people. Catch a few English farmers and set them to do what the Italian peasant does, year in and year out, without a murmur! Look at all the coast south of Naples. There is not a yard of it, scarcely, that hasn't been *made* by human hands. Look at the hill-towns; and think of the human toil that has gone to the making and maintaining of them since the world began.'

And swaying backwards and forwards he fell into the golden lines:

Adde tot egregias urbes, operumque laborem,
Tot congesta manu praeruptis oppida saxis,

Fluminaque antiquos subterlabentia muros.

'*Congesta manu! Ecco!*--there they are'--and he pointed down the river to the three or four distant towns, each on its mountain spur, that held the valley between them and Orvieto--pale jewels on the purple robe of rock and wood.

'So Virgil saw them. So the latest sons of time shall see them--the homes of a race that we chatter about without understanding--the most laborious race in the wide world.'

And again he rolled out under his breath, for the sheer joy of the verse:

Salve, magna parens frugum, Saturnia tellus, Magna virum.

The priest looked at him with a smile; preoccupied yet shrewd.

'I follow you with some astonishment. Surely--I remember other sentiments on your part?'

Manisty coloured a little, and shook his black head, protesting.

'I never said uncivil things, that I remember, about Italy or the Italians as such. My quarrel was with the men that run them, the governments that exploit them. My point was that Piedmont and the North had been too greedy, had laid hands too rapidly on the South and had risked this damnable quarrel with the Church, without knowing what they were running their heads into. And in consequence they found themselves--in spite of rivers of corrupt expenditure--without men, or money, or credit to work their big new machine with; while the Church was always there, stronger than ever for the grievance they had presented her with, and turned into an enemy with whom it was no longer possible to parley. Well!--that struck me as a good object lesson. I wanted to say to the secularising folk everywhere--England included--just come here, and look what your policy comes to, when it's carried out to the bitter end, and not in the gingerly, tinkering fashion you affect at home! Just understand what it means to separate Church from State, to dig a gulf between the religious and the civil life.--Here's a country where nobody can be at once a patriot and a good Christian--where the Catholics don't vote for Parliament, and the State schools teach no religion--where the nation is divided into two vast camps, hating and thrusting at each other with every weapon they can tear from life. Examine it! That's what the thing looks like when it's full grown. Is it profitable--does it make for good times? In your own small degree, are you going to drive England that way too?--You'll admit, Father--you always did admit--that it was a good theme.'

The priest smiled--a little sadly.

'Excellent. Only--you seemed to me--a little irresponsible.'

Manisty nodded, and laughed.

'An outsider, with no stakes on? Well--that's true. But being a Romantic and an artist I sided with the Church. The new machine, and the men that were running it, seemed to me an ugly jerry-built affair, compared with the Papacy and all that it stood for. But then--'

--He leant back in his chair, one hand snatching and tearing at the bushes round him, in his absent, destructive way.--

'Well then--as usual--facts began to play the mischief with one's ideas. In the first place, as one lives on in Italy you discover the antiquity of this quarrel; that it is only the Guelf and Ghibelline quarrel over again, under new names. And in the next--presently one begins to divine an Italy behind the Italy we know, or history knows!--Voices come to one, as Goethe would say, from the caves where dwell "Die Muetter"--the creative generative forces of the country.'--

He turned his flashing look on Benecke, pleased now as always with the mere task of speech.

'Anyway, as I have been going up and down their country, especially during the last six weeks; prating about their poverty, and their taxes, their corruption, the incompetence of their leaders, the folly of their quarrel with the Church; I have been finding myself caught in the grip of things older and deeper--incredibly, primevally old!--that still dominate everything, shape everything here. There are forces in Italy, forces of land and soil and race--only now fully let loose--that will remake Church no less than State, as the generations go by. Sometimes I have felt as though this country were the youngest in Europe; with a future as fresh and teeming as the future of America. And yet one thinks of it at other times as one vast graveyard; so thick it is with the ashes and the bones of men! The Pope--and Crispi!--waves, both of them, on a sea of life that gave them birth, "with equal mind"; and that with equal mind will sweep them both to its own goal--not theirs.'

He smiled at his own eloquence, and returned to his cigarette.

The priest had listened to him all through with the same subtle embarrassed look.

'This must have some cause,' he said slowly, when Manisty ceased to speak. 'Surely?--this change? I recall language so different--forecasts so gloomy.'

'Gracious!--I can give you books-full of them,' said Manisty, reddening, 'if you care to read them. I came out with a *parti-pris*--I don't deny it. Catholicism had a great glamour for me; it has still, so long as you don't ask me to put my own neck under the yoke! But Rome itself is disenchanting. And outside Rome!--During the last six weeks I have been talking to every priest I could come across in these remote country districts where I have been wandering. *Per Dio!*--Marcello used to talk--I didn't believe him. But upon my word, the young fellows whom the seminaries are now sending out in shoals represent a fact to give one pause!--Little black devils!--*Scusi!* Father,--the word escaped me. Broadly speaking, they are a political militia,--little else. Their hatred of Italy is a venom in their bones, and they themselves are mad for a spiritual tyranny which no modern State could tolerate for a week. When one thinks of the older men--of Rosmini, of Gioberti, of the priests who died on the Milan barricades in '48!'

His companion made a slow movement of assent.

Manisty smoked on, till presently he launched the *mot* for which he had been feeling. 'The truth of the matter seems to be that Italy is Catholic, because she hasn't faith enough to make a heresy; and anti-clerical, because it is her destiny to be a nation!'

The priest smiled, but with a certain languor, turning his head once or twice as though to listen for sounds behind him, and taking out his watch. His eyes meanwhile--and their observation of Manisty--were not languid; seldom had the mild and spiritual face been so personal, so keen.

'Well, it is a great game,' said Manisty again--'and we shan't see the end. Tell me--how have they treated *you*--the priests in these parts?'

Benecke started and shrank.

'I have no complaint to make,' he said mildly. 'They seem to me good men.'

Manisty smoked in silence.

Then he said, as though summing up his own thoughts,--

'No,--there are plenty of dangers ahead. This war has shaken the *Sabaudisti*--for the moment. Socialism is serious.--Sicily is serious.--The economic difficulties are serious.--The House of Savoy will have a rough task, perhaps, to ride the seas that may come.--But *Italy* is safe. You can no more undo what has been done than you can replace the child in the womb. The birth is over. The organism is still weak, but it lives. And the forces behind it are indefinitely, mysteriously stronger than the Vatican thinks.'

'A great recantation,' said the priest quickly.

Manisty winced, but for a while said nothing. All at once he jerked away his cigarette.

'Do you suspect some other reason for it, than the force of evidence?'--he said, in another manner.

The priest, smiling, looked him full in the face without replying.

'You may,' said Manisty, coolly. 'I shan't play the hypocrite. Father, I told you that I had been wandering about Italy on a quest that was not health, nor piety, nor archaeology. How much did you guess?'

'Naturally, something--*lieber Herr*.'

'Do you know that I should have been at Torre Amiata weeks ago but for you?'

'For me! You talk in riddles.'

'Very simple. Your letters might have contained a piece of news--and did not. Yet if it had been there to give, you would have given it. So I crossed Torre Amiata off my list. No need to go *there*! I said to myself.'

The priest was silent.

Manisty looked up. His eyes sparkled; his lips trembled as though they could hardly bring themselves to launch the words behind them.

'Father--you remember a girl--at the Villa?'

The priest made a sign of assent.

'Well--I have been through Italy--with that girl's voice in my ears--and, as it were, her eyes rather than my own. I have been searching for her for weeks. She has hidden herself from me. But I shall find her!--now or later--here or elsewhere.'

'And then?'

'Well, then,--I shall know some "eventful living"!'

He drew a long breath.

'And you hope for success?'

'Hope?' said Manisty, passionately. 'I live on something more nourishing than that!'

The priest lifted his eyebrows.

'You are so certain?'

'I must be certain'--said Manisty, in a low voice,--'or in torment! I prefer the certainty.'

His face darkened. In its frowning disorganisation his companion saw for the first time a man hitherto unknown to him, a man who spoke with the dignity, the concentration, the simplicity of true passion.

Dignity! The priest recalled the voice, the looks of Eleanor Burgoyne. Not a word for her--not a thought! His old heart began to shrink from his visitor, from his own scheme.

'Then how do you explain the young lady's disappearance?' he asked, after a pause.

Manisty laughed. But the note was bitter.

'Father!--I shall make her explain it herself.'

'She is not alone?'

'No--my cousin Mrs. Burgoyne is with her.'

Benecke observed him, appreciated the stiffening of the massive shoulders.

'I heard from some friends in Rome,' said the priest, after a moment--'distressing accounts of Mrs. Burgoyne's health.'

Manisty's look was vague and irresponsive.

'She was always delicate,' he said abruptly,--not kindly.

'What makes you look for them in Italy?'

'Various causes. They would think themselves better hidden from their English friends, in Italy than elsewhere, at this time of year. Beside, I remember one or two indications--'

There was a short silence. Then Manisty sprang up.

'How long, did you say, before the trap came? An hour and a half?'

'Hardly,' said the priest, unwillingly, as he drew out his watch.--'And you must give yourself three hours to Orvieto--'

'Time enough. I'll go and have a look at those frescoes again--and a chat with the woman. Don't interrupt yourself. I shall be back in half an hour.'

'Unfortunately I must write a letter,' said the priest.

And he stood at the door of his little bandbox of a house, watching the departure of his guest.

Manisty breasted the hill, humming as he walked. The irregular vigorous form, the nobility and animation of his carriage drew the gaze of the priest after him.

'At what point'--he said to himself,--'will he find her?'

CHAPTER XXII

Eleanor did not rise now, as a rule, till half way through the morning. Lucy had left her in bed.

It was barely nine o'clock. Every eastern or southern window was already fast closed and shuttered, but her door stood open to the *loggia* into which no sun penetrated till the afternoon.

A fresh breeze, which seemed the legacy of the storm, blew through the doorway. Framed in the yellow arches of the *loggia* she saw two cypresses glowing black upon the azure blaze of the sky. And in front of them, springing from a pot on the *loggia*, the straggly stem and rosy bunches of an oleander. From a distance the songs of harvesters at their work; and close by, the green nose of a lizard peeping round the edge of the door.

Eleanor seemed to herself to have just awakened from sleep; yet not from unconsciousness. She had a confused memory of things which had passed in sleep--of emotions and experiences. Her heart was beating fast, and as she sat up, she caught her own reflection in the cracked glass on the dressing-table. Startled, she put up her hand to her flushed cheek. It was wet.

'Crying!' she said, in wonder--'what have I been dreaming about? And why do I feel like this? What is the matter with me?'

After a minute or two, she rang a handbell beside her, and her maid appeared.

'Marie, I am so well--so strong! It is extraordinary! Bring everything. I should like to get up.'

The maid, in fear of Lucy, remonstrated. But her mistress prevailed.

'Do my hair as usual to-day,' she said, as soon as that stage of her toilette was reached, and she was sitting in her white wrapper before the cracked glass.

Marie stared.

'It will tire you, madame.'

'No, it won't. *Mais faites vite!*'

Ever since their arrival at Torre Amiata Eleanor had abandoned the various elaborate *coiffures* in which she had been wont to appear at the villa. She would allow nothing but the simplest and rapidest methods; and Marie had been secretly alarmed lest her hand should lose her cunning.

So that to-day she coiled, crimped, curled with a will. When she had finished, Eleanor surveyed herself and laughed.

'*Ah! mais vraiment, Marie, tu es merveilleuse!* What is certain is that neither that glass nor Torre Amiata is worthy of it. *N'importe.* One must keep up standards.'

'Certainly, madame, you look better to-day.'

'I slept. Why did I sleep? I can't imagine. After all, Torre Amiata is not such a bad place--is it Marie?'

And with a laugh, she lightly touched her maid's cheek.

Marie looked a little sullen.

'It seems that madame would like to live and die here.'

She had no sooner said the words than she could have bitten her tongue out. She was genuinely attached to her mistress; and she knew well that Eleanor was no *malade imaginaire*.

Eleanor's face changed a little.

'Oh! you foolish girl--we shall soon be gone. No, not that old frock. Look, please, at that head you've made me--and consider! *Noblesse oblige.*'

So presently, she stood before her table in a cream walking dress--perfect--but of the utmost simplicity; with her soft black hat tied round the ripples and clouds of her fair hair.

'How it hangs on me!' she said, gathering up the front of her dress in her delicate hand.

Marie made a little face of pity and concern.

'*Mais oui, Madame. Il faudrait le cacher un peu.*'

'Padding? *Tiens! j'en ai deja.* But if Mathilde were to put any more, there would be nothing else. One day, Marie, you see, there will be only my clothes left to walk about--by their little selves!'

She smiled. The maid said nothing. She was on her knees buttoning her mistress's shoes.

'Now then--*fini!* Take all those books on to the *loggia* and arrange my chair. I shall be there directly.'

The maid departed. Eleanor sat down to rest from the fatigue of dressing.

'How weak I am!--weaker than last month. And next month it will be a little more--and a little more--then pain perhaps--horrid pain--and one day it will be impossible to get up--and all one's poor body will fail one like a broken vessel. And then--relief perhaps--if dying is as easy as it looks. No more pangs or regrets--and at the end, either a sudden puff that blows out the light--or a quiet drowning in deep waters--without pain....And to-day how little I fear it!'

A *prie-dieu* chair, old and battered like everything else in the convent, was beside her, and above it her child's portrait. She dropped upon her knees, as she always did for a minute or two morning and evening, mostly out of childish habit.

But her thoughts fell into no articulate words. Her physical weakness rested against the chair; but the weakness of the soul seemed also to rest on some invisible support.

'What is the matter with me to-day?'--she asked herself again, in bewilderment. 'Is it an omen--a sign? All bonds seem loosened--the air lighter. What made me so miserable yesterday? I wanted him to come--and yet dreaded--dreaded it so! And now to-day I don't care--I don't care!'

She slipped into a sitting position and looked at the picture. A tiny garland of heath and myrtle was hung round it. The little fellow seemed to be tottering towards her, the eyes a little frightened, yet trusting, the gait unsteady.

'Childie!'--she said in a whisper, smiling at him--'Childie!'

Then with a long sigh, she rose, and feebly made her way to the *loggia*.

Her maid was waiting for her. But Eleanor refused her sofa. She would sit, looking out through the arches of the *loggia*, to the road, and the mountains.

'Miss Foster is a long time,' she said to Marie. 'It is too hot for her to be out. And how odd! There is the Contessa's carriage--and the Contessa herself--at this time of day. Run, Marie! Tell her I shall be delighted to see her. And bring another comfortable chair--there's a dear.'

The Contessa mounted the stone stairs with the heavy masculine step that was characteristic of her.

'***Vous permettez, madame!***'--she said, standing in the doorway--'at this unseasonable hour.'

Eleanor made her welcome. The portly Contessa seated herself with an involuntary gesture of fatigue.

'What have you been doing?' said Eleanor. 'If you have been helping the harvesters, *je proteste*!'

She laid her hand laughingly on the Contessa's knee. It seemed to her that the Contessa knew far more of the doings and affairs of her *contadini* than did the rather magnificent *fattore* of the estate. She was in and out among them perpetually. She quarrelled with them and hectored them; she had as good a command of the local dialect as they had; and an eye that pounced on cheating like an osprey on a fish. Nevertheless, as she threw in yet another evident trifle--that she cared more for them and their interests than for anything else in the world, now that her son was gone--they endured her rule, and were not actively ungrateful for her benefits. And, in her own view at any rate, there is no more that any rich person can ask of any poor one till another age of the world shall dawn.

She received Eleanor's remark with an embarrassed air.

'I have been doctoring an ox,' she said, bluntly, as though apologising for herself. 'It was taken ill last night, and they sent for me.'

'But you are too, too wonderful!' cried Eleanor in amusement. 'Is it all grist that comes to your mill--sick oxen--or humans like me?'

The Contessa smiled, but she turned away her head.

'It was Emilio's craze,' she said abruptly. 'He knew every animal on the place. In his regiment they called him the "vet.," because he was always patching up the sick and broken mules. One of his last messages to me was about an old horse. He taught me a few things--and sometimes I am of use--till the farrier comes.'

There was a little silence, which the Contessa broke abruptly.

'I came, however, madame, to tell you something about myself. Teresa has made up her mind to leave me.'

'Your daughter?' cried Eleanor amazed. '***Fiancee?***'

The Contessa shook her head.

'She is about to join the nuns of Santa Francesca. Her novitiate begins in October. Now she goes to stay with them for a few weeks.'

Eleanor was thunderstruck.

'She leaves you alone?'

The Contessa mutely assented.

'And you approve?' said Eleanor hotly.

'She has a vocation'--said the Contessa with a sigh.

'She has a mother!' cried Eleanor.

'Ah! madame--you are a Protestant. These things are in our blood. When we are devout, like Teresa, we regard the convent as the gate of heaven. When we are Laodiceans--like me--we groan, and we submit.'

'You will be absolutely alone,' said Eleanor, in a low voice of emotion, 'in this solitary place.'

The Contessa fidgetted. She was of the sort that takes pity hardly.

'There is much to do,'--she said, shortly.

But then her fortitude a little broke down. 'If I were ten years older, it would be all right,' she said, in a voice that betrayed the mind's fatigue with its own debate. 'It's the time it all lasts; when you are as strong as I am.'

Eleanor took her hand and kissed it.

'Do you never take quite another line?' she said, with sparkling eyes. 'Do you never say--"This is my will, and I mean to have it! I have as much right to my way as other people?" Have you never tried it with Teresa?'

The Contessa opened her eyes.

'But I am not a tyrant,' she said, and there was just a touch of scorn in her reply. Eleanor trembled.

'We have so few years to live and be happy in,' she said in a lower voice, a voice of self-defence.

'That is not how it appears to me,' said the Contessa slowly. 'But then I believe in a future life.'

'And you think it wrong ever to press--to *insist* upon--the personal, the selfish point of view?'

The Contessa smiled.

'Not so much wrong, as futile. The world is not made so--*chere madame*.'

Eleanor sank back in her chair. The Contessa observed her emaciation, her pallor--and the pretty dress.

She remembered her friend's letter, and the 'Signor Manisty' who should have married this sad, charming woman, and had not done so. It was easy to see that not only disease but grief was preying on Mrs. Burgoyne. The Contessa was old enough to be her mother. A daughter whom she had lost in infancy would have been Eleanor's age, if she had lived.

'Madame, let me give you a piece of advice'--she said suddenly, taking Eleanor's hands in both her own--'leave this place. It does not suit you. These rooms are too rough for you--or let me carry you off to the Palazzo, where I could look after you.'

Eleanor flushed.

'This place is very good for me,' she said with a wild fluttering breath. 'To-day I feel so much better--so much lighter!'

The Contessa felt a pang. She had heard other invalids say such things before. The words rang like a dirge upon her ear. They talked a little longer. Then the Contessa rose, and Eleanor rose, too, in spite of her guest's motion to restrain her.

As they stood together the elder woman in her strength suddenly felt herself irresistibly drawn towards the touching weakness of the other. Instead of merely pressing hands, she quickly threw her strong arms round Mrs. Burgoyne, gathered her for an instant to her broad breast, and kissed her.

Eleanor leant against her, sighing:

'A vocation wouldn't drag *me* away,' she said gently.

And so they parted.

*   *   *   *   *

Eleanor hung over the *loggia* and watched the Contessa's departure. As the small horses trotted away, with a jingling of bells and a fluttering of the furry tails that hung from their ears, the *padre parroco* passed. He took off his hat to the Contessa, then seeing Mrs. Burgoyne on the *loggia*, he gave her, too, a shy but smiling salutation.

His light figure, his young and dreamy air, suited well with the beautiful landscape through which it passed. Shepherd? or poet? Eleanor thought of David among the flocks.

'He only wants the crook--the Scriptural crook. It would go quite well with the soutane.'

Then she became aware of another figure approaching on her right from the piece of open land that lay below the garden.

It was Father Benecke, and he emerged on the road just in front of the *padre parroco*.

The old priest took off his hat. Eleanor saw the sensitive look, the slow embarrassed gesture. The *padre parroco* passed without looking to the right or left. All the charming pliancy of the young figure had disappeared. It was drawn up to a steel rigidity.

Eleanor smiled and sighed.

'David among the Philistines!--*Ce pauvre Goliath*! Ah! he is coming here?'

She withdrew to her sofa, and waited.

Marie, after instructions, and with that austerity of demeanour which she, too, never failed to display towards Father Benecke, introduced the visitor.

'Entrez, mon pere, entrez,' said Eleanor, holding out a friendly hand. 'Are you, too, braving the sun? Did you pass Miss Foster? I wish she would come in--it is getting too hot for her to be out.'

'Madame, I have not been on the road. I came around through the Sassetto. There I found no one.'

'Pray sit down, Father. That chair has all its legs. It comes from Orvieto.'

But he did not accept her invitation--at least not at once. He remained hesitating--looking down upon her. And she, struck by his silence, struck by his expression, felt a sudden seizing of the breath. Her hand slid to her heart, with its fatal, accustomed gesture. She looked at him wildly, imploringly.

But the pause came to an end. He sat down beside her.

'Madame, you have taken so kind an interest in my unhappy affairs that you will perhaps allow me to tell you of the letter that has reached me this morning. One of the heads of the Old Catholic community invites me to go and consult with them before deciding on the course of my future life. There are many difficulties. I am not altogether in sympathy with them. A married priesthood such as they have now adopted, is in my eyes a priesthood shorn of its strength. But the invitation is so kind, so brotherly, I must needs accept it.'

He bent forward, looking not at her, but at the brick floor of the *loggia*. Eleanor offered a few words of sympathy; but felt there was more to come.

'I have also heard from my sister. She refuses to keep my house any longer. Her resentment at what I have done is very bitter--apparently insurmountable. She wishes to retire to a country place in Bavaria where we have some relations. She has a small *rente*, and will not be in any need.'

'And you?' said Eleanor quickly.

'I must find work, madame. My book will bring me in a little, they say. That will give me time--and some liberty of decision. Otherwise of course I am destitute. I have lost everything. But my education will always bring me enough for bread. And I ask no more.'

Her compassion was in her eyes.

'You too--old and alone--like the Contessa!' she said under her breath.

He did not hear. He was pursuing his own train of thought, and presently he raised himself. Never had the apostolic dignity of his white head, his broad brow been more commanding. But what Eleanor saw, what perplexed her, was the subtle tremor of the lip, the doubt in the eyes.

'So you see, madame, our pleasant hours are almost over. In a few days I must be gone. I will not attempt to express what I owe to your most kind, most indulgent sympathy. It seems to me that in the "dark wood" of my life it was your conversation--when my heart was so sorely cast down--which revived my intelligence--and so held me up, till--till I could see my way, and choose my path again. It has given me a great many new ideas--this companionship you have permitted me. I humbly confess that I shall always henceforward think differently of women, and of the relations that men and women may hold to one another. But then, madame--'

He paused. Eleanor could see his hand trembling on his knee.

She raised herself on her elbow.

'Father Benecke! you have something to say to me!'

He hurried on.

'The other day you allowed us to change the *roles*. You had been my support. You threw yourself on mine. Ah! Madame, have I been of any assistance to you-- then, and in the interviews you have since permitted me? Have I strengthened your heart at all as you strengthened mine?'

His ardent, spiritual look compelled--and reassured her.

She sank back. A tear glittered on her brown lashes. She raised a hand to dash it away.

'I don't know, Father--I don't know. But to-day--for some mysterious reason--I seem almost to be happy again. I woke up with the feeling of one who had been buried under mountains of rocks and found them rolled away; of one who had been passing through a delirium which was gone. I seem to care for nothing--to grieve for nothing. Sometimes you know that happens to people who are very ill. A numbness comes upon them.--But I am not numb. I feel everything. Perhaps, Father'--and she turned to him with her old sweet instinct--of one who loved to be loved--'perhaps you have been praying for me?'

She smiled at him half shyly. But he did not see it. His head bent lower and lower.

'Thank God!' he said, with the humblest emphasis. 'Then, madame--perhaps--you will find the force--to forgive me!'

The words were low--the voice steady.

Eleanor sprang up.

'Father Benecke!--what have you been doing? Is--is Mr. Manisty here?'

She clung to the *loggia* parapet for support. The priest looked at her pallor with alarm, with remorse, and spoke at once.

'He came to me last night.'

Their eyes met, as though in battle--expressed a hundred questions--a hundred answers. Then she broke the silence.

'Where is he?' she said imperiously.' Ah!--I see--I see!'

She sat down, fronting him, and panting a little.

'Miss Foster is not with me. Mr. Manisty is not with you. The inference is easy.--And you planned it! You took--you **dared** to take--as much as this--into your own hands!'

He made no reply. He bent like a reed in the storm.

'There is no boldness like a saint's'--she said bitterly,--'no hardness--like an angel's! What I would not have ventured to do with my closest friend, my nearest and dearest--you--a stranger--have done--with a light heart. Oh! it is monstrous!-

-monstrous!'

She moved her neck from side to side as though she was suffocating--throwing back the light ruffle that encircled it.

'A stranger?'--he said slowly. His intense yet gentle gaze confronted hers.

'You refer, I suppose, to that most sacred, most intimate confidence I made to you?--which no man of honour or of heart could have possibly betrayed,'--she said passionately. 'Ah! you did well to warn me that it was no true confession--under no true seal! You should have warned me further--more effectually.'

Her paleness was all gone. Her cheeks flamed. The priest felt that she was beside herself, and, traversed as his own mind was with the most poignant doubts and misgivings, he must needs wrestle with her, defend himself.

'Madame!--you do me some wrong,' he said hurriedly. 'At least in words I have told nothing--betrayed nothing. When I left him an hour ago Mr. Manisty had no conception that you were here. After my first letter to him, he tells me that he relinquished the idea of coming to Torre Amiata, since if you had been staying here, I must have mentioned it.'

Eleanor paused. 'Subterfuge!' she cried, under her breath. Then, aloud--'You asked him to come.'

'That, madame, is my crime,' he admitted, with a mild and painful humility. 'Your anger hits me hard. But--do you remember?--you placed three lives in my hands. I found you helpless; you asked for help. I saw you day by day, more troubled, yet, as it seemed to me, more full of instincts towards generosity, towards peace. I felt--oh! madame, I felt with all my heart, that there lay just one step between you and a happiness that would compensate you a thousand times for all you had gone through. You say that I prayed for you. I did--often--and earnestly. And it seemed to me that--in our later conversations--I saw such signs of grace in you--such exquisite dispositions of the heart--that were the chance of action once more given to you--you would find the strength to seize the blessing that God offered you. And one evening in particular, I found you in an anguish that seemed to be destroying you. And you had opened your heart to me; you had asked my help as a Christian priest. And so, madame, as you say--I dared. I said, in writing to Mr. Manisty, who had told me he was coming northward--"if Torre Amiata is not far out of your road--look in upon me." Neither your name nor Miss Foster's passed my lips. But since--I confess--I have lived in much disturbance of mind!'

Eleanor laughed.

'Are all priests as good casuists as you, Father?'

His eyes wavered a little as though her words stung. But he did not reply.

There was a pause. Eleanor turned towards the parapet and looked outward towards the road and the forest. Her face and eyes were full of an incredible animation; her lips were lightly parted to let the quick breath pass.

Then of a sudden she withdrew. Her eyes moved back to Father Benecke; she bent forward and held out both her hands.

'Father--I forgive you! Let us make peace.'

He took the small fingers into his large palms with a gratitude that was at once awkward and beautiful.

'I don't know yet'--he said, in a deep perplexity--'whether I absolve myself.'

'You will soon know,' she said almost with gaiety. 'Oh! it is quite possible'--she threw up one hand in a wild childish gesture--'it is quite possible that to-morrow I may be at your feet, asking you to give me penance for my rough words. On the other hand--Anyway, Father, you have not found me a very dutiful penitent?'

'I expected castigation,' he said meekly. 'If the castigation is done, I have come off better than I could have hoped.'

She raised herself, and took up her gloves that were lying on the little table beside her sofa.

'You see'--she said, talking very fast--'I am an Englishwoman, and my race is not a docile one. Here, in this village, I have noticed a good deal, and the *massaja* gossips to me. There was a fight in the street the other night. The men were knifing each other. The *parroco* sent them word that they should come at once to his house--*per pacificarli*. They went. There is a girl, living with her sister, whose husband has a bad reputation. The *parroco* ordered her to leave--found another home for her. She left. There is a lad who made some blasphemous remarks in the street on the day of the Madonna's procession. The *parroco* ordered him to do penance. He did it. But those things are not English. Perhaps they are Bavarian?'

He winced, but he had recovered his composure.

'Yes, madame, they are Bavarian also. But it seems that even an Englishwoman can sometimes feel the need of another judgment than her own?'

She smiled. All the time that she had made her little speech about the village, she had been casting quick glances along the road. It was evident that her mind was only half employed with what she was saying. The rose-flush in her cheeks, the dainty dress, the halo of fair hair gave her back youth and beauty; and the priest gazed at her in astonishment.

'Ah!'--she said, with a vivacity that was almost violence--'here she is. Father--please--!' And with a peremptory gesture, she signed to him to draw back, as she had done, into the shadow, out of sight of the road.

But the advancing figure was plain to both of them.

Lucy mounted the hill with a slow and tired step. Her eyes were on the ground. The whole young form drooped under the heat, and under a weight of thought still more oppressive. As it came nearer a wave of sadness seemed to come with it, dimming the sunshine and the green splendour of the woods.

As she passed momentarily out of sight behind some trees that sheltered the gate of the courtyard, Mrs. Burgoyne crossed the *loggia*, and called to her maid.

'Marie--be so good as to tell Miss Foster when she comes in that I have gone out; that she is not to trouble about me, as I shall soon return; and tell her also that I felt unusually well and strong.'

Then she turned and beckoned to Father Benecke.

'This way, Father, please!'

And she led him down the little stair that had taken Lucy to the garden the night before. At the foot of the stairs she paused. The wall of the garden divided them from the courtyard, and on the other side of it they could hear Lucy speaking to the *massaja*.

'Now!' said Eleanor, 'quick I--before she discovers us!'

And opening the garden door with the priest's help she passed into the field, and took a wide circuit to the right so as to be out of view of the *loggia*.

'Dear madame, where are you going?' said the priest in some alarm. 'This is too fatiguing for you.'

Eleanor took no notice. She, who for days had scarcely dragged one languid foot after another, sped through the heat and over the broken ground like one of the goldfinches in the convent garden. The old priest followed her with difficulty. Nor did she pause till they were in the middle of the Sassetto.

'Explain what we are doing!' he implored her, as she allowed him to press his old limbs for a moment on his stick, and take breath.

She, too, leant against a tree panting.

'You said, Father, that Mr. Manisty was to leave you at midday.'

'And you wish to see him?' he cried.

'I am determined to see him,' she said in a low voice, biting her lip.

And again she was off, a gleam of whiteness gliding down, down, through the cool green heart of the Sassetto, towards the Paglia.

They emerged upon the fringe of the wood, where amid scrub and sapling trees stood the little sun-baked house.

From the distance came a sound of wheels--a carriage from Selvapendente crossing the bridge over the Paglia?

Mrs. Burgoyne looked at the house for a moment in silence. Then, sheltered under her large white parasol, she passed round to the side that fronted the river.

There, in the shade, sat Manisty, his arms upon his knees, his head buried in his hands.

He did not at first hear Mrs. Burgoyne's step, and she paused a little way off. She was alone. The priest had not followed her.

At last, as she moved, either the sound of her dress or the noise of the approaching wheels roused him. He looked up--started--sprang to his feet.

'Eleanor!--'

They met. Their eyes crossed. She shivered, for there were tears in his. But through that dimness there shone the fierce unspoken question that had leapt to them at the sight of his cousin--

'Hast thou found me, O mine enemy?'

CHAPTER XXIII

Eleanor was the first to break the silence.

'You have had a long pilgrimage to find us,' she said quietly. 'Yet perhaps Torre Amiata might have occurred to you. It was you that praised it--that proposed to find quarters at the convent.'

He stared at her in amazement.

'Eleanor--in God's name!' he broke out violently, 'tell me what this all means! What has been the meaning of this mad--this extraordinary behaviour?'

She tottered a little and leant against the wall of the house.

'Find me a chair, please, before we begin to talk. And--is that your fly? Send it away--to wait under the trees. It can take me up the hill, when we have finished.'

He controlled himself with difficulty and went round the house.

She pressed her hands upon her eyes to shut out the memory of his face.

'She has refused him!' she said to herself; 'and--what is more--she has made him believe it!'

Very soon his step was heard returning. The woman he had left in the shade listened for it, as though in all this landscape of rushing river and murmuring wood it the one audible, significant sound. But when he came back to her again, he saw nothing but a composed, expectant Eleanor; dressed, in these wilds, with a dainty care which would have done honour to London or Paris, with a bright colour in her cheeks, and the quiver of a smile on her lips. Ill! He thought he had seldom seen her look so well. Had she not always been of a thistle-down lightness? 'Exaggeration!--absurdity!' he said to himself fiercely, carrying his mind back to certain sayings in a girl's voice that were still ringing in his ears.

He, however, was in no mood to smile. Eleanor had thrown herself sideways on the chair he had brought her; her arms resting on the back of it, her delicate hands hanging down. It was a graceful and characteristic attitude, and it seemed to him affectation--a piece of her fine-ladyism.

She instantly perceived that he was in a state of such profound and passionate excitement that it was difficult for him to speak.

So she began, with a calmness which exasperated him:

'You asked me, Edward, to explain our escapade?'

He raised his burning eyes.

'What can you explain?--how can you explain?' he said roughly. 'Are you going to tell me why my cousin and comrade hates me and plots against me?--why she has inflicted this slight and outrage upon me--why, finally, she has poisoned against me the heart of the woman I love?'

He saw her shrink. Did a cruel and secret instinct in him rejoice? He was mad with rage and misery, and he was incapable of concealing it.

She knew it. As he dropped his head again in an angry stare at the grass between them, she was conscious of a sudden childish instinct to put out her hand and stroke the black curls and the great broad shoulders. He was not for her; but, in the old days, who had known so well as she how to soothe, manage, control him?

'I can't tell you those things--certainly,' she said, after a pause. 'I can't describe what doesn't exist.'

And to herself she cried: 'Oh! I shall lie--lie--lie--like a fiend, if I must!'

'What doesn't exist'?' he repeated scornfully. 'Will you listen to my version of what has happened--the barest, unadorned tale? I was your host and Miss Foster's. I had begun to show the attraction that Miss Foster had for me, to offer her the most trifling, the most ordinary attention. From the moment I was first conscious of my own feeling, I knew that you were against me--that you were influencing--Lucy'--the name dropped from his lips in a mingled anguish and adoration--'against me. And just as I was beginning to understand my own heart--to look forward to two or three last precious weeks in which to make, if I could, a better impression upon her, after my abominable rudeness at the beginning--*you* interfered--you, my best friend! Without a word our party is broken up; my chance is snatched from me; Miss Foster is spirited away. You and she disappear, and you leave me to bear my affront--the outrage done me--as best I may. You alarm, you distress all your friends. Your father takes things calmly, I admit. But even he has been anxious. Aunt Pattie has been miserable. As for me--'

He rose, and began to pace up and down before her; struggling with his own wrath.

'And at last'--he resumed, pausing in front of her--'after wandering up and down Italy, I find you--in this remote place--by the merest chance. Father Benecke said not a word. But what part he has played in it I don't yet understand. In another half-hour I should have been off; and again you would have made the veriest fool of me that over walked this earth. Why, Eleanor?--why? What have I done to you?'

He stood before her--a superb, commanding presence. In his emotion all un-shapeliness of limb or movement seemed to have disappeared. Transfigured by the unconsciousness of passion, he was all energy and all grace.

'Eleanor!--explain! Has our old friendship deserved this? Why have you done this thing to me?--And, my God!'--he began to pace up and down again, his hands in his pockets--'how well--how effectually you have gone to work! You have had--Lucy--in your hands for six weeks. It is plain enough what has been going on. This morning--on that hill--suddenly,'--he raised his hand to his brow, as though the surprise, the ecstacy of the moment returned upon him--'there among the trees--was her face! What I said I shall never remember. But when a man feels as I do he has no need to take thought what he shall say. And she? Impatience, coldness, aversion!--not a word permitted of my long pilgrimage--not a syllable of explanation for this slight, this unbearable slight that had been put upon me as her host, her guardian, for the time being! You and she fly me as though I were no longer fit to be your companion. Even the servants talked. Aunt Pattie and I had to set our-selves at once to devise the most elaborate falsehoods, or Heaven knows where the talk would have spread. How had I deserved such a humiliation?--Yet, when I meet Miss Foster again, she behaves as though she owed me not a word of excuse. All her talk of you and your health! I must go away at once--because it would startle and disturb you to see me. She had already found out by chance that I was here--she had begged Father Benecke to use his influence with me not to insist on seeing you--not to come to the convent. It was the most amazing, the most inexplicable thing! What in the name of fortune does it mean? Are we all mad? Is the world and everyone on it rushing together to Bedlam?'

Still she did not speak. Was it that his mere voice, the familiar torrent of words, was delightful to her?--that she cared very little what he said, so long as he was there, living, breathing, pleading before her?--that, like Sidney, she could have cried to him: 'Say on, and all well said, still say the same'?

But he meant to be answered. He came close to her.

'We have been comrades, Eleanor--fellow-workers--friends. You have come to know me as perhaps no other woman has known me. I have shown you a thousand faults. You know all my weaknesses. You have a right to despise me as an unstable, egotistical, selfish fool; who must needs waste other people's good time and good brains for his own futile purposes. You have a right to think me ungrateful for the kindest help that ever man got. You have a right as Miss Foster's friend--and per-haps, guessing as you do at some of my past history,--to expect of me probation and guarantees. You have a right to warn her how she gives away anything so precious as herself. But you have not a right to inflict on me such suffering--such agony of mind--as you have imposed on me the last six weeks! I deny it, Eleanor--I deny it altogether! The punishment, the test goes beyond--far beyond--your right and my offences!'

He calmed--he curbed himself.

'The reckoning has come, Eleanor. I ask you to pay it.'

She drew a long breath.

'But I can't go at that pace. You must give me time.'

He turned away in a miserable impatience.

She closed her eyes and thought a little, 'Now'--she said to herself--'now is the time for lying. It must be done. Quick! no scruples!'

And aloud:

'You understand,' she said slowly, 'that Miss Foster and I had become much attached to each other?'

'I understand.'

'That she had felt great sympathy for me in the failure of the book, and was inclined--well, you have proof of it!--to pity me, of course a great deal too much, for being a weakling. She is the most tender--the most loving creature that exists.'

'How does that explain why you should have fled from me like the plague?' he said doggedly.

'No--no--but--Anyway, you see Lucy was likely to do anything she could to please me. That's plain, isn't it?--so far?'

Her head dropped a little to one side, interrogatively.

He made no reply. He still stood in front of her, his eyes bent upon her, his hands in his pockets.

'Meanwhile'--the colour rushed over her face--'I had been, most innocently, an eavesdropper.'

'Ah!' he said, with a movement, 'that night? I imagined it.'

'You were not as cautious as you might have been--considering all the people about--and I heard.'

He waited, all ear. But she ceased to speak. She bent a little farther over the back of the chair, as though she were making a mental enumeration of the leaves of a tiny myrtle bush that grew near his heel.

'I thought that bit of truth would have stiffened the lies,' she thought to herself; 'but somehow--they don't work.'

'Well: then, you see'--she threw back her head again and looked at him--'I had to consider. As you say, I knew you better than most people. It was all remarkably rapid--you will hardly deny that? For a fortnight you took no notice of Lucy Foster. Then the attraction began--and suddenly--Well, we needn't go into that any more; but with your character it was plain that you would push matters on--that you would give her no time--that you would speak, *coute qua coute*--that you would fling caution and delay to the winds--and that all in a moment Lucy Foster would find herself confronted by a great decision that she was not at all prepared to make. It was not fair that she should even be asked to make it. I had become her friend, specially. You will see there was a responsibility. Delay for both of you--wasn't that to be desired? And no use whatever to go and leave you the address!--you'll admit that?' she said hurriedly, with the accent of a child trying to entrap the judgment of an angry elder who was bringing it to book.

He stood there lost in wrath, bewilderment, mystification. Was there ever a more lame, more ridiculous tale?

Then he turned quickly upon her, searching her face for some clue. A sudden perception--a perception of horror--swept upon him. Eleanor's first flush was gone; in its place was the pallor of effort and excitement. What a ghost, what a spectre she had become! Manisty looked at her aghast,--at her unsteady yet defiant eyes, at the uncontrollable trembling of the mouth she did her best to keep at its hard task of smiling.

In a flash, he understood. A wave of red invaded the man's face and neck. He saw himself back in the winter days, working, talking, thinking; always with Eleanor; Eleanor his tool, his stimulus; her delicate mind and heart the block on which he sharpened his own powers and perceptions. He recalled his constant impatience of the barriers that hamper cold and cautious people. He must have intimacy, feeling, and the moods that border on and play with passion. Only so could his own gift of phrase, his own artistic divinations develop to a fine suhtlety and clearness, like flowers in a kind air.

An experience,--for him. And for her? He remembered how, in a leisurely and lordly way, he had once thought it possible he might some day reward his cousin; at the end of things, when all other adventures were done.

Then came that tragi-comedy of the book; his disillusion with it; his impatient sense that the winter's work upon it was somehow bound up in Eleanor's mind with a claim on him that had begun to fret and tease; and those rebuffs, tacit or spoken, which his egotism had not shrunk from inflicting on her sweetness.

How could he have helped inflicting them? Lucy had come!--to stir in him the deepest waters of the soul. Besides, he had never taken Eleanor seriously. On the one hand he had thought of her as intellect, and therefore hardly woman; on the other he had conceived her as too gentle, too sweet, too sensitive to push anything to extremes. No doubt the flight of the two friends and Eleanor's letter had been a rude awakening. He had then understood that he had offended Eleanor, offended her both as a friend, and as a clever woman. She had noticed the dawn of his love for Lucy Foster, and had determined that he should still recognise her power and influence upon his life.

This was part of his explanation. As to the rest, it was inevitable that both his vanity and passion should speak soft things. A girl does not take such a wild step, or acquiesce in it--till she has felt a man's power. Self-assertion on Eleanor's part--a sweet alarm on Lucy's--these had been his keys to the matter, so far. They had brought him anger, but also hope; the most delicious, the most confident hope.

Now remorse shot through him, fierce and stinging--remorse and terror! Then on their heels followed an angry denial of responsibility, mingled with alarm and revolt. Was he to be robbed of Lucy because Eleanor had misread him? No doubt she had imprinted what she pleased on Lucy's mind. Was he indeed undone?--for good and all?

Then shame, pity, rushed upon him headlong. He dared not look at the face beside him with its record of pain. He tried to put out of his mind what it meant. Of course he must accept her lead. He was only too eager to accept it; to play the game as she pleased. She was mistress! That he realised.

He took up the camp-stool on which he had been sitting when she arrived and placed himself beside her.

'Well--that explains something'--he said more gently. 'I can't complain that I don't seem to you or anyone a miracle of discretion; I can't wonder--perhaps--that you should wish to protect Miss Foster, if--if you thought she needed protecting. But I must think--I can't help thinking, that you set about it with very unnecessary violence. And for yourself too--what madness! Eleanor! what have you been doing to yourself?'

He looked at her reproachfully with that sudden and intimate penetration which was one of his chief spells with women. Eleanor shrank.

'Oh! I am ill,' she said hastily; 'too ill in fact to make a fuss about. It would only be a waste of time.'

'Of course you have found this place too rough for you. Have you any comforts at all in that ruin? Eleanor, what a rash,--what a wild thing to do!'

He came closer to her, and Eleanor trembled under the strong expostulating tenderness of his face and voice. It was so like him--to be always somehow in the right! Would he succeed, now as always, in doing with her exactly as he would? And was it not this, this first and foremost that she had fled from?

'No'--she said,--'no. I have been as well here as I should have been anywhere else. Don't let us talk of it.'

'But I must talk of it. You have hurt yourself--and Heaven knows you have hurt me--desperately. Eleanor--when I came back from that function the day you left the Villa, I came back with the intention of telling you everything. I knew you were Miss Foster's friend. I thought you were mine too. In spite of all my stupidity about the book, Eleanor, you would have listened to me?--you would have advised me?'

'When did you begin to think of Lucy?'

Her thin fingers, crossed over her brow, as she rested her arm on the back of the chair, hid from him the eagerness, the passion, of her curiosity.

But he scented danger. He prepared himself to walk warily.

'It was after Nemi--quite suddenly. I can't explain it. How can one ever explain those things?'

'What makes you want to marry her? What possible congruity is there between her and you?'

He laughed uneasily.

'What's the good of asking those things? One's feeling itself is the answer.'

'But I'm the spectator--the friend.'--The word came out slowly, with a strange emphasis. 'I want to know what Lucy's chances are.'

'Chances of what?'

'Chances of happiness.'

'Good God!'--he said, with an impatient groan.--'You talk as though she were going to give herself any opportunity to find out.'

'Well, let us talk so, for argument. You're not exactly a novice, you know, in these things. How is one to be sure that you're not playing with Lucy--as you played with the book--till you can go back to the play you really like best?'

'What do you mean?' he cried, starting with indignation--'the play of politics?'

'Politics--ambition--what you will. Suppose Lucy finds herself taken up and thrown down--like the book?--when the interest's done?'

She uncovered her eyes, and looked at him steadily, coldly. It was an Eleanor he did not know.

He sprang up in his anger and discomfort, and began to pace again in front of her.

'Oh well--if you think as badly of me as that'--he said fiercely,--'I don't see what good can come of this conversation.'

There was a pause. At the end of it, Eleanor said in another voice:

'Did you ever give her any indication of what you felt--before to-day?'

'I came near--in the Borghese gardens,' he said reluctantly. 'If she had held out the tip of her little finger--But she didn't. And I should have been a fool. It was too soon--too hasty. Anyway, she would not give me the smallest opening. And afterwards--' He paused. His mind passed to his night-wandering in the garden, to the strange breaking of the terra-cotta. Furtively his gaze examined Eleanor's face. But what he saw of it told him nothing, and again his instinct warned him to let sleeping dogs lie. 'Afterwards I thought things over, naturally. And I determined, that night, as I have already said, to come to you and take counsel with you. I saw you were out of charity with me. And, goodness knows, there was not much to be said for me! But at any rate I thought that we, who had been such old friends, had better understand each other; that you'd help me if I asked you. You'd never yet refused, anyway.'

His voice changed. She said nothing for a little, and her hands still made a penthouse for her face.

At last she threw him a question.

'Just now--what happened?'

'Good Heavens, as if I knew!' he said, with a cry of distress. 'I tried to tell her how I had gone up and down Italy, seeking for her, hungering for any shred of news of you. And she?--she treated me like a troublesome intruder, like a dog that follows you unasked and has to be beaten back with your stick!'

Eleanor smiled a little. His heart and his vanity had been stabbed alike. Certainly he had something to complain of.

She dropped her hands, and drew herself erect.

'Well, yes,' she said in a meditative voice, 'we must think--we must see.'

As she sat there, rapt in a sudden intensity of reflection, the fatal transformation in her was still more plainly visible; Manisty could hardly keep his eyes from her. Was it his fault? His poor, kind Eleanor! He felt the ghastly tribute of it, felt it with impatience, and repulsion. Must a man always measure his words and actions by a foot-rule--lest a woman take him too seriously? He repented; and in the same breath told himself that his penalty was more than his due.

At last Eleanor spoke.

'I must return a moment to what we said before. Lucy Foster's ways, habits, antecedents are wholly different from yours. Suppose there were a chance for you. You would take her to London--expect her to play her part there--in your world. Suppose she failed. How would you get on?'

'Eleanor--really!--am a "three-tailed bashaw"?'

'No. But you are absorbing--despotic--fastidious. You might break that girl's heart in a thousand ways--before you knew you'd done it. You don't give; you take.'

'And you--hit hard!' he said, under his breath, resuming his walk.

She sat white and motionless, her eyes sparkling. Presently he stood still before her, his features working with emotion.

'If I am incapable of love--and unworthy of hers,' he said in a stifled voice,--'if that's your verdict--if that's what you tell her--I'd better go. I know your power--don't dispute your right to form a judgment--I'll go. The carriage is there. Good-bye.'

She lifted her face to his with a quick gesture.

'She loves you!'--she said, simply.

Manisty fell back, with a cry.

There was a silence. Eleanor's being was flooded with the strangest, most ecstatic sense of deliverance. She had been her own executioner; and this was not death--but life!

She rose. And speaking in her natural voice, with her old smile, she said--'I must go back to her--she will have missed me. Now then--what shall we do next?'

He walked beside her bewildered.

'You have taken my breath away--lifted me from Hell to Purgatory anyway,' he said, at last, trying for composure. 'I have no plans for myself--no particular hope--you didn't see and hear her just now! But I leave it all in your hands. What else can I do?'

'No,' she said calmly. 'There is nothing else for you to do.'

He felt a tremor of revolt, so quick and strange was her assumption of power over both his destiny and Lucy's. But he suppressed it; made no reply.

They turned the corner of the house. 'Your carriage can take ms up the hill,' said Eleanor. 'You must ask Father Benecke's hospitality a little longer; and you shall hear from me to-night.'

They walked towards the carriage, which was waiting a hundred yards away. On the way Manisty suddenly said, plunging back into some of the perplexities which had assailed him before Eleanor's appearance:

'What on earth does Father Benecke know about it all? Why did he never mention that you were here; and then ask me to pay him a visit? Why did he send me up the hill this morning? I had forgotten all about the convent. He made me go.'

Eleanor started; coloured; and pondered a moment.

'We pledged him to secrecy as to his letters. But all priests are Jesuits, aren't they?--even the good ones. I suppose he thought we had quarrelled, and he would force us for our good to make it up. He is very kind--and--rather romantic.'

Manisty said no more. Here, too, he divined mysteries that were best avoided.

They stood beside the carriage. The coachman was on the ground remedying something wrong with the harness.

Suddenly Manisty put out his hand and seized his companion's.

'Eleanor!'--he said imploringly--'Eleanor!'

His lips could not form a word more. But his eyes spoke for him. They breathed compunction, entreaty; they hinted what neither could ever say; they asked pardon for offences that could never be put into words.

Eleanor did not shrink. Her look met his in the first truly intimate gaze that they had ever exchanged; hers infinitely sad, full of a dignity recovered, and never to be lost again, the gaze, indeed, of a soul that was already withdrawing itself gently, imperceptibly from the things of earth and sense; his agitated and passionate. It seemed to him that he saw the clear brown of those beautiful eyes just cloud with tears. Then they dropped, and the moment was over, the curtain fallen, for ever.

They sighed, and moved apart. The coachman climbed upon the box.

'To-night!'--she said, smiling--waving her hand--'Till to-night.'

'*Avanti!*' cried the coachman, and the horses began to toil sleepily up the hill.

* * * * *

'Sapphira was nothing to me!' thought Eleanor as she threw herself back in the old shabby landau with a weariness of body that made little impression however on the tension of her mind.

Absently she looked out at the trees above and around her; at the innumerable turns of the road. So the great meeting was over! Manisty's reproaches had come and gone! With his full knowledge--at his humble demand--she held his fate in her hands.

Again that extraordinary sense of happiness and lightness! She shrank from it in a kind of terror.

Once, as the horses turned corner after corner, the sentence of a meditative Frenchman crossed her mind; words which said that the only satisfaction for man lies in being *dans l'ordre*; in unity, that is, with the great world-machine in which he finds himself; fighting with it, not against it.

Her mind played about this thought; then returned to Manisty and Lucy.

A new and humbled Manisty!--shaken with a supreme longing and fear which seemed to have driven out for the moment all the other elements in his character-- those baser, vainer, weaker elements that she knew so well. The change in him was a measure of the smallness of her own past influence upon him; of the infinitude of her own self-deception. Her sharp intelligence drew the inference at once, and bade her pride accept it.

They had reached the last stretch of hill before the convent. Where was Lucy? She looked out eagerly.

The girl stood at the edge of the road, waiting. As Eleanor bent forward with a nervous 'Dear, I am not tired--wasn't it lovely to find this carriage?' Lucy made no reply. Her face was stern; her eyes red. She helped Eleanor to alight without a word.

But when they had reached Eleanor's cool and shaded room, and Eleanor was lying on her bed physically at rest, Lucy stood beside her with a quivering face.

'Did you tell him to go at once? Of course you have seen him?'

'Yes, I have seen him. Father Benecke gave me notice.'

'Father Benecke!' said the girl with a tightening of the lip.

There was a pause; then Eleanor said:

'Dear, get that low chair and sit beside me.'

'You oughtn't to speak a word,' said Lucy impetuously; 'you ought to rest there for hours. Why we should be disturbed in this unwarrantable, this unpardonable way, I can't imagine.'

She looked taller than Eleanor had ever seen her; and more queenly. Her whole frame seemed to be stiff with indignation and will.

'Come!' said Eleanor, holding out her hand.

Unwillingly Lucy obeyed.

Eleanor turned towards her. Their faces were close together; the ghastly pallor of the one beside the stormy, troubled beauty of the other.

'Darling, listen to me. For two months I have been like a person in a delirium--under suggestion, as the hypnotists say. I have not been myself. It has been a possession. And this morning--before I saw Edward at all--I felt the demon--go! And the result is very simple. Put your ear down to me.'

Lucy bent.

'The one thing in the world that I desire now--before I die--(Ah! dear, don't start!--you know!)--the only, only thing--is that you and Edward should be happy--and forgive me.'

Her voice was lost in a sob. Lucy kissed her quickly, passionately. Then she rose.

'I shall never marry Mr. Manisty, Eleanor, if that is what you mean. It is well to make that clear at once.'

'And why?' Eleanor caught her--kept her prisoner.

'Why?--why?' said Lucy impatiently--'because I have no desire to marry him--because--I would sooner cut off my right hand than marry him.'

Eleanor held her fast, looked at her with a brilliant eye--accusing, significant.

'A fortnight ago you were on the *loggia*--alone. I saw you from my room. Lucy!--I saw you kiss the terra-cotta he gave you. Do you mean to tell me that meant nothing--*nothing*--from you, of all people? Oh! you dear, dear child!--I knew it from the beginning--I knew it--but I was mad.'

Lucy had grown very white, but she stood rigid.

'I can't be responsible for what you thought, or--for anything--but what I do. And I will never marry Mr. Manisty.'

Eleanor still held her.

'Dear--you remember that night when Alice attacked you? I came into the library, unknown to you both. You were still in the chair--you heard nothing. He stooped over you. I heard what he said. I saw his face. Lucy! there are terrible risks--not to you--but to him--in driving a temperament like his to despair. You know how he lives by feeling, by imagination--how much of the artist, of the poet, there is in him. If he is happy--if there is someone to understand, and strengthen him, he will do great things. If not he will waste his life. And that would be so bitter, bitter to see!'

Eleanor leant her face on Lucy's hands, and the girl felt her tears. She shook from head to foot, but she did not yield.

'I can't--I can't'--she said in a low, resolute voice. 'Don't ask me. I never can.'

'And you told him so?'

'I don't know what I told him--except that he mustn't trouble you--that we wanted him to go--to go directly.'

'And he--what did he say to you?'

'That doesn't matter in the least,' cried Lucy. 'I have given him no right to say what he does. Did I encourage him to spend these weeks in looking for us? Never!'

'He didn't want encouraging,' said Eleanor. 'He is in love--perhaps for the first time in his life. If you are to give him no hope--it will go hard with him.'

Lucy's face only darkened.

'How can you say such things to me?' she said passionately. 'How can you?'

Eleanor sighed. 'I have not much right to say them, I know,' she said presently, in a low voice. 'I have poisoned the sound of them to your ears.'

Lucy was silent. She began to walk up and down the room, with her hands behind her.

'I will never, never forgive Father Benecke,' she said presently, in a low, determined voice.

'What do you think he had to do with it?'

'I know,' said Lucy. 'He brought Mr. Manisty here. He sent him up the hill this morning to see me. It was the most intolerable interference and presumption. Only a priest could have done it.'

'Oh! you bigot!--you Puritan! Come here, little wild-cat. Let me say something.'

Lucy came reluctantly, and Eleanor held her.

'Doesn't it enter into your philosophy--tell me--that one soul should be able to do anything for another?'

'I don't believe in the professional, anyway,' said Lucy stiffly--'nor in the professional claims.'

'My dear, it is a training like any other.'

'Did you--did you confide in him?' said the girl after a moment, with a visible effort.

Eleanor made no reply. She lay with her face hidden. When Lucy bent down to her she said with a sudden sob:

'Don't you understand? I have been near two griefs since I came here--his and the Contessa's. And mine didn't stand the comparison.'

'Father Benecke had no right to take matters into his own hands,' said Lucy stubbornly.

'I think he was afraid--I should die in my sins,' said Eleanor wildly. 'He is an apostle--he took the license of one.'

Lucy frowned, but did not speak.

'Lucy! what makes you so hard--so strange?'

'I am not hard. But I don't want to see Mr. Manisty again. I want to take you safely back to England, and then to go home--home to Uncle Ben--to my own people.'

Her voice showed the profoundest and most painful emotion. Eleanor felt a movement of despair. What could he have said or done to set this tender nature so on edge? If it had not been for that vision on the *loggia*, she would have thought that the girl's heart was in truth untouched, and that Manisty would sue in vain. But how was it possible to think it?

She lost herself in doubts and conjectures, while Lucy still moved up and down.

Presently Cecco brought up their meal, and Eleanor must needs eat and drink to soothe Lucy's anxiety. The girl watched her every movement, and Eleanor dared neither be tired nor dainty, lest for every mouthful she refused Manisty's chance should be the less.

After dinner she once more laid a detaining hand on her companion.

'Dear, I can't send him away, you know--at once--to please you.'

'Do *you* want him to stay?' said Lucy, holding herself aloof.

'After all, he is my kinsman. There are many things to discuss--much to hear.'

'Very well. It won't be necessary for me to take part.'

'Not unless you like. But, Lucy, it would make me very unhappy--if you were unkind to him. You have made him suffer, my dear; he is not the meekest of men. Be content.'

'I will be quite polite,' said the girl, turning away her head. 'You will be able to travel--won't you--very soon?'

Eleanor assented vaguely, and the conversation dropped.

In the afternoon Marie took a note to the cottage by the river.

'Ask Father Benecke to let you stay a few days. Things look bad. What did you say? If you attacked me, it has done you harm.'

*   *   *   *   *

Meanwhile Lucy, who felt herself exiled from the woods, the roads, the village, by one threatening presence, shut herself up for a while in her own room, in youth's most tragic mood, calling on the pangs of thought to strengthen still more her resolve and clear her mind.

She forced her fingers to an intermittent task of needlework, but there were long pauses when her hands lay idle on her lap, when her head drooped against the back of her chair, and all her life centred in her fast beating heart, driven and strained by the torment of recollection.

That moment when she had stepped out upon the road from the shelter of the wood--the thrill of it even in memory made her pale and cold. His look--his cry--the sudden radiance of the face, which, as she had first caught sight of it, bent in a brooding frown over the dusty road, had seemed to her the very image of discontent.

'Miss Foster!--*Lucy!*'

The word had escaped him, in his first rush of joy, his spring towards her. And she had felt herself tottering, in a sudden blindness.

What could she remember? The breathless contradiction of his questions--the eager grasp of her hand--the words and phrases that were the words and phrases of love--dictated, justified only by love--then her first mention of Eleanor--the short stammering sentences, which as she spoke them sounded to her own ear so inconclusive, unintelligible, insulting--and his growing astonishment, the darkening features, the tightening lips, and finally his step backward, the haughty bracing of the whole man.

'Why does my cousin refuse to see me? What possible reason can you or she assign?'

And then her despairing search for the right word, that would not come! He must please, please, go away--because Mrs. Burgoyne was ill--because the doctors were anxious--because there must be no excitement. She was acting as nurse, but it was only to be for a short time longer. In a week or two, no doubt Mrs. Burgoyne would go to England, and she would return to America with the Porters. But for the present, quiet was still absolutely necessary.

Then--silence!--and afterwards a few sarcastic interrogations, quick, practical, hard to answer--the mounting menace of that thunderbrow, extravagant, and magnificent,--the trembling of her own limbs. And at last that sharp sentence, like lightning from the cloud, as to 'whims and follies' that no sane man could hope to unravel, which had suddenly nerved her to be angry.

'Oh! I was odious--odious!'--she thought to herself, hiding her face in her hands.

His answering indignation seemed to clatter through her room.

'And you really expect me to do your bidding calmly,--to play this ridiculous part?--to leave my cousin and you in these wilds--at this time of year--she in the state of health that you describe--to face this heat, and the journey home, without comforts, without assistance? It is a great responsibility, Miss Foster, that you take, with me, and with her! I refuse to yield it to you, till I have given you at least a little further time for consideration. I shall stay here a few hours longer. If you change your mind, send to me--I am with Father Benecke. If not--good-bye! But I warn you that I will be no party to further mystification. It is undesirable for us all. I shall write at once to General Delafield-Muir, and to my aunt. I think it will be also my duty to communicate with your friends in London or in Boston.'

'Mr. Manisty!--let me beg of you to leave my personal affairs alone!'

She felt again the proud flush upon her cheek, the shock of their two wills, the mingled anguish and relief as she saw him turn upon his heel, and go.

Ah! how unready, how *gauche* she had shown herself! From the beginning instead of conciliating she had provoked him. But how to make a plausible story out of their adventure at all? There was the deciding, the fatal difficulty! Her face burnt anew as she tried to think his thoughts, to imagine all that he might or must guess; as she remembered the glow of swift instinctive triumph with which he had recognised her, and realised from it some of the ideas that must have been his travelling companions all these weeks.

No matter: let him think what he pleased! She sat there in the gathering dark; at one moment, feeling herself caught in the grip of a moral necessity that no rebellion could undo; and the next, childishly catching to her heart the echoes and images of that miserable half-hour.

No wonder he had been angry!

'*Lucy!*'

Her name was sweetened to her ear for ever. He looked way-worn and tired; yet so eager, so spiritually alert. Never had that glitter and magic he carried about with him been more potent, more compelling.

Alack! what woman ever yet refused to love a man because he loved himself? It depends entirely on how she estimates the force of his temptation. And it would almost seem as though nature, for her own secret reasons, had thrown a special charm round the egotist of all types, for the loving and the true. Is it that she is thinking of the race--must needs balance in it the forces of death and life? What matters the separate joy or pain!

Yes. Lucy would have given herself to Manisty, not blind to risks, expecting thorns!--if it had been possible.

But it was not possible. She rose from her seat, and sternly dismissed her thoughts. She was no conscious thief, no willing traitor. Not even Eleanor should persuade her. Eleanor was dying because she, Lucy, had stolen from her the affections of her inconstant lover. Was there any getting over that? None! The girl shrank in horror from the very notion of such a base and plundering happiness.

CHAPTER XXIV

On the following morning when Lucy entered Eleanor's room she found her giving some directions to Marie.

'Tell Mamma Doni that we give up the rooms next week--Friday in next week. Make her understand.'

'*Parfaitement*, Madame.' And Marie left the room. Lucy advanced with a face of dismay.

'Ten days more!--Eleanor.

Eleanor tapped her lightly on the cheek, then kissed her, laughing.

'Are you too hot?'

'Dear!--don't talk about me! But you promised me to be gone before August.'

She knelt down by Eleanor's bedside, holding her hands, imploring her with her deep blue eyes.

'Well, it's only a few days more,' said Eleanor, guiltily. 'Do let's take it leisurely! It's so horrid to be hurried in one's packing. Look at all these things!'

She waved her hand desperately round the little room, choked up with miscellaneous boxes; then laid both hands on Lucy's shoulders, coaxing and smiling at her like a child.

Lucy soon convinced herself that it was of no use to argue. She must just submit, unless she were prepared to go to lengths of self-assertion which might excite Eleanor and bring on a heart attack.

So, setting her teeth, she yielded.

'Friday week, then--for the last, last day!--And Mr. Manisty?'

She had risen from her knees and stood looking down at Eleanor. Her cheek had reddened, but Eleanor admired her stateliness.

'Oh, we must keep Edward. We want him for courier. I gave you trouble enough, on the journey here.'

Lucy said nothing. Her heart swelled a little. It seemed to her that under all this sweetness she was being treated with a certain violence. She went to the balcony, where the breakfast had just been laid, that she might bring Eleanor's coffee.

'It *is* just a little crude,' Eleanor thought, uneasily. 'Dear bird!--the net is sadly visible. But what can one do?--with so little time--so few chances! Once part them, and the game is up!'

So she used her weakness once more as a tyranny, this time for different ends.

The situation that she dictated was certainly difficult enough. Manisty appeared, by her summons, in the afternoon, and found them on the *loggia*. Lucy greeted him with a cold self-possession. Of all that had happened on the previous day, naturally, not a word. So far indeed as allusions to the past were concerned, the three might just have travelled together from Marinata. Eleanor very flushed, and dressed in her elegant white dress and French hat, talked fast and well, of the country folk, the *padre parroco*, the Contessa. Lucy looked at her with alarm, dreading the after fatigue. But Eleanor would not be managed; would have her way.

Manisty, however, was no longer deceived. Lucy was aware of some of the glances that he threw his cousin. The trouble which they betrayed gave the girl a bitter satisfaction.

Presently she left them alone. After her disappearance Eleanor turned to Manisty with a smile.

'On your peril--not another word to her!--till I give you leave. That would finish it.'

He lifted hands and shoulders in a despairing gesture; but said nothing. In Lucy's absence, however, then and later, he did not attempt to control his depression, and Eleanor was soon distracting and comforting him in the familiar ways of the past. Before forty-eight hours had elapsed the relations between them indeed had resumed, to all appearance, the old and close intimacy. On his arm she crept down the road, to the Sassetto, while Lucy drove with the Contessa. Or Manisty read aloud to her on the *loggia*, while Lucy in the courtyard below sat chatting fast to a swarm of village children who would always henceforward associate her white dress and the pure oval of her face with their dreams of the Madonna.

In their *tete-a-tetes*, the talk of Manisty and Eleanor was always either of Lucy or of Manisty's own future. He had been at first embarrassed or reluctant. But she had insisted, and he had at length revealed himself as in truth he had never revealed himself in the days of their early friendship. With him at least, Eleanor through all anguish had remained mistress of herself, and she had her reward. No irreparable word had passed between them. In silence the old life ceased to be, and a new bond arose. The stifled reproaches, the secret impatiences, the *ennuis*, the hidden anguish of those last weeks at Marinata were gone. Manisty, freed from the pressure of an unspoken claim which his conscience half acknowledged and his will repulsed, was for his cousin a new creature. He began to treat her as he had treated his friend Neal, with the same affectionate consideration, the same easy sweetness; even through all the torments that Lucy made him suffer. 'His restlessness as a lover,--his excellence as a friend,'--so a man who knew him well had written of him in earlier days. As for the lover, discipline and penance had overtaken him. But now that Eleanor's claim of another kind was dead, the friend in him had scope. Eleanor possessed him as the lover of Lucy more truly than she had ever yet done in the days when she ruled alone.

One evening finding her more feeble than usual, he implored her to let him summon a doctor from Rome before she risked the fatigue of the Mont Cenis journey.

But she refused. 'If necessary,' she said, 'I will go to Orvieto. There is a good man there. But there is some one else you shall write to, if you like:--Reggie! Didn't you see him last week?'

'Certainly. Reggie and the first secretary left in charge, sitting in their shirtsleeves, with no tempers to speak of, and the thermometer at 96. But Reggie was to get his holiday directly.'

'Write and catch him.'

'Tell him to come not later than Tuesday, please,' said Lucy, quietly, who was standing by.

'Despot!' said Eleanor, looking up. 'Are we really tied and bound to Friday?'

Lucy smiled and nodded. When she went away Manisty sat in a black silence, staring at the ground. Eleanor bit her lip, grew a little restless, and at last said:

'She gives you no openings?'

Manisty laughed.

'Except for rebuffs!' he said, bitterly.

'Don't provoke them!'

'How can I behave as though that--that scene had never passed between us? In ordinary circumstances my staying on here would be an offence, of which she might justly complain. I told her last night I would have gone--but for your health.'

'When did you tell her?'

'I found her alone here for a moment before dinner.'

'Well?'

Manisty moved impatiently.

'Oh! she was very calm. Nothing I say puts her out. She thought I might be useful!--And she hopes Aunt Pattie will meet us in London, that she may be free to start for New York by the 10th, if her friends go then. She has written to them.'

Eleanor was silent.

'I must have it out with her!' said Manisty presently under his breath. In his unrest he rose, that he might move about. His face had grown pale.

'No--wait till I give you leave,' said Eleanor again, imploring. 'I never forget--for a moment. Leave it to me.'

He came and stood beside her. She put out her hand, which he took.

'Do you still believe--what you said?' he asked her, huskily.

Eleanor looked up smiling.

'A thousand times more!' she said, under her breath. 'A thousand times more.'

But here the conversation reached an *impasse*. Manisty could not say--'Then why?--in Heaven's name!'--for he knew why. Only it was not a *why* that he and Eleanor could discuss. Every hour he realised more plainly with what completeness Eleanor held him in her hands. The situation was galling. But her sweetness and his own remorse disarmed him. To be helpless--and to be kind!--nothing else apparently remained to him. The only gracious look Lucy had vouchsafed him these two days had been in reward for some new arrangement of Eleanor's sofa which had given the invalid greater ease.

He returned to his seat, smiling queerly.

'Well, I am not the only person in disgrace. Do you notice how Benecke is treated?'

'She avoids him?'

'She never speaks to him if she can help it. I know that he feels it.'

'He risked his penalty,' said Eleanor laughing. 'I think he must bear it.' Then in another tone, and very softly, she added--

'Poor child!'

Manisty thought the words particularly inappropriate. In all his experience of women he never remembered a more queenly and less childish composure than Lucy had been able to show him since their scene on the hill. It had enlarged all his conceptions of her. His passion for her was thereby stimulated and tormented, yet at the same time glorified in his own eyes. He saw in her already the *grande dame* of the future--that his labour, his ambitions, and his gifts should make of her.

If only Eleanor spoke the truth!

*   *   *   *   *

The following day Manisty, returning from a late walk with Father Benecke, parted from the priest on the hill, and mounted the garden stairway to the *loggia*.

Lucy was sitting there alone, her embroidery in her hands.

She had not heard him in the garden; and when he suddenly appeared she was not able to hide a certain agitation. She got up and began vaguely to put away her silks and thimble.

'I won't disturb you,' he said formally. 'Has Eleanor not come back?'

For Eleanor had been driving with the Contessa.

'Yes. But she has been resting since.'

'Don't let me interrupt you,' he said again.

Then he looked at her fingers and their uncertain movements among the silks; at the face bent over the workbasket.

'I want if I can to keep some bad news from my cousin,' he said abruptly.

Lucy started and looked up. He had her face full now, and the lovely entreating eyes.

'My sister is very ill. There has been another crisis. I might be summoned at any time.'

'Oh!'--she said, faltering. Unconsciously she moved a step nearer to him. In a moment she was all enquiry, and deep, shy sympathy--the old docile Lucy. 'Have you had a letter?' she asked.

'Yes, this morning. I saw her the other day when I passed through Rome. She knew me, but she is a wreck. The whole constitution is affected. Sometimes there are intervals, but they get rarer. And each acute attack weakens her seriously.'

'It is terrible--terrible!'

As she stood there before him in her white dress under the twilight, he had a vision of her lying with shut eyes in his chair at Marinata; he remembered the first wild impulse that had bade him gather her, unconscious and helpless, in his arms.

He moved away from her. For something to do, or say, he stooped down to look into her open workbasket.

'Isn't that one of the Nemi terra-cottas!'

He blundered into the question from sheer nervousness, wishing it unspoken the instant it was out.

Lucy started. She had forgotten. How could she have forgotten! There in a soft bed of many-coloured silks, wrapped tenderly about, yet so as to show the face and crown, was the little Artemis. The others were beneath the tray of the box. But this for greater safety lay by itself, a thin fold of cotton-wool across its face. In that moment of confusion when he had appeared on the *loggia* she had somehow displaced the cotton-wool without knowing it, and uncovered the head.

'Yes, it is the Artemis,' she said, trying to keep herself from trembling.

Manisty bent without speaking, and took the little thing into his hand. He thought of that other lovelier head--her likeness?--whereof the fragments were at that moment in a corner of his dressing-case, after journeying with him through the mountains.

As for Lucy it was to her as though the little head nestling in his hand must somehow carry there the warmth of her kisses upon it, must somehow betray her. He seemed to hold a fragment of her heart.

'Please let me put it away,' she said hurriedly. 'I must go to Eleanor. It is nearly time for dinner.'

He gave it up silently. She replaced it, smoothed down her silks and her work, and shut the box. His presence, his sombre look, and watching eye, affected her all the time electrically. She had never yet been so near the loss of self-command.

The thought of Eleanor calmed her. As she finished her little task, she paused and spoke again.

'You won't alarm her about poor Miss Manisty, without--without consulting with me?' she said timidly.

He bowed.

'Would you rather I did not tell her at all? But if I have to go?'

'Yes then--then you must.'

An instant--and she added hastily in a voice that wavered,' I am so very, very sorry--'

'Thank you. She often asks about you.'

He spoke with a formal courtesy, in his 'grand manner.' Her gleam of feeling had made him sensible, of advantage, given him back self-confidence.

The soft flutter of her dress disappeared, and he was left to pace up and down the *loggia* in alternations of hope and despair. He, too, felt with Eleanor that these days were fatal. If he lost her now, he lost her for ever. She was of those natures in which a scruple only deepens with time.

She would not take what should have been Eleanor's. There was the case in a nutshell. And how insist in these circumstances, as he would have done vehemently in any other, that Eleanor had no lawful grievance?

He felt himself bound and pricked by a thousand delicate lilliputian bonds. The 'regiment of women' was complete. He could do nothing. Only Eleanor could help.

$$*\qquad*\qquad*\qquad*\qquad*$$

The following day, just outside the convent gate, he met Lucy, returning from the village, whither she had been in quest of some fresh figs for Eleanor's breakfast. It was barely eight o'clock, but the sun was already fierce. After their formal greeting, Lucy lingered a moment.

'It's going to be frightfully hot to-day,' she said, looking round her with a troubled face at the glaring road, at the dusty patch of vines beyond it, at the burnt grass below the garden wall. 'Mr. Manisty!--you will make Eleanor go next Friday?--you won't let her put it off--for anything?'

She turned to him, in entreaty, the colour dyeing her pure cheek and throat.

'I will do what I can. I understand your anxiety,' he said stiffly.

She opened the old door of the courtyard and passed in before him. As he rejoined her, she asked him in a low voice--

'Have you any more news?'

'Yes. I found a letter at Selvapendente last night. The state of things is better. There will be no need I hope to alarm Eleanor--for the present.'

'I am so glad!'--The voice hurried and then paused. 'And of course, for you too,' she added, with difficulty.

He said nothing, and they walked up to the inner door in silence. Then as they paused on the threshold, he said suddenly, with a bitter accent--

'You are very devoted!'

She looked at him in surprise. Her young figure drew itself erect. 'That isn't wonderful--is it?--with her?'

Her tone pierced him.

'Oh! nothing's wonderful in women. You set the standard so high--the men can't follow.'

He stared at her, pale and frowning. She laughed artificially, but he could see the breath hurrying under the blue cotton dress.

'Not at all! When it comes to the serious difficulties we must, it seems, apply to you. Eleanor is thankful that you will take her home.

'Oh! I can be a decent courier--when I put my mind into it,' he said angrily. 'That, I dare say, you'll admit.'

'Of course I shall,' she said, with a lip that smiled unsteadily. 'I know it'll be invaluable. Please, Mr. Manisty, let me pass. I must get Eleanor her breakfast.'

But he still stood there, barring the way.

'Then, Miss Foster, admit something else!--that I am not the mere intruder--the mere burden--that you took me for.'

The man's soreness expressed itself in every word, every movement.

Lucy grew white.

'For Eleanor's sake, I am glad you came,' she said struggling for composure. But the dignity, the pride behind the agitation were so evident that he dared not go a step further. He bowed, and let her pass.

*   *   *   *   *

Meanwhile the Contessa was useful. After a very little observation, based on the suggestions of her letter from Home, she divined the situation exactly. Her affection and pity for Mrs. Burgoyne grew apace. Lucy she both admired and acquitted; while she half liked, half hated Manisty. He provoked her perpetually to judgment, intellectual and moral; and they fell into many a sparring which passed the time and made a shelter for the others. Her daughter had just left her; and the more she smarted, the more she bustled in and out of the village, the more she drove about the country, attending to the claims, the sicknesses, and the animals of distant *contadini*, the more she read her newspapers, and the more nimbly did her mind move.

Like the Marchesa Fazzoleni, she would have no pessimism about Italy, though she saw things in a less poetic, more practical way.

'I dare say the taxes are heavy--and that our officials and bankers and *impiegali* are not on as good terms as they might be with the Eighth Commandment. Well! was ever a nation made in a night before? When your Queen came to the throne, were you English so immaculate? You talk about our Socialists--have we any disturbances, pray, worse than your disturbances in the twenties and thirties? The *parroco* says to me day after day: "The African campaign has been the ruin of Italy!" That's only because he wants it to be so. The machine marches, and the people pay their taxes, and the farming improves every year, all the same. A month or two ago, the newspapers were full of the mobbing of trains starting with soldiers for Erythrea. Yet all that time, if you went down into the Campo de' Fiori you could find poems sold for a *soldo*, that only the people wrote and the people read, that were as patriotic as the poor King himself.'

'Ah! I know,' said Manisty. 'I have seen some of them. The oddest, naivest things!--the metre of Tasso, the thoughts of a child--and every now and then the cry a poet.'

And he repeated a stanza or two from these broad-sheets of the war, in a rolling and musical Italian.

The Contessa looked at him with cool admiration; and then aside, at Lucy. Certainly, when this Englishman was taking pains, his good-looks deserved all that could be said of them. That he was one of the temperaments to which other lives minister without large return--that she had divined at once. But, like Lucy, she was not damped by that. The Contessa had known few illusions, and only one romance; her love for her dead son. Otherwise she took the world as it came, and quarrelled with very few of its marked and persistent phenomena.

They were sitting on a terrace beneath the north-western front of the Palazzo. The terrace was laid out in a formal garden. Fountains played; statues stood in rows; and at the edge cypresses, black against the evening blue and rose, threw back the delicate dimness of the mountains, made their farness more far, and the gay foreground--oleanders, geraniums, nasturtiums--more gay.

Eleanor was lying on a deck-chair, smiling often, and at ease. Lucy sat a little apart, busy with her embroidery. She very seldom talked, but Eleanor could not make a movement or feel a want without her being aware of it.

'But, Madame, I cannot allow you to make an enemy out of me!'--said Manisty to the Contessa, resuming the conversation. 'When you talk to me of this Country and its future, ***vous prechez un converti***.'

'I thought you were the Jonah of our day,' she said, with her abrupt and rather disdainful smile.

Manisty laughed.

'A Jonah who needn't complain anyway that his Nineveh is too ready to hear him.'

'Where is the preaching?' she asked.

'In the waste-paper basket,' said Manisty, throwing away his cigarette. 'Nowadays, apparently it is the prophets who repent.'

Involuntarily his eye wandered, sought for Lucy withdrew. She was hidden behind her work.

'Oh! preach away,' cried the Contessa. 'Take up your book again. Publish it. We can bear it.'

Manisty searched with both hands for his matches; his new cigarette between his lips.

'My book, Madame'--he said coolly--' outlived the pleasure its author took in writing it. My cousin was its good angel; but not even she could bring a blunder to port. Eleanor!--*n'est-ce pas?*'

He gathered a spray of oleander that grew near him, and laid it on her hand, like a caress. Eleanor's emaciated fingers closed upon it gently. She looked up, smiling. The Contessa abruptly turned away.

'And besides--' said Manisty.

He puffed away steadily, with his gaze on the mountains.

'I wait,' said the Contessa.

'Your Italy is a witch,' he said, with a sudden lifting of eyes and voice, 'and there are too many people that love her!'

Lucy bent a little lower over her work.

Presently the Contessa went away.

Eleanor lay with eyes closed and hands crossed, very white and still. They thought her asleep, for it was common with her now to fall into short sleeps of pure exhaustion. When they occurred, those near her kept tender and generally silent watch, joining hands of protection, as it were, round her growing feebleness.

After a few minutes, however, Manisty bent across towards Lucy.

'You urged me once to finish the book. But it was she who told me the other day she was thankful it had been dropped.'

He looked at her with the half irritable, half sensitive expression that she knew so well.

'Of course,' said Lucy, hurriedly. 'It was much best.'

She rose and stooped over Eleanor.

'Dear!--It is getting late. I think I ought to call the carriage.'

'Let me,' said Manisty, biting his lip.

'Thank you,' said Lucy, formally. 'The coachman understood we should want him at seven.'

When he came back, Lucy went into the house to fetch some wraps.

Eleanor opened her eyes, which were singularly animated and smiling.

'Listen!'

He stooped.

'Be angry!' she said, laying a light grasp on his arm. 'Be quite angry. Now--you may! It will do no harm.'

He sat beside her, his head bent; gloomily listening, till Lucy reappeared.

But he took the hint, calling to his aid all his pride, and all his singular power of playing any role in his own drama that he might desire to play. He played it with energy, with desperation, counting meanwhile each hour as it passed, having in view always that approaching moment in London when Lucy would disappear within the doors of the Porters' house, leaving the butler to meet the demands of unwelcome visitors with such equivalents of 'Not at home' as her Puritan scruples might allow; till the newspapers should announce the safe sailing of her steamer for New York.

He ceased to propitiate her; he dropped embarrassment. He ignored her. He became the man of the world and of affairs, whose European interests and relations are not within the ken of raw young ladies from Vermont. He had never been more brilliant, more interesting, more agreeable, for Eleanor, for the Contessa, for Benecke; for all the world, save one. He described his wanderings among the Calabrian highlands. He drew the peasants, the priests, the great landowners of the south still surrounded with their semi-feudal state; he made Eleanor laugh or shudder with his tales of the brigandage of the sixties; he talked as the artist and the scholar may of the Greek memories and remains of the Tarentine coast. Then he turned to English politics, to his own chances, and the humours of his correspondence. The Contessa ceased to quarrel with him. The handsome Englishman with the colour of a Titian, and the features of an antique, with his eloquence, his petulance, his conceit, his charm, filled the stage, quickened the dull hours whenever he appeared. Eleanor's tragedy explained itself. The elder woman understood and pitied. As for Lucy Foster, the Contessa's shrewd eyes watched her with a new respect. At what stage, in truth, was the play, and how would it end?

Meanwhile for Lucy Foster alone, Manisty was not agreeable. He rose formally when she appeared; he placed her chair; he paid her all necessary courtesies. But his conversation never included her. Her coming generally coincided--after she was ceremoniously provided for--with an outbreak of talk between him and Eleanor, or between him and Benecke, more eager, animated and interesting than before. But Lucy had no part in it. It was not the early neglect and incivility of the villa; it was something infinitely colder and more wounding; the frigidity of disillusion and resentment, of kindness rebuffed and withdrawn.

Lucy said nothing. She went about her day's work as usual, making all arrangements for their departure, devoting herself to Eleanor. Every now and then she was forced to consult with Manisty as to arrangements for the journey. They spoke as mere acquaintances and no more than was necessary; while she, when she was alone, would spend much time in a silent abstraction, thinking of her uncle, of the duties to which she was returning, and the lines of her future life. Perhaps in the winter she might do some teaching. Several people in Greyridge had said they would employ her.

And, all the time, during the night hours when she was thus wrestling down her heart, Manisty was often pacing the forest paths, in an orgie of smoke and misery, cursing the incidents of the day, raging, doubting, suffering--as no woman had yet made him suffer. The more truly he despaired, the more he desired her. The strength of the moral life in her was a revelation, a challenge to all the forces of his own being. He was not accustomed to have to consider such things in women. It added to her a wealth, a rarity, which made the conquest of her the only object worth pursuing in a life swept bare for the moment of all other passions and zests. She loved him! Eleanor knew it; Eleanor declared it. Yet in ten days' time she would say,--'Good bye, Mr. Manisty'--with that calm brow which he already foresaw as an outrage and offence to love. Ah! for some means to cloud those dear eyes--to make her weep, and let him see the tears!

CHAPTER XXV

Hullo, Manisty!--is that you? Is this the place?'
The speaker was Reggie Brooklyn, who was dismounting from his bicycle at the door of the convent, followed by a clattering mob of village children, who had pursued him down the hill.

'I say, what a weird place!' said Reggie, looking about him,--'and at the other end of nowhere. What on earth made Eleanor come here?'

Ho looked at Manisty in perplexity, wiping the perspiration from his brow, which frowned beneath his fair curls.

'We were hero last year,' said Manisty, 'on that little tour we made with the D.'s. Eleanor liked it then. She came here when the heat began, she thought it would be cool.'

'You didn't know where she was ten days ago,' said the boy, looking at him queerly. 'And General Muir didn't know, for I heard from some one who had seen him last week.'

Manisty laughed.

'All the same, she is here now,' he said drily.

'And Miss Foster is here too?'

Manisty nodded.

'And you say that Eleanor is ill?'

The young man had still the same hostile, suspicious air.

Manisty, who had been poking at the ground with his stick, looked up. Brooklyn made a step backward.

'*Very* ill,' he said, with a face of consternation. 'And nobody knew?'

'She would not let us know,' said Manisty slowly. Then he added, with the authority of the older man, the man in charge--'now we are doing all we can. We start on Friday and pick up a nurse at Genoa. When we get home, of course she will have the best advice. Very often she is wonderfully bright and like herself. Oh! we shall pull her round. But you mustn't tire her. Don't stay too long.'

They walked into the convent together, Brooklyn all impatience, Manisty moody and ill at ease.

'Reggie!--well met!' It was Eleanor's gayest voice, from the vine-leafed shadows of the *loggia*. Brooklyn sat down beside her, gazing at her with his troubled blue eyes. Manisty descended to the walled garden, and walked up and down there smoking, a prey to disagreeable thoughts.

After half an hour or so Reggie came down to the convent gate to look out for the ricketty diligence which had undertaken to bring his bag from Orvieto.

Here he was overtaken by Lucy Foster, who seemed to have hurried after him.

'How do you do, Mr. Brooklyn?' He turned sharply, and let her see a countenance singularly discomposed.

They looked at each other a moment in silence. He noted with amazement her growth in beauty, in expression. But the sadness of the mouth and eyes tortured him afresh.

'What is the matter with her?' he said abruptly, dropping her timidly offered hand.

'An old illness--mostly the heart,' she said, with difficulty. 'But I think the lungs are wrong too.'

'Why did she come here--why did you let her?'

The roughness of his tone, the burning of his eyes made her draw back.

'It seemed the best thing to do,' she said, after a pause. 'Of course, it was only done because she wished it.'

'Her people disapproved strongly!'

'She would not consider that.'

'And here in this rough place--in this heat--how have you been able to look after her?' said the young man passionately.

'We have done what we could,' said the girl humbly. 'The Contessa Guerrini has been very kind. We constantly tried to persuade her to let us take her home; but she couldn't bring herself to move.'

'It was madness,' he said, between his teeth. 'And now--she looks as though she were going to die!'

He gave a groan of angry grief. Lucy turned aside, leaning her arm against the convent gateway, and her face upon it. The attitude was very touching; but Brooklyn only stared at her in a blind wrath. 'What did you ever come for?'--was his thought--'making mischief!--and robbing Eleanor of her due!--It was a bad bargain she wanted,--but she might have been allowed to have him in peace. What did you come meddling for?'

At that moment the door of the walled garden opened. Manisty came out into the courtyard. Brooklyn looked from him to Lucy with a tight lip, a fierce and flashing eye.

He watched them meet. He saw Lucy's quick change of attitude, the return of hardness and composure. Manisty approached her. They discussed some arrangement for the journey, in the cold tones of mere acquaintance. Not a sign of intimacy in manner or words; beyond the forced intimacy of those who have for the moment a common task.

When the short dialogue was over, Manisty mumbled something to Brooklyn to the effect that Father Benecke had some dinner for him at the house at the foot of the hill. But he did not wait for the young man's company. He hurried off with the slouching and yet swinging gait characteristic of him, his shoulders bent as it were under the weight of his great head. The young man and the girl looked after him. Then Reggie turned impulsively.

'I suppose it was that beastly book--partly--that knocked her up. What's he done with it?'

'He has given it up, I believe. I heard him say so to Eleanor.'

'And now I suppose he will condescend to go back to politics?'

'I know nothing of Mr. Manisty's affairs.'

The young man threw her a glance first of distrust--then of something milder and more friendly. They turned back to the convent together, Lucy answering his questions as to the place, the people, the Contessa, and so forth.

A step, quick and gentle, overtook them.

It was Father Benecke who stopped and greeted them; a venerable figure, as he bared his white head, and stood for a moment talking to Brooklyn under the great sycamore of the courtyard. He had now resumed his clerical dress; not, indeed, the soutane; but the common round collar, and long black coat of the non-Catholic countries. The little fact, perhaps, was typical of a general steadying and settling of his fortunes after the anguish of his great catastrophe.

Lucy hardly spoke to him. His manner was soft and deprecating. And Miss Foster stood apart as though she liked neither it nor him. When he left them, to enter, the Convent, Reggie broke out:--

And how does *he* come to be here? I declare it's the most extraordinary tangle! What's he doing in there?'

He nodded towards the building, which seemed to be still holding the sunlight of the day, so golden-white it shone under the evening sky, and against the engirdling forest.

'Every night--almost--he comes to read with Eleanor.'

The young man stared.

'I say--is she--is she going to become a Catholic?'

Lucy smiled.

'You forget--don't you? They've excommunicated Father Benecke.'

'My word!--Yes!--I forgot. My chief was awfully excited about it. Well, I'm sure he's well quit of them!'--said the young man fervently. 'They're doing their level best to pull this country about everybody's ears. And they'll be the first to suffer--thank heaven!--if they do upset the coach. And so it was Benecke that brought Manisty here?'

Lucy's movement rebuked him; made him feel himself an impertinent.

'I believe so,' she said coldly. 'Good-night, Mr. Brooklyn. I must go in. There!--that's the stage coming down hill.'

He went to tell the driver to set down his bag at the house by the bridge, and then he walked down the hill after the little rumbling carriage, his hands thrust into the pockets of his blue flannel coat.

'She's not going to marry him!--I'll bet anything she's not! She's a girl of the right sort--she's a brick, she is!'--he said to himself in a miserable, a savage exultation, kicking the stones of the road furiously down hill, after the disappearing diligence. 'So that's how a woman looks when her heart's broken!--Oh! my God--Eleanor!--my poor, poor Eleanor!'

And before he knew what had happened to him, the young fellow found himself sitting in the darkness by the roadside, grappling with honest tears, that aston-ished and scandalised himself.

*   *   *   *   *

Next day he was still more bewildered by the position of affairs. Eleanor was apparently so much better that he was disposed to throw scorn on his own burst of grief under the starlight. That was the first impression. Then she was apparently in Manisty's charge. Manisty sat with her, strolled with her, read to her from morning till night. Never had their relations been more intimate, more affectionate. That was the second impression.

Nevertheless, that some great change had taken place--above all in Eleanor--became abundantly evident to the young man's quickened perception, before an-other twenty-four hours had passed away. And with this new sense returned the sense of irreparable tragedy. Eleanor stood alone--aloof from them all. The more unremitting, the more delicate was Manisty's care, the more tender was Lucy's de-votion, the more plainly was Brooklyn aware of a pathetic, a mysterious isolation which seemed already to bring the chill of death into their little company.

The boy's pain flowed back upon him, ten-fold augmented. For seven or eight years he had seen in Eleanor Burgoyne the woman of ideal distinction by whom he judged all other women. The notion of falling in love with her would have seemed to him ridiculous. But his wife, whenever he could indulge himself in such a luxury, must be like her. Meanwhile he was most naively, most boyishly devoted to her.

The sight of her now, environed as it were by the new and awful possibilities which her state suggested, was a touch upon the young man's nature, which seemed to throw all its energies into a fiery fusion,--concentrating them upon a changed and poignant affection, which rapidly absorbed his whole being. His pity for her was almost intolerable, his bitterness towards Manisty almost beyond his control. All very well for him now to be the guardian of her decline! Whatever might be the truth about the American girl, it was plain enough that while she could still reckon on the hopes and chances of the living, Eleanor had wasted her heart and powers on an egotist, only to reap ingratitude, and the deadly fruit of 'benefits forgot.'

What chafed him most was that he had so little time with her; that Manisty was always there. At last, two days after his arrival, he got an hour to himself while Manisty and Father Benecke were walking, and Lucy was with the Contessa.

He began to question her eagerly as to the future. With whom was she to pass the remainder of the year--and where?

'With my father and Aunt Pattie of course,' said Eleanor, smiling. 'It will be Scotland I suppose till November--then London.'

He was silent for a few moments, the colour flooding his smooth fair face. Then he took her hand firmly, and with words and gestures that became him well, he solemnly asked her to marry him. He was not fit to tie her shoes; but he could take care of her; he could be her courier, her travelling companion, her nurse, her slave. He implored her to listen to him. What was her father to her--he asked her plainly--when had he ever considered her, as she should be considered? Let her only trust herself to him. Never, never should she repent that she had done him such an inconceivable honour. Hang the diplomatic service! He had some money; with her own it would be enough. He would take her to Egypt or the Cape. That would revive her.

Eleanor heard him very calmly.

'You dear, dear boy!' she said, when he paused for lack of breath. 'You remind me of that pretty story--don't you remember?--only it was the other way about-- of Lord Giffard and Lady Dufferin. He was dying--and she married him--that she might be with him to the end. That's right--for the woman. It's her natural part to be the nurse. Do you think I'm going to let *you* ruin your career to come and nurse me? Oh! you foolish Reggie!'

But he implored her; and after a while she grew restless.

'There's only one thing in the world you can do for me!--' she said at last, push- ing him away from her in her agitation.

Then reaching out from her sofa, she opened a drawer in a little table beside her, and took out a double photograph-case, folded together. She opened it and held it out to him.

'There!--help me bring those two together, Reggie--and I'll give you even more of my heart than I do now!'

He stared, open-mouthed and silent, at the portraits, at the delicate, illumined face.

'Come here'--she said, drawing him back towards her. 'Come and let us talk.'

*   *   *   *   *

Meanwhile Manisty and Father Benecke were climbing the long hill, on the return from their walk. There had been no full confidence between these two. Manisty's pride would not allow it. There was too sharp humiliation at present in the thought of that assurance with which he had spoken to Benecke by the river-side.

He chose, therefore, when they were alone, rather to talk to the priest of his own affairs, of his probable acceptance of the Old Catholic offers which had been made him. Benecke did not resent the perfunctory manner of his talk, the half-mind that he gave to it. The priest's shrewd humility made no claims. He understood perfectly that the catastrophe of his own life could have no vital interest for a man absorbed as Manisty was then absorbed. He submitted to its being made a topic, a *passe-temps*.

Moreover, he forgave, he had always forgiven Manisty's dominant attitude towards the forces which had trampled on himself. Often he had felt himself the shipwrecked sailor sinking in the waves, while Manisty as the cool spectator was hobnobbing with the wreckers on the shore. But nothing of this affected his love for the man. He loved him as Vanbrugh Neal had loved him; because of a certain charm, a certain indestructible youth and irresponsibility at the very heart of him, which redeemed half his errors.

'Ah! my dear friend,' Manisty was saying as they neared the top of the hill--with his largest and easiest gesture; 'of course you must go to Bonn; you must do what they want you to do. The Old Catholics will make a great deal of you. It might have been much worse.'

'They are very kind. But one transplants badly at sixty-six,' said the priest mildly, thinking perhaps of his little home in the street of his Bavarian town, of the pupils he should see no more, of the old sister who had deserted him.

'*Your* book has been the success,' said Manisty, impatiently. 'For you said what you meant to say--you hit your mark. As for me--well, never mind! I came out in too hot a temper; the men I saw first were too plausible; the facts have been too many for me. No matter. It was an adventure like any other. I don't regret it! In itself, it gave one some exciting moments, and,--if I mistook the battle here--I shall still fight the English battle all the better for the experience! ***Allons donc***!--"To-morrow to fresh woods and pastures new!'"

The priest looked at his handsome reckless air, with a mixture of indulgence and repulsion. Manisty was 'an honourable man,' of many gifts. If certain incalculable elements in his character could be controlled, place and fame were probably before him. Compared with him, the priest realised profoundly his own meaner, obscurer destiny. The humble servant of a heavenly ***patria***, of an unfathomable truth, is no match for these intellectual soldiers of fortune. He does not judge them; he often feels towards them a strange forbearance. But he would sooner die than change parts!

*   *   *   *   *

As the convent came in sight, Manisty paused.

'You are going in to see her?'

The priest assented.

'Then I will come up later.'

They parted, and Father Benecke entered the convent alone.

Five days more! Would anything happen--or nothing? Manisty's wounded vanity held him at arm's length; Miss Foster could not forgive him. But the priest knew Eleanor's heart; and what else he did not know he divined. All rested with the American girl, with the wounded tenderness, the upright independence of a nature, which, as the priest frankly confessed to himself, he did not understand.

He was not, indeed, without pricks of conscience with regard to her. Supposing that she ultimately yielded? It was he who would have precipitated the solution; he who would in truth have given her to Manisty. Might he not, in so doing, have succoured the one life only to risk the other? Were Manisty's the hands in which to place a personality so noble and so trusting as that of the young girl?

But these qualms did not last long. As we have seen he had an invincible tenderness for Manisty. And in his priestly view women were the adjuncts and helpers of men. Woman is born to trouble; and the risks that she must take grow with her. Why fret about the less or more? His own spiritual courage would not have shrunk from any burden that love might lay upon it. In his Christian stoicism--the man of the world might have called it a Christian insensibility--he answered for Lucy.

Why suppose that she would shrink, or ought to shrink? Eve's burden is anyway enormous; and the generous heart scorns a grudging foresight.

As to Mrs. Burgoyne--ah! there at least he might be sure that he had not dared in vain. While Lucy was steel to him, Eleanor not only forgave him, but was grateful to him with a frankness that only natures so pliant and so sweet have the gift to show. In a few hours, as it seemed to him, she had passed from fevered anguish into a state which held him often spellbound before her, so consonant was it to the mystical instincts of his own life. He thought of her with the tenderest reverence, the most sacred rejoicing. Through his intercourse with her, moreover, while he guided and sustained her, he had been fighting his own way back to the sure ground of spiritual hope and confidence. God had not withdrawn from him the divine message! He was about to step forth into the wilderness; but this light went with him.

On the stairs leading to Mrs. Burgoyne's rooms he met Reggie Brooklyn coming down. The young man's face was pale and strained. The priest asked him a question, but he ran past without an answer.

Eleanor was alone on the *loggia*. It was past eight o'clock, and the trees in the courtyard and along the road were alive with fire-flies. Overhead was the clear incomparable sky, faintly pricked with the first stars. Someone was singing 'Santa Lucia' in the distance; and there was the twanging of a guitar.

'Shall I go away?' he said, standing beside her. 'You wished me to come. But you are fatigued.'

She gave him her hand languidly.

'Don't go, Father. But let me rest a little.'

'Pay me no attention,' he said. 'I have my office.'

He took out his breviary, and there was silence.

After a while, when he could no longer see even the red letters of his little book and was trusting entirely to memory, Eleanor said, with a sudden clearness of voice,--

A strange thing happened to me to-day, Father. I thought I would tell you. For many many years I have been haunted by a kind of recurrent vision. I think it must have come, to begin with, from the influence of a clergyman--a very stern, imaginative, exacting man--who prepared me for confirmation. Suddenly I see the procession of the Cross; the Lord in front, with the Crown of Thorns dripping with blood; the thieves following; the crowd, the daughters of Jerusalem. Nothing but that--but always very vivid, the colours as bright as the colours of a Van Eyck--and bringing with it an extraordinary sense of misery and anguish--of everything that one wants to forget and refuse in life. The man to whom I trace it was a saint, but a forbidding one. He made me afraid of him; afraid of Christianity. I believed, but I never loved. And when his influence was withdrawn, I threw it all behind me, in a great hurry. But this impression remained--like a nightmare. I remember the day I was presented; there, in the midst of all the feathers and veils and coronets, was the vision,--and the tumult of ghastly and crushing thoughts that spread from it. I remember hating Christianity that day; and its influence in the world.

'Last night, just before the dawn, I looked out; and there was the vision again, sweeping over the forests, and up into the clouds that hung over Monte Amiata. And I hated it no more. There was no accompanying horror. It seemed to me as natural as the woods; as the just-kindling light. And my own soul seemed to be rapt into the procession--the dim and endless procession of all times and nations--and to pass away with it,--I knew not where....

Her voice fell softly, to a note of dream.

'That was an omen,' he said, after a pause, 'an omen of peace.'

'I don't know,--but it soothed! As to what may be *true*, Father,--you can't be certain any more than I! But at least our dreams are true--to *us*.'... 'We make the heaven we hope indeed our home! All to the good if we wake up in it after all! If not, the dream will have had its own use here. Why should we fight so with our ignorance? The point is, as to the *quality* of our dreams! The quality of mine was once all dark--all misery. Now, there is a change,--like the change from London drizzle and rain to the clearness of this sky, which gives beauty to everything beneath it. But, for me, it is not the first time--no, not the first--'

The words were no longer audible, her hands pressed against each other, and he traced that sudden rigidity in her dim face which meant that she was defending herself against emotion.

'It is all true, my friend,' he said, bending over her,--'the gospel of Christ. You would be happier if you could accept it simply.'

She opened her eyes, smiling, but she did not reply. She was always eager that he should read and talk to her, and she rarely argued. But he never felt that intellectually he had much hold upon her. Her mind seemed to him to be moving elusively in a sphere remote and characteristic, where he could seldom follow. *Anima naturaliter Christiana*; yet with a most stoic readiness to face the great uncertainties, the least flattering possibilities of existence: so she often appeared to him.

Presently she dragged herself higher in her chair to look at the moon rising above the eastern mass of the convent.

'It all gives me such extraordinary pleasure!' she said, as though in wonder--'The moon--the fire-flies--those beautiful woods--your kindness--Lucy in her white dress, when I see her there at the door. I know how short it must be; and a few weeks ago I enjoyed nothing. What mystery are we part of?--that moves and changes without our will. I was much touched, Father, by all you said to me that great, great day; but I was not conscious of yielding to you; nor afterwards. Then, one night, I went to sleep in one mind; I woke up in another. The "grace of God," you think?--or the natural welling back of the river, little by little, to its natural bed? After all I never wilfully hurt or defied anybody before--that I can remember. But what are "grace" and "nature" more than words? There is a Life,--which our life perpetually touches and guesses at--like a child fingering a closed room in the dark. What else do we know?'

'We know a great deal more,' he said firmly. 'But I don't want to weary you by talking.'

'You don't weary me. Ah!'--her voice leapt--'what *is* true--is the "dying to live" of Christianity. One moment, you have the weight of the world upon you; the next, as it were, you dispose of the world and all in it. Just an act of the will!--and the thing verifies itself like any chemical experiment. Let me go on--go on!' she said, with mystical intensity. 'If the clue is anywhere it is there,--so far my mind goes with you. Other races perceive it through other forms. But Christ offered it to us.'

'My dear friend,' said the priest tenderly--'He offers us *Himself*.'

She smiled, most brightly.

'Don't quarrel with me--with my poor words. He is there--***there!***'--she said under her breath.

And he saw the motion of her white fingers towards her breast.

Afterwards he sat beside her for some time in silence, thinking of the great world of Rome, and of his long conflict there.

Form after form appeared to him of those men, stupid or acute, holy or worldly, learned or ignorant, who at the heart of Catholicism are engaged in that amazing struggle with knowledge which perhaps represents the only condition under which knowledge--the awful and irresistible--can in the long run safely incorporate itself with the dense mass of human life. He thought of scholar after scholar crushed by the most incompetent of judges; this man silenced by a great post, that man by exile, one through the best of his nature, another through the worst. He saw himself sitting side by side with one of the most-eminent theologians of the Roman Church; he recalled the little man, black-haired, lively, corpulent, a trifle underhung, with a pleasant lisp and a merry eye; he remembered the incredible conversation, the sense of difficulty and shame under which he had argued some of the commonplaces of biology and primitive history, as educated Europe understands them; the half patronising, half impatient glibness of the other.--

'Oh! you know better, my son, than I how to argue these things; you are more learned, of course. But it is only a matter for the Catechism after all. Obey, my friend, obey!--there is no more to be said.'

And his own voice--tremulous:

'I would obey if I could. But unhappy as I am, to betray truths that are as evident to me as the sun in heaven would make me still unhappier. The fate that threatens me is frightful. *Aber ich kann nicht anders*. The truth holds me in a vice.'--

'Let me give you a piece of counsel. You sit too close to your books. You read and read,--you spin yourself into your own views like a cocoon. Travel--hear what others say--above all, go into retreat! No one need know. It would do you much good.'

'Eminence, I don't only study; I pray and meditate; I take pains to hear all that my opponents say. But my heart stands firm.'

'My son, the tribunal of the Pope is the tribunal of Christ. You are judged; submit! If not, I am sorry--regret deeply--but the consequence is certain.'

And then his own voice, in its last wrestle--

'The penalty that approaches me appears to me more terrible the nearer it comes. Like the Preacher--"I have judged him happiest who is not yet born, nor doth he see the ills that are done under the sun." Eminence, give me yet a little time.'

'A fortnight--gladly. But that is the utmost limit. My son, make the "sacrificium intellectus!"--and make it willingly.'

Ah!--and then the yielding, and the treachery, and the last blind stroke for truth!--

What was it which had undone him--which was now strangling the mental and moral life of half Christendom!

Was it the **certainty** of the Roman Church; that conception of life which stakes the all of life upon the carnal and outward; upon a date, an authorship, a miracle, an event?

Perhaps his own certainty, at bottom, had not been so very different.

But here, beneath his eyes, in this dying woman, was another certainty; erect amid all confusion; a certainty of the spirit.

And looking along the future, he saw the battle of the certainties, traditional, scientific, moral, ever more defined; and believed, like all the rest of us, in that particular victory, for which he hoped!

*   *   *   *   *

Late that night, when all their visitors were gone, Eleanor showed unusual animation. She left her sofa; she walked up and down their little sitting-room, giving directions to Marie about the journey home; and at last she informed them with a gaiety that made mock of their opposition that she had made all arrangements to start very early the following morning to visit the doctor in Orvieto who had attended her in June. Lucy protested and implored, but soon found that everything was settled, and Eleanor was determined. She was to go alone with Marie, in the Contessa's carriage, starting almost with the dawn so as to avoid the heat: to spend the hot noon under shelter at Orvieto; and to return in the evening. Lucy pressed at least to go with her. So it appeared had the Contessa. But Eleanor would have neither. 'I drive most days, and it does me no harm,' she said, almost with temper. 'Do let me alone!'

When she returned, Manisty was lounging under the trees of the courtyard waiting for her. He had spent a dull and purposeless day, which for a man of his character and in his predicament had been hard to bear. His patience was ebbing; his disappointment and despair were fast getting beyond control. All this Eleanor saw in his face as she dismounted.

Lucy, who had been watching for her all the afternoon, was at the moment for some reason or other with Reggie in the village.

Eleanor, with her hand on Marie's arm, tottered across the courtyard. At the convent door her strength failed her. She turned to Manisty.

'I can't walk up these stairs. Do you think you could carry me? I am very light.'

Struck with sudden emotion he threw his arms round her. She yielded like a tired child. He, who had instinctively prepared himself for a certain weight, was aghast at the ease with which he lifted her. Her head, in its pretty black hat, fell against his breast. Her eyes closed. He wondered if she had fainted.

He carried her to her room, and laid her on the sofa there. Then he saw that she had not fainted, and that her eyes followed him. As he was about to leave her to Marie, who was moving about in Lucy's room next door, she touched him on the arm.

'You may speak again--to-morrow,' she said, nodding at him with a friendly smile.

His face in its sudden flash of animation reflected the permission. He pressed her hand tenderly.

'Was your doctor useful to you?'

'Oh yes; it is hard to think as much of a prescription in Italian as in English-- but that's one's insular way.'

'He thought you no worse?'

'Why should one believe him if he did?' she said evasively. 'No one knows as much as oneself. Ah! there is Lucy. I think you must bid us good-night. I am too tired for talking.'

As he left the room Eleanor settled down happily on her pillow.

'The first and only time!' she thought. 'My heart on his--my arms round his neck. There must be impressions that outlast all others. I shall manage to put them all away at the end--but that.'

When Lucy came in, she declared she was not very much exhausted. As to the doctor she was silent.

But that night, when Lucy had been for some time in bed, and was still sleepless with anxiety and sorrow, the door opened and Eleanor appeared. She was in her usual white wrapper, and her fair hair, now much touched with grey, was loose on her shoulders.

'Oh! can I do anything?' cried Lucy, starting up.

Eleanor came up to her, laid a hand on her shoulder, bade her 'be still,' and brought a chair for herself. She had put down her candle on a table which stood near, and Lucy could see the sombre agitation of her face.

'How long?' she said, bending over the girl--'how long are you going to break my heart and his?'

The words were spoken with a violence which convulsed her whole frail form. Lucy sprang up, and tried to throw her arms round her. But Eleanor shook her off.

'No--no! Let us have it out. Do you see?' She let the wrapper slip from her shoulders. She showed the dark hollows under the wasted collar-bones, the knife-like shoulders, the absolute disappearance of all that had once made the difference between grace and emaciation. She held up her hands before the girl's terrified eyes. The skin was still white and delicate, otherwise they were the hands of a skeleton.

'You can look at *that*,' she said fiercely, under her breath--'and then insult me by refusing to marry the man you love, because you choose to remember that I was once in love with him! It is an outrage to associate such thoughts with me--as though one should make a rival of someone in her shroud. It hurts and tortures me every hour to know that you have such notions in your mind. It holds me back from peace--it chains me down to the flesh, and to earth.'

'Eleanor!' cried the girl in entreaty, catching at her hands. But Eleanor stood firm.

'Tell me,' she said peremptorily--'answer me truly, as one must answer people in my state--you do love him? If I had not been here--if I had not stood in your way--you would have allowed him his chance--you would have married him?'

Lucy bent her head upon her knees, forcing herself to composure.

'How can I answer that? I can never think of him, except as having brought pain to you.'

'Yes, dear, you can,' cried Eleanor, throwing herself on her knees and folding the girl in her arms. 'You can! It is no fault of his that I am like this--none--none! The doctor told me this afternoon that the respite last year was only apparent. The mischief has always been there--the end quite certain. All my dreams and disappointments and foolish woman's notions have vanished from me like smoke. There isn't one of them left. What should a woman in my condition do with such things? But what *is* left is love--for you and him. Oh! not the old love,' she said impatiently--persuading, haranguing herself no less than Lucy--'not an ounce of it! But a love that suffers so--in his suffering and yours! A love that won't let me rest; that is killing me before the time!'

She began to walk wildly up and down. Lucy sprang up, threw on some clothes, and gradually persuaded her to go back to her own room. When she was in bed again, utterly exhausted, Lucy's face--bathed in tears--approached hers:

'Tell me what to do. Have I ever refused you anything?'

*   *   *   *   *

The morning broke pure and radiant over the village and the forest. The great slopes of wood were in a deep and misty shadow; the river, shrunk to a thread again, scarcely chattered with its stones. A fresh wind wandered through the trees and over the new-reaped fields.

The Angelus had been rung long ago. There was the bell beginning for Mass. Lucy slipped out into a cool world, already alive with all the primal labours. The children and the mothers and the dogs were up; the peasants among the vines; the men with their peaked hats, the women shrouded from the sun under the heavy folds of their cotton head-gear; turned and smiled as she passed by. They liked the Signorina, and they were accustomed to her early walks.

On the hill she met Father Benecke coming up to Mass. Her cheek reddened, and she stopped to speak to him.

'You are out early, Mademoiselle?'

'It is the only time to walk.'

'Ah! yes--you are right.'

At which a sudden thought made the priest start. He looked down. But this time, he at least was innocent!

'You are coming in to tea with us this afternoon, Father?'

'If Mademoiselle does me the honour to invite me.'

The girl laughed.

'We shall expect you.'

Then she gave him her hand--a shy yet kind look from her beautiful eyes, and went her way. She had forgiven him, and the priest walked on with a cheered mind.

Meanwhile Lucy pushed her way into the fastnesses of the Sassetto. In its very heart she found a green-overgrown spot where the rocks made a sort of natural chair; one great block leaning forward overhead; a flat seat, and mossy arms on either side.

Here she seated herself. The winding path ran above her head. She could be perceived from it, but at this hour what fear of passers by?

She gave herself up to the rush of memory and fear.

She had travelled far in these four months!

'Is this what it always means?--coming to Europe?' she asked herself with a laugh that was not gay, while her fingers pulled at a tuft of hart's-tongue that grew in a crevice beside her.

And then in a flash she looked on into her destiny. She thought of Manisty with a yearning, passionate heart, and yet with a kind of terror; of the rich, incalculable, undisciplined nature, with all its capricious and self-willed power, its fastidious demands, its practical weakness; the man's brilliance and his folly. She envisaged herself laden with the responsibility of being his wife; and it seemed to her beyond her strength. One moment he appeared to her so much above and beyond her that it was ridiculous he should stoop to her. The next she felt, as it were, the weight of his life upon her hands, and told herself that she could not bear it.

And then--and then--it was all very well, but if she had not come--if Eleanor had never seen her--

Her head fell back into a mossy corner of the rock. Her eyes were blind with tears. From the hill came the rumble of an ox-waggon with the shouts of the drivers.

But another sound was nearer; the sound of a man's step upon the path. An exclamation--a leap--and before she could replace the hat she had taken off, or hide the traces of her tears, Manisty was beside her.

She sat up, staring at him in a bewildered silence. He too was silent,--only she saw the labouring of his breath.

But at last--

'I will not force myself upon you,' he said, in a voice haughty and self-restrained, that barely reached her ears. 'I will go at once if you bid me go.'

Then, as she still said nothing, he came nearer.

'You don't send me away?'

She made a little despairing gesture that said, 'I can't!'--but so sadly, that it did not encourage him.

'Lucy!'--he said, trembling--'are you going to take the seal off my lips--to give me my chance at last?'

To that, only the answer of her eyes,--so sweet, so full of sorrow.

He stooped above her, his whole nature torn between love and doubt.

'You hear me,' he said, in low, broken tones--'but you think yourself a traitor to listen?'

'And how could I not?' she cried, with a sudden sob. And then she found her speech; her heart unveiled itself.

'If I had never, never come!--It is my fault that she is dying--only, only my fault!'

And she turned away from him to hide her face and eyes against the rock, in such an agony of feeling that he almost despaired.

He controlled himself sharply, putting aside passion, collecting his thoughts for dear life.

'You are the most innocent, the most true of tender friends. It is in her name that I say to you--Lucy, be kind! Lucy, dare to love me!'

She raised her arm suddenly and pointed to the ground between them.

'There'--she said under her breath, 'I see her there!--lying dead between us!'

He was struck with horror, realising in what a grip this sane and simple nature must feel itself before it could break into such expression. What could he do or say?

He seated himself beside her, he took her hands by force.

'Lucy, I know what you mean. I won't pretend that I don't know. You think that I ought to have married my cousin--that if you had not been there, I should have married her. I might,--not yet, but after some time,--it is quite true that it might have happened. Would it have made Eleanor happy? You saw me at the villa--as I am. You know well, that even as a friend, I constantly disappointed her. There seemed to be a fate upon us which made me torment and wound her when I least intended it. I don't defend myself,--and Heaven knows I don't blame Eleanor! I have always believed that these things are mysterious, predestined--matters of temperament deeper than our will. I was deeply, sincerely attached to Eleanor-- yet!--when you came--after those first few weeks--the falsity of the whole position flashed upon me. And there was the book. It seemed to me sometimes that the only way of extricating us all was to destroy the book, and--and--all that it implied--or might have been thought to imply,--' he added hurriedly. 'Oh! you needn't tell me that I was a blundering and selfish fool! We have all got into a horrible coil--and I can't pose before you if I would. But it isn't Eleanor that would hold you back from me, Lucy--it isn't Eleanor!--answer me!--you know that?'

He held her almost roughly, scanning her face in an agony that served him well.

Her lips moved piteously, in words that he could not hear. But her hands lay passive in his grasp; and he hastened on.

'Ever since that Nemi evening, Lucy, I have been a new creature. I will tell you no lies. I won't say that I never loved any woman before you. I will have no secrets from you--you shall know all, if you want to know. But I do say that every passion I ever knew in my first youth seems to me now a mere apprenticeship to loving you! You have become my life--my very heart. If anything is to be made of a fellow like me--it's you that'll give me a chance, Lucy. Oh! my dear--don't turn from me! It's Eleanor's voice speaks in mine--listen to us both!'

Her colour came and went. She swayed towards him, fascinated by his voice, conquered by the mere exhaustion of her long struggle, held in the grasp of that compulsion which Eleanor had laid upon her.

Manisty perceived her weakness; his eyes flamed; his arm closed round her.

'I had an instinct--a vision,' he said, almost in her ear, 'when I set out. The day dawned on me like a day of consecration. The sun was another sun--the earth reborn. I took up my pilgrimage again--looking for Lucy--as I have looked for her the last six weeks. And everything led me right--the breeze and the woods and the birds. They were all in league with me. They pitied me--they told me where Lucy was--'

The low, rushing words ceased a moment. Manisty looked at her, took both her hands again.

'But they couldn't tell me'--he murmured--'how to please her--how to make her kind to me--make her listen to me. Lucy, whom shall I go to for that?'

She turned away her face; her hands released themselves. Manisty hardly breathed till she said, with a trembling mouth, and a little sob now and then between the words--

'It is all so strange to me--so strange and so--so doubtful! If there were only someone here from my own people,--someone who could advise me! Is it wise for you--for us both? You know I'm so different from you--and you'll find it out perhaps, more and more. And if you did--and were discontented with me--I can't be sure that I could always fit myself to you. I was brought up so that--that--I can't always be as easy and pleasant as other girls. My mother--she stood by herself often--and I with her. She was a grand nature--but I'm sure you would have thought her extravagant--and perhaps hard. And often I feel as though I didn't know myself,--what there might be in me. I know I'm often very stubborn. Suppose--in a few years--'

Her eyes came back to him; searching and interrogating that bent look of his, in which her whole being seemed held.

What was it Manisty saw in her troubled face that she could no longer conceal? He made no attempt to answer her words; there was another language between them. He gave a cry. He put forth a tender violence; and Lucy yielded. She found herself in his arms; and all was said.

Yet when she withdrew herself, she was in tears. She took his hand and kissed it wildly, hardly knowing what she was doing. But her heart turned to Eleanor; and it was Eleanor's voice in her ears that alone commanded and absolved her.

*   *   *   *   *

As they strolled home, Manisty's mood was of the wildest and gayest. He would hear of no despair about his cousin.

'We will take her home--you and I. We will get the very best advice. It isn't--it shan't be as bad as you think!'

And out of mere reaction from her weeks of anguish, she believed him, she hoped again. Then he turned to speculate on the voyage to America he must now make, on his first interviews with Greyridge and Uncle Ben.

'Shall I make a good impression? How shall I be received? I am certain you gave your uncle the worst accounts of me.'

'I guess Uncle Ben will judge for himself,' she said, reddening; thankful all the same to remember that among her uncle's reticent, old-fashioned ways none was more marked than his habit of destroying all but an infinitesimal fraction of his letters. 'He read all those speeches of yours, last year. You'll have to think--how you're going to get over it.'

'Well, you have brought me on my knees to Italy,' he said, laughing. 'Must I now go barefoot to the tomb of Washington?'

She looked at him with a little smile, that showed him once more the Lucy of the villa.

'You do seem to make mistakes, don't you?' she said gently. But then her hand nestled shyly into his; and without words, her heart vowed the true woman's vow to love him and stand by him always, for better for worse, through error and success, through fame or failure. In truth her inexperience had analysed the man to whom she had pledged herself far better than he imagined. Did her love for him indeed rest partly on a secret sense of vocation?--a profound, inarticulate divining of his vast, his illimitable need for such a one as she to love him?

* * * * *

Meanwhile Eleanor and Reggie and Father Benecke waited breakfast on the *loggia*. They were all under the spell of a common excitement, a common restlessness.

Eleanor had discarded her sofa. She moved about the *loggia*, now looking down the road, now gathering a bunch of rose-pink oleanders for her white dress. The *frou-frou* of her soft skirts; her happy agitation; the flush on her cheek;--neither of the men who were her companions ever forgot them afterwards.

Manisty, it appeared, had taken coffee with Father Benecke at six, and had then strolled up the Sassetto path with his cigarette. Lucy had been out since the first church bells. Father Benecke reported his meeting with her on the road.

Eleanor listened to him with a sort of gay self-restraint.

'Yes--I know'--she said, nodding--'I know.--Reggie, there is a glorious tuft of carnations in that pot in the cloisters. Ask Mamma Doni if we may have them. *Ecco*--take her a *lira* for the baby. I must have them for the table.'

And soon the little white-spread breakfast-table, with it rolls and fruit, was aglow with flowers, and a little bunch lay on each plate. The *loggia*, was in *festa*; and the morning sun flickered through the vine-leaves on the bright table, and the patterns of the brick floor.

'There--there they are!--Reggie!--Father!--leave me a minute! Quick--into the garden! We will call you directly.'

And Reggie, looking back with a gulp from the garden-stairs, saw her leaning over the *loggia*, waving her handkerchief; the figure in its light dress, tossed a little by the morning breeze, the soft muslin and lace eddying round it.

They mounted. Lucy entered first.

She stood on the threshold a moment, looking at Eleanor with a sweet and piteous appeal. Then her young foot ran, her arms opened; and with the tender dignity of a mother rejoicing over her child Eleanor received her on her breast.

$$* \qquad * \qquad * \qquad * \qquad *$$

By easy stages Manisty and Lucy took Mrs. Burgoyne to England. At the end of August Lucy returned to the States with her friends; and in October she and Manisty were married.

Mrs. Burgoyne lived through the autumn; and in November she hungered so pitifully for the South that by a great effort she was moved to Rome. There she took up her quarters in the house of the Contessa Guerrini, who lavished on her last days all that care and affection could bestow.

Eleanor drove out once more towards the Alban hills; she looked once more on the slopes of Marinata and the white crown of Monte Cavo; the Roman sunshine shed round her once more its rich incomparable light. In December Manisty and Lucy were expected; but a week before they came she died.

A German Old Catholic priest journeyed from a little town in Switzerland to her burial; and a few days later the two beings she had loved stood beside her grave.

They had many and strong reasons to remember her; but for one reason above all others, for her wild flight to Torre Amiata, the only selfish action of her whole life, was she--at least, in Lucy's heart--through all the years that followed the more passionately, the more tragically enthroned.

The Codes Of Hammurabi And Moses
W. W. Davies

QTY

The discovery of the Hammurabi Code is one of the greatest achievements of archaeology, and is of paramount interest, not only to the student of the Bible, but also to all those interested in ancient history...

Religion   **ISBN:** *1-59462-338-4*   **Pages:**132

MSRP $12.95

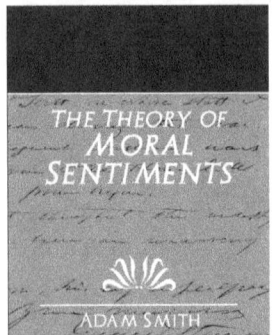

The Theory of Moral Sentiments
Adam Smith

QTY

This work from 1749. contains original theories of conscience amd moral judgment and it is the foundation for systemof morals.

Philosophy **ISBN:** *1-59462-777-0*   **Pages:**536

MSRP $19.95

Jessica's First Prayer
Hesba Stretton

QTY

In a screened and secluded corner of one of the many railway-bridges which span the streets of London there could be seen a few years ago, from five o'clock every morning until half past eight, a tidily set-out coffee-stall, consisting of a trestle and board, upon which stood two large tin cans, with a small fire of charcoal burning under each so as to keep the coffee boiling during the early hours of the morning when the work-people were thronging into the city on their way to their daily toil...

Childrens   **ISBN:** *1-59462-373-2*

Pages:84

MSRP $9.95

My Life and Work
Henry Ford

QTY

Henry Ford revolutionized the world with his implementation of mass production for the Model T automobile. Gain valuable business insight into his life and work with his own auto-biography... "We have only started on our development of our country we have not as yet, with all our talk of wonderful progress, done more than scratch the surface. The progress has been wonderful enough but..."

Pages:300

Biographies/   **ISBN:** *1-59462-198-5*   *MSRP $21.95*

www.bookjungle.com *email: sales@bookjungle.com fax: 630-214-0564 mail: Book Jungle PO Box 2226 Champaign, IL 61825*

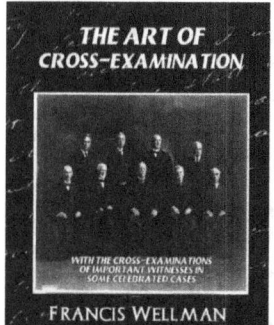

The Art of Cross-Examination
Francis Wellman

QTY

I presume it is the experience of every author, after his first book is published upon an important subject, to be almost overwhelmed with a wealth of ideas and illustrations which could readily have been included in his book, and which to his own mind, at least, seem to make a second edition inevitable. Such certainly was the case with me; and when the first edition had reached its sixth impression in five months, I rejoiced to learn that it seemed to my publishers that the book had met with a sufficiently favorable reception to justify a second and considerably enlarged edition. ..

Pages:412

Reference   **ISBN: *1-59462-647-2***   *MSRP $19.95*

On the Duty of Civil Disobedience
Henry David Thoreau

QTY

Thoreau wrote his famous essay, On the Duty of Civil Disobedience, as a protest against an unjust but popular war and the immoral but popular institution of slave-owning. He did more than write—he declined to pay his taxes,   and was hauled off to gaol in consequence. Who can say how much this refusal of his hastened the end of the war and of slavery ?

Law   **ISBN: *1-59462-747-9***   **Pages:48**

MSRP $7.45

Dream Psychology Psychoanalysis for Beginners
Sigmund Freud

QTY

Sigmund Freud, born Sigismund Schlomo Freud (May 6, 1856 - September 23, 1939), was a Jewish-Austrian neurologist and psychiatrist who co-founded the psychoanalytic school of psychology. Freud is best known for his theories of the unconscious mind, especially involving the mechanism of repression; his redefinition of sexual desire as mobile and directed towards a wide variety of objects; and his therapeutic techniques, especially his understanding of transference in the therapeutic relationship and the presumed value of dreams as sources of insight into unconscious desires.

Pages:196

Psychology   **ISBN: *1-59462-905-6***   *MSRP $15.45*

The Miracle of Right Thought
Orison Swett Marden

QTY

Believe with all of your heart that you will do what you were made to do. When the mind has once formed the habit of holding cheerful, happy, prosperous pictures, it will not be easy to form the opposite habit. It does not matter how improbable or how far away this realization may see, or how dark the prospects may be, if we visualize them as best we can, as vividly as possible, hold tenaciously to them and vigorously struggle to attain them, they will gradually become actualized, realized in the life. But a desire, a longing without endeavor, a yearning abandoned or held indifferently will vanish without realization.

Pages:360

Self Help   **ISBN: *1-59462-644-8***   *MSRP $25.45*

They had many and strong reasons to remember her; but for one reason above all others, for her wild flight to Torre Amiata, the only selfish action of her whole life, was she--at least, in Lucy's heart--through all the years that followed the more passionately, the more tragically enthroned.

QTY

The Fasting Cure *by Sinclair Upton*   ISBN: *1-59462-222-1*   **$13.95**
In the Cosmopolitan Magazine for May, 1910, and in the Contemporary Review (London) for April, 1910, I published an article dealing with my experiences in fasting. I have written a great many magazine articles, but never one which attracted so much attention... New Age/Self Help/Health Pages 164

Hebrew Astrology *by Sepharial*   ISBN: *1-59462-308-2*   **$13.45**
In these days of advanced thinking it is a matter of common observation that we have left many of the old landmarks behind and that we are now pressing forward to greater heights and to a wider horizon than that which represented the mind-content of our progenitors... Astrology Pages 144

Thought Vibration or The Law of Attraction in the Thought World   ISBN: *1-59462-127-6*   **$12.95**
by William Walker Atkinson   Psychology/Religion Pages 144

Optimism *by Helen Keller*   ISBN: *1-59462-108-X*   **$15.95**
Helen Keller was blind, deaf, and mute since 19 months old, yet famously learned how to overcome these handicaps, communicate with the world, and spread her lectures promoting optimism. An inspiring read for everyone... Biographies/Inspirational Pages 84

Sara Crewe *by Frances Burnett*   ISBN: *1-59462-360-0*   **$9.45**
In the first place, Miss Minchin lived in London. Her home was a large, dull, tall one, in a large, dull square, where all the houses were alike, and all the sparrows were alike, and where all the door-knockers made the same heavy sound... Childrens/Classic Pages 88

The Autobiography of Benjamin Franklin *by Benjamin Franklin*   ISBN: *1-59462-135-7*   **$24.95**
The Autobiography of Benjamin Franklin has probably been more extensively read than any other American historical work, and no other book of its kind has had such ups and downs of fortune. Franklin lived for many years in England, where he was agent... Biographies/History Pages 332

Name	
Email	
Telephone	
Address	
City, State ZIP	

☐ **Credit Card**   ☐ **Check / Money Order**

Credit Card Number	
Expiration Date	
Signature	

Please Mail to: Book Jungle
                    PO Box 2226
                    Champaign, IL 61825
or Fax to: *630-214-0564*

ORDERING INFORMATION

web: *www.bookjungle.com*
email: *sales@bookjungle.com*
fax: *630-214-0564*
mail: *Book Jungle PO Box 2226 Champaign, IL 61825*
or PayPal *to sales@bookjungle.com*

Please contact us for bulk discounts

DIRECT-ORDER TERMS

**20% Discount if You Order
Two or More Books**
Free Domestic Shipping!
Accepted: Master Card, Visa,
Discover, American Express

www.ingramcontent.com/pod-product-compliance
Lightning Source LLC
Chambersburg PA
CBHW081140020726
47504CB00009B/1943